# A DIVIDED SPY

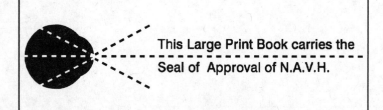

This Large Print Book carries the
Seal of Approval of N.A.V.H.

THOMAS KELL SERIES

# A DIVIDED SPY

## CHARLES CUMMING

**THORNDIKE PRESS**

*A part of Gale, Cengage Learning*

GALE
CENGAGE Learning·

Farmington Hills, Mich • San Francisco • New York • Waterville, Maine
Meriden, Conn • Mason, Ohio • Chicago

## GALE
### CENGAGE Learning·

Thorndike Press® Large Print Thriller.
The text of this Large Print edition is unabridged.
Other aspects of the book may vary from the original edition.
Set in 16 pt. Plantin.

### LIBRARY OF CONGRESS CATALOGING-IN-PUBLICATION DATA

Names: Cumming, Charles, 1971– author.
Title: A divided spy / by Charles Cumming.
Description: Large print edition. | Waterville, Maine : Thorndike Press, a part of Gale, Cengage Learning, 2017. | Series: Thorndike Press large print thriller | Series: Thomas Kell Series
Identifiers: LCCN 2017009857| ISBN 9781432839574 (hardcover) | ISBN 1432839578 (hardcover)
Subjects: LCSH: Large type books. | BISAC: FICTION / Espionage. | GSAFD: Spy stories.
Classification: LCC PR6103.U484 D58 2017b | DDC 823/.92—dc23
LC record available at https://lccn.loc.gov/2017009857

Published in 2017 by arrangement with Macmillan Publishing Group, LLC/St.Martin's Press

Printed in the United States of America
1 2 3 4 5 6 7 21 20 19 18 17

For Julia Wisdom

We are, I know not how, somewhat double in ourselves, so that what we believe we disbelieve, and cannot rid ourselves of what we condemn.

— MICHEL DE MONTAIGNE

Truth doesn't always come from truthful men.

— JAMES SALTER

■ ■ ■ ■

# LONDON

■ ■ ■ ■

# 1

Put it all on red. Put it all on black.

Jim Martinelli stacked five thousand pounds of chips into two six-inch piles. He held each of the piles in the tips of his fingers. One of them was fractionally higher than the other, the other slightly crooked at the base. He stared at them. His whole future, the mountain of his debt, just twenty disks of plastic in a casino. Double the money and he could keep Chapman at bay. Lose it and he was finished.

Arms across the baize, a blur of hands as the players around him reached out to place their bets. The suit from Dubai putting single chips on eighteen through thirty-six, the other Arab putting a grand on red. The Chinese tourist to Martinelli's left put a carpet of blue chips in the upper third, smothering the table with piles of five and six. Big wins for him tonight. Big losses. Then he put twenty grand on ten and walked away from the table. Twenty thousand pounds on a one–in–thirty-five chance. Even in the worst times, in the craziest urges of the last two years, Martinelli had never been stupid enough to do something like that. Perhaps he wasn't as messed up as he thought. Maybe he still had things under control.

The wheel was spinning. Martinelli stayed out of the play. It didn't feel right; he wasn't getting a clear reading on the numbers. The Chinese tourist was hovering near the bar, now almost twenty feet away from the table. Martinelli tried to imagine what it must be like to have so much money that you could afford to blow twenty grand on a single moment of chance. Twenty grand was four months' salary at the Passport Office, more than half of his debt to Chapman. Two wins in the next two rounds and he would be holding that kind of dough. Then he could cash out, go home, call Chapman. He could start to pay back what he owed.

The croupier was tidying up. Centering chips, straightening piles. In a low, firm voice he said: "No further bets, please, gentlemen," and turned toward the wheel.

*The house always wins,* Martinelli told himself. *The house always wins . . .*

The ball was beginning to slow. The

Chinese tourist was still hovering near the bar, back turned to the play, his little chimney of twenty grand on ten. The ball dropped and began to jump in the channels, the quiet innocent clatter as it popped from box to box. Martinelli laid a private bet with himself. *Red. It's going to be red.* He looked down at his pile of chips and wished that he had staked it all.

"Twenty-seven, red," said the croupier, placing the wooden dolly on a low pile of chips in the center of the baize. Martinelli felt a sting of irritation. He had missed his chance. Across the room, the tourist was returning from the bar, watching the croupier clear away the losing bets, the cheap plastic rustle of thousands of pounds being dragged across the baize and scooped into the tube. There was no expression on his face as the stack on ten was pulled; nothing to indicate loss or sorrow. Washed out and inscrutable. The face of a gambler.

Martinelli stood up, nodded at the inspector. He left his chips on the table and walked downstairs to the bathroom. They were playing Abba on the sound system, a song that reminded Martinelli of driving long distances with his father as a child. The door of the gents was ajar, paper towels littering the floor. Martinelli scraped them to one side with his foot and checked his reflection in the mirror.

His skin was pallid and gleaming with sweat. In the bright fluorescent light of the bathroom the tiredness under his eyes looked like bruises from a fight. He had worn the same shirt two nights in a row and could see that a thin brown line of dirt had formed inside the collar. He bared his teeth, wondering if a chunk of olive or peanut had been lodged in his gums all night. But there was nothing. Just the pale yellow stains on his front teeth and a sense that his breath was stale. He took out a piece of gum and popped it into his mouth. He was exhausted.

"All right, Jim? How's it going for you tonight?"

Martinelli swung around.

"Kyle."

It was Chapman. He was standing in the door, looking at a stack of leaflets in a plastic box beside the sink. Advice for gamblers, advice for addicts. Chapman picked one up.

"What does it say here?" he began, reading from the leaflet in his abrasive London accent. *"How to play responsibly."*

Chapman smiled at Martinelli. The eyes were dead, menacing. He turned the page.

*"Remember. Gambling is a way for responsible adults to have some fun."*

Martinelli had never had the balls to read the leaflet. They said that the addict had to *want* to quit. He felt his stomach dissolve and had to steady himself against the wall.

*"Most of our customers do not see gambling as a problem. But for a very small minority, Jim, we know that this is not the case."*

Chapman looked up. He moved the side of his mouth in a way that made Martinelli feel like he was going to spit at him.

*"If you think you are having trouble controlling your gambling, this leaflet contains important information on where to seek help."* Chapman lowered the leaflet and looked into Martinelli's eyes. "Do you need help, Jim?" He tilted his head to one side and grinned. "Do you want to talk to someone?"

"I've got five grand on the table. Upstairs."

"Five? Have you?" Chapman sniffed loudly, as if he were struggling to clear his sinuses. "You and I both know that's not what we're talking about, don't we? You're not being straight, Jim."

Chapman took a step forward. He raised the leaflet and held it in front of him, like a man singing a hymn in church.

*"Only gamble what you can afford to lose,"* he said. *"Set yourself personal limits. Only*

spend a certain amount of time at the tables." He stared at Martinelli. "Time, Jim. That's what you've run out of, isn't it?"

"I've told you," he said. "Five grand. Upstairs. Let me play."

Chapman walked toward the basins. He looked at himself in the mirror, admiring what he saw. Then he kicked out his leg behind him and slammed the bathroom door.

"I can tell you that you've got a problem," he said. "I can tell you that if you don't give me what's owed by tomorrow morning, I won't be — how do they say — responsible for my actions."

"I understand that." Martinelli could feel himself freezing up, his mind going numb.

"Oh, you understand that, do you?"

"Can you just let me past?" Martinelli pressed away from the wall and moved toward the basins. "Can you open the door, please? I want to go upstairs."

Chapman appeared to admire his display of courage. He nodded and opened the door. An ominous smile was playing on his face as he indicated that Martinelli could leave.

"Don't let me stop you," he said, stepping to one side with the flourish of a matador.

"You go and see what you can do, Jim. Be lucky."

Martinelli climbed the stairs two at a time. He needed to be back at the tables in the way that a man who has been held underwater craves to reach the surface and to suck in a deep breath of air. He headed back to his seat and saw that a play was coming to an end. The pop and clatter of the ball, the rapt attention of the gamblers waiting for it to settle.

"Six. Black," said the croupier.

Martinelli saw that the Chinese tourist had a split of five grand on five and six. A small fortune. The croupier placed the dolly on the winning square and began to sweep the losing chips from across the table. Then he paid out what he owed — more than eighty grand to the Chinese in a stack of twenty, with no discernible reaction from either man.

Martinelli took it as a sign. He waited until the table was clear, then moved his stack of chips onto black. All or nothing. Take it or leave it. The house always wins. Fuck Kyle Chapman.

Then it was just a question of waiting. The bloke from Dubai put his usual spread on eighteen through thirty-six, the other Arab going big on six-way splits along the baize.

It worried Martinelli that the Chinese stayed out of the play and wandered over to the bar. It was like a bad omen. Maybe he should take back his chips.

"No more bets, please, gentlemen," said the croupier.

Too late. Martinelli could do nothing but stare at the wheel, praying for the chance on black, mesmerized — as he had always been — by the counterpoint of spokes and ball, the one hypnotically slow, the other a blur as it raced beneath the rim.

Slowing now, the ball about to drop. Nauseated with anxiety, Martinelli took his eyes away from the wheel and saw Kyle Chapman standing in his eyeline. He had come back upstairs. He wasn't looking at the wheel. He wasn't looking at the baize. He was looking directly at the man who owed him thirty thousand pounds.

Martinelli's eyes went back to the table. All or nothing. Feast or famine. He heard the rattle and click of the ball, watched it drop and vanish beneath the rim like a magic trick.

The inspector looked down. He would see it first. The croupier leaned over the wheel, preparing to call the number.

Martinelli closed his eyes. It was like an

ax falling. He always felt sick at this moment.

*I should have put it all on red,* he thought.
*The house always wins.*

■ ■ ■ ■

# FIVE WEEKS LATER

■ ■ ■ ■

# 2

Thomas Kell stood on the westbound platform at Bayswater station, one eye on a copy of the *Evening Standard,* the other on the man standing three meters to his left wearing faded denim jeans and a brown tweed jacket. Kell had seen him first on Praed Street, reflected in the window of a Chinese restaurant, then again twenty minutes later coming out of a branch of Starbucks on Queensway. Average height, average build, average features. Tapping his Oyster card on the reader at Bayswater, Kell had turned to find the man walking into the station a few paces behind him. He had ducked the eye contact, staring at his well-worn shoes. That was when Kell sensed he had a problem.

It was just after three o'clock on a Wednesday afternoon in June. Kell counted eleven other people waiting on the platform, two of them standing directly behind him.

Drawing on a long-forgotten piece of self-defense, he placed his right leg farther forward than his left, shifted his weight back on to his rear heel as the train clattered into the station — and waited for the shove in the back.

It never came. No crowding up, no crazed Chechen errand boy trying to push him onto the tracks as a favor to the SVR. Instead the District Line train deposited half a dozen passengers onto the platform and eased away. When Kell looked left, he saw that the man in the faded jeans had gone. The two men who had been standing behind him had also boarded the train. Kell allowed himself a half smile. His occasional outbreaks of paranoia were a kind of madness, a yearning for the old days; the corrupted sixth sense of a forty-six-year-old spy who knew that the game was over.

A second train, moments later. Kell stepped on board, took a fold-down seat, and reopened the *Standard.* Royal pregnancies. Property prices. Electoral conspiracies. He was just another traveler on the Tube, traceless and nondescript. Nobody knew who he was nor who he had ever been. On the fifth page, a photograph of an aid worker murdered by the maniacs of ISIS; on the seventh, more wretched news from

Ukraine. It was of no consolation to Kell that in the twelve months he had spent as a private citizen following the murder of his girlfriend, Rachel Wallinger, the regions on which he had worked for the greater part of his adult life had further disintegrated into violence and criminality. Though Kell had deliberately avoided making contact with anyone in the Service, he had occasionally run into former colleagues in the supermarket or on the street, only to be treated to lengthy discourses on the "impossible task" facing MI6 in Russia, Syria, Yemen, and beyond.

"The best we can hope for is a kind of stasis, somehow to keep a *lid* on things," a former colleague had told him when they bumped into one another at a Christmas party. "God knows it was easier in the age of the despots. There are some mornings, Tom, when I'm as nostalgic for Mubarak and Gaddafi as a Dunkirk Tommy for the white cliffs of Dover. At least Saddam gave us something to *aim* for."

The train pulled into Notting Hill Gate. In the same conversation, the colleague had offered his "sincere condolences" over Rachel's death and intimated to Kell how "devastated" the "entire Service" had been over the circumstances of her assassination in Istanbul. Kell had changed the subject. Rachel's memory was his alone to curate; he wanted no part in others' recollections of the woman to whom he had lost his heart. Perhaps he had been naïve to fall so quickly for a woman he had barely known, and a fool to trust her, yet he guarded the memory of his love as jealously as a starving animal with a scrap of food. Every morning, for months, Kell had thought of Rachel at the moment of waking, then steadily throughout the day, a debilitating punctuation to his solitary, unchanging existence. He had raged at her, he had talked with her, he had drenched himself in memories of the short period in which they had been involved with one another. The loss of the *potential* that Rachel had possessed to knit together the broken strands of Kell's life constituted the most acute suffering he had ever known. Yet he had survived it.

"You must be having a midlife crisis," his ex-wife, Claire, had told him at one of their occasional reunion lunches, commenting on the fact that Kell had given up alcohol, was taking himself off to the gym three times a week, and had broken a twenty-year, twenty-a-day smoking habit. "No alcohol, no fags. No *spying*? Next thing you'll be buying an open-topped Porsche and taking twenty-two-year-olds to the polo at Windsor Great Park."

Kell had laughed at the joke even as he inwardly acknowledged how little Claire understood him. She knew nothing, of course, about his relationship with Rachel, nothing about the operation that had led to her death. This was just the latest in a lifetime of secrets between them. As far as Claire was concerned, Kell would always be the same man: an intelligence officer through and through, a spy who had spent more than two decades in thrall to the luster and the intrigue of espionage. Their marriage had failed because he had loved the game more than he had loved her.

"You're wedded to your agents, Tom," Claire had said during one of many similarly unequivocal conversations that had heralded the end of the marriage. "Amelia Levene is your family, not me. If you had to choose between us, I have no doubt that you would pick MI6."

Amelia. The woman whose career Kell had saved and whose reputation he had salvaged. The chief of the Secret Intelligence Service, appointed three years earlier, now approaching the end of her tenure, with the Middle East on fire, Russia in political and economic turmoil, and Africa ravaged by Islamist terror. Kell had neither seen nor heard from her since the afternoon of Rachel's funeral, an occasion at which they had deliberately ignored one another. By recruiting Rachel to work for SIS behind his back, Amelia had effectively signed her death warrant.

Earl's Court. Kell stepped off the train and registered the familiar acid taste of his implacable resentment. It was the one thing he had been unable to control. He had come to terms with the end of his marriage, he had mastered his grief, reasoned that his professional future lay beyond the walls of Vauxhall Cross. Yet Kell could not still a yearning for vengeance. He wanted to seek out those in Moscow who had given the order for Rachel's assassination. He wanted justice.

The Richmond service was due in a few minutes. A pigeon swooped in low from the Warwick Road, flapped toward the opposite platform and settled beside a bench. There was a District Line train standing empty behind it. The pigeon hopped on board. As if on cue, the doors slid shut and the train moved out of the station.

Kell turned and joined the huddle of passengers on platform 4, heads ducked down in text messages, Twitter feeds, games of

Angry Birds. A huge bearded man with a "Baby on Board" badge attached to the lapel of his jacket stood beside him. Kell half expected to spot his old friend from Bayswater: faded denim jeans and a brown tweed jacket. A woman behind him was talking in Polish on a mobile phone; another, shrouded in a black niqab, was scolding a small child in Arabic. These were the citizens of the new London, the international masses whom Amelia Levene was charged to protect. More than twenty years earlier, Kell had joined SIS in a spirit of undiluted patriotism. To save lives, to defend and protect the kingdom, had seemed to him both a noble and an exhilarating pursuit for a young man with adventure in his blood. Now that London was a city of Africans and Americans, of Hollande-fleeing French, of Eastern Europeans too young to have known the impediments of communism, he felt no different. The landscape had changed, yet Kell still felt wedded to an *idea* of England as the country evolved, even as that idea shifted and slipped beneath his feet. There were days when he longed to return to active duty, to stand once again at Amelia's side. But he had allowed the personal to overcome the political.

The train pulled into the platform. Carriages as empty as his days flickered in the afternoon light. Kell stepped aside to allow an elderly woman to board the train, then took his seat and waited.

# 3

Kell was at his flat in Sinclair Road within twenty minutes. He had been inside for less than five when his phone rang, a rare landline call that Kell assumed would be from Claire. The number was otherwise known only to SIS Personnel.

"Guv?"

It didn't take long for Kell to pick the voice. Born and raised in Elephant and Castle, then two decades in Tech-Ops at MI5.

"Harold?"

"The one and only."

"How did you get this number?"

"Nice to hear from you, too."

"How?" Kell asked again.

"Do we have to do this?"

It was a fair question. With half a dozen clicks of a mouse, Harold Mowbray could have found out Kell's blood type and credit rating. Now private sector, he had worked

31

closely with Amelia on two occasions in the previous three years: Kell's home number might even have come directly from "C."

"Okay. So how have you been?"

"Good, guv. Good."

"Arsenal doing all right?"

"Nah. Gave them up for Lent. Too many pretty boys in midfield."

Kell found himself reaching for a cigarette that wasn't there. He thought back to the previous summer, sitting with Mowbray in a Bayswater safe house killing time waiting for a mole. Harold had known that Kell was in love with Rachel. He had come to the funeral, paid his respects. Kell trusted him insomuch as he had always been efficient and reliable, but knew that theirs was a professional relationship that would never transcend Mowbray's loyalty to whoever was paying his bills.

"So what's up?" he asked. "You selling something? Want me to buy your season ticket to Highbury?"

"Keep up. Arsenal moved out of Highbury years ago. We've been playing at the Emirates since 2006."

It occurred to Kell that, save for a perfunctory exchange in Pret a Manger at lunch, this was the first conversation he had held with another human being in more than twenty-four hours. The night before he had cooked spaghetti bolognese at home and watched back-to-back episodes of *House of Cards.* In the morning he had gone to the gym, then wandered alone around an exhibition at the National Portrait Gallery. Sometimes he would go for days without any meaningful interaction whatsoever.

"Still," said Mowbray, "we need to have a chat."

"Isn't that what we're doing?"

"Face to face. *Mano a mano.* Too long and complicated for the phone."

That could mean only one thing. Work. Blowback from a previous operation, or a dangled carrot on something new. Either way, Mowbray didn't trust Kell's landline to keep it a secret. Anybody could be listening in. London. Paris. Moscow.

"You remember that Middle Eastern place we used to go to on the American gig?"

"Which one?" "The American gig" had been the molehunt. Ryan Kleckner. A CIA officer in the pay of the SVR, Russia's foreign intelligence service.

"The one with the waitress."

"Oh, *that* one." Kell made a joke of it, but understood that Mowbray was being deliberately obscure. There was only one Middle Eastern restaurant that both of them had been to on the Kleckner operation. West-bourne Grove. Persian. Kell had no recollection of the waitress, pretty or otherwise. Mowbray was simply making sure that their table wouldn't be covered in advance.

"Can you make dinner tonight?" he asked.

Kell thought about stalling but was too intrigued by the invitation. Besides, he was looking at another night of leftovers and *House of Cards.* Dinner with Harold would be a fillip.

"Meet you there at eight?" he suggested.

"You will know me by the smell of my cologne."

# 4

Kell arrived at the restaurant at quarter to eight, early enough to ask for a quiet spot at the back with line of sight to the entrance. To his surprise, Mowbray was already seated at a table in the center of the small, brick-lined room, his back to a group of jabbering Spaniards.

It was fiercely hot, the open mouth of a *tanoor* bread oven blowing a furnace heat into Kell's face as he walked inside. A waitress, whom he vaguely recognized, smiled at him as Mowbray stood up behind her. Iranian music was playing at a volume seemingly designed to guarantee a degree of conversational privacy.

"Harold. How are you?"

"*Salam,* guv."

"*Salam, khoobi,*" Kell replied. The heat of the *tanoor* as he sat down was like a summer sun against his back.

"You speak Farsi?" They were shaking hands.

"I was showing off," Kell said. "Enough to get by in restaurants."

"Menu Farsi," Mowbray replied, smiling at his own remark. "Iranians don't like being confused for Arabs, do they?"

"They do not."

Mowbray looked to be recovering from a bad case of sunburn. His forehead was scalded red and there were flaking patches of dry skin around his mouth and nose.

"Been away?" Kell asked.

"Funny you should mention that." Mowbray flapped a napkin into his lap and grinned. "Went to Egypt with the wife."

"Why funny?"

"You'll see. Shall we order?"

Kell wondered why he was playing hard to get. He opened his menu as the waitress passed their table. Mowbray looked up, caught Kell's eye, and winked.

"So," he said, spring-loading another joke. "You can have a skewer of minced lamb with *taftoon* bread, *two* skewers of minced lamb with *taftoon* bread, a skewer of marinated lamb cubes with *taftoon* bread, *two* skewers of marinated lamb cubes with *taftoon* bread, a skewer of minced lamb *and* a skewer of marinated lamb cubes with *taftoon . . .*"

"I get it," said Kell, smiling as he closed the menu. "You order. I'm going to the bathroom."

There was a strong smell of hashish leading up to the gents. Kell stopped to look at a wall of turquoise tiles inlaid on the staircase, breathing in the smoke. He wanted to trace the source of the smell, to find whoever had rolled the joint in a backroom office and to share it with them. In the bathroom he washed his hands and glanced in the mirror, wondering why Mowbray was coming to him with tall tales from Egypt. What was the scoop? ISIS? Muslim Brotherhood? Maybe he was the bagman for a job offer in the private sector, an ex-SIS suit using Kell's friendship with Mowbray as a lure. There had been five or six such offers in the previous twelve months, all of which Kell had turned down. He wasn't interested in private security, nor did he want to be a nodding donkey on the board of Barclays or BP. On the other hand, if the pitch was something Russian, something that would get Kell close to the men who had ordered Rachel's assassination, he would give it serious consideration.

"I forgot," Mowbray announced as Kell

settled back into his seat. "They don't serve booze."

"Don't worry about it. I gave it up."

"Fuck off."

"Seven months dry."

"Now why would you want to go and do a thing like that?"

"Tell me about Egypt."

Mowbray leaned forward and put a hand in his pocket. Kell thought he was going to produce a photograph or a flash drive, but he kept it there as he spoke. If Kell hadn't known that Mowbray was capable of far greater subtleties, he might have assumed that he was triggering a recording device.

"Hurghada."

"What about it?"

"One-horse town on the east coast. Mainland Egypt, Red Sea, facing Sinai."

"I know where it is, Harold."

"Last three years, Karen and me have been flying there for a bit of winter sun; easyJet goes three times a week. Car picks us up and drives us an hour south to a place called Soma Bay. Four hotels and a golf course, back to back, arse end of nowhere. Fresh water piped in from the Nile turns the fairways green, fills the swimming pools. Coral reefs and scuba diving for the grownups, camel rides on the beach for the kids.

In the tourist industry they call it a 'hot flop.' "

The food arrived. Mashed aubergines with garlic and herbs. Feta cheese mixed with tarragon and fresh mint. A bowl of hummus was placed in front of Kell, nestled beside a basket of flatbread.

"There's your *taftoon,*" he said, encouraging Mowbray to continue.

"Anyway, we always stay at the same place. German owned, German efficient, German-occupied sunbeds. Never seen a Yank there, never met a Frog. The occasional Brit, from time to time, but mostly German pensioners and Russian oligarch types with dyed hair and third wives who probably weren't alive under Gorbachev. Am I painting the picture?"

"Vividly," said Kell, and took a bite of *taftoon.*

"So, guv, here's the thing. Here's the reason I wanted to see you. Something very strange happened, something I can still hardly believe."

Mowbray looked like he meant it. There was an expression of amused consternation on his face.

"They do breakfasts," he said, nodding slowly and looking across the table, as though half expecting Kell to finish his sentence. "They do breakfasts every morning . . ."

"What a breakthrough in hospitality," Kell replied. "I must go and stay there."

Mowbray was staring across the table, eyes fixed somewhere around Kell's left ear.

"On the second-last day we were there, this couple walks in. Two men. You get that kind of thing at the hotel. They're comfortable with gays, lots of it about, even for a Muslim country." Mowbray sipped his tap water, trying to slow himself down. "Karen looks up and makes a noise of disapproval." He checked himself. "No, not disapproval, she's not homophobic or anything. More conspiratorial than that. Like a joke between us. 'Look at the fruits,' you know?"

"Sure," said Kell.

"They were both dressed in white shirts and white trousers. That's very German, too. Ninety percent of the guests look like they're playing at Wimbledon or members of some cult. Pristine white, like an advert for one of those soap powders that really deliver at low temperatures." Kell resisted telling Mowbray to "get on with it" because he knew how he liked to operate. "And there's an age gap between them," he said, "maybe fifteen or twenty years. The older bloke is the one facing me. German money,

40

you can tell. He sits down with what looks like a fruit salad, black-rimmed glasses, suntan. I can't see the boyfriend, but he's younger, fitter. Late thirties, at a guess. The old boy is camp, a bit effeminate, but this one looks straight, macho. There's something about him that triggers me, but I can't yet tell what it is."

Kell had stopped eating. He knew what Mowbray was going to tell him, a giddy premonition of something so improbable that he dismissed it out of hand.

"Anyway, Karen had finished her orange juice. Wanted to get another one. She'd hurt her foot on the coral so I offered to go instead. There's an egg station at the buffet and I waited there while the chef made me an omelette. Got the wife's orange juice, got some yogurt, then started to walk back toward our table. That was when I saw his face. That was when I recognized him."

"Who?" said Kell. "Who was it?"

"The boyfriend was Alexander Minasian."

# 5

Kell stared at Mowbray in disbelief.

"Don't fuck around," he said, because the chance sighting was so sensational that Kell had to reckon that Mowbray was making a joke.

"As clear as I'm sitting here facing you," he said. "No way it was anybody else."

Alexander Minasian was the SVR officer responsible for the recruitment of Ryan Kleckner, a high-level CIA mole in the Middle East who had funneled Western secrets to Moscow for more than two years. In an operation instigated by Amelia Levene, Kell had identified Kleckner, run him to ground in Odessa, and handed him over to Langley. In response to the loss of Kleckner, Moscow had given the order to kill Rachel. Kell held Minasian personally responsible. He wanted his head on a plate.

"Minasian has a wife," Kell said quietly. The heat of the kiln was burning into his back. "At least that's what we thought. It never entered the equation that he was gay. It's not SVR house style. They wouldn't countenance it. They're not big on homosexuality in Putin's Russia. You probably noticed."

Mowbray's reaction — a slow shake of the head, mouth pursed so that minute traces of food were visible on the inside of his lips — told Kell that he was convinced by what he had seen. He picked up his glass and turned it in his hand, a man waiting to be believed. Kell began to work from memory, his knowledge of Minasian still as insubstantial as the official SIS file. Nobody knew where Minasian had come from, where he was currently stationed, how he had recruited Kleckner.

"Minasian's wife is the daughter of a St. Petersburg oligarch. Andrei Eremenko. Draws a lot of water in Moscow. Close to the Kremlin." Kell had spent long hours looking into Eremenko's business affairs, searching for any overlap with Minasian, any clue as to his whereabouts or personality. "If he finds out his son-in-law is *gay* . . ."

"He's not going to be very happy about it." Mowbray finished Kell's sentence and set his glass back on the table. "Nor is Mrs. Minasian, for that matter. Wives can be sensitive about that stuff."

"Perhaps she already knows," Kell suggested. In his experience, wives often knew far more of their husband's misdemeanors than they ever publicly acknowledged. Many of them preferred to exist in a state of denial. Let the man philander, let him play his vain and tawdry games. Just keep it in-house. At all costs, protect the nest.

"That's what I wondered."

Kell was silent as he continued to analyze what he had been told. It was unthinkable that the SVR would have a gay officer on its books, married or otherwise. SIS had only begun recruiting openly homosexual employees in the previous ten or fifteen years; modern Russia was antediluvian by comparison. If Minasian's secret was exposed, his career would end overnight.

"Who else have you spoken to about this?"

Kell dreaded the simple reply, "C," because it would instantly shrink his options. The wheels of his imagination had begun to turn, a dormant ruthlessness circling Minasian's vulnerability like a bird of prey. If his nemesis was hiding a secret of this magnitude, he was vulnerable to an extent that was almost beyond belief. But if Amelia knew about it, she would sideline Kell on any subsequent operation, doubtless citing "personal issues" and "clouded judgment."

"I haven't told a soul," Mowbray replied, though his eyes slid to one side and he tapped his mouth with a napkin as he spoke. Kell studied the face and could not be certain that Mowbray was telling the truth. A tiny section of sunburned skin around his nose looked as if it were about to flake off.

"Not even Karen?" he asked. Spousal pillow talk was an occupational hazard among veteran spies; the habit of secrecy became harder and harder to sustain as the years went by.

"Never discuss work with the wife," Mowbray replied quickly. "Never. Something we agreed on from day one. Last time she asked me was ninety-one or ninety-two, when they arrested a bunch of IRA in London. She was watching John Simpson on the *Nine O'Clock News,* said: 'Did you have something to do with this?' I told her to mind her own business."

"But she saw Minasian?"

"Oh, yeah. All the time."

"What does that mean? She met him?"

"No. Neither of us did that. But we were staying at the same hotel. Caught the whole show."

Kell saw the glint in Mowbray's eye, the suggestion of an even greater prize.

"Call it trouble in paradise," he explained with a predictable grin. "Our man from Moscow wasn't getting on very well with his boyfriend. They kept fighting. Arguing."

"All of this played out in public?" Kell was beginning to wonder if Harold had stumbled on a setup, Minasian role-playing the moody boyfriend for the purpose of an undisclosed SVR operation at the hotel. Perhaps the relationship had even been staged for Mowbray's benefit, or Mowbray himself had been turned by the Russians.

"Not exactly." The older man was leaning forward again, still grinning. "You see, I made a point of watching them whenever I could. Surreptitious photos, eavesdropping in the bar."

"Jesus." Kell had an image of Mowbray prowling around a sun-blasted Egyptian tourist resort with a long-lens camera and a boom microphone. "Any chance I could see those photos?"

Mowbray had been biding his time, waiting for the invitation. Setting his knife and fork to one side, he shot Kell a look of mischievous self-satisfaction and reached back into his jacket pocket. Inside were half a dozen color photographs, the size of postcards, four of which spilled onto the ground as he retrieved them.

"Fuck," he muttered. It was like watching a conjuror trying to learn a new trick. "Here you go."

Kell took the photographs and experienced an extraordinary feeling of exhilaration. He turned to check his background. A chef in stained check trousers was standing three feet behind him, stretching a ball of dough on a small cushion. Kell's body was cloaked in heat. He craved alcohol.

The first photograph showed Minasian standing alone at the edge of a swimming pool, in bright sunlight. He was wearing Ray-Ban sunglasses and navy blue swimming shorts. Fit for his age, defined musculature, an expressionless mouth. The man who had given the order to kill Rachel. He felt a visceral hatred toward him. There was a woman's blurred shoulder in the left foreground of the shot, presumably Karen. Mowbray had used her as a decoy.

The next three photographs were all taken by long lens from an elevated position, angled down toward a garden in which Minasian was standing with his lover. When Kell asked, Mowbray confirmed that he had been sitting on the balcony of his room at the back of the hotel and had overheard the two men arguing. In the first shot of the sequence, they were embracing, Minasian topless, the older man wearing a pale pink short-sleeved shirt, white shorts, and plimsolls. He was tanned with chalk-white hair that was bald at the crown. In the second shot, the older man appeared to be extremely upset, his eyes stained with tears, Minasian leaning back as if to disengage from what was happening in front of him. In the third shot — Kell assumed that he had looked at the sequence out of chronological order — Minasian was gesticulating with his right arm in a manner deemed threatening enough for the older man to be shielding himself by raising his hand and turning to one side. Was he afraid of being hit? The next photograph, apparently taken with a different lens, from a new angle, showed the older man crouching down in a separate section of the garden, hands covering his face.

"What was going on?" Kell asked.

"They were shouting at each other like a couple of teenagers." The waitress removed the bowls of hummus and mashed aubergine. There was a clatter as something fell over in the kitchen. "Big fight between two queens about 'lying' and 'broken promises' and Minasian being a 'prick.' I couldn't make much of it out."

"They were always speaking English?"

"Mostly. Far as I could tell, the old boy didn't speak Russian. He's German. From Hamburg."

"How do you know that?"

"Because I'm not an idiot, guv."

"Nobody said you were, Harold."

Kell took a bite of lamb and invited Mowbray to continue. He was about to order a beer when he remembered that the restaurant was dry. A single glimpse of the secret world had been enough to strip him of a seven-month commitment to remain booze free.

"His name is Bernhard Riedle."

"How are you spelling that?"

Mowbray wrote down the name on a piece of paper and passed it to Kell.

"I got into the hotel e-mail. Piece of piss. Jumped on their wi-fi, hacked into the account used by the reservations manager, read Riedle's messages."

"Undetected?"

Kell felt uneasy. Mowbray wasn't trained in surveillance. If Minasian had caught even a scent of his interest — the eavesdropped conversations, the clandestine photographs — he might have turned the tables and engineered an investigation of his own into the nosy couple from England.

"Of course undetected," Mowbray reassured him. "Did the whole thing from my room. Took fifteen minutes. Anyway, here's the interesting bit. Minasian stayed under a pseudonym. Riedle called him 'my partner Dmitri' in the e-mails."

"Makes sense," said Kell. "He's married. Riedle could be covering for him. Did you get a passport? A surname?"

"No, sir."

"But Minasian would have had to show one when he checked in. So either Riedle really does think his boyfriend is called 'Dmitri' or he's conscious that Alexander Minasian works for the SVR and is traveling under alias."

"How do you figure that?"

Mowbray looked momentarily confused, as if Kell had identified a flaw in his thesis. For his own part, Kell was surprised that Mowbray had failed to join the dots.

"If I go on holiday with my girlfriend 'Anne Smith' and she travels on a passport calling herself 'Betty Jones,' I'm going to ask her how come she has two identities. Unless she's from the Office."

"True," said Mowbray. "You are." There was a sheepish pause while he made a silent calculation. Kell sensed his embarrassment and urged him to continue.

"Well," he said, rubbing the back of his

head. "We can discount the idea that Riedle is a spook. Once I got home I did some digging around. He's an architect."

"From Hamburg?"

"Originally, yes. That's where he has his practice, anyway. Right now, though, he's spending a lot of time in Brussels."

"Reason?"

"Some kind of office building. Swish headquarters for a Belgian television company. He's designing it, living in an apartment there while it goes up."

"With Minasian paying him the occasional visit?"

"Negative, Houston."

"They broke up?"

"They broke up," Mowbray replied.

Kell immediately saw this not as a setback, but as an opportunity. A man in love is less likely to betray his partner. A man with a broken heart can be manipulated into acts of vengeance.

"You said Riedle was feeling sorry for himself? That's what you meant? Minasian dumped him?"

Mowbray twisted his chafed nose and looked to one side, timing the delivery of a chunk of bad news. The waitress, who had passed their table several times in the preceding minutes, trying to ascertain if the two middle-aged gentlemen intended to finish their meals, finally made her decision and began collecting their plates of half-eaten food.

"He dumped him," said Mowbray. "Gigantic lovers' tiff."

"After the argument you witnessed? That was it? They separated?"

Mowbray nodded, staring at the table.

"The photos you saw, then Riedle crying on his own in the garden. That was the last time we saw Minasian. I assume he left that night. There was a twenty-two hundred Air Egypt flight from Hurghada to Cairo. He could have gone anywhere after that."

"And Riedle?"

"Stayed another two days. Had breakfast in his room, ate dinner alone with a look on his face like his life was over."

"How do you figure that?" Kell asked. "Just from a look on his face? Maybe he's that kind of person."

Mowbray pitched backward in his seat, as if Kell had been unnecessarily confrontational. Kell apologized with a raised hand and took the opportunity to order two glasses of mint tea. He was aware that his adrenaline was running high, an eagerness to ensnare Minasian clashing against long-practiced instincts for caution and context.

"What I meant was . . ."

"Don't worry, guv." Mowbray offered a conciliatory hand of his own. "I know what you meant. How did we know he was suffering? Why was he wandering around like a lovestruck adolescent?"

"Precisely. How did you know?"

Mowbray pulled out a packet of cigarettes and set them on the table. Kell looked at them and resented his own self-discipline.

"Riedle spent a lot of time at the pool, reading off an iPad. Struck up a friendship with one of the boys down there. Egyptian kid, good-looking."

"Gay?"

Mowbray realized what he had said and shook his head vigorously, chasing off the inference.

"No. Nothing like that. Married, wife and kid in Luxor. Early thirties. Laid out our sunbeds in the morning. Brought us drinks. Put up the umbrellas when the sun got too hot. You know the kind of thing."

"Sure."

"Well, I got talking to him and he said how Riedle was unhappy. He'd broken up with his boyfriend. They'd been seeing each other for over three years, had the latest in a long line of nasty rows. 'Dmitri' had left the hotel, gone off with a new boyfriend."

"He told all that to a *pool boy*?"

Mowbray seemed to be aware that the interaction sounded far-fetched.

"Bernhard struck me as the confessional sort. Needy, artistic, you know? Any sympathetic ear will do for a type like that. 'I'm in pain, come and listen to me. I've built a new house, come and look at it. I'm miserable, make me feel better.' And we tell strangers our secrets, don't we? He's never going to see the pool boy again, never going to build him a house in Luxor. He was a convenient shoulder to cry on for a couple of miserable days in paradise."

Kell felt a strange and disorienting sense of kinship with Riedle, the empathy of the brokenhearted man. He remembered his own dismay at Rachel's treachery, then the long months of grieving that followed her death. He accepted the mint tea from the waitress, who smiled at Mowbray as she placed a glass on the table in front of him. Kell was surprised when Mowbray asked for the bill. What was the hurry?

"You've told nobody about this?" he asked.

"Nobody, guv. Just you. I knew what it would mean to you, after everything that happened. Wanted to give you the opportunity."

Kell found himself saying "Thank you" in a way that caused Mowbray to produce a conspiratorial nod. A small burden of complicity had been established between them. Yet it was disconcerting to consider that choice of word: "opportunity." An opportunity for what? Kell knew that nothing would ever erase the pain he had suffered over the loss of Rachel. Vengeance would not bring her back to life, nor alter the dynamics of his relationship with Amelia. Recruiting Minasian would bring Kell a modicum of respect from colleagues at SIS for whom he felt little but contempt. So why do it? Why not stand up, shake Mowbray's hand, put fifty quid on the table to cover the bill, and walk out of the restaurant? His better future lay outside SIS — he *knew* this, he had come to terms with it — and yet Kell felt powerless to suppress his hunger for revenge.

"You know that I'm going to go after him, don't you?" he said.

"I assumed that, yes," Mowbray replied.

The waitress brought the bill.

## 6

They had made it easy for Jim Martinelli.

Kyle Chapman had asked for his address in Peterborough. He had said that four separate U.K. passport application forms would arrive at his home within the next seven days. He told Martinelli that if he took the forms to work, processed them in the usual way in his capacity as an application examiner, and guaranteed that the passports would then be sent out to the individuals concerned, his debt of thirty thousand pounds would be cleared.

Chapman gave Martinelli a warning. He said that if he attempted to contact any law-enforcement official in relation to the passports, or kept any of the information contained in the application forms, he would be killed. Chapman told Martinelli that he was working on behalf of a "businessman in Tirana" with connections to organized criminal groups in the U.K. who would "happily" hunt him down and "enjoy listening to you begging for your life in some warehouse in Peterborough where the only thing that moves is a rat taking a shit and a fucked-off Albanian touching an electric cable to your testicles." Chapman added that if, at any point, he or his client became aware that Martinelli was suffering from "stress" or had taken sick leave, or was in any way considering a change of job within the next six to twelve months, he would suffer the same fate. It was a simple exchange. The passports for the debt. No behavioral problems at work. No midnight confessions to the Samaritans after "half a bottle of Smirnoff and a good cry." If he delivered the passports, he would be free of his debt. Nobody would ever come near him again, nobody would ever finger him for abusing his position. Chapman and his associate in Albania were "men of their word who believed in loyalty and good professional conduct."

Martinelli had agreed. He had felt that he had no choice. Five days later, the passport applications had arrived at his home. Two of them had the photographs of Caucasian males attached, the third a picture of a woman in her mid-twenties, possibly with roots in northeast Africa or the Arabian peninsula. The fourth showed a fit-looking male in his early twenties who was almost certainly of Indian or Pakistani heritage. His was the only name that Martinelli committed to memory, because he had felt — looking into the young man's blank, pitiless eyes — that he was betraying not only himself by allowing such a man to possess a falsely obtained British passport, but also, potentially, the lives of many others.

The young man's name was Shahid Khan.

# 7

As soon as he had shaken Mowbray's hand outside the restaurant, Kell set to work.

He needed to discover more about Minasian, to find a way of running him to the ground. He knew that the Russian would have left no trace of himself in Hurghada, save for a false passport and a few brisk, pixelated appearances on hotel CCTV. With that in mind, Kell instructed his old friend and ally, Elsa Cassani, a freelance computer specialist based in Rome, to try to find out the surname on which "Dmitri" had been traveling in Egypt. To his surprise, her efforts failed. There was no record on the hotel computer of Bernhard Riedle's companion; the room had been registered and billed solely in Riedle's name. Kell assumed that if "Dmitri" had presented a passport, the details had either been lost or transcribed by hand.

That meant going after Riedle. If Kell

could befriend him and earn his trust, he could stripmine Riedle for information about Minasian's habits, his character traits, his strengths and weaknesses. Such a psychological portrait would prove invaluable when the time came to try to recruit him. Above all, Riedle could provide Kell with a means of communicating with Minasian. Used correctly, the heartbroken lover could be the lure that would draw Kell's quarry out into the open.

With Elsa having drawn a blank, Kell put his doubts about Mowbray to one side and hired him on £750 a day for "as long as it takes to get me face to face with Dmitri." Such was Kell's determination to pursue Minasian without involving Amelia Levene that he was prepared to spend much of the two-hundred-thousand-pound fee SIS had deposited in his bank account following the Kleckner operation. It had always felt like blood money to Kell; to use it in pursuit of Rachel's killer felt not only just, but liberating.

Mowbray was immediately successful. By Saturday he had located Bernhard Riedle's address in Brussels and ascertained that he was living in a block of luxury serviced apartments in the Quartier Dansaert. Kell found the agents online and took out a three-week rental of his own on an apartment in the same building. He then traveled with Mowbray to Brussels on the Eurostar, taking two rooms at the Hotel Metropole. The next afternoon, less than five days after meeting Mowbray in Westbourne Grove, Kell had moved into the apartment.

# 8

Weekends were always the hardest. When he was busy with work, Bernhard Riedle could find distraction in a site visit, in a conversation with a structural engineer, even in lunch with his client. But when the meetings stopped, when the builders went home on a Friday evening and the office in Hamburg closed for business, Riedle was alone with his agony. He drank constantly, he sat on his own in the vast apartment, unable to read, to concentrate on watching the television, to do anything other than obsess about Dmitri.

He thought about him incessantly. Though there was no evidence for this, he was convinced that Dmitri had left his wife and that all of the promises he had made to Bernhard were now being made to a younger, more vital lover, a partner with whom he would build a meaningful future. He pictured them deep in conversation, laughing and sharing intimacies; devouring one another's bodies. Everything physical between them more satisfying for Dmitri, their intellectual life more stimulating and more meaningful than it had ever been with Bernhard. He could hear Dmitri betraying him in conversation, speaking contemptuously of his character. What they had shared over their three years together — the trips to Istanbul, to London and New York — had already become a subject of ridicule. The peculiar hardness in Dmitri's personality, the chill ruthlessness Bernhard had fought so hard to ignore, was now all that remained of him. He felt discarded and forgotten. He felt weak and he felt old. He wanted, more than anything he had ever wanted in his life, to have the opportunity to confront Dmitri, to rail at him for his cruelty and selfishness, and then to restore their relationship to what it had once been. He felt that he could not live without Dmitri's love. If he could not have it, he would kill himself. He was going mad.

Brussels was a prison. They had spent so much time in the city in recent months that every street corner held a memory of their relationship. Restaurants in which they had eaten, parks in which they had walked, cinemas where they had watched films, holding hands and touching in the darkness. The bed in which Bernhard slept was the bed in which he had made love to Dmitri, stroked his hair, read to him from the books they adored. It was only in bed that Dmitri had allowed himself to be vulnerable, to articulate his deepest fears and insecurities. On occasions he had encouraged Bernhard to beat him, to punish him — these had been the only times when Bernhard had felt that he had any semblance of control over their relationship. He had been intoxicated by the intimate depravity of their private selves. There had been nothing false between them in this bed. There had been no secrets. Now Bernhard could only sleep by taking a pill that would knock out the night, leaving him exhausted for work the following morning. In his first waking moments, he would be assaulted by images of Dmitri with his new lover. As a consequence, he walked the streets with a feeling of bottled hate — he had never known such humiliation, such a distilled sense of betrayal and loss. This was the wretched character of Bernhard Riedle's life. He was at the mercy of a man who seemed utterly contemptuous of him. He was fifty-nine years old and knew — because he had no illusions about such things — that he would never again experience a love as intense and as fulfilling as that which he had experienced with Dmitri.

It was a Saturday night in June. Tourists in the Grande Place. Teenagers drinking cheap beer, couples with selfie sticks taking flash photographs in front of the Hôtel de Ville. Bernhard despised them, not least because he envied them their youth and apparent happiness. The square stank of horse manure and cheap melted chocolate and it was almost impossible to take more than a few steps without tripping over a small child. Bernhard felt less alone among the crowds, but wished that he had taken one of the smaller side streets through the old town instead of subjecting himself to the cheerful chaos of the square. He had eaten an early dinner in a poor and expensive Italian restaurant, leaving half of his food untouched, a bottle of Verdicchio emptied. Before dinner he had consumed two beers on an empty stomach and now felt the familiar symptoms of a depressive drunkenness. He was wary of encountering an associate from the building project, or even the client himself. It would take very little for Bernhard to break down; a small gesture of kindness, an expression of empathy, and he might even collapse in tears. He did not want to undermine his reputation nor be exposed for the lonely and broken fool that he had become.

He decided to return home, to take a sleeping pill, then to go to church in the morning. He had begun to pray last thing at night, pleading with God to ease his suffering, to show Dmitri the error of his ways. It was time to take his prayers to a place in which he might find some modicum of spiritual solace. He knew that Dmitri believed only in himself and in his own strength. He would doubtless hold Bernhard in even greater contempt for the naïveté of his newfound devotion. So be it. He had to try to find some semblance of calm, a way to end the turbulence into which he had been thrown since Egypt.

Riedle walked toward his apartment block in the Quartier Dansaert, the crowds ebbing away as he reached Rue des Chartreux. The entrance to the building was set back from the street by a short, dimly lit passageway in which couples sometimes lurked for a furtive kiss, and where Bernhard's neighbors tied up their bicycles and strollers. By the time he reached it, the bustle of the night had receded to an absolute stillness, the only noise in the neighborhood the echo of Bernhard's footsteps as he turned toward the door.

What happened next happened quickly.

There was a man of Somalian appearance standing in the passageway, most likely a drug addict. His jacket was torn, his shoes stained. Bernhard could smell the sharp acidic filth of his clothes and sweat.

*"Entschuldigen Sie mich,"* he said, instinctively speaking in German. The Somali was blocking his route to the door and took a step toward him.

*"Argent,"* he said, the French aggressive and guttural. *"Portefeuille. Maintenant."*

As Bernhard processed the realization that he was being mugged, a second man walked into the passageway behind him, shutting off any hope of escape. This man was taller than the Somali and almost certainly of Eastern European descent. He loomed over Bernhard. There was a livid birthmark to the left of his nose.

*"Un moment, s'il vous plait,"* he said, turning back to the Somali, desperately searching for his wallet. Bernhard reached into the pocket of his trousers and pulled out a handful of loose change. Some of the money spilled onto the ground as he tried to pass it to the Somali.

"Fucking money now," said the Eastern European.

"*Oui, oui.* Yes, okay," Bernhard told him, spinning around. That was when he saw the knife, hidden within the folds of the man's leather jacket. Bernhard let out a gasp, still desperately searching for his wallet. Had he been pickpocketed in the Grande Place? He was terrified of being cut. Of all things, at that moment he thought not of Dmitri — who would surely have been able to protect him from his assailants — but of ISIS, of kidnap, of heads sliced apart by machetes. He wondered if the men were terrorists.

"Watch."

The Eastern European had flicked at the antique Omega Constellation on Bernhard's wrist, sending pain shooting along his forearm. He winced and cried out as the man hissed at him in French to remain silent.

"*Argent.*"

Before Bernhard had a chance to remove the watch, the Somali had grabbed him by the right arm, almost knocking him to the ground. A car drove past but did not stop. Bernhard wanted to shout out but knew that they would run him through with the knife. He was pitiably afraid. He had never known such fear, even when attacked as a young man, for his habits, for his dress, for the sin of being gay. Those attacks had conferred upon him a certain nobility and he had at least experienced them with other men, in groups of two or three. On this occasion, however, he was quite alone. He could be killed for the watch, for the contents of his wallet, and the men would never be caught.

Then, a miracle. One of the tenants from the apartment block came into the passage from the street, jangling a set of keys, whistling a tuneless song. He was about forty-five, lean, and reasonably fit. The man looked up, realized what was happening, and acted with astonishing speed. In clear, confident French, he approached the men, stepping in front of Bernhard as he did so.

*"Mais qu'est-ce qu'il se passé? Dégage de là."*

Bernhard felt himself pushed against the wall as the Somali moved past him to confront the neighbor. The next thing Bernhard knew, the neighbor had disarmed the Eastern European, knocking his knife to the ground. It spun away to the far side of the passage as the Somali doubled over from a savage kick in his groin. Meanwhile, the Eastern European was nursing a cut on his arm. He cried out in pain and ran onto the street, leaving his friend behind. The neighbor — who was dressed in jeans and a dark sweater — dispatched a second, heavy blow to the Somali, this time to the side of his neck. He fell onto the cobbled tiles of the passageway, where blood had dripped onto the ground. The neighbor then grabbed Bernhard, put a key in the lock, and guided him inside the entrance of the apartment building before slamming the door behind them. All of this had taken less than twenty seconds.

"Are you all right? *Ça va?*" he asked, holding Bernhard's forearms and fixing his eyes with a manic, adrenalized stare. As Bernhard registered that his savior was British, he became dimly aware of the rapid kick and scrape of a man trying to kickstart a motorbike on the street.

"*Oui. Ça va.* Yes," he replied, shaking his head in bewildered gratitude, thanking the Englishman as effusively as he could manage. So great was his relief that he felt he might be on the verge of laughter.

"Did they attack you?" the man asked. "Did they take anything?"

"No," Bernhard replied. "You were extraordinary. I do not know what happened. Thank you."

"Stay here," said the neighbor and reopened the door. He walked back along the passageway until he was standing outside on the street. The Somali had disappeared. The neighbor then took a piece of cloth or a tissue from his pocket, bent down, and mopped up the blood that had spilled on the ground. At that moment, Bernhard heard the motorbike catch and roar, buzzing past the Englishman, who swore loudly — "Fuck you!" — as the Eastern European made his escape.

"Did you get the license plate?" Bernhard asked when the man had come back into the foyer.

"I'm afraid not," he replied.

"Never mind. Probably it was a stolen bike."

"Yes," he said. "Probably it was."

# 9

The two men stood face to face in the lobby. One of them was in a state of advanced shock. The other was pleased that the plan he had so meticulously prepared had come off without a hitch.

Thomas Kell, the brave, resourceful English neighbor who had come to the aid of Bernhard Riedle, placed a comforting hand on the German's back and felt the quick surge and drop of his chest as he struggled to control his breathing. Riedle put out a hand to steady himself against the wall of the lobby and looked across at Kell.

"I cannot thank you enough," he said. "Without your help . . ."

"Don't mention it," Kell replied. "Are you sure you're all right?"

Riedle had a kind, friendly face, solid and bespectacled. It was a face Kell warmed to immediately. Riedle took a moment to gather himself, then quite literally dusted himself down, running his hands along his sleeves and down his thighs as though trying to drive away all evidence of contact with his attackers.

"You said you didn't lose anything?" Kell asked. "They didn't take any of your money?"

"You didn't give them a chance," Riedle replied, breaking into a relieved smile. "They took nothing."

Kell introduced himself as "Peter" and explained that he had been coming back from eating dinner at a local restaurant. Riedle — to Kell's surprise — introduced himself as "Bernie," a nickname that had not come up in any of the surveillance of his e-mail traffic. Taking advantage of the German's mood of heartfelt gratitude, Kell suggested that he accompany him to his apartment and sit with him until he had completely recovered from the shock of the attack. To Kell's relief, Bernhard happily agreed to the idea, adding that he was mesmerized by the skill and professionalism with which his neighbor had disarmed and chased off his assailants.

"Were you once a soldier?" he asked as they walked side by side up the stairs.

"Not as such," Kell replied. "In a former life I worked as a diplomat, often in some fairly hairy places. Kenya. Iraq. Afghanistan. I was taught a bit of self-defense, you know? Luckily I very rarely get a chance to use it."

"Well, I am extremely grateful to you." They had reached the door. Riedle took out a set of keys. He was several inches shorter than Kell, who could see a small summer insect trapped in the light white hairs on the crown of his head. "I don't know what I would have done if you had not appeared," he said, turning the key and ushering his guest inside. Kell walked into the hall and heard the thunk and click of a sliding bolt as Riedle closed the door behind them. "He had a knife. You cut him."

"He cut himself." Kell noted the same off-the-peg watercolors, candlesticks, and soft furnishings that adorned his own apartment, two floors above. Clearly the developers had bought dozens of the same items in a job lot, distributing them evenly throughout the building. The layout of the rooms was also identical. A kitchen off the hall, a bedroom and bathroom to the rear of the apartment. "But not seriously," he said. "The blade must have touched his wrist as I went to disarm him."

Riedle listened intently, though Kell was spinning a further deceit. The man who had been holding the knife was a former Polish intelligence officer named Rafal Suda whom Kell had met many years earlier while working on an SIS operation in Gdansk. Rafal had snapped open a small vial of theatrical blood that had dripped, effectively enough, onto the cobbles. His accomplice, Xavier Baeyens, a retired Belgian Customs official, had acquired the motorbike on which Suda had made his escape. He had stripped the plates, fudged the insurance, and put enough petrol in the tank to get to Bruges.

"Should I call the police?" Riedle asked.

It was a question Kell had been expecting and one for which he had prepared a suitably tortured answer.

"It's difficult," he said. "The same thing happened to a friend of mine in London recently. Broad daylight, cameras everywhere, two witnesses to a mugging at knifepoint. She lost her bag, her wedding ring, a cell phone, about three hundred pounds in cash. The police did nothing. They tried, of course, but it was impossible to track down the men who had attacked her. She got lost in weeks of bureaucracy and eventually nothing came of it."

Riedle was momentarily frustrated. He wanted justice. Kell could see it in his face.

"But they looked like drug dealers and local criminals," he said. "There might be photographs on file at the . . . the . . ." He struggled for the correct English term. "Commissariat? Precinct?"

"Police station," said Kell.

"Yes. We could identify them."

The brave English neighbor managed to look suitably dismayed by this idea.

"If you need to do that, Bernie, of course I'd be happy to help. But I'm very busy with work and, being one hundred percent honest, slightly reluctant to get dragged into a court case. I live in London, I'd have to keep coming back and forth to Brussels. You seem unharmed. Nothing was stolen, so you have no need to file an insurance claim. But of course if you *want* to . . ."

Riedle nodded. He could hardly ask Peter to waste time speaking to the police, to assist in pressing charges or to travel regularly from London to Brussels to stand as a witness in any ensuing trial. It was just a street mugging, after all. He had lost nothing but his dignity. It would be best for Riedle to comply with the wishes of the man who had so uncomplainingly come to his rescue.

"Of course, of course," he said, turning toward the kitchen. He gestured at Kell to sit down. "Better to have a drink and forget all about it. These scum will never be found."

As Kell muttered "Yes," the mobile phone in his jacket buzzed with an incoming text. He assumed it was Harold, sitting upstairs in the rented apartment on the fourth floor, doubtless helping himself to a large tumbler of Kell's single malt. Mowbray had been waiting in the lobby as Kell approached the passageway on Rue des Chartreux, ready to intercept any neighbor who threatened to leave the building while the mugging was taking place.

Kell checked the phone. It was a text from Rafal. He had met up with Xavier. They had abandoned the motorbike. Kell gave them the all-clear and thanked them for a job well done. Suda was due to return to Poland the next day, Xavier to take a ten-day holiday in Accra. Kell was putting the phone back in his pocket when Riedle appeared from the kitchen.

"Can I make you a drink?"

Kell asked for whiskey. His commitment to remaining on the wagon had lasted only until his first night in Brussels, when he had succumbed to the temptation of a glass of Talisker. He was not yet back on the cigarettes, but reckoned the Minasian operation would have him on twenty a day before the end of the month. As a precaution, he had bought a packet of Winston Lights and stowed them, still sealed, in the drawer beside his bed.

"Ice?" Riedle asked.

"No, thank you. Just a splash of water to open it up."

Riedle disappeared and returned with the drink. Kell sat down in a suede-covered armchair identical to the one upstairs in which he had read Rafal and Xavier's surveillance reports on Riedle's movements around Brussels. The staged mugging had been planned for the night before, only to be called off at the last moment when a taxi had pulled up on the opposite side of the street, just as Xavier was taking up position.

"I like this expression," said Riedle, passing Kell the whiskey. Kell thanked him with a brisk nod. "To 'open it up.' The water does this with the flavor, yes? I do not drink whiskey."

Riedle himself was holding a long-stemmed glass of red wine and appeared to be slightly unsteady on his feet. Xavier had been tailing him all evening and had reported the consumption of two beers in the old town before eight o'clock, then an entire bottle of white wine at an Italian restaurant in the Rue de la Montagne. Shock usually took the edge off drunkenness, but Riedle had been saved from the lions and might easily be slipping into a state of euphoria.

"Cheers."

Kell lifted the whiskey — blended, to judge by the smell — and the two men touched glasses.

It had begun.

# 10

They were smiling as they handed the envelope to Azhar Ahmed Iqbal. There were three of them. The oldest of the men, whom Azhar had never seen before, said that it was a genuine British passport that had come by diplomatic bag from Amman. An official in the U.K. Passport Office had been compromised by brave and resourceful agents of ISIS and had produced the passport in return for a sum of money.

Azhar opened the envelope. The passport was hard and cold to the touch. It was clean and new and would not easily bend in his hands. They were still smiling at him as they watched him look at it and flick through the pages.

Three months earlier, Azhar had been taken into a room in Raqqa and had sat on a stool beside a blank white wall. Someone had taken his photograph. One of the men, a good fighter from Tunisia who had worked as a barber, had shaved off Azhar's beard and cut his hair so that he would look good in front of the camera. Azhar saw that this photograph had now been laminated inside the passport. He looked successful and educated. He looked like a businessman. It was exactly what they wanted.

"You like the way you look?" Jalal asked with a sly grin.

"Yeah. I like it," Azhar replied.

"But now you are not Azhar Ahmed Iqbal from Leeds, no? You are no longer Omar Assya. Who are you, my friend?"

Azhar looked down at the name printed beneath the photograph. He had been using the *kunya* "Omar Assya" for at least three years as a way of obscuring his identity from the West Yorkshire Police. He had grown used to it.

"Shahid Khan." Azhar did not mind the name. They had made him a year older. But then he saw his place of birth. "From *Bradford*?" he said. "Why did you say I was from fookin' Bradford?"

All the men laughed. When they had calmed down, when Azhar had finished talking about the rivalry between Leeds and Bradford, and when he had started to get used to being called "Shahid," Jalal told him that he had to protect the passport at all costs. He should also carry it around with him so that it became slightly worn and looked less new. Before returning to the United Kingdom, Shahid was to fly to Dubai and then to Cairo so that the passport would show arrival and departure stamps from the UAE and Egypt. This would help to dispel any suspicion if a member of the U.K. Border Police at Heathrow looked more closely at the passport and decided to question Shahid about his movements. Should this happen, Shahid was to say that he had been attending his cousin's wedding in Dubai and had returned home via Cairo so that he could visit the pyramids. If he was subjected to more intense scrutiny — if, for example, he was taken into an interview room by an officer of the British MI5 — Shahid was to rely on the biographical details of his real life. So: Shahid Khan went to the same school as Azhar Ahmed Iqbal; he had the same cousins, the same brothers and sisters, as Azhar Ahmed Iqbal. That way he could tell his favorite family stories and make his background sound more realistic. The trick was to stay as close to the truth as possible. It was when you started to lie that you ran into trouble.

"What about my job?" Azhar asked. "What do I do for work?"

Jalal said that this was a good question that proved that they had chosen the right soldier for the operation in England. He told "Shahid" that he was to say he was unemployed and about to move to London to look for work. He was to say that he had spent the last of his savings on the trips to Dubai and Cairo. Jalal would see to it that a Facebook page and mobile phone account were set up in Shahid Khan's name. He would have other profiles on the Internet that would fool the British MI5. Jalal told Shahid that he had time in which to adapt to his new identity and to ask more questions like the one he had just been clever enough to ask. Jalal insisted that it was "extremely unlikely" that Shahid would be questioned by the British. Thousands of young Muslim men passed through Heathrow airport every day. They would make sure that his flight arrived at the busiest time of day. Shahid would be well dressed — they would provide good clothes for him — and he would look educated and respectable. It was the will of Allah that Shahid Khan be allowed to pass into his former country.

Shahid had absolute faith in Jalal's judgment. It was Jalal who had taught him about the beauty of the Caliphate. Shahid embraced him. He embraced the other men.

They told him that he was brave and would soon be spoken of as a hero who had avenged the Prophet. Shahid believed them. It was all that he wanted. To be a hero in their eyes, in the eyes of the true believers, and to do God's will.

## 11

Kell and Riedle talked until two o'clock in the morning.

Kell had sensed immediately that it would take at least two or three such encounters before Riedle would begin to open up about "Dmitri." It was obvious from a certain detachment in his conversation that the German wanted to present himself in a good light, particularly in the aftermath of the mugging, which had plainly unsettled him. He was a proud man. A successful man. Kell knew from Elsa's research that Riedle was responsible for a large team of architects in Hamburg and had been a partner at his firm for more than ten years. He listened closely as Riedle explained the work he was doing in Brussels, occasionally adding stories of his own about his phantom career as a diplomat in the Foreign Office. Riedle, who spoke faultless English as a result of spending seven years working in

London, was evidently highly regarded within architectural circles, but tended to keep himself to himself. He valued his privacy and had few close friends. With the exception of his three-year relationship with the married Minasian, Riedle's lifestyle appeared to be morally unimpeachable: Elsa and Mowbray had not flagged up any predilection for rent boys or problems with drugs or gambling. His interests stretched from English and American literature to Chinese contemporary art to the street food of Mexico and the music of Brazil. He was educated, thoughtful, and unfailingly polite. Kell liked him.

At no point in the evening did Riedle mention his sexuality. Kell hinted that his own marriage had broken down several years earlier, but quickly moved the subject on when he sensed that Riedle was uneasy. Don't rush him, he told himself, moving through the rusty gears of a hundred yesteryear recruitments. Let the relationship flourish in its own good time. If Riedle thinks that you are discreet, that you are astute and wise, that you are, above all, sympathetic to his cause, he will become your agent. Allow him to warm to you, to trust you, finally to confide in you; Kell's influence would be the drop of water that causes the whiskey to open up.

And so it came to pass. The two neighbors made a plan to meet for dinner two nights later at Forgeron, a fashionable brasserie in a district of Brussels frequented by Belgian hipsters and optimistic couples on second dates. Riedle appeared at half past seven wearing a lively gray tweed suit, brown brogues, and a pale pink shirt offset by a cream tie spotted with large blue polka dots. He was sporting a new, thicker pair of glasses that were almost identical to those worn by every architect Kell had ever encountered. He was tempted to make a joke about typecasting but instead complimented Riedle on the choice of venue.

"Yes. It's wonderful here," he said, reminding Kell of a music-hall impresario as he gazed around the room. "I have reserved a table on the balcony."

Kell looked up. The "balcony" was a narrow raised metal walkway on the first floor, no more than five feet wide, set with tables for two. Riedle confirmed their reservation with the maître d' and the two men were led upstairs by a waitress who shot Kell an exaggeratedly friendly look, judging him to be Riedle's boyfriend and wanting to appear supportive. There was a low roof above the balcony and an overweight man occupying the first of three tables. The man's chair was jutting out so that Kell was obliged to perform an elaborate ducking maneuver in order to pass him. The waitress had selected the farthest table on the walkway and took their orders for drinks. Kell was pleased when he heard Riedle asking for a kir. The sooner there was alcohol inside him, the better.

There were pleasantries and exchanges of small talk while they studied their menus and drank their aperitifs. Riedle, who had his back to the brasserie, raised a toast to Kell and insisted that he was going to pay for dinner "as a thank-you for saving me." During their conversation at the apartment, Kell had explained that he was working on an investment project in Brussels, a suitably vapid job description that he hoped would discourage any further interest. Nevertheless, Riedle asked if his meetings were going well, and Kell was able to say that it was "early days" and that "a number of parties still needed to be sounded out" before the "proper financing" could be guaranteed. Riedle's own account of a difficult meeting with a services consultant that afternoon took them halfway through their first course, by which time they were drinking a bottle of Chablis. Kell had ordered smoked salmon blinis, Riedle a vichyssoise.

"How is your food?" Riedle asked.

"Not identifiably Russian," Kell replied, and was glad to see a momentary discomfort flicker in his companion's eyes. He had chosen the dish as a private joke, but now realized that it might lead him toward Minasian. "How's your soup?"

"Fine."

Taking advantage of a slight pause, Kell inched toward Dmitri.

"The blinis are fine, but I've broken a personal promise. Just as one should never eat bouillabaisse outside Marseilles, I believe you should never order these" — he indicated his plate — "outside Moscow."

"You have been to Russia?" Riedle asked. Kell could feel him lifting from the bottom of the river, circling upward through the dark waters, rising slowly to the bait.

"Many times," he replied. "The caviar is not as good as it once was — and it's certainly more expensive nowadays — but I still go there for business."

"You were a diplomat there?"

"No. Briefly in Armenia in the mid-nineties when I filled in for somebody on sick leave, but never Moscow." Kell had to be careful not to push too hard. "Minasian" was an Armenian surname. Though it was almost certainly the case that Dmitri had presented himself to Riedle as a Russian citizen, he might occasionally have spoken nostalgically of his forebears in the Caucasus. The best cover is the simplest cover, one that draws on truthful elements in the spy's background. "Have you been yourself?" he asked, sipping his Chablis without an apparent care in the world. "Moscow? St. Petersburg?"

"I do not trust Russians," Riedle replied with an almost petulant finality. "I have personal reasons. I despise their politics, their leadership."

"It's certainly a worry . . ."

"I sometimes think that the Russian character is the end of kindness, you know? The end of everything that is nice and good in this world."

Kell was not a fisherman, but knew the angler's rapturous delight in feeling that first bite on the lure. The sudden tug, the ripple on the surface of the water, the line running out as the fish ran free.

"I'm not sure I understand you," he said, though he understood all too well.

"As I say, personal reasons." Riedle finished his soup and set the spoon down gently. "I have to be careful what I say. I don't want to come across as racist or as a bigot . . ."

"You are among friends, Bernie. You can say what you like. I'm not here to judge you."

That was all it took. Riedle pulled the sleeve of his jacket, squeezed a ruby cufflink, and was away.

"When I think of the Russian temperament, I think of sin," he said, looking at Kell as though he was both morally ashamed and politically disappointed by what he was about to say. "I think of money and the greed for money. A state apparatus that robs its own people, politicians filling their pockets at the expense of the men and women they are elected to represent. I think of violence. Journalists silenced, opposition politicians murdered for the exercise of free speech. Corruption and death always going hand in hand." He took a sip of water, like a pianist composing himself before embarking on the final movement of a concerto. "When I think of Russia I think of deceit. Husbands deceiving wives. Young women seducing older men because they crave nothing but money and status. Deceit in business, of course. Do you follow me? The Slavic temperament is human nature at its most base. There is no kindness in Russia.

Everything is so raw and brutal. They are like animals."

It was an astonishing diatribe, and one to which Kell responded with the obvious question.

"You said you had personal reasons for feeling this way?"

A waiter had inched along the balcony and begun to clear away their plates of food. Kell hoped that the interruption would not cause Riedle to soften his prejudice or, worse, change the subject.

"I don't wish to bore you with those," he said, ordering a bottle of Chianti. "I can't only talk about myself this evening, Peter."

"No. Do." Kell sensed that talking about himself was exactly what Bernhard Riedle wanted to do. "I'd be interested to hear your reasons. I sometimes find myself thinking the same way about Russia, particularly when it comes to murdered dissidents."

Riedle took his eyes away from Kell and looked past him toward the large street window. He appeared to be lost in thought. It was like watching a man in a dealership trying to decide whether or not to buy an expensive car.

"I had a relationship with a Russian," he said finally, the bustle and noise of the restaurant rendering his voice almost inaudible. "A man," he added. Riedle was examining Kell's reaction with sudden intensity. "Does this make you uncomfortable?"

Kell wondered if there had been something in his facial response to indicate disapproval, but quickly ascertained that Riedle was merely testing for any evidence of homophobia.

"Not at all," he replied. "Does the man live in Hamburg?"

Riedle shook his head.

"You were together a long time?"

"Three years."

"When did you break up?"

Riedle swallowed a long, glass-emptying mouthful of Chablis.

"Last month," he replied, and looked over the railing that ran along the length of the walkway, down toward the entrance of the restaurant. Kell could see a cook standing over a bed of crushed ice, shucking oysters. "I was in Egypt," he said, again bringing his eyes back to the table. "A holiday. Things had not been good for a long time. He decided finally to end things."

"I'm very sorry to hear that." Kell had a memory of Claire blithely informing him that she was in a new relationship, less than a month after their separation. "Nothing worse than a breakup," he said. "How are you coping?"

Riedle was both surprised and comforted by the question. "Not well," he said. "To be honest, Peter, I am suffering."

Kell leaned toward him, doing his job. "I've been there," he said. "You don't sleep. You can't eat. You're angry, you feel lost. It doesn't get any easier with age. If anything, these things become worse."

"Yes," Riedle replied. "You felt this with your wife when your marriage ended?"

Kell hesitated for a moment, because he hated drawing Claire into operational conversation. It was tawdry and disloyal to use her for the purposes of deception; there had to be something in his life that remained sacred. Everything else, for years and years, had been infected by spying.

"My marriage was different," he said. "My wife and I met when we were very young. We grew apart. We became different people as the years went by." Kell might have added that there had been times when he had blamed Claire for the entire squeezed and cut-down shape of his life; that he had been liberated by their separation. Or he might have said that there were still moments, when they met for lunch or saw one another at a social occasion, when he felt an almost gravitational pull toward her, a longing to be reintegrated into their former life. Instead, he said something comparatively bland, but undeniably true: "I think she found the demands of my job very difficult. There was also an added, very painful complication in that we were never able to have children."

The waiter brought their main courses and the bottle of Chianti. It was then that Riedle mentioned Minasian for the first time.

"I'm embarrassed to admit that Dmitri — my lover, my boyfriend — was married."

Kell allowed himself to process the revelation, seemingly for the first time, before responding.

"These things happen," he said. "Adultery is commonplace. Men find themselves conflicted. Particularly in Russia, I imagine, where the attitude to a person's sexuality is so toxic. Embarrassment is pointless, Bernie. Shame is what we feel when we are worried about what other people are thinking about us."

"This is a very liberal view, Peter." Riedle smiled with avuncular disapproval, touching one of the polka dots on his expensive cream tie. The light caught in his designer spectacles and flashed off a lens. "Dmitri was tormented by his deceit. Or, at least, he pretended to be."

It was a first meaningful glimpse into the Minasian personality. Kell said: "What do you mean, 'pretended'?" as he scribbled notes in his mind.

Riedle lifted his knife and fork and carved into the fatty edge of a lamb cutlet. "Perhaps I am being unfair," he said. "His wife has been ill for many years. Some kind of muscular difficulty which leaves her in great pain."

Kell suspected that this was a lie. There was nothing in the files about Svetlana Minasian suffering from a debilitating illness, muscular or otherwise.

"That's awful," Kell said, a judgment that caused Riedle to wince. He wanted no expressions of sympathy for the woman; she had simply been an obstacle blocking his access to Dmitri.

"It is and it is not," he replied. "She prevents him from living the life he wants to live. From being the man he wants to be. She is also highly critical of him, closed off in her thinking. Spoiled and judgmental."

Kell wondered how much of this was true. He suspected that Minasian had constructed flaws in Svetlana's character that would both console Riedle and justify his emotional distance from the marriage.

"And children? Do they have any?"

Riedle shook his head. "No." There was a strange kind of satisfaction in his reply; it suggested the complete absence of a sexual relationship between Minasian and his wife. "I think Dmitri was very sophisticated, very clever when it came to presenting himself to me in a certain way," Riedle said, with a perceptiveness that took Kell by surprise. "He knew what I wanted and he knew how to give it. He also knew how to take it away."

"Take what away? You mean his love for you?"

Like a breeze coming through an open window, Kell remembered the enveloping intimacy he had known with Rachel, the deepest and most fulfilling love he had ever felt for a woman; a love ripped away in a few short days by the realization that she had been lying to him. He thought of Amelia's cunning and of his own role in deceiving Riedle. Minasian was the common denominator. "Dmitri" controlled them all.

"I mean that there is something sadistic about him. Something deeply manipulative and cruel. That is the conclusion I have come to, not just because of the way he has disregarded me since our relationship ended, but also because I can now look back on his behavior when we were together in a different way."

"In what way?"

"He was often selfish and bullying. He knew that I was not as strong as he was. He knew that I was profoundly in love with him. But rather than take responsibility for this, to be careful with my feelings, he used it as a tool, a weapon against me." For some time, Riedle chewed his food, saying nothing. Kell also remained silent, waiting. "A person should have a duty of care for someone they profess to love, no?" Riedle's expression suggested that his question could brook no argument. "I think Dmitri was obsessed by ideas of power. This is the only way I can understand things, looking back. Have you read *Nineteen Eighty-Four*?"

"Not for a long time."

"It is one of Dmitri's favorite novels." Kell silently absorbed the irony of this revelation, but said nothing. "There is an exchange, toward the end of the book, when Winston Smith is being tortured. A discussion about power. Winston is asked how a man exerts power over another man. Do you remember his answer?"

"By making him suffer?" Kell suggested.

"Precisely!"

Riedle beamed at Kell with astonished admiration, as if he had at last met a person who could not only understand his plight, but explain Dmitri's behavior into the bargain. Kell smiled. He was trying to link together what Riedle was saying. Much of it was startling, yet a jilted lover, an angry and heartbroken boyfriend, will think and say anything that might make sense of tangled emotions. Kell needed to be able to separate Riedle's prejudices from the hard, observable facts about Dmitri's behavior. Kell reminded himself that he had only two objectives: to build a detailed psychological profile of Minasian, and to use Riedle to lure him out of the shadows. Everything else was tangential.

"It sounds to me as though it's a good thing that you're no longer with this man. If what you're saying is true, he didn't make you very happy. It sounds like a form of torture."

"It is true. Believe me. But isn't it also the case that the things in life which give us the most pleasure also cause us the most pain?"

"I'll drink to that."

Kell lifted his glass but had misjudged the moment. Riedle was uncomfortable and quickly returned to his recollections.

"Dmitri was everything to me. I thought

of us as a perfect match, despite the gap in age between us."

"How old was he?" Kell asked.

"Thirty-four when we met. He is almost thirty-eight now. I have just become fifty-nine." Riedle appeared briefly to slip into a private memory. Kell knew that Minasian had lied to Riedle about his age; according to his file at SIS, he was almost forty-one. "We laughed together," Riedle said. "I could tell him everything and he could solve my problems. He was capable of immense kindness, of great insights. We shared a love of the same literature, the same interests. The truth is that he fascinated me in every element of his personality."

"But he knew this and he took advantage of it."

"Yes!" Riedle's response was quick, almost convulsive. Kell noticed the table behind him coming to a sudden halt in conversation. "Yes, he took advantage of that." Riedle cut off another chunk of lamb. He spoke as he chewed. It was the first time the German's impeccable table manners had faltered. "What is most painful is the loss of this side of his personality. The side that could make me happy. It is not easy at my age to meet a man, particularly one who possessed this ability to bring such contentment to me." Kell thought of Rachel, her ghost eavesdropping on their conversation, and concluded — not for the first time — that human beings were fools to expect other people to shore them up. He was about to repeat his earlier assertion that Riedle was well shot of the relationship when something happened that stripped him of his composure. Looking down toward the entrance, he saw a beautiful woman in her early twenties walking into the restaurant in the company of a man who was at least twice her age. The man was wearing a black suit and his hair was slicked back with gel. A large birthmark was visible to the left of his nose.

It was Rafal Suda.

Kell fixed his eyes back on Riedle and smiled a crocodile smile. If the German looked down, he would see Suda. It was that simple. The man who had mugged him only two nights earlier was standing less than eight feet away, making audible small talk with the maître d'. If Riedle recognized him, there would be a confrontation. There would be police involvement and Kell would be obliged to act as a witness. The operation would be over before it had begun. Any hope of locating Minasian by using Riedle as a lure would evaporate.

In an effort to keep the conversation flowing, Kell repeated his assertion that Riedle was lucky to be free of Dmitri, a man who had exerted such a baleful influence over his private life. He spoke for as long as it took for Suda and his date to be led toward the interior of the restaurant. When they were beyond Riedle's line of sight, Kell encouraged the German to respond. As he listened to his reply, Kell could see Suda, out of the corner of his eye, being led to the first table on the parallel balcony. He was no farther away than the length of a London bus. It was a slice of wretched luck. Forgeron had seating for up to a hundred customers in the main section toward the back of the restaurant, but Suda had been seated in one of the few places from which he could still be seen by Riedle.

The German was talking. Kell was trying to absorb what he was saying about Minasian while simultaneously formulating a plan for getting Suda out of the restaurant. A warning text message would do it, but Suda would almost certainly have abandoned the mobile he had used on the Riedle operation. Kell had no other number, only an e-mail address. What were the chances of a middle-aged Polish spook checking his in-box while a statuesque blonde was gazing adoringly into his eyes over a platter of oysters? Slim, at best. No, he had to think of an alternative approach — and all the while keep Riedle talking.

"What were Dmitri's politics?" he asked. Kell looked down at Riedle's plate. The German had almost finished his lamb cutlets. That was the next problem. With a kir and several glasses of wine inside him, a man of Riedle's age might need to go to the bathroom in the break between courses. Should he do so, he would need to turn around and to inch along the balcony, all the while looking out over the restaurant, directly toward Suda's table.

"He rarely spoke about politics," he said. "I asked him, of course, and we had arguments about what was going on in Ukraine."

"What kind of arguments?"

"Oh, the usual ones." Riedle speared a stem of purple-sprouting broccoli, no more than two or three mouthfuls left before he would finish. "That Crimea should be restored to Russia, that it was given to Kiev without permission by Khrushchev . . ."

"I would agree with that," Kell replied.

"But I saw the separatist aggression in the east as a senseless waste of lives, innocent people dying for the cause of meaningless nationalism."

"I would also agree with that," Kell concurred, desperately scrabbling for ideas. He felt like a public speaker with ten more minutes to fill and not an idea in his head. "And what we've been seeing in Russia is the extraordinary success of the Kremlin propaganda machine. There are educated, liberal intellectuals in Moscow who believe that Ukrainian soldiers have *crucified* Russian children, that any opposition to Russian influence in the region has been orchestrated by the CIA . . ."

The use of "we" was a hangover from Office days, the party line at SIS. Kell had made a mistake. Riedle, thankfully, appeared not to have noticed. Instead he nodded approvingly at what Kell had said and then — Kell felt the dread again — turned in his seat and looked down toward the entrance, distracted by a movement or sound that Kell had not detected.

"But otherwise he wasn't a political animal?" Kell asked, trying to bring Riedle's eyes back to the table. It had been a mistake to ask about politics. Riedle was a sensualist, an emotional man in the grip of heartbreak. He didn't want to be talking about civil wars. He wanted to be talking about his feelings.

"No, he was not. He had studied political

philosophy at Moscow University."

A waiter was bringing a bottle of Champagne to Suda's table. When the cork popped, Riedle might turn around and look toward his table. All of Kell's energy was directed at preventing that from taking place. He needed to hold Riedle in a sort of trance of conversation, to make it impossible for him to look away.

"What was his job?" Kell asked. He removed his jacket in the gathering heat.

"Like you," Riedle replied. "Private investment. Raising financing for different projects around Europe."

A classic SVR cover.

"Which allowed him to travel extensively? To spend time with you?"

The woman was giggling, Suda raising a loud toast.

"Precisely." Something had caused Riedle to smile. "It's funny. I always felt like the sophisticated one. The older Western European intellectual teaching the boy from Russia. This was false, of course. Dmitri was much cleverer, much better educated than I am. But he was often very quiet. I used to think of it as shyness. Now I think of it as a *lack* of something."

"He sounds like somebody with very little generosity of spirit."

"Yes!" Riedle almost thumped the table in enthusiastic endorsement of Kell's insight. "That is exactly what he was like."

"Generosity of spirit is so rare," Kell said, continuing to improvise conversation. Could he send a note via a member of staff? Not a chance. Nor could he leave Riedle alone at the table; the German might use the time to start gazing around the restaurant. "If a person is essentially self-interested," Kell said, moving a floret of cauliflower in slow circles around his plate, "if their only goal is the satisfaction of their own vanity, their own appetites, even at the expense of friends or loved ones, that can be enormously distressing for the person left behind."

"You understand a great deal, Peter," Riedle replied, lifting a final mouthful of lamb toward his gaping mouth. Kell watched the rising fork as he might have watched a clock ticking down to zero hour. He was convinced that Riedle was going to leave the table as soon as he had finished eating. "Tell me about your own experience," Riedle asked. "Tell me how you coped with the end of your marriage."

If it would guarantee the German's undivided attention for the next hour, Kell would happily now have told him the most intimate and scandalous details of his relationship with Claire. Besides, wasn't it one of the golden rules of recruitment? Share your vulnerabilities. Confide in a prospective agent. Tell him whatever he needs to hear in order to establish complicity. But before he had a chance to answer, Riedle added a coda.

"First, however, will you excuse me?" He was dabbing his mouth with his napkin and preparing to stand up. "I must go to the bathroom."

At that same moment, Kell looked across the room and saw Rafal Suda in the midst of precisely the same ritual. The dabbed napkin. The soundless request to his companion. It was as though the two men had made a secret plan to meet. Rising to his feet, Suda laughed as his date cracked a toothy joke. If Riedle left now, he would bump into Suda within thirty seconds.

"Would you mind if I went first?" Kell asked and did something that he had never done in all his life as an intelligence officer. He clutched at his waist and pretended to be hit by a searing pain in his stomach.

"But of course," Riedle replied, settling back into his seat. "Are you all right, Peter?"

Kell struggled to his feet, wincing in apparent agony. "Fine," he gasped, "Fine," and ducked to avoid a low-hanging lamp. "Happens from time to time. Just give me five minutes, will you, Bernie? I'll be right back."

# 12

Kell was only a few feet behind Suda as he walked into the bathroom. A man in a dark gray suit came out at the same time and held the door for him as they passed one another.

*"Merci,"* Kell said, going inside.

Suda was standing at a urinal, staring down into the bowl. He was alone in the room. There were two cubicles beyond him, both of which Kell checked for occupants before lighting the blue touchpaper.

"What the fuck are you doing here?"

Suda looked back, urinating, and swore in Polish.

"Tom."

"I'm eating dinner ten feet away from your fucking table with Bernhard fucking Riedle. Why are you still in Brussels?"

The shock oozed into Suda's face as he began to reply, his blue-black birthmark creased with fatigue. Still urinating, he was unable fully to turn around. Kell was riding the adrenaline of the previous fifteen minutes and did not hold back.

"You realize if he sees you, I'm fucked? You realize if he so much as turns around and looks at your underage, I-still-haven't-graduated-from-high-school girlfriend and recognizes the man sitting opposite her, that my operation — for which you were extraordinarily well paid and which has cost me outside of ten thousand pounds and almost two weeks of planning — will not only be over, but will involve you being arrested in front of a room full of people carrying iPhones — iPhones with cameras and zoom lenses and microphones — and me standing right beside Riedle as he asks me to positively identify the street criminal who tried to mug him two nights ago?"

Suda was zipping up his trousers and trying to interrupt, but Kell wasn't done.

"I'm not interested what excuse you have, why you felt that you had to stay in Brussels with your newly adolescent, fake-eyelash, breast-enhanced babysitter, rather than go home to your wife and children in Warsaw as you promised me you would do when I hired you, but here's what's going to happen, Rafal. There's a kitchen outside. You go into it. You walk very quickly and very confidently to the back of that kitchen and you leave by any exit possible. You leave the way the staff leave. If anybody tries to stop you, pay them. Do you have money?"

Suda nodded. It was like scolding a schoolboy who had been caught cheating in an exam.

"Good," he said. "I will tell a waiter that I saw you leaving, that you had to go out the back because your wife had walked into the restaurant and that you gave me money. I will pay your bill. The waiter will then explain to Kim Kardashian that you're waiting for her outside. Maybe she'll finish her oysters. Maybe she won't. You can call her. Do what you want. But if you don't get out of here and get permanently out of Riedle's sight, I will personally see to it that no intelligence agency, no corporate espionage outfit, no police department, no bank or multinational will ever give you any business again. You won't teach. You won't drive cabs. You won't change a fucking lightbulb in this shitty Belgian bathroom. All you will do is get out of this restaurant. Do not pass go. Do not collect two hundred pounds. *Leave.*"

# 13

Suda did as he was told.

Kell watched him walk briskly through the swinging doors of the kitchen and waited outside to make sure that he did not double back. He then took the maître d' to one side, explained that he had met a man in the bathroom who was at risk of being compromised by his wife while dining with his mistress, paid Suda's bill in cash, tipped the maître d' a further twenty euros to break the news gently and discreetly to the girlfriend, then made his way back to Riedle.

Several minutes had passed since Kell had left the table, but the German was relaxed and companionable, fussing and fretting over Kell's condition. *Have you had these incidents before? Do you require a doctor? Perhaps it was something in your food?* Kell brushed aside his concerns, realizing — as their conversation continued — that Minasian would almost certainly have taken advantage of Riedle's innate decency; there was a neediness about him, a desire to win affection through acts of kindness and generosity, which to a sadist like Minasian would have been like the scent of blood to a shark.

"I was thinking, while you were away, that I feel rather ashamed."

"Ashamed, Bernie? Why?"

Kell wondered why Riedle hadn't yet taken the opportunity to go to the bathroom. His napkin was still balled on the table.

"It is embarrassing for a man of my age, a man almost sixty, to be at the mercy of an infatuation, don't you think? To be so brokenhearted. So weak. I feel like a fool."

"Don't," Kell replied firmly, and tried to comfort Riedle with a shake of the head. "I think it shows that you are alive. That you haven't given up on people, become stale or jaded." Riedle asked him to translate the word "jaded" and Kell offered "tired" as a lazy synonym. "We all have a need for company. Most of us, anyway. What you are going through speaks to our deep need to feel connected, to share our lives with somebody who understands us, who makes us feel cherished. We want to feel free to be who we are. We want somebody who will help to open up the best side of ourselves."

Rachel flooded Kell's memory, her poise and her laughter, the way in which she had so quickly intuited so much about him. He felt the loss of her as a pain every bit as searing as that which he had faked only ten minutes earlier, clutching his stomach for Riedle's benefit.

"To care for somebody and to be cared for," Kell continued, now thinking of Claire and of everything that had gone missing between them. "To be excited about seeing them, hearing what they have to say, talking to them. Isn't that what it's all about? You obviously had that with Dmitri, when things were good between you. A person can be fifty-nine or nineteen and experience those things. There's no shame in mourning them when they have been taken away from you."

"Then I thank you for your understanding," Riedle sighed with a gesture of collapsing gratitude, and finally stood up to go to the bathroom.

As he inched along the walkway, Kell looked across to the opposite balcony, where the maître d' was only now informing Suda's companion that her date had left for the evening via the back door. She took the news with laudable restraint, checking her face in a compact mirror before standing up, adjusting her hair, and walking down-stairs. As she tottered to the ground floor on four-inch heels, she took a smartphone from her purse and checked the screen for messages. At the same moment, Kell felt his own phone pulse in his trouser pocket.

It was a text from Suda.

> I will tell Stephanie that it was a Polish police matter, not anything to do with my wife.

*Tell her what you like,* Kell muttered as a second text came in.

> I will take her to Hotel Metropole. I apologize, Tom. My plane leaves for Warsaw at 8 tomorrow. In the morning. R.

Kell deleted the messages without replying and watched Stephanie collect her coat at the entrance. She must have felt his gaze because she looked up and stared at Kell, an almost imperceptible tremor of longing in her eyes. A beautiful young woman aware of her power over men, and testing it all the time. Kell thought of her in Rafal's arms in a bed at the Hotel Metropole. Then he thought of Rachel and Claire, of Riedle and Minasian, of the whole sorry dance of sex and yearning, of love and betrayal.

There was one more glass of wine left in the bottle of Chianti. He finished it.

## 14

The two men walked home together, Riedle bidding farewell to Kell in the lobby of the apartment building where, just two days earlier, they had met for the first time. Kell rode the lift to the fourth floor, already taking the pen with which he would write down detailed notes about the dinner from his jacket pocket. It was an old habit from Office days. Get home, write up the telegram, no matter how late at night, then send it to London.

Kell entered the apartment. He was hanging up his jacket when he heard a cough from the living room. Walking inside, he saw Mowbray sitting on the sofa, a glass of single malt in front of him and a grin on his face like Arsenal had won the European Cup in extra time.

"You're looking very pleased with yourself, Harold."

"Am I, guv? Well, that makes sense." He

leaned further back on the sofa. "How was your dinner? Bernie try and hold your hand?"

"Very funny."

"Seriously, you wanna be careful, boss. Bloke like that, lonely and unhappy. Nice, good-looking British diplomat comes along, listens to his sad stories, protects him from antisocial elements on the mean streets of Brussels. He might be falling in love with you."

Kell was pouring a whiskey of his own and felt a sting at the edge of his vanity. He didn't normally mind Mowbray's joshing, but liked to maintain a level of hierarchical respect in his dealings with colleagues.

"So why are you looking so smug?" he asked, sitting in an armchair at right angles to the sofa. Kell kicked off his shoes, trusting his memory sufficiently to be able to write the report in an hour's time.

"Did Bernie say anything about how he used to contact lover boy?"

Kell shook his head. "We haven't got that far yet. First night I met him he mentioned something about a friend "always losing his phones and changing numbers." I assumed that was Minasian, that he had four or five different mobiles he used for contacting Riedle. Why do you ask?"

Kell took a sip of his whisky, sensing that Mowbray had made a breakthrough. The communications link between Riedle and Minasian was the holy grail of the operation. Find that and they could start to track the Russian, to lure him across the channel to London.

"I think I've cracked it," he said.

Kell moved forward. "Tell me."

"You know I put key-log software in his laptop? Every password entered, every sentence typed."

"Sure."

There was a laptop on the table in front of them. Mowbray opened it up. "So it turns out they kept it simple. Least as far as e-mail is concerned. I've been able to hack into his account. They encrypted their messages."

It was the smart play, the easiest and most secure way for Minasian to communicate with Riedle without raising his suspicions or drawing the attention of the SVR.

"PGP?" Kell asked, an acronym for a popular piece of encryption software that he understood in only simple terms.

"Very good!" Mowbray replied, amazed that Kell — who was famously antediluvian when it came to technology — was even aware that PGP existed. "So Elsa got hold of the private key which Bernie stored on his laptop and Bob became my uncle. After that it's just like reading a regular e-mail correspondence."

Mowbray swiveled the laptop toward Kell and said: "Take a look." There were only three e-mails sitting in the account: two from Riedle, one from Minasian. Kell assumed that the others had been deleted or filed elsewhere. As Mowbray stood up and went outside onto the balcony to smoke a cigarette, Kell clicked on the most recent message.

It was dated ten days earlier and had been given the headline "Betrayal." It was both a plea from Riedle, begging Minasian to come to Brussels so that they could patch things up, and a sustained attack on his character and behavior. Reading it, Kell felt as if he were intruding on a private grief so intense as to be almost embarrassing in its candor.

You are not the man I recognize, the man I love. You are so cruel to me, so hard and objective. What happened to us? Your attitude when we talked on the phone yesterday degraded everything that we once shared.

That phrase — "when we talked on the

phone" — was as welcome to Kell as water in a drought, because it held out the possibility that Minasian would risk contacting Riedle again, perhaps making a call on Skype that Mowbray's microphones would pick up.

You coldly announce that you are still in love with Vera, that you are now disgusted by your <u>true</u> sexuality, by what passed between us. How do you think that makes me feel? You tell me that you still love her, that you now find Vera attractive, when we both know this is a <u>lie</u>. You have never wanted to be with her in that way. Why now? Why the change? Then you told me on the telephone that you feel more relaxed in her company than you ever did with me. What kind of a person says those things?

A sociopath says those things, thought Kell. Someone incapable of compassion, of feeling anything but contempt for those who might ask something of them.

I always admired your commitment to the "truth." There had been so many lies in my own life when we met that I found your determination to act honestly in all things captivating. But I realize now that you are a hypocrite. Your "truth" is just what suits you at the time. It disguises your ruthlessness, because you are indeed ruthless and unkind. You lie to Vera, you lie to me, you lie to your unborn children. You lie to <u>yourself</u>.

Kell no longer knew if he was reading the e-mail for operational reasons or purely out of human fascination. He worried that Riedle's anger and spite, if it continued, would drive Minasian further and further away. At times he sounded like a man who had lost all reason and context.

You have left me, but you have not tried to soften the blow or to use the simple white lies people use in these situations when they <u>care</u> about not hurting a lover. What I hope for, what I <u>need</u>, is a small amount of compassion, of kindness, some sense that what we have been through together over the past three years means something to you. All I am asking for is a sense that you understand and are sensitive to the depth of my love for you. You know, better than anyone has ever known, how I think and how I feel and how difficult my life is now that you are not in it — and yet you treat me as if I was no more important to you than a boy picked up in a sauna.

There was more. Much more. The suggestion that Minasian, a year earlier, had been introduced to one of Riedle's friends and had slept with him. The accusation that he had taunted Riedle continuously with stories about the men (and women) he met in different European cities while working for the bank. There had clearly been a sadomasochistic element to the relationship that Minasian had encouraged and enjoyed. Added to what Riedle had told Kell at dinner about Minasian's aggressive, sullen behavior, the relationship amounted to a catalogue of emotional abuse. Kell wanted to go downstairs, to knock on Riedle's door, ask him why the hell he had put up with it for so long, and then pour him a large Scotch.

He clicked to the second e-mail. It was, as Kell expected, a brief reply from Minasian, written four days after Riedle's message, with no subject line. The language was distant, cold, and supremely controlled.

I hoped that you would behave with more dignity, more courage. If you write to me like this again I will have nothing more to do with you. I refuse to engage with your insults and accusations.

Kell noted the absence of any consoling words. Nothing to acknowledge Riedle's pain or the accusation of infidelity. Nevertheless, Minasian was holding out the possibility of further interaction in the future.

Riedle had replied within twelve hours. Kell clicked to this final e-mail.

I am very sorry. I was angry. Please don't vanish. I am happy to be friends. I just want to keep you in my life and to try to understand what is happening to us.

You are so strong. I don't think you have ever known heartbreak. I know that you have felt isolated and alone. I know that you have felt a panic about the structure of your life. But you have never known what it is to feel passed over, exchanged — the madness of loss. You have never lost somebody that you were not ready to lose, a person who felt, as I do, that you were holding his entire happiness in the palm of your hand. It's like you have closed your hand. Made a fist. I need to be treated with delicacy, with kindness and compassion. Please provide this. I am begging you.

I am very sorry for the things I said. I did not mean them. Please consider what I said about Brussels. I can come and meet you anywhere, even if it's just for lunch (or a cup of coffee!). In Egypt you said you had a period coming up in Paris. That would be perfect — I can be at the Gare du Nord in less than two hours from Brussels.

Kell drained the whiskey, thinking of Paris, of Brasserie Lipp, remembering Amelia's kidnapped son and the operation three years earlier, in which Kell had played the pivotal role in securing his release. On a pad beside the computer he began to write notes. The first word he wrote, in capitals, was CONTROL, beneath which he began to sketch out his ideas in more detail.

1. Power and control central to M's personality. Must retain a position of dominance. What is he afraid of if he <u>loses</u> control? What is the vulnerability/insecurity we can exploit? The secret about his sexuality — or something else?
2. For R to be this upset/deranged, there must be huge charisma. Charm, apparent empathy, patience, sensuality. M extremely attractive — to young and old, male and female. He demands adoration.

125

He nurtures it. So this must be partly cultivated, artificial behavior.

Chameleon. Adapts himself to give people what they need for as long as he needs them.

3. According to R, M is highly judgmental/opinionated. Does he also react badly to criticism? Gloating self-image? Ask R in more detail.

4. What does M want? What can we give him? Do we flatter, or squeeze?

"What are you writing?"

Mowbray had appeared beside him. Kell covered up part of the notes with his elbow, like a card player wary of revealing his hand.

"Just some initial thoughts on Minasian."

"Yeah? Sounds like a nice fella, doesn't he?" Mowbray's shirt smelled of cigarette smoke. "Real piece of work. Chewed up our Bernie and spat him out."

"Yes," Kell agreed. "He was out of his depth. Can't have had any idea what he was getting into."

Mowbray leaned over, his breath stale with whiskey.

"*Flatter or squeeze.* What does that mean?"

"Exactly what it says." Kell was annoyed

that Mowbray was being intrusive. "Either I make Minasian feel like top dog, tell him how great he is, feed his ego and his self-image, or I find out what it is that he's hiding — and squeeze him."

"Hiding? You mean above and beyond the fact that he's married to the daughter of a Russian oligarch but secretly likes taking it up the jacksie?"

Kell couldn't contain a burst of laughter. "That may be all there is to it," he said. "Just that secret. Just Riedle. But I was interested by something Bernie said at dinner, very early on. That he thinks of Russians as corrupt, greedy. Wouldn't surprise me if Minasian is involved in something illegal. Something financial, possibly linked to Svetlana's father."

"You think he would have told Bernie about that?"

"Who knows?" Kell closed the laptop. "The system out there would certainly present a man in Minasian's position with myriad opportunities to squirrel away some cash for a rainy day. He's a vain man. A controlling man. A narcissist, for want of a better word. If he's threatened by his father-in-law's wealth, if Svetlana's lifestyle is an affront to his masculinity and his sense of his own grandeur, if Minasian feels that he has to bring home more than an SVR salary, then — yes — he could be involved in corrupt activity."

Mowbray returned to the sofa and appeared to be mulling over Kell's theory. Kell scribbled "MONEY?" on the notepad, underlining it twice, and wondered what Elsa might be able to find out about Minasian's financial affairs if pointed in the right direction.

"How much store do you set by those?" Mowbray asked, flicking his head toward the laptop.

"What do you mean?" Kell asked.

"I mean how much can we ever know somebody, just by reading what they've written, or what someone else has said about them? It's all prejudice, isn't it? I know there are people out there who think the world of Harold Mowbray. And I know there are people out there who think I'm more or less a complete arsehole." Kell smiled. "Seriously, boss." Mowbray was looking around for his glass. "This Alexander Minasian. Maybe he's not as bad as we all think. Maybe we're reading him wrong. Maybe one day you'll get face to face with him and discover you have more in common with him than you ever imagined."

# 15

Egypt Air flight MS777 from Cairo International Airport had touched down at London
Heathrow a few minutes behind schedule at
1544 on a cloudless English afternoon in
May.

Shahid Khan had spent most of the journey trying, unsuccessfully, to sleep. He had
been in a state of profound anxiety and
could feel the judgment and suspicion of
his fellow passengers weighing down on him
like a thick rope coiled around his neck and
shoulders. He had been traveling for five
days. He had hated Dubai and wondered
why Jalal had insisted that he go there from
Istanbul. There were other countries, other
cities, that did not require a visa for U.K.
citizens. Shahid had looked them up online.
Why subject him to Dubai? To *strengthen*
him? To remove any doubts about his future
actions? Shahid did not need such help. He
did not understand Jalal's reasons. He was

at peace with the path that had been chosen for him. It was the will of Allah. Shahid looked forward to the day of his martyrdom as he looked forward to the defeat of Assad's dogs, to the destruction and the humiliation of the American empire. This was his dream and the dream of the brothers and sisters he had left behind in the Caliphate. Many of them would not live to see this dream fulfilled. Shahid himself would not live to see it. But he would help to bring it about. This was a glorious and a pure thing.

The passengers disembarked into the terminal building. Shahid went with them, following the signs to Passport Control. In fourteen months of fighting in Syria he had not suffered with any illness, but in Cairo he had eaten food from a vendor in the street and suffered terrible sickness and cramps in his hotel room. Perhaps this was why he was in such an agitated state. He had lost weight and was still feeling sick. He had only been able to drink water on the airplane and eat a few dry biscuits. And now he had to make it through the passport queue, past the customs officers and the plainclothes detectives — the most difficult moment of his journey. Shahid knew the obstacles in front of him. Jalal had spoken about them in detail and had told him how to behave.

*Join any queue,* he had said. *Not the shortest one. Check the messages on your mobile phone, read a book or a newspaper. Take your jacket off if you are sweating. Do not evade eye contact and do not try to trick them. You are just another passenger. You are just another face. In the eyes of the British authorities, you are of no importance.*

Shahid felt inside his jacket for the passport. He touched it. Also the mobile phone, provided to him by Jalal, and the wallet. Shahid had been given over one thousand pounds in cash. Jalal had promised that his contact at Heathrow — a man named Farouq who had fought *jihad* — would give him a thousand more. Shahid took out the wallet. It had a London Oyster card inside it, also till receipts, a book of stamps, even the membership card from a gym. How had Jalal organized all of this? He was so thorough and clever in his thinking. His planning and his foresight were gifts from God.

Shahid looked at the men and the women walking all around him. There were many men like him in casual clothes wearing denim jeans and gray or black jackets. Jalal had been right. It was important to look like the others, to blend in.

They came to the passport queue. Shahid

waited at the end of a long, snaking line. People were complaining about the delay. Shahid wished that the queue had been shorter. It was agony to wait. He stared at his phone and shuffled forward as the queue moved, but he could not think about anything else except facing the guards. He was able to look at the Facebook page that Jalal had created and to see that a number of the friend requests he had made to strangers on the site had been accepted. This was surely good. It would make the page more believable if he was questioned in the airport. Jalal had filled the phone with numbers and contacts, but they were not people Shahid knew. He had been told never to try to communicate with any of his brothers and sisters in the Caliphate. Likewise, he was forbidden to contact any member of his family in England. Shahid had to understand this. He had to understand that his family had been told by the British government that Azhar Ahmed Iqbal had been killed while fighting for ISIS near the city of Mosul, in northern Iraq. His father believed that his son was dead.

The queue took thirty minutes. At last, Shahid was facing the row of officials. A space came up at one of the desks in front of him and he walked up to it. He looked up and saw that the guard was Muslim. Her head was covered by a black hijab. He smiled at her. The woman did not smile back. Shahid felt that she could see right through his heart to the secret that lay inside him.

He placed the passport on the counter. The woman took it and opened it while studying his face. There were two men on the far side of the desk, watching the room. Shahid knew that they were plainclothes officials and was sure that they were suspicious of him.

"Good afternoon, sir," she said. "Where have you come from today?"

"From Cairo," Shahid replied. He had not spoken for more than four hours and his voice was dry and cracked.

The woman placed the passport inside a machine that emitted a cold blue light. There was a red rash on her wrists and the backs of her hands. She looked at a computer screen that was partly obscured behind the counter. Shahid felt sure that she was going to question him. He felt sure that the computer would tell her that the passport was a fake. ISIS had been duped by their contact in Tirana. He would be arrested by the two men in plainclothes and sent for trial. They would imprison him.

The guard looked up. She placed the passport on the counter and smiled. Shahid took it back.

"Thank you, Mr. Khan," she said. "Welcome home."

# 16

Kell could not sleep.

Mowbray had left just before one, heading back to the Metropole with a quip about sharing an adjoining room with Rafal and Stephanie.

"That headboard starts to bump, I'm calling the concierge," he said, shaking Kell's hand and heading off into the night.

Kell had lain awake for an hour in the semidarkness of his rented, featureless bedroom, wondering what Minasian would be doing in Paris. Business or pleasure? A relationship-mending break with Svetlana? A stolen weekend with a new lover? Without Amelia's help, there would be no way of finding him in Paris. Even with the assistance of SIS, the chances of Minasian leaving a trail for Kell and his ilk to follow were minimal. The e-mails were his only solid lead. Riedle remained the key.

Just after two thirty he went into the

kitchen and swallowed two aspirin with an inch of Talisker. He longed for a cigarette. It was perhaps a sign of the softening of Kell's operational temperament that he was concerned about Riedle's well-being. He imagined the moment when he would have to tell the German the truth about "Dmitri." To break his heart still further by revealing that the man with whom he had fallen in love and shared three of the most exciting and turbulent years of his life was, in fact, a Russian intelligence officer. Riedle would have to come to terms not only with the loss of Dmitri, but also with the realization that he had been lied to and manipulated, again and again — not least by Kell himself. And to what end? To satisfy Kell's desire for vengeance? To recruit Minasian so that he could take him in triumph to Amelia, dropping an SVR officer at her feet like a dog with a captured bird? There was no guarantee that Riedle would even agree to assist SIS in any operation against Minasian. Certainly he harbored great anger and resentment toward his former lover, but Kell was in no doubt that if "Dmitri" returned, asking to be understood and forgiven, Riedle would take him back in an instant. Far from Kell's options opening up in the wake of the discovery of the e-mail exchange, they were shutting down.

He went into the sitting room and re-trieved the laptop.

Mowbray had not signed out of Riedle's e-mail account. Kell felt the aspirin and the whisky working through him as he looked more closely at the screen. There were no longer three messages in the in-box. There were four. At some point in the previous two hours, Alexander Minasian had re-sponded.

Kell clicked on the message.

I have been thinking about your letters to me. There is a great deal that I violently disagree with, but I cannot ignore the fact that you feel very angry and upset with me. For this, I want to say sorry.

This is not a justification, but an explana-tion: I honestly believed it would be better for you if I was not in contact with you, re-appearing in your mind. I limited myself to brief e-mails. I thought it was better to remove all emotion.

I will be in England from 29 or 30 June until 2 July, staying at our place under my normal name. You obviously have very strong feelings about the way I behaved. I would be happy to meet and talk. I believe that many of the things you have written are dishonest and unfair. If I had not written this message to you, you would have even stronger feelings in that respect. If you leave a note for me in the usual way, I will try to come and see you. I hope that my schedule will permit this.

Kell read the e-mail three times. Minasian was coming to London. He was reaching out to Riedle, seemingly trying to make amends. Perhaps much of what Riedle had said was true. The two men really had been in love. They had shared something that was proving impossible to break. Certainly Minasian's message did not fit with the personality type Kell had constructed in his mind. Sociopaths did not say sorry. Narcissists did not take into consideration the feelings or the circumstances of their victims. Or, rather, they did so only if they required something from them in terms of their own continued well-being. Was it possible that Minasian was having second thoughts about his reconciliation with Svetlana?

Kell read the e-mail a fourth time, immediately drawing an opposite conclusion. There was no suggestion of reconciliation in the message, only a desire on Minasian's part not to be regarded as unfeeling or cruel. A determination, in other words, to

138

influence Riedle's emotions. Minasian's principal driver was power. He needed to exercise control even over the denouement of their relationship.

Thirsty for another whisky, Kell poured himself a second inch of Talisker and resolved to think practically; to stop trying to understand every nuance of Minasian's personality and to put a particular spin or interpretation on his behavior based on insufficient evidence. Yet he was feeling the long night of drinking. A dangerous combination of adrenaline and stubbornness was threatening to cloud Kell's judgment. He convinced himself that his best course of action was to reply to the e-mail immediately, masquerading as Riedle. He felt that he could easily re-create the German's style and syntax. He would extract the name of Minasian's favorite hotel from Riedle in the morning, instruct Elsa or Mowbray to block his access to the account, then arrange to meet "Dmitri" in London. It would be a classic false flag operation.

To that end, Kell created a blank document and began to compose his reply. Before he did so, he took the sealed packet of Winston Lights from the drawer beside his bed, opened the sitting-room window, and lit his first cigarette in more than six months. The nicotine worked on him with the snap of an amphetamine; he gasped at the pleasure of the first drag, inhaling deeply as the smoke filled his chest. He tapped the ash into his now empty whisky glass, balanced the cigarette on the end of the table, and began to type.

I am so happy to hear from you, Dmitri.

Kell saw that he had already made a mistake. At no point, in any of the drafts, had either man used the other's name. Anonymity was paramount. He deleted "Dmitri," took another drag from the cigarette, and continued.

I am so happy to hear from you. Thank you for your kind message. Of course I will come to London!

Kell looked at what he had written. He wondered if it sounded like Riedle. The German had used exclamation marks in his own messages, but perhaps this one was misplaced. Kell removed it. A curl of smoke drifted up into his eyes, stinging them.

I am so happy to hear from you. Thank you for your kind message. Of course I will come to London. I will travel over on the 28th and stay until the end of the month. Let's sit down and talk about everything. It will make me so joyful to see you.

Kell double-clicked on the paragraph and copied it from the document. He would paste his reply into an encrypted e-mail for Minasian to read in the morning.

He took a last drag of the Winston and dropped the butt into the glass. He had not enjoyed the second half of the cigarette. His mouth was dry and there was now a taste on his tongue like the surface of a road. He knew, without quite being able to admit it to himself, that he was drunk. He looked at his watch. It was twenty to four in the morning.

*Take a break,* he told himself. *Think.*

He went into the kitchen and ran the cold tap. Kell had intended to pour himself a glass of water, but instead cupped the water in his hands and threw it against his face so that his neck and the front of his shirt became soaked and cold.

He needed to stop. He had no control. He was not leaving himself open to chance or to basic human error. What if Riedle woke up at five and checked the account, desperate for a sign of life from Minasian? What if

141

he saw what Kell was intending to send?

Kell went back into the sitting room and deleted the document. He marked Minasian's e-mail as "Unread," turned off the MacBook, returned to his bedroom, and swallowed two more aspirin. He was exhausted. He was so determined to find Minasian that he had been prepared to jeopardize everything just to gain a minuscule advantage of time. There was only one sensible way to proceed: to allow Riedle to respond to Minasian's invitation and then to track him to London.

Kell returned to the bedroom, relieved that he had not been foolish enough to send the e-mail. He fell asleep almost immediately to the sound of a child sobbing in a neighboring apartment.

# 17

Bernhard Riedle rang with the good news shortly before eleven.

"Peter? I just wanted to tell you. Something very good has happened."

Kell had been awake for only five minutes, brain-fogged by the long night of drinking and five hours' sleep. He was stumbling around the kitchen in a pair of boxer shorts, searching for a clean mug.

"Bernie. Hi. What's up?"

"It's Dmitri. He's been in touch. He wants us to meet."

"That's great." Kell opened the fridge and saw that he had forgotten to buy milk. "Did he call? Did you talk things over?"

"No. He never telephones. We always e-mail. It is safer that way. Because of Vera."

"Vera?"

"His wife. You don't remember?"

Kell looked out the window at the rooftops of Brussels. Svetlana, Vera. Alexander, Dmitri. Thomas, Peter.

"Oh, yes. Sorry. Haven't had my cup of coffee yet."

Riedle proceeded to tell Kell what he already knew. That Minasian had apologized for seeming distant and cold and had suggested meeting up in London to clear the air.

"When?" Kell asked.

"The last week of June."

He laid some early foundations.

"That's terrific. I'll be in London from the twenty-sixth. We could meet up while you're in town."

"You want to meet Dmitri?" The tone of Riedle's question suggested that he did not think this suggestion was entirely impractical.

"No, no. I didn't mean that. I just meant that I'll be in London. If you find yourself free for lunch or dinner one night . . ."

"Oh."

There was a delay on the line, a drop in the signal.

"Bernie?"

"Yes, sorry." The connection was restored. "So let's do that."

The two men continued to discuss Riedle's nascent travel plans, a conversation that allowed Kell to form a basic idea of how his own schedule would pan out in the coming days and weeks.

"Where will you be staying in London?" he asked.

"I usually take a room north of Soho," Riedle replied. "The Charlotte Street Hotel. Do you know it?"

"I know it."

Elsa could have ascertained as much from Riedle's e-mail account, but Kell had a deeper purpose.

"And Dmitri?" he asked.

"What about him?"

"Where will he be staying? In the same hotel?"

"Oh, no." Riedle produced a quiet chuckle. "We like to keep things separate from Vera. Dmitri said he will be at his favorite place. A hotel where we have such happy memories."

A hotel that I'm going to soak in surveillance, thought Kell. A hotel where Alexander Minasian isn't going to be able to move without a camera capturing every pixel of his wretched existence. All Kell needed was photographic proof of a sexual relationship with Riedle. Presented with evidence of that kind, Minasian would have no choice but to comply with whatever Kell asked of him.

"And where's that?" he asked.

"Dmitri always stays at Claridge's."

# 18

Shahid Khan had received the text message from "Farouq" while he was waiting for his suitcase in the baggage hall. It was an instruction to meet him in the short-stay car park. Farouq had described himself as a tall man of fifty-five with "close-cropped gray hair" wearing a dark brown suit. Shahid spotted him within moments of walking outside.

"Peace be upon you," he said, greeting him in Arabic.

Farouq shook his head.

"I don't talk like that," he replied. "Neither should you. You are not this person any more. You are not a religious man."

Shahid felt chastened. He had been in London for less than an hour and had already made a mistake. He had apologized to Farouq and they walked to the car in silence. Shahid watched him. There was something cold and determined about the man Jalal had sent to meet him.

Once they were inside the car Farouq gave him the money and said: "I am going to drive you to Victoria station. You get the train to Brighton and you start everything now. You remember what you have been told?" Shahid nodded. "You use the money to rent a room in a guesthouse. Find a job in the area. Join a gym. Open a bank account. Make friends."

"Yes," Shahid replied. "Jalal told me everything."

"No names," the man snapped back. "No details. I don't know who you are. You don't know who I am. At the moment I am just a person giving you a lift to Victoria."

Shahid wanted to tell Farouq about his past. He wanted him to know that he had fought bravely in the Caliphate, that he had been selected for martyrdom because of his high intelligence and courage. He wanted to feel that he had earned the respect of men like Farouq.

"You are Syrian?" he asked. The man's accent, his features, and his coloring were near-identical to men of a similar age that he had seen in the Caliphate.

"I am your contact. That is all," Farouq replied.

They were driving out of the car park.

Farouq told Shahid that there was a number in his mobile phone for a man called "Kris." Shahid was to write it down and keep it somewhere safe. If he was ever concerned about anything, if he had questions, if he needed to talk, he should call Kris from a public telephone, or with the use of a third-party mobile. They would arrange to meet. He was to be Shahid's sole point of contact in the U.K. Kris would also be the person who would provide him with the weapons necessary to carry out the operation.

"You are Kris?"

Farouq shook his head. Shahid could not decide if he was relieved by this, or dismayed. He did not like to think that he would not see Farouq again.

"You must never say anything about the operation on an open line or in any written communication."

"I know that," Shahid replied. "I've been taught that."

"Good." The Syrian had brought the car onto the M4 and they were heading east into London. "Do you have doubts?" he asked.

Shahid wondered if the question was a trick planted by Jalal. Did they have concerns about him? Or did they expect Shahid to be uncertain at this stage, to have moments of fear and hesitation?

"I have no doubts," he replied.

"You will carry out your duty to avenge the Prophet?" There was an unmistakable note of bewilderment in Farouq's voice, as though such a sacrifice would have been beyond his own personal capabilities. Shahid felt strengthened by this. He now knew that he was braver than the man Jalal had sent to escort him. He understood that there were very few men with a faith and courage equal to his own.

"I will carry out my duty," he replied, and looked out the window at a car that had broken down at the side of the motorway. It was strange to be back in England. It was cold here. He felt that he was a long way from home. He had grown up in this place, but he had grown away from it. Out there, in the suburbs of London, in the squats of Liverpool and Manchester, in the mosques of Birmingham and Southampton, lay an army of men and women who would support him in his quest. He was their symbol of hope; he would be their hero. Shahid felt that he was at the center of a vast crowd, larger than any group or demonstration ever seen in the cities of the West, a crowd visible only to true Muslims and true believers; millions of men and women cheering him on, willing Shahid Khan to fulfill his destiny. He could not see them, but he could feel them. They gave him an insuperable strength.

"I know what I'm doing," he told Farouq. "I know what I was sent here to do."

# 19

Claridge's made up Kell's mind. A hotel of that size meant telling SIS. Without the assistance of his former Service, he would be outgunned on surveillance. Done properly, an operation to recruit Minasian would require undercover officers working as staff in the hotel; rooms rigged for sight and sound; eyes in the lobby and dining rooms. You could do a lot of things off the books at SIS, but you couldn't get control of Claridge's with only Elsa and Harold Mowbray for company.

There were several days until the Russian was due in London. Kell doubted that Minasian would risk traveling to the U.K. with Svetlana, but suspected that oligarch money would be paying for their room. He wondered why Minasian was taking the chance of being collared on British soil. This, after all, was the man who had given the order for the murder of Rachel Wallinger. What was so important to the SVR that it required Minasian's presence in London? Kell confronted the very real possibility that his nemesis had quit the secret world — or been fired in the wake of the Kleckner operation — and was now working in the private sector. If that was the case, he was effectively useless as an agent. Brussels would have been a waste of time and Kell's imminent meeting with Amelia a further humiliation.

He texted her from the customs hall at St. Pancras in the late afternoon. To his surprise, Amelia rang back within five minutes.

"Tom?"

"Hello," he said, as flatly as he could manage.

"How are you?" she asked, her voice animated and warm. "How have you been?"

"I've been fine, thank you." Kell experienced the extraordinary sensation of being grateful for all the years that he had known Amelia. In the absence of Claire, she was the closest thing he possessed to family. He knew in that moment that it would be hopeless to try to fight his affection for her. "Something's come up," he said. "I need to talk to you."

Amelia was too much of an old hand to ask for more detail on an insecure line.

Instead, she said: "Of course. Tonight? Are you free?"

He had not expected such an immediate opportunity. Kell explained that he was at St. Pancras, needed to go home to drop his bags, but would be free by seven.

"Perfect. I have to go to an event in Knightsbridge. That ghastly hotel where Clive had his fiftieth. Do you remember it?"

"I remember," Kell replied.

"Good. Then why don't we meet there at half past six? I'll put your name down."

Kell was now on the station concourse, walking through a mall lined on either side by restaurants and shops. He passed an old man playing Chopin on a public piano.

"What sort of event?" he asked.

"Long story," Amelia replied. "You'll need to put on a suit."

Kell was on time. There was no sign of Amelia in the lobby of the hotel, just a handful of businessmen in leather armchairs, hunched over tablets and smartphones. Two clipboard-wielding models wearing plastic smiles were standing beside a bank of lifts.

"Are you here for the show, sir?" one of them asked.

"I am," Kell replied, though he had no

idea what the "show" would entail.

He was ushered toward the closest of three lifts and instructed to "hit B3." Alone in the cabin, Kell dropped to a subterranean crypt where two more models — prettier and more glamorous than their predecessors — were checking names off a guest list. There was a background thump of state-of-the-art techno and a trio of Slavic bouncers in identical gray jackets trying their best to look intimidating. One of them stared at Kell with muscled contempt as he emerged from the lift, then appeared to experience feedback on his security earpiece and winced in pain.

Within a few moments, Kell had reached the front of a short queue.

"Can I help you, sir?"

The taller of the two models was gazing at him through a cake of foundation. Glancing down at the guest list — reading upside down — Kell saw his own name beside that of "Amelia Levene." At the top of the page he recognized the logo of a boutique fashion house and wondered why on earth the chief of the Secret Intelligence Service was attending functions hosted by European clothes designers.

"I'm on the list," he said, pointing at his name. "Tom Kell."

A tick and a smile and Kell was welcomed into the party, taking a flute of Champagne from a tray as he passed into a dark, low-lit room stocked with thirtysomething financiers and women on their third facelift. A camp, undersized Italian wearing an embroidered purple smoking jacket walked up and greeted him.

*"Ciao."*

"Hello," said Kell.

The Italian flashed a smile of radioactive whiteness while making a big deal of maintaining eye contact. It was immediately obvious that he had mistaken Kell for someone else.

"You are Michael? With Deutsche Bank?"

"I'm afraid not." Kell felt oddly flattered by the misconception. "I'm Tom."

"Luigi," the man replied.

They shook hands. A vastly overweight man wearing a pair of Technicolor pajamas walked past them, flanked by flunkies. With a conspiratorial whisper, Luigi explained that he was "a top Korean DJ." There was a powerful smell of aftershave in the slipstream of his entourage.

"North or South?" Kell asked. Luigi failed to get the joke.

They continued to speak for several minutes, during which Luigi revealed that he had organized the fashion show, had moved to London from Milan at the age of twenty-one, and had never heard of Amelia Levene. To their right, a group of seemingly significant figures from the fashion world were having their photographs taken against a sponsorship board. Luigi recognized one of the women — her face obliterated by collagen — and promptly excused himself from the conversation.

"Nice talking to you," Kell told him, and seized a canapé from a passing waitress.

He was now alone at the edge of the room, Amelia more than twenty minutes late. In a deep armchair nearby, a young woman in a tight cream dress was draped over a man at least forty years her senior with dyed hair. The man reminded Kell of Burt Lancaster. They looked irretrievably bored both by the party and by each other.

"There you are. I'm so sorry."

Amelia had materialized beside him. She was wearing black silk trousers and a collarless white shirt and reached out to touch the shoulder of Kell's suit jacket. It had been more than a year since they had last seen one another and Kell reacted to Amelia's particular blend of poise and unattainable beauty as he had always done: by feeling strangely unformed and youthful in her presence. He caught a trace of Hermès Calèche, the perfume she always wore, and the scent of it kicked up memories of all the years that he had known her.

"Amelia."

"Were you struggling?" She was looking around the room at the hordes of unsmiling guests. "It's like a training exercise in here. How long can candidates survive in a room full of fashion journalists with Champagne breath?"

Kell would ordinarily have laughed, but something inside him stalled on Amelia's easy familiarity. He wanted to feel that she was uncomfortable in his presence; that she would acknowledge the recklessness with which Rachel had been treated in Istanbul. Intuiting this, Amelia became more circumspect and laid a hand on Kell's arm.

"It's very good to see you, Tom. I'm sorry to have kept you waiting."

"No apology necessary."

"You look well."

Kell knew that it was an empty compliment and did not return it.

"Why are we here?" he asked.

"My goddaughter is one of the models. I promised I'd put in an appearance." Amelia was holding a glass of Champagne and scanned the room a second time. Kell assumed that she was checking for contacts and colleagues, perhaps a cocktail circuit spook from the French or Italian embassies. "Tell me how you've been. You look fit. You look so well. I can't believe how lovely it is to see you."

"I'm fine," Kell replied, his voice still deliberately flat and uninflected. He felt a sense of wary distrust, like walking alone down an empty street at night. "And you?"

Amelia let out an uncharacteristically theatrical sigh.

"Busy," she said, with the clear suggestion that work was more than usually exhausting. Kell could only guess at the overwhelming complexity of her position: from Donetsk to Riyadh, from Tripoli to Beijing, he could not remember a time when the Service had been under so much pressure.

"I need to ask you about Alexander Minasian," he said, adding his consuming obsession to the burden of her responsibilities.

The mention of Minasian's name had a startling effect. In Amelia's suddenly hardened attitude, Kell sensed a deep-lying guilt that she had failed to bring the Russian to justice. Rachel had died as a consequence of Amelia placing her in harm's way; she was also the daughter of Paul Wallinger, a man with whom Amelia had conducted a long affair. She owed it to both of them to exact some measure of revenge against Minasian, yet she had failed to do so.

"Of course," she said, again touching Kell on the arm. "What would you like to know?"

"Is he still SVR?"

"As far as I'm aware. We think he's still operational in Kiev."

"He's being watched?"

"I'm afraid not." Amelia rarely apologized or admitted to fault, but on this occasion managed to convey a sense that she was ashamed by the Service's inability to track Minasian. "Too many Requirements. I'm stretched in every direction. We simply can't spare the people."

"I understand."

"I saw a report in which it was confirmed that Minasian had lost a brother in Chechnya about ten years ago."

"He was a soldier?" Kell asked.

Amelia nodded. "Fighting the good fight. I can't remember his name offhand. Information came through a separate channel, somebody looking at Andrei Eremenko, the father-in-law. Moscow keeps tabs on him, on Svetlana. She's been struggling to have a baby."

Kell nodded and said: "I know." The tiniest flicker of suspicion flashed across

Amelia's eyes.

"How did you know?"

"You first." Kell knew only what Riedle had told him; that "Dmitri" had no children. "Tell me about Svetlana."

"What do you want to know?"

"Any illnesses? Any kind of muscular problem?"

He was remembering what Riedle had said about "Vera" suffering from an ailment that left her "in great pain." Amelia shook her head, suggesting that Kell was barking up the wrong tree.

"Does she visit him in Kiev?" he asked.

Amelia answered quickly and decisively: "No."

"How often does he go home?"

"I'd have to check the records, but from memory he's been sighted in Moscow only once in the last year. Coming out of their apartment. Why the interest in Svetlana?"

Kell again avoided the question.

"Do we know any more about Istanbul? About the order to kill Rachel?"

Amelia turned away. Kell felt that he could glimpse the guilt and the rage churning inside her.

"Very little," she replied. "The Cousins were worried that we'd want an inquiry into the Kleckner business. The extent of his treachery, the deal with Jim Chater, his somewhat mysterious death." Jim Chater was the CIA officer whom Kleckner had manipulated and betrayed; "the Cousins" was in-house jargon for the CIA. Amelia implied with a look that Langley had arranged Kleckner's murder. "That sucked up a lot of time. I'm sorry to say that we eventually acquiesced. Again, events elsewhere meant that Istanbul receded into the background." It was no surprise to Kell that the Service had not fulfilled its responsibilities toward Rachel. A few years earlier, he himself had been chewed up by that particular blend of bureaucratic cynicism and legal intransigence at which most monolithic institutions excel. "To be entirely honest," Amelia said, "none of us felt that we would ever get anywhere in terms of arresting the man who killed Rachel, in terms of putting together a criminal case that —"

Kell interrupted her. He didn't want to hear excuses. He knew, as well as she did, that the high priests of Vauxhall Cross specialized in back-covering cynicism. Amelia was now their empress and would happily have sealed the Wallinger file rather than risk trial by media. Hers, after all, was an intelligence service like all the rest. Should an officer find himself exposed to public scrutiny, he would be hung out to dry. Everybody understood this. Nobody rode to anyone's rescue. To all questions from outsiders there was a mantra: "We can neither confirm nor deny." This nurtured and protected the culture of secrecy, the one true faith to which they all subscribed. Furthermore, Kell had never put any trust in the Turkish courts. Moscow would have tied London in legal knots for a generation rather than put Minasian on the stand. No, the only way to avenge Rachel was to go after Minasian direct.

"What if I told you that I had a line into the SVR? What if I told you that I had an opportunity to burn Minasian?"

Amelia had picked up a scallop canapé from a passing waitress. As she raised it to her lips, she hesitated for a fraction of a second, looking up at Kell before slowly inserting the food into her mouth. Several seconds passed while she absorbed what he had told her.

"I'd say that I was extremely interested in watching that happen," she said, swallowing her food. "Let's find a quiet corner to continue this conversation. We've got about half an hour before Sophie is due on the catwalk. I'm all yours."

■ ■ ■ ■

Kell related the events of the previous few weeks: Mowbray's initial sighting of Minasian and Riedle at the hotel in Hurghada; the staged mugging at the apartment in Brussels; Riedle's account of Minasian's repugnant behavior during their relationship; the Russian's imminent visit to London. Throughout Kell's account, Amelia maintained a look of fixed and inscrutable concentration, only breaking her silence occasionally to check a point of fact.

"Claridge's?" she asked, as Kell was drawing to the end.

"Claridge's," he replied. "Paid for by Svetlana. Vera. Whatever you want to call her. With Daddy's money, anyway. The Eremenko billions."

They were sitting alone on a sofa in a corner of the low-lit basement, huddled together like an illicit couple while guests moved around them in a hum of small talk and gossip. Their body language was so private, and the tone of their conversation so conspiratorial, that Amelia and Kell had been interrupted only once by a passing waiter offering to refill their glasses. Amelia had shooed him off.

She now edged away from Kell, reached into her handbag, and checked the screen of her phone. It was not clear whether she was consulting the time or checking for messages from the Office. It may have been that Amelia simply needed a few moments in which to process what she had been told and to decide upon her reaction. When she had deliberated long enough, she put the phone back in her bag, turned toward Kell, and took a deep, somewhat melodramatic breath.

"Tom." It was like sitting with a doctor who was about to deliver a diagnosis of inoperable cancer. Amelia put a hand on Kell's knee, adding once again to the impression of a slightly forced and patronizing intimacy. "I know that losing Rachel in the circumstances in which we lost her was extraordinarily difficult for you. You feel angry, you feel guilty."

"With respect, you don't know how I feel."

It was Amelia's turn to ignore Kell's remark.

"You want some measure of revenge for what happened. For Rachel's murder to *mean* something. A day of reckoning."

"Don't *you*?"

"All of us have felt powerless in this respect, Tom. Rachel's death was, among many other things, a humiliating time. We suffered because we had been unable to save her."

What Amelia had said was true, yet her remarks did not take account of her own complicity in Rachel's death. She had placed her in harm's way and had failed adequately to protect her. Kell was still waiting for some indication that Amelia bore a sense of responsibility for what had happened.

"You know that I have the greatest respect for you," she said. "Both as an intelligence officer and as a friend, I owe you a great deal, Tom." Kell knew that he was being softened up. The medical diagnosis was imminent. "Nevertheless, I have to say that what you've told me sounds very much like a trap. I don't buy it. I don't believe it. I think you're being manipulated. I think Harold Mowbray is in the pay of Alexander Minasian."

# 20

Kell felt a thump of humiliation and turned away. He found himself staring at Luigi, who waved at him across the room with a ripple of slim fingers. Kell looked back at Amelia, numbed by what she had told him.

"Why would you think that?"

It had always been his secret doubt: the wretched possibility that Harold had been offered a hundred grand to betray him. Amelia obviously had inside information. Minasian's supposed homosexuality, his relationship with Riedle, the imminent trip to London: it was all too good to be true. Kell had been played for a fool by a man he had trusted as a friend.

"Instinct," Amelia replied.

Kell was surprised by her answer. He had been expecting conclusive evidence that Mowbray had been caught talking to the Russians: proof of a wire transfer; recordings of a clandestine conversation with the SVR.

"Instinct?" he said. "Is that all?"

Amelia suggested with a dismissive movement of her eyes that instinct was all that the chief of the Secret Intelligence Service required in order to arrive at a fixed conclusion.

"It doesn't add up," she said. "It's too easy."

In his twenty-year career in the secret world, Kell — in common with many of his colleagues — had developed a theory that most of the Service's greatest successes had come about, in part, because of cock-up and human error. He had never been a believer in perfect plans and immaculate conspiracies. Her Majesty's enemies may have been clever and resourceful, but they were seldom so farsighted, so operationally sophisticated, that they could entirely eradicate the possibility of routine accidents and mistakes. For a woman of Amelia's experience to cast doubt on Kell's story simply because it was "too easy" ran counter to every instinct he possessed as a spy. It was when things were most obvious that they were often most true.

"What doesn't add up?" he asked, though he knew exactly how Amelia was going to respond.

"Well, for a start, even if you disregard the extraordinarily small possibility that Minasian's sexuality has not been flagged up at some point by Moscow, you are asking me to imagine that a pedigree Russian foreign intelligence officer — the best of the best — takes the frankly insane risk of visiting a Western tourist hotel over the Easter holidays in the company of his secret boyfriend. You said that the hotel was popular with German tourists of a certain age and economic class? What if one of them happens to be BND?"

Kell could feel his anger rising as rapidly as his determination to prove Amelia wrong. He answered immediately.

"You know yourself that nobody in the BND has ever *seen* Minasian. He's a ghost. When he was running Kleckner we had a meeting with Stefan fucking Helling trying to find out what he looked like. Remember? Nobody in the entire German espiocracy had a clue."

Amelia was obliged to concede Kell's point, but continued nonetheless.

"Look. It just seems too cute. They have an argument right under Harold's window. Poor Bernhard breaks into floods of tears. Minasian does a body swerve and leaves the resort. Meanwhile Harold just happens to find out Riedle's name, address, and serial number and call you up in London."

A waitress passed behind their sofa with an almost-empty bottle of Champagne. Kell was thirsty and flagged her down.

"That's what Harold *does,*" he replied. He thanked the girl as she filled his glass, then waited until she had walked on. "He takes surveillance photographs, he breaks into reservations systems. Are you telling me Elsa is part of this conspiracy, too?"

Amelia shot Kell a jaded look, implying that Elsa was as eminently corruptible as any other freelance analyst on the books at Vauxhall Cross. Was it not the case that she had been uncharacteristically incompetent on the current investigation? Elsa had not even been able to provide Kell with Minasian's pseudonym at the Egypt hotel. Was that accidental or evidence of something more malign?

"Don't you believe in love?" Kell asked.

"Don't I believe in *what*?" Amelia assumed an outraged hauteur. *"Love?"*

Kell took a sip of Champagne.

"Think about Minasian," he said. "A married man, dutiful, loving toward Svetlana, proud to be serving the Motherland. But he has *needs.* He has a secret sexuality that *must* be serviced. We've had these guys

170

before. Hard men in the IRA with wives back in Belfast and a boyfriend in the unit."

"Exactly." Amelia snapped her reply, a return of serve fizzing low over the net. "In the *unit*. They kept it local. They kept it intimate. I know the man you're thinking of and I know the way he managed things. He maintained control over every element of his secret life by sharing it only with one person in his unit over whom he exercised complete tactical and moral influence."

Kell tried to respond. Amelia again cut him down.

"Let me finish my point." All the warmth and easy familiarity of her manner had dissipated. "Why doesn't a man as clever and as careful as Minasian find a boyfriend in Kiev or Moscow? Why doesn't he manage it in-house? Why does he fly from Ukraine to Cairo, from London to Brussels, carrying on like a dog in heat? Does he *want* to get caught?"

"Love," Kell said again.

Amelia threw back her arms and gazed at the ceiling.

"I give up," she said. "You've gone soft, Tom."

There was a strange tenderness in the remark. With the exception of her relationship with Paul Wallinger, Amelia had lived so much of her own life at an emotional distance from the possibility of love that she could at times seem almost desiccated.

"I haven't gone soft," Kell replied. "Believe me, I have seen enough with Claire, heard enough about Minasian, realized the truth of Rachel's behavior toward me, to make me as cynical and as closed off to that sort of thing as you can imagine." It didn't look as though Amelia had entirely understood what Kell was trying to tell her, but he pressed on. "I just happen to believe in Bernie Riedle. I have sat with him. I have listened to him. I have staged a mugging outside his apartment after which he almost wept with shock and gratitude. This is not a Method actor. This is a man who is in love with Alexander Minasian. And he believes that Alexander Minasian is still in love with him."

"Do *you* believe that?" Amelia asked, and for the first time Kell glimpsed the possibility that she could be persuaded out of her prejudice.

"Yes," he said firmly, though he was not at all sure that what he was about to say was even partly true. "I believe that Minasian is still in love with Riedle, in the sense that even the most heartless, self-interested individuals are capable of experiencing feelings of tenderness and affection, no matter how corrupted they may be."

There was a momentary break in their conversation, punctured by the amplified sound of an object being tapped against the side of a glass. A burst of feedback, then a disembodied voice filled the darkened room.

"Ladies and gentlemen, the event is about to start. Will you please make your way to your seats?"

It was Kell's first — and, he hoped, last — experience of the fashion catwalk. Fifteen minutes of male models walking between rows of seated *fashionistas* wearing a series of increasingly bizarre outfits: violet leather biking jackets offset by cream silk scarves as broad as bedsheets; aquamarine culottes worn with pale plimsolls and straw boating hats; tablecloth-check linen suits with three-quarter-length trousers. Kell sat beside Amelia, who had been given a seat in the front row. She was watching the proceedings with rapt fascination, occasionally leaning across to whisper a mischievous "Oooh, he's rather dashing" in Kell's ear. Across the runway, Luigi was seated at the right hand of Burt Lancaster, his fists clenched and knuckles white, eyes set in fierce concentration.

"Here she is," said Amelia as the bone-thin Sophie finally appeared at the end of the runway. She was wearing a beautiful black evening dress, open at the shoulders and across the back, and passed Amelia's seat like a specter, making no eye contact with her godmother.

"Tell me about Mowbray in Odessa," Amelia asked, once she had left the runway. All of the male models had now gathered on the narrow stage.

"What about him?" Kell replied. He was aware of Luigi staring at them in quiet disapproval. Guests were not supposed to chitchat during the show.

"Who saw Minasian?" Amelia asked. "Did Harold spend time with him in the arrivals area?"

Kell could still replay every frame of what had happened at the port a year earlier. He knew that Mowbray had been nowhere near Minasian.

"Danny and Carol took him down after Kleckner came off the ship. Harold was outside the terminal at the time, making sure the SVR didn't grab him from the customs hall. He knew what Minasian looked like from our photograph, but they never got face to face. Danny Aldrich filled him with ketamine. He was out almost immediately."

Sophie had appeared for a second time, now wearing a sleeveless vest and a pair of black silk trousers not dissimilar — at least to Kell's untrained eye — to the ones being worn by her godmother.

"And later?" Amelia asked.

"Nothing." Kell glanced across at Luigi and tried to warm him up with a flattering smile. "Harold was around before we took off in the plane. He and Danny drove back to Odessa, flew out that night. Minasian never set eyes on him."

Amelia was looking to her left, tracking Sophie's approach. She passed their seats and returned backstage. Kell wasn't worried by Amelia's questions. He felt only a sense of impatience that it was taking her so long to trust his judgment.

"The Russians know where I live," he said. "It wouldn't be at all difficult for them to track me down. If what you're saying is true, that Harold has been turned and is working against me, it's an extraordinarily elaborate way of exacting revenge for blowing Kleckner. Easier to throw me under a train, no?"

"Perhaps Minasian doesn't know you've left us and wants to recruit you?" Amelia suggested. There was a burst of applause as the audience reacted to one of the outfits.

"Perhaps this is his way of drawing you in."

Kell laughed at the idea. "Then why doesn't somebody come and find me at the Havelock in Brook Green?" Kell adopted a cod Russian accent. "Hello, Meester Kell. My name eez Vladimir. I know you unhappy. Let me buy you pint."

Amelia smiled, but as she turned back to him, he saw that her eyes were soft with concern.

"*Are* you unhappy?" she asked. In years gone by, Kell would have fallen on her tenderness with gratitude, but he was now too hardened against her. It was simpler to treat all expressions of kindness as a manipulation. "I don't even work for you any more," he said. "What could I possibly tell Minasian that would be of any use to the SVR?"

"You've always underestimated your importance, Tom. You could tell them a great deal."

Kell again ignored the deliberate flattery; Amelia had too many tricks up her sleeve for anything she said to be taken at face value. A new song was playing, a synthesized version of "Don't Stand So Close to Me" that Kell didn't recognize.

"Who have you got in the SVR?" he asked. The question was deliberately provocative, but he was in the mood to push her.

"Never you mind," Amelia replied.

Kell knew that she was being disingenuous. The Service had had nobody on the books a year earlier; the chances of a successful SVR recruitment in the intervening period were vanishingly small.

"You still don't have anybody, do you?" he said. "At least, anyone of any stature."

A knowing grin curled across Amelia's face, disappearing as quickly as it had appeared. Kell again looked across the runway and nodded at Luigi. This time, the Italian nodded back.

"Nobody," Kell repeated. He was taunting her now. Amelia did not respond. The show was drawing to a close and all five male models had lined up on the stage. They left a gap between them, through which a bearded Italian of indeterminate age and inflexible forehead emerged from backstage to rapturous applause. He was flanked on one side by Sophie, on the other by a second female model, equally emaciated. Both had their arms wrapped around him. Kell assumed that he was the man who had designed the clothes.

"Do you think Andrei Eremenko would look good in culottes?" he asked, turning to face Amelia as both of them began to clap.

He could feel her wariness clearing like clouds burning off on a summer morning.

"Just the thing to wear in the bar at Claridge's this season, darling," she replied.

That was when Kell knew that she had changed her mind.

# 21

Svetlana Eremenko landed at Heathrow Airport three days later. According to MI5 surveillance she was met by a uniformed chauffeur who carried her modest luggage to an armor-plated Mercedes in the short-term car park. It was a Monday morning but there was little traffic on the M4. Within an hour she was checking in for a five-night stay at Claridge's, paying £480 per night for the privilege and charging it to a credit card that was traced to a company owned by Andrei Eremenko.

Amelia had insisted on a light-touch approach at the hotel, on the sensible basis that the continuing secure e-mail exchanges between Riedle and Minasian would provide Kell with all the information he needed in order to track the two men's whereabouts. There was no sense in informing Claridge's that a Russian citizen of interest to Her Majesty's government would soon be joining his wife in suite 184; that would only heighten the risk of Minasian smelling a rat and taking the first plane back to Kiev. For the same reason, MI5 would not be flooding the lobby with surveillance. Amelia wanted Minasian to feel as relaxed and as anonymous as possible for a pedigree Russian intelligence officer who would already suspect that his wife was flagged by the Brits. There would be no doorman or chambermaid or concierge paid to offer information on Minasian's movements, just as there would be no cameras or microphones installed in the Eremenko suite. The chances of Minasian saying or doing anything compromising at the hotel were negligible.

"Besides," said Amelia, "as soon as he gets to the hotel he's going to insist on switching rooms. They always do. Moscow rules. We could go to the very great trouble of bugging every phone and plant pot in the building, but I'd rather leave poor Svetlana in relative peace and just keep an eye on Riedle. Bernie will lead us to the mountain, won't he, Tom? Bernie holds the keys to the castle."

She was right. In order to pitch Minasian, to have something to hold against him, Kell needed proof of his homosexuality. At the moment he had nothing; only Riedle's verbal account of the relationship, some photographs from Hurghada, and a few anodyne e-mails, none of which could be conclusively pinned on the Russian. The goal was to get the two men together in a room, to record and film their interactions, then to extract Minasian and present him with the full extent of his folly. Faced with cooperation or ruin, Kell was certain that Minasian would choose to save his own skin.

Since Brussels, the number of messages between Riedle and Minasian had begun to intensify. Minasian had confirmed that he would be arriving in the U.K. on 30 June, a Tuesday. Riedle had immediately reserved a seat on a Monday-morning Eurostar from Brussels. Finding the Charlotte Street Hotel fully booked, Riedle had taken a room at a hotel on Piccadilly, less than a mile from Claridge's. Kell had made an appointment to see the manager. Mowbray, whose fees were now being paid by SIS, equipped Riedle's room with surveillance equipment and Kell was given a pass key allowing him access to every secure area in the hotel. No other members of staff were informed about the intrusion. The manager had been required to sign a copy of the Official Secrets Act and instructed not to report the operation to his superiors. He refused payment and told Kell that he would report "any unusual activity from Mr. Riedle" should anything arise.

Vauxhall Cross still had little idea why Svetlana Eremenko had come to London. Amelia had allowed Kell to put foot surveillance on her whenever she stepped outside Claridge's, and GCHQ were listening to her phone. For the most part, however, she seemed content to sleep late at the hotel and to enjoy the shops and cafés of Mayfair. Late on the Monday afternoon she walked as far as Marylebone High Street and bought some paperbacks in Daunt Books. The following morning she was tailed to the Summer Exhibition at the Royal Academy. At all times she was alone. One report described her as "modestly dressed, courteous and friendly," as if to distinguish her from the stereotype of the super-rich Russian. It was assumed that Svetlana was communicating with her husband via WhatsApp — which was notoriously difficult to hack — or with a secondary mobile phone of which GCHQ had no knowledge. Her bags had not been searched at Heathrow nor had her room been investigated during her absences from the hotel.

Kell himself was obliged to stay clear of

Svetlana at all times. There was every possibility that Minasian was already in London, traveling under alias, working counter-surveillance on his wife, checking for signs of trouble. If he spotted Kell at Claridge's, or saw him wandering around the lobby of Riedle's hotel in Piccadilly, he would cut and run.

Riedle, however, was a different matter. The two men had agreed to meet in London and Kell was keen to speak to him, not least because he might have information about meeting "Dmitri" that had not been disclosed via e-mail. A separate surveillance team was on hand to "house" Riedle from St. Pancras station to his hotel in Piccadilly. Checking in at a similar time to Svetlana, Riedle had spent most of the day working in his room, breaking off to visit the hotel gym at around six o'clock.

To limit the possibility of being seen in his company, Kell had invited Riedle to dinner at Archibald's, an obscure private members' club in Bloomsbury to which Minasian would have no access. Kell himself was not a member, but SIS had an arrangement with the club that had proved fruitful in the past. Unlike the Travellers Club or White's, Archibald's was not a Foreign Office watering hole and there was little chance of Kell being recognized. Nevertheless, he arrived an hour early, through the basement entrance, and arranged for a secluded table in the dining room with no line of sight to the street. Riedle, having been in town for less than six hours, was delighted to have been admitted to one of the inner sanctums of the British Establishment, and wore an uncharacteristically sober gray suit for the occasion.

"So it's happening?" Kell asked as their main courses were served. "You're seeing him in London?"

Riedle took a sip of claret and nodded.

"Yes. He comes here tomorrow." That confirmed the message Minasian had sent to Riedle, setting the date of his arrival in London as Tuesday, 30 June. "He has to spend some time with Vera seeing a doctor about her medical condition, then he says he will be free in the afternoons, perhaps on Wednesday or Thursday."

The team were still not clear what was meant by Svetlana's "medical condition." On her walks around London she had shown no signs of physical discomfort or pain. Kell assumed that Minasian had simply spun Riedle a lie.

"You'll meet at your hotel?"

Riedle shook his head quickly, implying

that Kell was pushing at the edge of what he was comfortable disclosing.

"Well, that's great," he said, without probing further. He was concerned that Minasian would be spooked by the idea of meeting in Riedle's hotel and instead insist on a last-minute switch to a different location. "And you feel fine about things?" he asked. "You're sure it's a good idea?"

"I am sure." Riedle plainly wanted to draw the subject to a close. They were eating lamb cutlets again, served with oversteamed vegetables and roast potatoes. School food, thought Kell, as he spooned mint jelly onto his plate.

"I would just like to say something."

Riedle had put down his knife and fork and lowered his voice to an almost reverent hush.

"Of course."

Kell wondered what was coming. For an awful, paranoid moment, he wondered if Riedle had grasped the extent to which he was being manipulated. Perhaps he knew the true nature of "Dmitri's" profession and had understood that Peter was a false friend. There was a resigned look on his face, candid and melancholic.

"I want to thank you, Peter." Kell leaned back in his seat, relieved. "You have been a very good friend to me. You have helped enormously." Riedle suddenly reached out his hand. Kell was concerned that Riedle was going to try to touch him. "You may not realize this," he continued, twirling the stem of his wineglass as it rested on the table, "but it is true. One of the strange things about my suffering is that it is in many ways the opposite of what a person might expect to experience at a time like this. Usually when we have suffered loss, we yearn to return to the person who has destroyed us. We want to mend the wound. It has not been like that with me. Not at all."

"You mean you don't want to reconcile with Dmitri? Then why are you meeting him?"

Kell was sure that something was going to go wrong: an e-mail exchange between the two men on the eve of the reunion that would push Minasian away; a quick, face-to-face argument giving the cameras and microphones nothing in terms of leverage. Riedle seemed stronger and more determined than had been the case in Brussels. His eyes had a fixed, stubborn quality. It was as though he were steeling himself for revenge.

"I will meet him because I hate him and

because I love him. Does this make sense?"

"Perfect sense."

Kell put down his own knife and fork and smiled, trying to convey that he was keen to understand in greater detail precisely what Riedle wanted to tell him.

"I hate Dmitri. I am intensely angry with him for the way he has treated me and for the way that he has made me feel. But I also love him. How can I not? He is everything that I need and admire. I wanted someone to hear me and to understand the extent to which I had been made to suffer by this man, but also by the extent to which I had been liberated to *feel* such love. You were the person who listened, who understood. *You* were the man. I sensed that you knew what it was still to love somebody whom you also hate."

Save for the tinkling of glass and cutlery, and the low, ordered murmur of male conversation, there was silence in the dining room. Kell felt a vivid combination of worry and regret. He knew that he had manipulated Riedle past a point at which such a manipulation was ethically defensible and yet he felt a strange sense of pride in having helped a man through his suffering.

"Thank you for saying that," he replied. "It's kind of you to say so. I've really enjoyed our conversations, Bernie. I'm glad that I've been able to help."

Both men began to eat again. Kell felt that he should say something more.

"We have a saying in English," he began. "There's a thin line between love and hate. I'm sure you have a similar phrase in German."

Riedle chewed and nodded, without offering an example.

"It's one of the fascinating things in human nature," Kell continued. "We are drawn to people who might destroy us, yet we often tire of those who show us unconditional love. It must be something to do with a fear of death and stasis. A great love affair makes us feel alive, vivid and free. But that feeling comes at a price. We are never truly happy while we are at the mercy of another person."

"Yes," Riedle replied, looking out across the ancient club. He was smiling in a benign and slightly distracted fashion.

"It must be to do with that. Something to do with stasis. And with death."

## 22

Kell returned home to find that Riedle had already written a message to Minasian. Though he had always known that their friendship might become an operational risk, he was nevertheless deeply concerned by what he read:

> I have just come back from dinner at Archibald's Club with my new friend, Peter. An extraordinary building, an old-fashioned English gentlemen's club in Bloomsbury. Photographs of Queen Elizabeth on the wall and shoe polish in the bathrooms! I have not told you about Peter, have I?

Riedle was trying to provoke a reaction, but Kell suspected that this was not how Minasian would interpret the message. A man of such bulletproof self-confidence would not be unsettled by petty jealousy; he would, however, want to know about "Peter" for professional reasons. How had they met? Why was Bernhard dining with him in London? If Riedle told him about the mugging in Brussels, Minasian would almost certainly conclude that "Peter" was the pseudonym of a British intelligence officer.

Kell lit a cigarette, opened the window in his living room, and poured a glass of wine. He could do nothing but wait. Spotting a copy of *Nineteen Eighty-Four* on his shelves, he took it down and began to read, drawn into the world of Doublethink and the Ministry of Love for the first time since his teens. Kell checked his laptop every four or five minutes for a reply from Minasian, but nothing had appeared in the account. At around midnight, surveillance at the Piccadilly hotel reported that Riedle had gone to bed. Kell took a shower to kill more time, but there was still no activity from Minasian fifteen minutes later.

Just after one o'clock, he took a sleeping pill, set his alarm for seven, and called it a night.

He woke at six. Minasian had replied to Riedle's message. The wording was almost exactly as Kell had anticipated. A couple of lines in response to Archibald's e-mail, then:

No. You have not told me about Peter. Who is he? How did you meet?

Kell called Amelia immediately.

"There may be a slight problem."

"There's always a slight problem."

"Bernie is trying to make our boy jealous by telling him about Peter."

"About you?" Amelia asked.

"Yes."

Kell was still in bed, propped up in front of the laptop, eyes sticky with sleep, his brain clearing out the remnants of the sleeping pill.

"He's told him about Brussels? About the fight?"

"Not yet." Kell set the laptop to one side and stood up. "If he does, I'm going to delete the message before Minasian gets a chance to read it. It's worth the risk."

Amelia did not hesitate. "Agreed," she said.

"Any sign of him?"

"Who? Minasian?" There was a momentary pause, perhaps while Amelia checked her surveillance reports. "None."

"And Svetlana?"

"Housed to Claridge's last night."

Kell could hear the mumble of Radio 4 in the background and assumed that Amelia was in her kitchen at the grace-and-favor SIS flat in London. They agreed to stay in touch throughout the day, though Amelia explained that she would be in a meeting "with the PM" from two o'clock onward.

"I'm leaving it with you, Tom," she said. "Do what you have to do."

Kell immediately called surveillance at the Piccadilly hotel and requested minute-by-minute updates on Riedle's behavior and movements. Just before eight he was told that the target had woken up. Having gone to the bathroom, Riedle's first act had been to open his computer. Watching a live feed at Vauxhall Cross, the surveillance officer reported that Riedle was "typing something into the keyboard." When he had finished, Kell logged in to the secure e-mails.

Sure enough, his reply was sitting in the in-box:

I will tell you about him tomorrow. Too complicated to explain now. I have booked a room in the usual way. 98 Sterndale Road, Flat 4. The postcode is W14 0HX. I have it for one night only. What time do you think you will arrive?

Kell was intensely relieved. The meeting off-site in Sterndale Road — rather than in

Riedle's hotel room — was doubtless yet another layer of Minasian paranoia, but the time delay was sufficient to give Tech-Ops the chance to rig the apartment. Kell typed the address into his iPhone. The property was no more than five minutes on foot from his own flat in Sinclair Road. He guessed that Riedle had booked it on Airbnb, or a similar online agent, and contacted Vauxhall Cross to arrange entry to the property.

"Soak the place," he told them when the senior member of the surveillance team called him back twenty minutes later. "Get every nook and cranny. Bedrooms, bathrooms, balconies, cupboards. I'm going to need clear dialogue, clear images. This is a high-value target, a once-only opportunity. Everything has to go like clockwork."

"Yes, sir. Thank you, sir," the man replied, and Kell experienced the strange and invigorating sensation of the blacklisted man who has finally been invited back into his favorite club.

# 23

It was then just a question of waiting for Alexander Minasian.

He had told Riedle that he would arrive in London on Tuesday the thirtieth, but by sunset there was no sign of him at Claridge's. Three different surveillance officers working on rotation in the lobby reported sightings of Svetlana Eremenko, but at no point during the day did she leave the hotel. Kell knew that Minasian might have slipped up to her room via a staff entrance, or even by donning a simple disguise, but it concerned him when Svetlana was seen eating dinner alone in the hotel restaurant with only a paperback for company.

He checked the e-mail contact between Riedle and Dmitri but there had been no further messages between the two men. Minasian had agreed to meet Riedle at Sterndale Road "at about 3 P.M., if I can get away from Vera." That was their final exchange.

Had Minasian been spooked by "Peter" or by Archibald's? Or was it simply in his nature to dissemble and confuse? Kell could not know. He could only sit and wait, reading the surveillance updates, watching the occasional rally at Wimbledon, and ringing out for food.

At ten thirty, he called Amelia at home.

"He's not here."

"I am aware of that," she said.

"If he doesn't come, we've got nothing."

"I am also aware of that."

"How was the prime minister?" Kell was irritated by her supercilious tone.

"Sunburned," she replied.

The conversation did not last long. Amelia confirmed what Kell already knew — that Riedle and Svetlana were both in their hotel rooms — and tried to console him with the thought that Minasian was probably already in the U.K., "shaking off an imaginary tail in Cambridge or Gatwick or Penrith."

"You know how that lot operate," she said. "Always think they've got company, even when they're supposed to be on shopping holidays in sunny England with their beautiful young wives. You want to know my guess?"

"I do," Kell replied.

"Our man Alexander is fast asleep in his

little bed in Kiev. Tomorrow morning, first thing, he'll take a cab to the airport, fly into Heathrow under alias, skip through Passport Control, and meet Svetlana for lunch."

"What about Sterndale Road?" Kell asked. "What about Riedle? They've only got their love nest until Thursday morning."

There was a noise down the line, as though Amelia thought that Kell was being unnecessarily pessimistic.

"How long is he going to need with Riedle?" She sounded exasperated. "At some point in the afternoon, he'll make his excuses to Svetlana, hop in a cab to Brook Green, have his little chat with Bernie, they'll go to bed for a bit. Then Alexander will head back to Claridge's." Kell lit a cigarette, listening. "That's all we'll need," she said. "Confirmation on the mikes that the two of them have been to bed together. Once we have that, we have everything. Visual proof, audio proof, the lot. Then you'll have what you need, Tom. The head of John the Baptist."

# 24

Shahid Khan found the new life easier than he had thought it would be. It had been simple to forget his old ways and to blend in. He looked good and he knew that people liked him. He was fit and he was strong and not shy to talk to anyone who crossed his path. The guys in the gym asked him for tips on fitness and he helped them with circuits and weights. It gave Shahid pleasure to know that he was fooling them. They thought that he was their friend, their "buddy." Shahid drew satisfaction from this because their friendship and camaraderie meant nothing to him. He was playing a role. He was doing it so that nobody would suspect him, so that when the day of his martyrdom arrived, these same people would tell their friends and families that Shahid Khan had seemed like such a "normal" young man, so easygoing and friendly, not a care in the world. They were all fools.

They had not been able to see the anger inside him. Shahid Khan was not a "normal" person. He was exceptional.

He played the same role when he was working at the supermarket. The girls on the checkouts looked at Shahid and smiled at him; some of them even teased him about his Yorkshire accent. Young mothers in heavy makeup with small children shopping in the mornings and afternoons cut him sly glances as Shahid stacked the shelves. They asked him questions that he knew they did not need to ask. Where could they find ice cream? Where could they find sliced bread? They wanted him. He could tell by the way they smiled. Shahid knew they were lonely and empty, women with nothing inside them except base desires. They had no learning or education, no understanding of how to raise a family properly in the eyes of God. Their children were always covered in food and screaming. Shahid felt pity for them growing up in a world like this, with fathers who had abandoned them and mothers who thought only of themselves and their own desires. On Friday and Saturday nights he had seen the drinking and the fights on the streets of Brighton. Girls exposed themselves and drank alcohol and behaved like there was no difference between a man and a woman. Shahid saw how important money was to these people and yet how lazy they were. At the supermarket, for instance, the staff who worked alongside him were always trying to cheat the system. They took time off or stole food from the shelves. They worked and then they boasted about taking money from the council for housing benefit, for dole. They were open about this, as if they wished to be honored for their lies. They had no pride, just as the women who exposed themselves in the streets and on the beaches had no honor. Shahid thought of the nobility and the courage of the women he had seen in the Caliphate. They knew that it was their duty to serve God, to serve their men.

Shahid had found a room in a house in Rottingdean. His landlady was a Christian woman who went to church every Sunday. Kitty. He rarely saw her. The house was divided into two parts. He lived at the back in a bedsit that he had decorated according to Jalal's instructions. There were posters on the walls of Arsenal footballers, of American actresses, of Bruce Lee. Shahid kept no poetry or religious materials in view of the landlady. He did not wish to raise her suspicions. He kept his Koran hidden behind a stack of DVDs. He prayed at night, in the darkness of his room, and again first thing in the morning. Shahid had never attended mosque in Brighton. He could not risk being seen by the cameras or by the agents of MI5 who had infested sacred Muslim places of worship. He yearned for mosque but understood that he would be forgiven by God after he had completed his act of martyrdom. He would be rewarded. This was the radiance of Islam.

# 25

At 9:43 on Wednesday morning, Alexander Minasian was sighted emerging from the revolving doors at Claridge's in the company of his wife, Svetlana, and an "unidentified male" estimated to be "in his late fifties or early sixties." He was wearing black shoes, dark blue chino trousers, a white shirt, and gray sports jacket. Nobody knew how Minasian had entered the hotel or when he had arrived. No morning flight from Kiev had landed in time to allow him to get to the hotel so quickly and there was no flag on his passport. He had most likely traveled under alias and slipped into the lobby in the early hours of the morning having worked countersurveillance on Riedle, possibly for several days. That he was still in London and happy to be seen in Svetlana's company was a credit to the team working on the operation. Minasian thought he was clean and plainly had no idea that both his wife and his erstwhile boyfriend were being watched by the Security Service.

Surveillance reported that Minasian, Svetlana, and the older man were ushered into the same bulletproof limousine that had fetched Svetlana from Heathrow two days earlier. They were driven along Brook Street toward Hanover Square and followed north by an SIS black cab to an address on Upper Wimpole Street. It was at this point that surveillance contacted Kell with the update.

Kell was sitting at home in his kitchen, drinking a cup of coffee in front of two laptops, three mobile phones, and a Ben Macintyre op-ed in *The Times*.

"A man matching GAGARIN's description has just driven with VALENTINA to Upper Wimpole Street, sir. One nine one." "GAGARIN" had been given to Minasian as a code name, on the basis that he bore a passing resemblance to the Russian cosmonaut. A quick search on Wikipedia had revealed that Yuri Gagarin had been married to a woman named "Valentina." "A second male in the vehicle with them. Older, about sixty. Black suit, white shirt. Didn't seem like muscle."

Kell knew in his bones that the older man was Andrei Eremenko. He was about to say as much when the hunch was confirmed.

"I've had Vauxhall call up images of TOLSTOY, sir. I'd say it's a match. Looks like him."

It was the third time in his career that Kell had heard Surveillance refer to a Russian target as TOLSTOY. They needed to read some new books.

"Thank you," he replied. "Was GAGARIN carrying anything?"

Kell wanted to know if Minasian had an overnight bag, something large enough to contain a change of clothes.

"Affirmative. Small backpack. VALEN-TINA just her usual handbag. Nothing on TOLSTOY."

Kell was stubbing out a cigarette. He had been smoking almost continuously for forty-eight hours.

"Okay," he said. "Switch the cars and keep an eye on them when they come out."

Though Kell was relieved that Minasian was in London, he was also unsettled by the thought that the man whom he held responsible for Rachel's murder was now just a few miles away in Westminster. His presence was tangible. Kell wanted to confront him, but felt trapped. It was like being a boxer who had trained for a fight in which he would never participate. How extraordinarily easy it would be to walk out of his flat and hail a cab, to drive to Upper Wimpole Street and challenge Minasian face to face. No tradecraft. No surveillance. No plots. Just a reckoning between men. And yet that option was denied to him by the demands of the operation. The political had superseded the personal. Kell and Amelia had set themselves on the path of an elaborate revenge that, if handled properly, would leave Minasian's life and career in tatters. The gentle, blameless Svetlana would be married to a traitor of the Motherland and her father's business career ruined by association. And for what? The prestige of running a Russian intelligence officer? To honor Rachel's memory? Staring at the laptops and the phones, the notepads and the half-empty cups of coffee, at all the paraphernalia of scrutiny and surveillance, Kell wondered — not for the first time — if it was all going to be worth it.

To distract himself, he typed "191 Upper Wimpole Street" into Google, on the assumption that the family had been invited to a meeting or brunch at a private residence. What he saw cast him back into the twilight of his own marriage, to numberless visits of the same kind at Claire's side, each of them more desperate than the last:

The Wimpole Clinic offers an extensive range of fertility services. Our team of specialist consultants in the fields of fertility and gynecology are expert in all aspects of assisted conception, endoscopic surgery, and male fertility. We can provide comprehensive assistance to couples who are not able to conceive on their own.

The coincidence was startling. It transpired that Minasian had been telling a version of the truth when he complained to Riedle that "Vera" was suffering from a medical condition that left her "in great pain." That pain was not physical; it was psychological. Claire had been devastated by her inability to have children, so much so that Kell attributed the deterioration of their marriage chiefly to the agony of her infertility. He had been resigned to living out the rest of his life without children, but Claire had sought solace in the arms of other men, wrongly believing that they might give her the child she had always craved. Minasian was now living through the same torment. Was it his own fault that Svetlana was unable to conceive? Had Riedle been correct in suggesting that the sexual relationship between them was nonexistent? And why was Eremenko accompanying his daughter and son-in-law on such a private and potentially distressing visit? Daddy's money was almost certainly paying for Svetlana's treatment, but there was something humiliating — even emasculating — about his direct involvement.

Kell picked up the phone. Amelia was at her desk. When he told her that Minasian and Svetlana were attending an appointment at the clinic, he heard the quiet, empty shock in her voice as memories of her own long battle with conception came flooding back.

"Is that so?" she said softly. "Poor girl."

There was a long pause, as much as five or six seconds, a period in which the decency inside Kell, his momentary sympathy for Minasian, completely evaporated. An idea of such wretched cynicism had taken hold of him that he was almost ashamed of himself for conceiving it. Yet he could not shake it off. To Kell's astonishment, Amelia had arrived at the same conclusion. They were both thinking in exactly the same way. They had made the same ruthless calculation, but it was Amelia who was bold enough to articulate it.

"We can use this," she said. "You realize that, don't you?"

"I do," Kell replied.

"Where is the best fertility treatment in the world?"

"London."

"Exactly. If Minasian wants to have children, he needs to be sure that we'll let Svetlana into the country. Once she starts her treatment, she'll be flying in every six weeks. Put a block on her passport and that's not going to happen."

Kell was dismayed by Amelia's logic, not least because her ultimate disregard for Svetlana matched his own. In Amelia's position, he would have played exactly the same hand. This was the business they were in. No compassion, no sympathy, no kindness. Honor among thieves, perhaps. Honor among spies, never. They were committed to taking Minasian as their prize and would stop at nothing to do so.

# 26

Shahid longed to act, to do what he had been sent to do.

In Brighton he had come to see, with blessed clarity, what he had been taught about the West, first by Javed Rahman, the preacher in Leeds who had brought him to true Islam, and later by Jalal. They had taught him that liberty was a poison inside human beings. They had used a phrase Shahid had always remembered: "Freedom is made of thorns." The openness of European society, the liberal values of America and the West, led directly to moral depravity. Therefore that society needed to be cleansed. Shahid understood this fully now. The cleansing could only take place if those who lived by such values were wiped away.

So he waited, day and night, for the signal. Whenever he grew impatient and hungry to act, Shahid thought of the silent army of true Muslims in every community in Europe and around the world who believed in what he was going to do. Those people, the oppressed and the humble, gave him strength. Jalal had told him that the attack must come at the "most timely political moment." Those who had established the Caliphate, who wanted it to expand and to grow in strength, predicted that Shahid's martyrdom would fill the governments and the populations of the West with fear; his bravery would draw the United Kingdom and her allies into acts of retaliation and vengeance. The ultimate goal was war.

Whenever he was not working or training in the gym, Shahid scoured the newspapers, listened to the radio, and watched television. He read every story he could find about ISIS and the Middle East. He studied the political situation in America, in Russia, and closely followed events in the United Kingdom. He wanted to be able to anticipate when the order would come. If his brothers and sisters in the Caliphate suffered a reverse — if, say, a holy warrior was killed by a drone strike or a prisoner of the infidel released from captivity — would Shahid be signaled to act? Or would they prefer him to strike when ISIS had been victorious in battle, to indicate to the world — to believers and nonbelievers alike — that the

Caliphate was indestructible and its dominance inevitable?

Finally, on an evening late in June, as Shahid was returning home from work, he received the message from Kris. It was just as Jalal had said it would be: a simple text message, using prearranged language, indicating when the operation was to go ahead. Yet it dismayed Shahid to learn of the delay. He could not understand why they wanted him to wait.

Time and venue agreed: July 11, 6 P.M.

## 27

Bernhard Riedle woke in the dead of night, then again at dawn, and, finally, at eight o'clock, thanks to an alarm call from the hotel. He knew that he had barely slept and yet he felt vital and well rested. The two days in London had allowed him to complete some essential paperwork but, more important, to settle much of his anxiety and heartbreak. He knew that Dmitri would not have arranged to meet him at the flat had he not been experiencing second thoughts about their separation. By agreeing to see him, he was effectively contradicting much of what he had said in Egypt, not least that he saw "no chance or possibility" that they would ever be reunited, and that the relationship between them had "never worked." Both of these statements Bernhard could now happily consign to the scrapheap. Dmitri had come to his senses.

Nevertheless, Bernhard still felt a sense of

injustice and anger. He knew that he must find the strength to confront Dmitri about his cruel behavior, and to extract an apology for the way that he had conducted himself. This would be difficult. When they were together, Dmitri had an extraordinary effect on him; all Bernhard wanted was to hold him and to be close to him. He would find it very difficult to be strong and to maintain his dignity. Nevertheless, at the very least he required an acknowledgment of wrongdoing; without it, how could he trust Dmitri not to behave in a similar fashion again? Did he have the strength to ask for such a thing and to risk losing him forever? Was personal pride more important than personal happiness? These were the questions that troubled Bernhard as he made his way to the lobby for breakfast.

He checked out of the hotel just before ten o'clock. It was a fiercely hot morning. Piccadilly was thick with tourists and he had to stand in the full glare of the sun for more than five minutes while waiting for a taxi. Bernhard instructed the driver to take him to the Westfield shopping center in White City and asked for directions to Waitrose. He wanted to buy some basic provisions for the apartment and to stock up on some of Dmitri's favorite things.

More crowds, more heat, at Westfield. Bernhard found a shaded colonnade leading to the supermarket and gratefully hid from the sun. He wished that he could at least text Dmitri to find out at exactly what time he planned to arrive. His last e-mail had said three o'clock, but on many occasions in the past he had been an hour early, or several hours late to their meetings. Bernhard hated sitting around and waiting. There was something humiliating about it. It seemed so ridiculous not at least to be able to contact Dmitri now that they were both in London. What was he so afraid of? Could he not escape Vera's attention for even five minutes? Did she check his cell phone every time it rang?

Waitrose was air-conditioned and blessedly free of crowds. Bernhard took a trolley and went directly to the alcohol section, picking up a bottle of chilled Laurent-Perrier Champagne and one of Quincy, which was the closest wine on display to Sancerre, Dmitri's favorite from the Loire. He suspected that they would remain in the flat that evening — London was too populous and full of Russians to risk being seen together in a restaurant — but knew that neither of them would feel like cooking. There were plenty of delivery companies in

West London; they could choose whatever they felt like eating when the time was right. But Bernhard knew how much Dmitri enjoyed breakfast and was determined to spoil him. There were organic eggs on sale, as well as packets of *jamón ibérico,* sourdough bread, and orange juice. He also bought coffee and soy milk. With his trolley almost full, Bernhard walked to the checkout, paid for two long-life carrier bags, then made his way back along the colonnade to the taxi rank.

## 28

Kell read the surveillance report from Waitrose. Champagne, orange juice, eggs, con-
doms. Any fears he might have had that
Riedle was planning to hurt or injure Minasian immediately subsided. He was obviously planning for a romantic evening and
hoping that Minasian would stay overnight.

Vauxhall Cross had ascertained that the
one-bedroom property on Sterndale Road
had indeed been rented out on Airbnb.
Tech-Ops had entered the flat at two o'clock
in the morning and rigged it for Riedle's
visit. Cameras and microphones had been
placed in the living room, the bathroom,
the bedroom, and the kitchen. At the same
time, a member of the surveillance team had
taken a room at the back of a hotel on
Shepherd's Bush Road that had line of sight
to the entrance, albeit one that was partially
obscured by the branch of a tree. A team on
the street had kept a lookout for Minasian

while the flat was being prepared. He had never showed.

Riedle had rented the top-floor apartment, one of three in the building. The ground-floor flat was occupied by an Australian single mother and her nine-year-old son, both of who would be at home during Riedle's visit. The first-floor property was empty. The owner of Riedle's flat had told Airbnb that he would be home on 2 July by 6 p.m. For this reason, Riedle had been asked to vacate the premises by two o'clock.

Minasian, Svetlana, and Andrei Eremenko spent almost two hours at the fertility clinic. When they emerged into the fierce midday sunshine, Eremenko's driver was waiting for them. They drove south to Piccadilly. As they were entering the Wolseley for a lunch reservation at 12:30, Kell received confirmation that Riedle had been housed to Sterndale Road. Simon, the surveillance officer in the hotel across the street, had watched Riedle entering the property and could see him changing the bedsheets in the bedroom on the south side of the building. Surveillance footage from the flat was now transmitted live to Kell's laptops and he was able to watch Riedle unpacking groceries in the kitchen just a few moments later.

Wary of spooking Minasian at the last

minute, Kell called off the black cab that had tailed Eremenko's limousine to the Wolseley.

"Let them eat lunch in peace," he told Vauxhall Cross. "The mountain will come to Mohammed."

Forty minutes later there was a ring at the front door. Kell had been expecting Harold Mowbray since one. He walked barefoot to the intercom and buzzed him inside.

"Beers," he said, plonking a four-pack of Stella Artois on the kitchen counter. Mowbray's short-sleeved shirt was soaked with sweat. "Fuck me it's hot outside and fuck me this flat stinks of cigarettes."

"ATLANTIC is in the building."

Riedle had been given the code name by Kell, a nod to the well-known hotel in Hamburg.

"I just walked two blocks from his front door on the way back from Tesco." Mowbray put two pepperoni pizzas in the freezer. "How long 'til liftoff?"

Kell knew the time without needing to consult his watch. Every minute was ticking past in slow motion. It was twelve minutes past one.

"Minasian said he'd be there by three. That could mean two, that could mean four, that could mean five, that could mean ten."

"Could mean he doesn't show up at all."

Kell conceded the point with a nod and lit yet another cigarette. "It's always like this," he said.

Mowbray was leaving the kitchen. "Yeah. What's that line you're fond of quoting? 'Spying is waiting.'"

"Spying is waiting," Kell concurred.

As he walked into the living room, briefly consulting the live feeds from Sterndale Road, Kell told Mowbray that Minasian, Svetlana, and Eremenko were eating lunch at the Wolseley and that he had dropped all surveillance on GAGARIN.

"Place on Green Park, right?"

"That's the one." Kell sat down, switched on the television, and watched a rally at Wimbledon on mute. "We just have to wait," he said, knowing that he wouldn't tell Mowbray about the fertility clinic, about the plan to squeeze Minasian on Svetlana's passport. That was operational information, not idle chitchat. He took a drag on the cigarette and wondered what the doctors had told her. "You want to work in shifts?" he said. "You watch the laptops, I'll watch the phones?"

"Deal," said Mowbray.

Mowbray sat at the large table in the center of the living room. Kell had put all his books and papers in piles in the corner of the room. He had cleared his desk of detritus and removed a photograph of Rachel from the wall. Mowbray swiveled the three laptops toward him, then stood up, crossed the room, and opened the window. Birdsong and the chatter of children. All of London life going on around them. He had pressed the kettle in the kitchen. Kell could hear it crackle and hiss to the boil.

"Looks like Bernie's all settled in." Mowbray was back in front of the screens.

"He had a shower about twenty minutes ago," Kell replied.

"Not surprised. Fucking hot out . . ."

One of the mobiles rang. The link to Simon in the hotel. Kell answered it.

"Boss?"

"Yup."

"Vehicle outside. Could be an Uber."

"What makes you say that?"

"Lexus. Guy just got out of the back."

*Let it be him,* thought Kell. *Let it be Minasian.*

"What's he wearing?"

"Don't know if he's going to ninety-eight. He's talking to the driver."

"What does he look like?"

"Tree in the way, guv. Those fucking leaves. Could be GAGARIN, could not be

GAGARIN . . ."

"What's he wearing?" Kell heard the attack in his own voice, the anxiety, and backed off. "What can you see?"

"Black shoes. Black trousers."

It had been reported that Minasian was wearing black shoes and dark blue trousers. It could be a match.

"Hair? Give me something else."

"Dark. Cut short. Balding at the back. Early thirties. Short, squat. Maybe Greek or Turkish? Mediterranean. I can't see his face. Red shirt, black blazer."

Balding didn't sound right. Minasian had a full head of hair. And the coloring and height were wrong. Furthermore, the Russian had been wearing a white shirt and gray sports jacket. It was possible that he had changed after leaving the Wolseley, but it was unlikely that he had yet finished lunch.

"It's not him," he said, looking across the room. Mowbray was staring at Kell. "It's not GAGARIN."

There was a momentary silence. Kell put the phone on speaker and Simon's voice filled the room.

"Vehicle staying where it is. Hazard lights. He's walking up to the door, guv. Walking up to ninety-eight."

"Could be for the neighbor," Kell suggested flatly. "Mother of the nine-year-old boy?"

"Who the fuck *is* it?" said Mowbray.

"Not clear on that," said Simon. "Hold, please. Hazards still flashing. Engine on the Lexus running."

# 29

Bernhard Riedle heard the sudden burst on the doorbell and felt his heart surge. Dmitri was early. He checked his reflection in the bathroom mirror then picked up the intercom.

"Hello?"

"Delivery for flat three."

Riedle felt a slump of disappointment. He pressed the button for entry.

"Are you inside?" he asked as the lock buzzed and the door clicked open. "Do you require a signature?"

"Please," said the delivery man. Riedle hung up, picked up the keys to the apartment, and prepared to walk downstairs. He decided against putting on any socks or shoes and headed for the front door. It was cool in the narrow corridor outside the flat. The walls were dirty, the paint chipped along the skirting board.

"Just coming," Riedle called out as he

reached the turn at the top of the stairs.

"Down here," said the man, and Riedle could now see him.

He did not look like a deliveryman. He was wearing no uniform and did not appear to be carrying any identification. He was in his early thirties, smartly dressed, and seemed at first glance to be a neighbor or perhaps a friend visiting the occupants of the ground-floor flat. As Riedle reached the bottom of the stairs, he noticed that the man was not carrying a parcel or envelope of any kind. There was no box on the ground, though the front door was ajar. Perhaps the items for delivery were outside in a van.

"Mr. Riedle? Bernhard Riedle?"

"Yes," he said, and stopped: "But how did you know I was here?"

The man fired once, blowing out the back of Riedle's head with a silenced handgun. Riedle's body was thrust backward toward the door of the ground-floor apartment. The man then fired a second shot into his chest, holstered the weapon, turned around, and walked out onto the street.

## 30

"Subject just got back in the Lexus. Front seat. Vehicle has moved away."

"Where's ATLANTIC?" Mowbray muttered, staring at the live feeds. There were no cameras rigged in the stairwell or hall of the apartment. When Riedle had answered the intercom and walked downstairs, they had lost audio-visual.

"Did you get a number plate?" Kell asked. He knew that something was badly wrong.

"Partial," Simon replied. His voice sounded hesitant, uncertain.

"Where the fuck's he gone?" Mowbray stood back to allow Kell to look at the screens. Bedroom. Bathroom. Kitchen. Sitting room. There was no movement inside the apartment. Nothing.

"What can you see from the hotel?"

A slice of feedback on the speaker, then:

"Could be he met the neighbor. She's downstairs with the kid."

"That wasn't my question," Kell replied. "What can you *see*?"

"Nothing, sir."

Kell turned to Mowbray. A lawnmower had started up in a neighboring garden, forcing him to raise his voice.

"The screens. Are they accurate? Can they be refreshed? Have we got some kind of glitch?"

Mowbray shook his head. "They're fine, boss. Doesn't work like that. They don't all go down at the same time. Different circuits." Mowbray could sense that Kell was already working off the worst-case scenario. "Simon's probably right," he said, in an effort to console him. "Bernie's just having a chat with the neighbor, killing time. He'll be back any moment."

"No." Kell was shaking his head. He had understood what had happened, all of the ways in which he had failed to see how easily Riedle had been tricked. "He won't be coming back."

Mowbray looked at Kell. Their worst fears were confirmed by Simon's voice on the speaker, low and disbelieving.

"Jesus."

"What is it?" Kell asked quietly.

"We've got movement. Mother and son. They just came out the front door. She's shielding him."

"Why?" Kell asked, but he knew the answer to his own question.

Simon's voice was quick and shocked, sentences folding into sentences as he described the scene in front of him.

"She's distraught. They're crying. We've got a crowd gathering. I've got people standing back. The kid's in tears. Something's happened, boss. I think there's been a shooting."

Mowbray's mouth hung open, as though frozen in mid-breath. Kell looked at him and placed a hand on his back, as if to take on the full burden of responsibility for what had happened. He understood everything now, in the way that ideas materialize in an instant and order themselves out of nothing. Minasian had sent a private team to erase his little problem. He had lured Riedle to London, then had him taken out, safe in the knowledge that Scotland Yard would never be able to join the dots.

"Stay where you are," he told Simon. It was the first law of surveillance. Never leave your post, no matter what you see, no matter what you feel you can do to intervene.

"I'm staying," came the reply. "I count two bystanders on phones, boss. Looks like emergency calls. They're calling it in. The neighbor is being comforted. She's got the kid in her arms. He's still crying. They're both still crying."

Kell heard the ping of a message on Amelia's dedicated mobile. He picked it up. The screen said: "News?"

"Problem," he typed back.

"Again?!" Amelia replied.

How strange it was to think that she might have smiled as she typed that. Kell put the phone in his back pocket and picked up his private mobile. He told Mowbray to stay in front of the screens, instructed Simon to text him with updates. Then he grabbed his jacket and keys and ran out onto the street.

## 31

Kell jogged along Masbro Road in the heat of the afternoon, his shirt drenched in sweat, the operation crumbling around him. He called surveillance at Thames House, ordering teams back to the Wolseley and Claridge's. There was still a small chance that Minasian was with Svetlana and that he could be arrested for complicity in Riedle's murder. It was also entirely probable that the Russian had said his good-byes, shouldered his rucksack, and taken a taxi to Gatwick or Heathrow. Traveling under alias, Minasian would be out of U.K. airspace within three hours. Most likely Kell would never set eyes on him again.

He rang Amelia's number.

"You said there was a problem."

It sounded as if she were walking somewhere in a hurry. Her voice, like his own, was breathless and rushed. She had so many other problems to deal with, and now Kell was presenting her with this.

"ATLANTIC is down," he said, slowing to a standstill. Kell felt that he was giving SIS the ammunition with which to finish off the dregs of his career. "There was a shooting. They took him out."

"Dear God. *Who* took him out?"

"Who do you think?"

Simon had reported by text that the police were now outside Sterndale Road and that there had already been a report of a shooting in the area on Twitter. Kell told Amelia that he was on his way to the scene.

"You're *what*?" She sounded bewildered and angry. "Why? Tom, no. That's an appalling idea. Do not show your face at Sterndale Road."

Kell knew her too well. She was not trying to protect him. She was looking after number one. Her instinct was to distance SIS from the shooting. If Riedle's death was pinned to the SVR, or it was discovered that he had been under surveillance, it would be Amelia who took the hit.

"I know what I'm doing," he said.

"Do not show your face, Tom. I am ordering you."

It was a fair request. Every citizen was now a reporter and amateur cameraman. There would be smartphones outside Stern-

229

dale Road, passersby capturing faces in the crowd and instantly posting the results on Facebook and Instagram. Within a couple of hours the *Daily Mail* would have shaky amateur footage from the scene. How would it look if Kell was recognized and identified? Yet he found himself saying to Amelia: "I know what I'm doing" and ending the call before she had a chance to respond. He wanted to see what had happened for himself. He knew, with absolute certainty, that it had been a professional hit, just as he knew that he was taking the last few steps in his long career. After this, there would be nothing. Amelia would cut him out. In future years, Kell would be spoken of as the man who had lost Rachel Wallinger, the man who had lost Bernhard Riedle. Nothing he had done in his career before — or might ever do in the future — would dispel those facts, nor salvage his reputation.

The phone rang. Kell clicked it to mute. Let Amelia steam. He rounded the bend at the eastern end of Sterndale Road, hearing the sound of laughter in a garden as he passed a house on the corner. Bright sunlight on his face. A ponytailed schoolgirl in a purple uniform was skipping ahead of him, swinging a satchel. Kell felt increasingly dejected. Without "Peter," without

Brussels, without the whole charade of entrapment, Bernhard Riedle would still be alive. It was Istanbul all over again. A person was dead because their life had been touched by Thomas Kell. He felt as though he were walking into a permanent solitude of shame and regret.

Mowbray called the mobile.

"What's going on?" he said.

"I'm heading down there." Kell knew what Mowbray's answer would be, but still found himself asking: "Anything on the laptops?"

"Nothing, guv."

Mowbray sounded emptied out, all of the wit and energy drained from his voice. Kell heard a text message coming into the phone, most probably from Simon. The side of his face was so soaked in sweat that the handset was sucking against his ears as he spoke.

"Just stay in the flat, okay? Let me know if you hear anything from Claridge's or the Wolseley."

"I already did." It sounded like Mowbray was reading from notes. "They said there was no sign of the group at the restaurant. Left at around two fifteen. Claridge's has TOLSTOY in his room, VALENTINA in the lobby. Nobody's seen GAGARIN. Maître d' at the Wolseley said she thinks he left before the other two. Caught a cab on Piccadilly."

"Of course he did," Kell replied resignedly, and hung up.

He was now halfway down Sterndale Road. He could hear sirens screaming in the distance. Cars had stopped in a line ahead of him and emergency lights were strobing at the end of the street. Kell checked the text message. It was indeed from Simon, confirming that an ambulance had arrived at the scene and that police officers were busy sealing off the block.

Kell was now less than three hundred meters away from the doorway in which Riedle had been shot. He came to a halt and wiped the sweat from his face with both sleeves of his shirt. He was carrying his jacket and took out a packet of cigarettes. He needed to be able to think clearly, to compose himself, to work out what to do. As he lit the cigarette, Kell heard another siren coming in from the south, almost certainly from the police station at Hammersmith. He looked at his watch. Not yet three o'clock. The shooting would be on the news within the hour.

He continued to walk west, cars doing U-turns ahead of him, taking side streets to escape the jam. He could now see two police officers patrolling the final block on the street. They had stretched three separate ribbons of blue-and-white tape across the road, in front of which a small crowd had gathered. Kell was shocked to see a child among them, holding his father's hand as they gawped at the scene. There was an ambulance parked outside the property, as well as three police vehicles. An even larger crowd was being held back by police tape on the opposite side, closer to Simon's hotel. Kell could see the window of Simon's room. He called his mobile.

"Sir."

"I'm about a hundred and fifty meters from your hotel. On the northern side of Sterndale Road. Can you see me?"

A momentary pause. Simon said: "Yes, sir. I can see you."

"Anything to report?"

"Nothing."

Then Kell saw something that made him rear back in disbelief. He instinctively stepped off the pavement and shielded himself behind a parked white van.

"Jesus."

Directly ahead of him, there was a man standing at the edge of the crowd. Black shoes, dark blue chino trousers, a white shirt. He was in his mid-thirties and wearing a gray sports jacket.

"What is it?"

"GAGARIN," Kell replied. "I have eyes on GAGARIN." In his consternation, he abandoned all protocol and dispensed with the code name. "I'm standing less than fifty feet from Alexander Minasian."

# 32

On Kell's orders, Simon walked out of the hotel room, locked the door, and ran downstairs. Within moments he was standing among the crowds at the police cordon on Shepherd's Bush Road. Looking east down Sterndale, he was able to confirm that the man standing at the edge of the opposite police cordon was Alexander Minasian.

"You're sure?" Kell asked, though he himself was in no doubt.

"Ninety-nine percent," Simon replied. "I've only seen surveillance photographs, a couple of frames of video, but that's got to be him. I don't want to keep looking, risk eye contact, but it's a match."

"You have sunglasses on?"

"Yes, sir."

"He won't notice you from that range. Tell me exactly what you see."

Kell was less than the length of six cars from Minasian, but still close enough to the van to conceal himself if the Russian turned around. He had not yet done so. In fact, Minasian appeared not to have moved for a considerable period of time. He was standing with his hands on his head, looking directly at the ambulance parked outside number 98. A passerby, noticing him, would have assumed that Minasian — in common with several other people nearby — was in a state of shock.

"He looks freaked out, boss. Looks as amazed as the rest of us." Kell could see Simon standing just beyond the second of the two police cars. "Why is he here?" he muttered. "Why take the risk?"

Kell realized what had happened. Minasian had not given the instruction for Riedle's murder. It had come from someone else. Somebody who had found out about their relationship and was determined to stop it. He crossed to the southern side of Sterndale Road, still speaking to Simon.

"We'll find that out," he said. "Can you get over to this side? Go down Dewhurst Road, the one parallel to this. We need to follow him, get him under some kind of control. I'll call it in. If we can get teams ahead of GAGARIN and behind, there's a net we can close. We must not lose him."

"I understand."

Kell was grateful for Simon's sangfroid. He was only in his early twenties, just a kid on a run-of-the-mill surveillance job. By making him leave his post, Kell was putting him into an operational context for which he would be minimally prepared.

"See you in a couple of minutes," he said, and ended the call. He was through to Mowbray within ten seconds.

"Harold?"

"Guv."

"I've got visual on GAGARIN."

"You've got what-the-fuck?"

"Get down here. Sterndale Road. Corner of Dunsany Road. Get a cab or a bike if you can, we'll need to be mobile if he moves. Call the Office. Tell them to flood as many people into this area as they can spare. Give them your number, get them to circulate the photographs. Tell them GA-GARIN is dressed as described. No change in appearance."

"Why don't you just arrest him?"

Kell could hear Mowbray already moving around the flat, grabbing whatever he would need.

"Not here. Not when I can be filmed or photographed. We need to get him into a choke point, somewhere discreet."

"You're the boss," Mowbray replied.

Simon had already made it to the corner of Dunsany Road. Kell saw him slow from a sprint to a brisk walk and they made nodding eye contact. Minasian was about twenty feet away from him, still staring at the stunned activity outside Riedle's building. Kell had not yet seen his face. Minasian's hands were now back by his sides and he was standing perfectly still, making no attempt to shield his identity or to blend in more naturally with the crowd.

Kell sensed that he was about to move. Sure enough, with Simon just a few feet away, Minasian turned to his left. There was a tree beside Kell that he used for partial cover, but he was too intrigued to resist studying Minasian more closely. This was the first time that the two men had been so close to one another: in Odessa, Minasian had been a name on a radio; on the plane in Kiev, just a voice on a phone. Now, finally, he could see the man himself. Minasian had a surprisingly youthful face, unlined and clear-skinned, beneath a mop of dark brown hair, combed and parted neatly to one side. In another era, he might indeed have been an eager Soviet astronaut, or perhaps a rural doctor, affable and ruddy-cheeked.

"He must be heading for Brook Green,"

Simon said. He was looking at Kell as they spoke. "I've got low power on my phone, boss. I'm sorry."

Kell knew that there was little point in complaining. He needed Simon to stay sharp and to remain calm for as long as they were in contact. "Don't worry," he said, raising a conciliatory hand. "Conserve battery. Text me. Switch off your wi-fi. That will give you a few extra minutes. I'll walk behind you, parallel."

Kell was wondering how long it would take for Amelia to scramble a team. Minasian was now about fifteen meters ahead of Simon on the opposite side of the street. The Russian was walking with an almost methodical slowness toward Brook Green, a small, triangular park at the edge of Shepherd's Bush Road. He looked, from his lowered head and slightly hunched back, like a man coming to terms with a terrible shock. Minasian had evidently been on his way to meet Riedle, only to discover that he had been shot. Why, then, had he remained at the scene? Why had he stood for so long, observing the activity around the flat? Was it possible that the impact of Riedle's assassination had affected him to such an extent that he had momentarily lost all reason and common sense? Perhaps. For months Kell had thought of Minasian as a perfect spy, ruthless and intimidating, yet in the brilliant sunshine of this extraordinary afternoon, he looked lost. There was no obvious tradecraft in his behavior, no discernible antisurveillance. Kell was tailing him as easily as he could have tailed the schoolgirl twirling her satchel.

Such a state of affairs could not last. Even as Kell dialed Amelia's number, he knew that Minasian would soon work out that he was a marked man. If the SVR had killed Riedle, Minasian was next; at the very least, his career was over. If the killer had been dispatched by Svetlana it meant not only that his wife knew of his affair with Riedle, but that their secret correspondence had also been breached. How else had the killer known about the rendezvous in Sterndale Road?

Amelia's phone switched to voice mail. Was she ignoring his call? As Kell left a message, he tried to imagine what he would do in Minasian's position. Return to Claridge's? Make a run for the airport? He was convinced that the Russian would act in character. In other words, that he would do nothing rash, nothing to suggest that he was guilty of any crime. A combination of intellectual pride and professional vanity would compel Minasian to finesse his way out of the crisis into which he had fallen. He would find a way of denying his relationship with Riedle; of explaining why he happened to have been passing Sterndale Road. Kell knew that he was facing a significant challenge. It would be one thing to grab Minasian and to put him under interrogation. It would be quite another to force him to act against his own interests and in the service of the British government.

Simon had reached the one-way street running east to west alongside Brook Green. Minasian was ahead of him, walking on a stretch of road used by black cabs; at any moment he might hail one and be gone. Realizing this, Kell used his phone to order an Uber, hoping that a car would come quickly enough to allow him to follow Minasian if he grabbed a taxi.

The Russian crossed the road. Simon was still about fifteen meters behind him. There were women in bikinis sunbathing in the park, two men in jeans with their shirts off flying a Frisbee across a narrow expanse of grass. Minasian approached the first of two caged public tennis courts and came to a halt, watching a rally between a man and a woman. It was possible that he was now trying to ascertain if he was being followed.

Simon did not break stride but instead — to Kell's admiration — hailed a young woman walking a small dog as though she were an old friend, immediately engaging her in conversation. It was superb tradecraft. His body language suggested a relaxed and familiar relationship between them. When Simon bent to pet the dog, the woman smiled and encouraged him to do so. At the same time, Minasian turned toward the second tennis court, reassured that he was alone. A coach and a young teenager were about to start a lesson. The surface of the court was littered with bright yellow balls, which they were busily picking up. The Russian took out his phone and began to type a message as the coach kicked several of the balls toward the service line. Kell took the opportunity to make a call of his own to Mowbray, only to see a message from Amelia that astonished him.

Stand down. Pointless. Let him go.

It was incomprehensible. Had Amelia become so corporatized, so risk-averse, that she would let a compromised SVR officer float away in central London? Kell swore aloud, even as he fought the surely inconceivable idea that Amelia had known in advance about Riedle's murder. A second message came through to allay his suspicions.

Leave it with me. Office will fully investigate. Not your responsibility.

Kell was about to respond when a call from Mowbray interrupted him.

"Guv?"

"What's happening?"

"It's the Office. They won't authorize it. They won't send any teams."

Kell asked Mowbray who he had spoken to at Vauxhall Cross.

" 'C,' " he replied. "She won't wear it. Says we should let GAGARIN take off. I can't argue with that. She's paying my bills. I have to do what she says."

"Like fuck you do," Kell told him. "We're bringing him in. Where are you?"

"Far end of Sterndale Road." It was obvious from Mowbray's tone of voice that his loyalty to Kell trumped any misgivings he might have had about Amelia. "Where do you want me?"

Kell knew that there were at least two streets perpendicular to Mowbray's position that would get him north of Minasian within three or four minutes. He instructed him to head south toward the park and then to look for the tennis courts.

"I've got an Uber on its way," he said, "Simon nearby. You on foot?"

"Yup."

"No bike? No cab?"

"Couldn't find one. Traffic's terrible."

The conversation was interrupted by another incoming call. Kell switched to answer it.

"Hello?" he said.

There was a long delay. Somebody on a speakerphone. In the time it took him to answer, Kell was able to ascertain that Minasian was still watching the tennis and that Simon had taken a seat on the grass.

"Hello. This is your Uber driver."

The accent was Middle Eastern, the English rudimentary. A Frisbee fell to the grass within a few feet of Simon.

"Yes. Where are you?"

Another long delay. Kell repeated his question, watching Simon, watching Minasian. The tennis coach was giving the teenager a tip about his forehand.

"Very bad traffic. I am W14."

Kell turned back toward the wall. A small boy in a bright red helmet shot past him riding a child's bicycle.

"Okay." A siren screamed on Shepherd's

Bush Road. Kell was obliged to raise his voice. "I'm on the north side of the park," he shouted. "Brook Green. Can you see me?" It felt absurd to be calling in the support of an Uber driver in order to tail an SVR officer, but what other options were left to him? A taxi could come past at any point. If Minasian turned around and jumped in, he would be gone in a moment. Reporting the number plate would be pointless; use of the recognition technology needed clearance from Amelia.

"I can see you . . ."

The line went dead. Kell swore within earshot of a passing mother and child but had no time to ring back. Mowbray was on hold.

"I'm coming onto Brook Green, guv," he said. He sounded out of breath, age catching up with him. "Remind me what GAGARIN's wearing."

Kell described Minasian's clothing. "Can you see a playground?"

"Affirmative."

"Beyond that, two tennis courts. Our side, the man with dark brown hair. Watching a coach and a teenage boy, gray jacket slung over his right shoul—"

"I see him. Jesus."

Mowbray was twenty seconds away from

the tennis courts, Simon a similar distance on the opposite side. Minasian was effectively surrounded. But as Kell turned around, he saw a black cab on Shepherd's Bush Road, orange light lit, indicating left toward the park. Simultaneously, Minasian looked in the same direction. The taxi would be passing him in under thirty seconds.

"Shit."

"What is it?" Mowbray asked, still on the line.

"Taxi coming. I've got an Uber on its way, but the driver could be in Dalston for all I know."

"GAGARIN's hailing it."

Kell turned and saw what Mowbray had seen. Minasian had stepped away from the tennis courts and was waving his right hand in the air, trying to attract the attention of the driver.

"I'm going for it," he shouted, running to intercept the taxi. "Get alongside GA-GARIN. We're taking him with us."

Kell raised his arm, ran to the edge of the park, and stepped into the road, forcing the cab to brake in front of him.

"Sorry, mate," Kell said, as he leaned through the window. "Didn't mean to step out that far."

"Geezer in front saw me first," the driver

replied, pointing ahead to Minasian.

"That's all right, he's a friend of mine, we're all going the same way," Kell replied, and climbed into the back seat as the driver released the lock. Looking through the windscreen, Kell could see Minasian lowering his hand. Mowbray, who was still connected on the mobile, was only four or five meters away from him. The two men would soon be face to face.

"He's going to recognize you from Egypt," Kell said.

"So what?" Mowbray replied, and as Kell instructed the driver to pull up alongside the two men, he heard Mowbray engaging Minasian in conversation.

"You're coming with us, chum . . ."

"Just here, please," Kell told the driver, opening the door as the taxi slowed to a halt.

Only then did Alexander Minasian seem to realize what was happening to him. Blue eyes flickered very quickly from side to side and his body tipped forward as he absorbed what Mowbray had told him. Just as quickly, Minasian tried to recover his composure, but the sight of Kell inside the cab astonished him. He looked panicked, like a condemned man who has glimpsed the scaffold for the first time. Simon was suddenly beside him, blocking off any possible escape route toward the park.

"Alexander!" Kell called out, leaning forward from the back seat of the cab. He produced a beaming smile. "Why don't we give you a lift?"

# 33

With a barely perceptible push in the lower back, Mowbray steered Minasian into the taxi. Kell indicated that he should sit in the fold-down seat opposite his own and made way for Mowbray beside him. Simon entered by the opposite door. With no safe house nor clearance from Amelia, Kell had little choice but to instruct the driver to take them to his flat on Sinclair Road. He was certain that Minasian would insist on returning to Claridge's within a few hours, citing the risk of being reported absent by the SVR. That would give him only a very narrow window of time in which to pitch the Russian and to set up the basic parameters of their relationship. The conversation would be complex and fraught with risk. Kell had the Riedle notes to work from, combined with years of experience in recruitment and interrogation, but he had never been up against a serving Russian officer. Minasian was cornered and compromised, but he was not going to make life easy.

There was the added problem of the taxi driver, who had sounded concerned as Minasian was bundled into the back of the cab.

"Everything all right?" he had said as the doors slammed shut. "What's the story, fellas?"

To allay his suspicions, and to avoid any compromising conversation from the back seat, Kell replied with a hearty "Fine, thanks, sorry about the confusion" and quickly engineered a diversionary chat as the taxi moved east along Brook Green.

"Did you see those guys playing Frisbee?"

"I did!" Mowbray replied, playing along with the ruse. Minasian was staring at Kell with nerveless blue eyes, powerless to prevent what was happening. Kell stared back, mesmerized by the sudden proximity of the man who had dominated his thoughts for so long. Minasian was of average height, but evidently strong and fit. Kell was struck not only by his surprisingly youthful appearance, but also by the quality of his clothes and general appearance. Not for him the down-at-heel uniform of the Russian working class; this, after all, was a man who stayed at Claridge's and lunched at the Wolseley. His shirt and trousers were designer brands, his jacket tailored, the polished shoes made from hand-stitched leather. The steel edge of a chunky wristwatch was visible beneath the sleeve of Minasian's cuff-linked shirt and his fingernails were trim and clean; they had evidently been manicured. Kell had a mental image of a snake slipping out of its skin and into another. As the driver turned left toward Blythe Road, Kell leaned forward, reached into Minasian's jacket pocket, and, encountering no resistance or objection, withdrew both his wallet and a well-used BlackBerry. There was a burst of eau de cologne.

"Did you know that Frisbees began life as containers for pizza?" he said, drawing a smile from Mowbray as he began to flick through the contents of the wallet. Russian credit cards and a driving license — all in Minasian's real name — as well as a substantial amount of currency in euros, rubles, and sterling. The wallet was lizard skin with an Asprey stamp. "Somebody saw a couple throwing one back and forth on a beach and offered to buy it from them for a dollar."

"Is that right?" Mowbray replied, dead-pan.

"Whoever it was, he realized he was sitting on a fortune." Kell took the cover off the BlackBerry and removed the SIM and battery. "Got the design patented, made the tins in hard plastic, the rest is history."

Minasian was gazing out the window. He looked detached and calm.

"Just here, please," said Kell.

They were at least twenty meters from his door. The taxi pulled over and Kell paid. Mowbray and Simon flanked the Russian as they waited for the driver to pull away. They were concerned that he might try to run. Kell knew better. Minasian was coming along not only because he had no choice, but because he believed that he could win whatever battle lay ahead of him.

"The apartment is just over there," Kell said as the taxi growled around the corner. "No need for you to come inside, Simon," he added, and saw a look of disappointment flit across the young man's face. "Stay out here for a bit. Keep an eye on the street."

Minasian was looking up and down the road, doubtless trying to memorize his location. Simon took out his phone. Kell knew that he would soon be called home by his superiors, on the orders of "C." Amelia would want to know where they had taken GAGARIN. She might even send a team to extract him.

"Just through here," Kell said as they

walked into the hall.

One of the neighbors had left a box of empty bottles for recycling near the door of the flat on the ground floor. There were parcels and letters on the large fuse box that served as a shelf for mail. Kell led Minasian upstairs, Mowbray following behind them as Kell unlocked his front door.

"Come in." Kell was suddenly hungry. He realized that it would be a long time before he was able to eat a proper meal. "Make yourself at home."

Minasian walked inside. He passed the kitchen and went into the living room, looking for all the world like a man sizing up a property for rent.

"Why don't you take a seat?"

Minasian spun around and looked at Kell as if he had suggested something quite uncommon. The Russian had not yet spoken. He frowned and dropped into a hardbacked chair. Kell found an iPhone charger, connected it to a power source, propped up his phone on a pile of books, and aimed the lens at Minasian.

"This conversation will be recorded," he said.

Minasian shrugged as Mowbray drew the curtains to reduce the brightness of the sunlight streaming through the windows.

The air in the flat was stale, the temperature muggy, but Mowbray switched on a small desk fan rather than open the window. The risk of traffic distortion on the audio was too great.

"Glass of water?" Kell suggested. "Coffee? Tea?"

"Coffee," Minasian replied. It was the first word he had said. His voice was deeper than Kell had expected, the Russian accent not as pronounced.

"How do you take it, Alex?" Mowbray asked, moving toward the kitchen. "Sugar? Dash of white?"

Minasian did not reply. For a considerable time, nothing was said. Kell lit a cigarette and maneuvered a chair until he was sitting opposite Minasian. He checked the initial footage from the iPhone for framing and focus, then replaced it.

"Can you confirm your name, please?"

"Why?" Minasian asked.

"Because you have no choice."

Minasian reacted with a look of impatient disdain that Kell suspected would become familiar.

"Name," he said.

"You know who I am."

"Name."

Mowbray emerged from the kitchen car-

254

rying a tray on which he had placed two cups of coffee, a bowl of sugar, some milk, and a plate of biscuits. There was a low table between the two men and he set the tray down, nodding at Minasian.

"There you go, Alex. I made it black. Just the way you like it."

*"Menya zovut Aleksandr Minasyan."*

"In English," Kell replied.

Minasian's response was reluctant and near-inaudible.

"My name is Alexander Alexeyich Minasian."

"Again."

"My name . . ." There was a stubborn, humiliated pause. "Is Alexander Alexeyich Minasian."

"Who do you work for?"

Minasian looked at Kell, half pleadingly. Kell demonstrated by his reaction that he expected Minasian to comply.

*"Ya ofitser Es Ve Er."*

"Are you married?"

Minasian spluttered a contemptuous laugh.

"Excuse me?"

"I said are you married."

"You know that I am."

"Please tell us your wife's name." Kell wanted to humiliate Minasian, to see the suffering of the man who had made him suffer. Yet he knew that he must control his anger, his yearning for revenge.

"You know this also," Minasian replied.

"Tell us her name."

"Eremenko. Svetlana."

"And who is Bernhard Riedle? Who *was* Bernhard Riedle?"

On this occasion, Minasian did not hesitate.

"He was a friend," he said, his eyes dropping to the floor. "He was a decent man."

Kell spooned two sugars into his coffee and indicated to Mowbray that he should leave the room. As he did so, heading toward the bedroom at the back of the flat, Minasian leaned forward.

"How do you know that I am not being followed?"

"I don't," Kell replied briskly.

It was the truth, though he had guessed from Minasian's behavior in Sterndale Road — not to mention the longevity of his relationship with Riedle — that he was not a man who was ordinarily tracked by his own people.

"Then you are taking a big risk, no?"

"You would know all about taking risks, Alexander."

Minasian interpreted the remark as a

compliment and allowed himself a momentary smile. It was astonishing to see the effect of this on his face, as though his earlier sullenness had been a mask that he could decide to wear or remove on a whim. The lurching mood swings in Minasian's temperament, described in such detail by Riedle, were beginning to play out in front of his eyes.

"If I am not back at my hotel by seven o'clock," he said, "my wife will be alarmed."

"Well, we can't have that."

"You have given me no means of communicating with her."

Kell took the BlackBerry and battery out of his jacket pocket, holding them up in both hands.

"You mean this? You want to contact her?"

"It would be a good idea for us."

Kell shook his head. "Maybe later. First, could we talk about what you were doing in Sterndale Road?"

Minasian looked down at the plate of biscuits and ignored the question.

"You live here?" he asked Kell, gazing around the room.

It was no surprise that Minasian had worked it out. They had walked past a pile of letters in the hall, one of which had been a bank statement addressed to Kell. Even if the Russian had failed to see it, there were too many personal touches, too many idiosyncrasies in the apartment for the location to pass as a safe house. From his chair, Minasian could see a black-and-white photograph of a Masai warrior, a memento from a long-ago posting in Nairobi; a framed letter in Hebrew from a senior official in the Israeli government, sent to Kell just a few weeks after he had arrived as an undeclared "diplomat" in Tel Aviv; and a gold cigarette lighter, engraved with the initials P.M., given to him by Amelia two years earlier. On the bookshelves, to Minasian's left, there were numerous weighty tomes on foreign affairs and political philosophy, as well as diplomatic memoirs and half a yard of John le Carré. It would not have taken a detective of particularly sharp insight to conclude that this was Kell's home.

"I do," he conceded. In all conversations of this sort, it was better to tell the truth whenever possible. Confidence was forged more quickly in an atmosphere of honesty.

"Then why have you brought me here?"

"Time," Kell replied, again being as candid as the situation would allow. "We won't be able to talk for very long. As you said, Alexander, you must soon be getting back to your wife."

Minasian appeared to concede Kell's point and looked back at the plate of biscuits without any further comment.

Kell repeated his question.

"What were you doing in Sterndale Road?"

Minasian looked up and his gaze assumed a soulful, penetrative quality that suggested both high intelligence and absolute candor. In this moment, it was a face seemingly innocent of wrongdoing. There was no malice in it.

"You know why I was there," he said.

"Do I?"

Minasian continued to look at Kell. He knew what SIS wanted. A video confession of his relationship with Riedle. It was just a question of how long Minasian would delay the inevitable, and therefore salvage a little pride.

"I'm sorry about Bernie," Kell said, trying a different approach. "I really am. He *was* a good man."

No discernible reaction from the Russian. Minasian used silence as both a disguise and as a tool of control.

Kell pressed on: "It must have been a terrible shock to you."

Minasian's mouth twisted into an expression of distaste. He looked across the room at the bookshelves.

"You are Peter," he said quietly. It was not a question. It was a statement.

"I am Peter," Kell replied.

"You were lovers?"

Kell laughed out loud and turned toward the kitchen, as though expecting to share the moment with Mowbray.

"No," he said. "Peter was not a threat to you."

Minasian appeared to appreciate the subtlety of Kell's answer and smiled to himself, nodding slowly. But the apparent softening in his demeanor was short-lived.

"Why did the British have him killed?"

"We didn't."

Kell took a first sip of the coffee. It was cooler than he had anticipated. Perhaps they had been talking for longer than he imagined.

"Not you. Your superiors."

"They didn't either."

A strange combination of sadness and disappointment played out across Minasian's face. Kell was struck again by the beguiling candor of his eyes and felt for a moment, against all rational judgment, that he was dealing with a man of deep sensitivity and moral principle. Such an ability to deceive through appearances was a priceless quality for a spy and one that Kell found himself coveting. He could see how effective Minasian must have been in recruiting Ryan Kleckner, appealing simultaneously to the American's sophomoric political ideas and to his monstrous vanity. As for Riedle, no wonder he had fallen so hard: a man as attractive and charismatic as Minasian would have strung him along as skillfully as a matador exhausting a bull.

"He was assassinated."

"Yes, he was," Kell replied. "But not by us." He felt it necessary to add: "I'm sorry."

"You do not need to say this. It is of no interest to me what you feel."

Kell was beginning to doubt his longheld belief that Minasian had encouraged Rachel's murder. He felt that the decision had come from Moscow and that Minasian had been overruled when he tried to stop it. He had no evidence for this other than a sense that the man sitting in front of him was too canny, too cautious and all-seeing, to have made such a rash move. Rachel's death had been a senseless act, not only morally indefensible but strategically pointless. Minasian was surely far too subtle to sink to such depths or to sully his reputation so needlessly.

"Do you know why he was killed?" Kell asked.

"You would know the answer to that question," Minasian replied.

Kell noticed that the Russian was allowing a very small amount of his shock and grief to color his mood. He had to try to keep Minasian in this state. It was no good allowing him to retreat into silence and obfuscation.

"I don't blame you for what happened to Rachel," he said, hoping to close the gap between them. "You know that I was in love with her. I know that you tried to broker our deal in good faith. I know that the order to kill her came from Moscow."

Minasian took the bait. His eyes locked on to Kell's.

"I am glad you know that," he replied. "I hoped that your sources would find it out. I do not operate in this way. That is the truth, Thomas."

Kell registered the use of his first name and felt a coldness pass across the surface of his skin. It was as though Minasian had been expecting their confrontation all along.

"I know that the order to kill Rachel came from Moscow," he repeated, "just as I know that my Service had nothing to do with what happened today. To Bernie. I believe you were betrayed by your own people."

Minasian looked toward the lens of the iPhone, longing to switch it off so that he could speak with total openness.

"Believe what you want," he said. "I know my own *people*. I know my own side."

Kell seized on this.

"Really? You think the SVR would tolerate a homosexual officer? Come to think of it, would *anybody* in the Russian political and intelligence community tolerate the man that you are, the man that you need to be? Why else have you lived in such secrecy for so long? Why else are you forced to live your life as a lie?"

It was the principal point of weakness in Minasian's personality and Kell intended to press on it repeatedly until it reaped rewards.

"You can do better than this, surely?" Minasian replied, revealing an unsurprising gift for withering condescension. Kell was not deterred.

"I don't need to do any better," he said, "because what I'm saying is the truth. You work for an organization — in fact, you serve a *country* — that considers you a third-class citizen, a mutant, depraved and amoral, purely because of something as simple and immutable as your sexuality."

He thought of Blunt and Burgess, clutched into the loving embrace of the NKVD for precisely the same reason. "You serve the very people who would condemn you for the man that you are, for the way that you *feel*. You're in a hypocritical position, Alexander. You have no integrity."

The words came out more or less as Kell would have wished them to come out, and they had more or less the impact that he had hoped for. He was trying to deliver blows to Minasian's vanity, to slice through the fragile narcissism of a man who knew, deep in his psyche, that he was fraudulent. Long ago, Minasian had been resourceful enough to set up his personality in such a way that he could survive — even flourish — within the hypocrisy that Kell had identified. Yet Kell was convinced that at the center of his character lurked an isolated and fearful man, an individual so at odds with society that the secret world had been the one place in which he could safely find refuge and still function.

"I am interested by your methods," Minasian replied. For the first time his voice sounded uncertain. "It's fascinating to see the way the British work."

"Let's not fuck around," Kell replied quickly. "I'm trying to pay you the compliment of not telling you how much we already know about you and how much shit you're in. I'm trying to treat you as an equal and I'm happy to offer you any way out of the terrible situation into which you and your wife have fallen."

"My *wife*?"

Minasian was unable to conceal his shock. He had instantly understood what Kell was telling him. *We know about your fertility problems. We can make this easy or we can make this hard.* Minasian was being compromised by a Service that had been gently blackmailing its targets for decades and calling it "common sense" and "the British way." In Moscow, they roughed you up and shot you. In London, they took you for oysters; only later did you find out you'd picked up the bill.

"Svetlana," Kell replied, and felt a trace of shame at his own ruthlessness. He lifted up his cup of coffee, his face partly concealed behind the mug as he drank. "Do you want to talk about her? Do you think she knew about Bernhard? Do you think that's what happened today?"

Minasian leaned back in his chair, exhaled heavily, and folded his arms. He had reached a decision. The Russian knew that he was cornered and that it would be pointless not to cooperate further with SIS. If he left the interview without a promise of collaboration, Kell would shop him to Moscow. Minasian was most likely resigned to the inevitability of working for Kell and had concluded that he could maintain greater control over his destiny by agreeing to do so quickly.

"This is a dirty trade we have chosen, is it not?" he said.

"Sometimes," Kell replied coolly. It sounded like a line Minasian had remembered from a movie.

"I think I know what happened to Bernhard," Minasian said. He stood up, took one of Kell's cigarettes, lit it, and returned to the chair. Kell handed him an ashtray, his heart thumping as the confession began to pour out. "I think I know where I was lazy."

"Lazy?"

"You know this, too."

"Why don't you tell me," Kell replied, "and we'll see if our theories match."

Minasian smiled again — that secret, mischievous glint that transformed his face — and drew on the cigarette with resigned pleasure.

"I loved him. Did you know that?"

Kell felt the delicious rush of adrenaline

that accompanies the moment a target snaps.

"I suspected it," he replied, though this was far from the truth. From everything that he had discerned from Riedle, the relationship between the two men had been emotional one-way traffic. Riedle had loved Minasian deeply, hopelessly. Minasian had provoked and then tested that love primarily for the purpose of being fueled by it. Kell remembered one of Riedle's more hysterical outbursts: "He derives a sadistic satisfaction from torturing me. He drinks the blood from my wounds." Kell had to keep telling himself that the man sitting in front of him was a sociopath; that any demonstration of normal human decency or compassion was almost certainly an act.

"Bernhard was a good man," Minasian continued. "He was very generous, very interesting. Kind and patient."

"Yes," Kell said, lighting a cigarette of his own. Minasian's respectful tone, his simple and direct manner, was completely persuasive.

"We had fought," he continued, the voice level and matter-of-fact. "I was not always happy in his company. I think this explains why I was sometimes aggressive toward him."

It looked as though Minasian needed Kell to agree with this assessment of his behavior, so he nodded.

"If I am honest," the Russian continued, "I felt trapped by his love. He adored me. And I did adore him. But Svetlana had to come first. My work had to come first. I was torn between them and I felt guilty. Guilty about my feelings, even about my desires. The marriage and my career had to survive."

"Of course," Kell replied. Like all world-class liars, Minasian was able, first and foremost, to convince himself of his own sophistry and deceit. If he could convince himself, it followed that he could convince others. Kell even suspected that the Russian took pleasure in seeing his lies play out in public. Everything that he was saying was a performance — for Kell, for the camera, for himself. Had Kell not had the chance to meet Riedle and to hear his side of the story, he might have believed every word of what Minasian was telling him.

"I expected to see him one last time," he said. "I wanted to see him. He was the most important person in my life for the last three years. When I was with him, I was at my most alive, more so even than in my work. I was going there today to talk to him. I was looking forward to it."

"And to stay the night?" Kell asked.

Minasian shook his head quickly. "I don't think so." He looked troubled as he said this. "It would have been difficult, with Svetlana."

They stared at one another. Kell had done his best to appear empathetic to Minasian's expressions of sadness and regret, while Minasian himself had looked increasingly forlorn, almost as if he were starting to blame himself for Riedle's death.

"Let me ask you this," said Kell. "Why did you stay so long at Sterndale Road? Why did it take you so long to walk away? It was only by chance that we saw you."

Minasian shrugged, looking up at the ceiling. He appeared to contemplate Kell's question deeply and waited a considerable amount of time before answering it.

"Do you remember when you were a child?" he said finally, "after swimming?" The Russian brought his eyes back to Kell's. They were vast and sad. He looked so young, so trusting. "You would stand under the warm shower and you would not want to get out because you knew that you would be cold afterward."

"Yes," Kell replied.

"It was like that."

Minasian's innocence at this moment was undeniably touching. Despite all that he knew about his character, the ruthlessness beneath the seemingly harmless exterior, Kell could not help feeling a burst of sympathy. Minasian had made the decision to confess. He had crossed the Rubicon. He knew that "Peter" had spoken at length to Riedle about the collapse of their relationship and therefore that Kell knew a great deal about him. Minasian was now trying to build a counternarrative that would slowly convince Kell of his inherent decency and blamelessness. Why? Because it would give him room to maneuver at a later stage in their relationship. By then, if the Service had come to trust "GAGARIN," Riedle's version of his character would be ignored as the hysterical exaggerations of a jilted lover.

"Do go on," Kell said, fascinated by the strategy.

"What would you like to know?" Minasian asked.

Kell posed the first question that came into his head.

"You said earlier that you were 'lazy.' What did you mean by that?"

Minasian rested his cigarette in the ashtray and stretched his arms above his head. His white linen shirt had come loose at the waist, revealing a taut, muscular belly, smooth and hairless.

"Everybody makes mistakes," he replied. "Even God."

Kell smiled, not least because he recognized the quote.

"Isaac Babel?"

The Russian cracked a vulpine smile.

"Very impressive," he said. "You know Russian literature?"

"Some," Kell replied.

"Babel was a wonderful writer." Minasian raised his hands and crossed his forearms so that they were resting on top of his head. Kell glimpsed the watch again, the status symbol. "A Ukrainian, in fact. From Odessa."

"I know," said Kell. "Shot by the NKVD, wasn't he? For adultery. Sleeping with another officer's wife."

"If you believe that." Minasian's tone implied that NKVD liquidations were the stuff of Western propaganda. Kell brought the conversation back to Riedle.

"We were talking about mistakes," he said. "About bad luck. Somebody knew that you were communicating with Bernie. Is that possible? Somebody other than us?"

"Perhaps," Minasian replied. "I cannot think of any other way."

"Your Service?"

Minasian picked up the cigarette. "No," he said.

"Something like that would be enough to get you fired, yes?"

"Of course."

There was a sound of hammering from building works across the street. Kell waited until it had subsided before testing out a theory.

"Tell me about Svetlana's father."

Minasian's eyes flicked up at Kell's.

"Andrei?"

"Yes."

The Russian took a long draw on the cigarette, buying himself time. Kell watched him stub it out and knew that he had hit a nerve.

"What do you want to know?" he said, looking toward the kitchen. Minasian's back was now partly turned.

"What kind of a man is he?" Kell asked. "What kind of father-in-law? How does he treat his daughter?"

"It is complicated." Minasian suddenly looked more uncomfortable than at any time in the interview.

"How is it complicated?"

The Russian's eyes darted to one side and his mouth contorted into a pained grimace.

He did not want to say something that might compromise his position still further. Kell remained silent, allowing Minasian to reveal as much, or as little, as he chose.

"There is no doubt that Andrei draws strength and political influence from having me as a son-in-law," he began.

"How so?" Kell asked, startled by Minasian's frankness.

"In Russia, to have a close family member in the intelligence services is to obtain a certain status. A guarantee of safety."

"Safety from what?"

"From the vultures in the Kremlin."

Kell was astonished by the choice of vocabulary. "That's how you would describe the men who employ you? As *vultures*?"

Minasian ducked the question.

"Andrei would like me to remain in the SVR. That is all I am saying. We are part of a big, happy family, Thomas. His business interests are completely protected as long as I remain in the Service."

"That's not all you're saying."

"What else am I saying?"

"Your wife is Andrei's only child, yes?"

Minasian nodded.

"And he loves her, of course?"

"Of course."

"So it stands to reason that he wants his

daughter to have a good and faithful husband."

A shimmer of irritation appeared on Minasian's face. The moment was gone in a second, but Kell felt that he had been afforded a glimpse into his deep-state personality. Kell waited for a moment and took a deep, apologetic breath, as though he wished he did not have to voice the theory that he was now obliged to articulate.

"What if Andrei suspected that you were cheating on Svetlana?" he asked. "Is that possible?"

Minasian nodded resignedly. "Of course. Everything in our world is possible."

"So, given that, what if he hired somebody to investigate you? Somebody to follow you around and go through your stuff whenever you were overseas, away from Kiev or Moscow?"

Minasian reacted to the idea as if it had never occurred to him, though Kell was sure that he was lying.

"You really think this is what happened?" he asked.

"Stay with me." Kell had smoked his own cigarette to the base of the filter and now stubbed it out, scorching the tips of his fingers as he did so. "You needed an alphanumeric code to communicate with Bernie, yes? A public key and a private key."

"Something like this."

"You kept the private key written down in the lining of your suitcase, under a floorboard, or sewn into the curtains of the spare room? It was too long to commit to memory."

Minasian compressed a smile. "Something like this."

"So let's imagine that the private investigators hired by your father-in-law found that code. They knew what to do with it. They isolated the e-mail account and they opened up your correspondence with Riedle."

Minasian's admiring silence spoke volumes. Kell had worked it out.

"They reported back to Andrei. They told him that his son-in-law was having an affair. Not with a housewife from Vienna or a waitress in the Marais, but with an architect from Hamburg. A fifty-nine-year-old man. They told him that his son-in-law was secretly gay."

Minasian stood up and again took one of Kell's cigarettes, lighting it and then standing by the closed curtains as he smoked. Kell was aware that he was now out of shot on the film, but did not want to break the moment by adjusting the angle on the lens.

"You would know better than I do what

your father-in-law's views are on homosexuality," he said. "Just from looking at the guy, knowing his background and his record, I'd say he probably isn't the most liberal-minded person I've ever set eyes on." Minasian looked as if he had swallowed something unpleasant. "Let's face it, Alexander. He was probably incredibly angry with you, embarrassed and unsettled. If you weren't who you are, if you weren't of value to him, if you weren't the only chance he's got of having grandchildren, who's to say what might have happened? It could have been *you* getting shot this afternoon, not Bernie."

Minasian turned quickly, a sour expression on his face barely discernible against the square of light in the living-room window.

"I think Andrei Eremenko made a decision based on rage and based on business. He felt that Bernhard Riedle had the potential to obliterate your career in the SVR and therefore to destroy his daughter's life and threaten his relationship with the Kremlin. Still with me?"

Minasian was listening to Kell with the same stillness with which he might have listened to the doctor on Upper Wimpole Street just a few hours earlier. He did not say "yes" to Kell's question; he did not say "no." He simply stared at him.

"In fact, it wouldn't surprise me if Andrei has a little word with you at some stage in the next twenty-four hours. *Stop cheating on my daughter. Stay away from your boyfriends. Be a man.* It wouldn't surprise me if he lets you know that *he* was the one responsible for ordering Riedle's assassination. That's why you didn't want to get out of the shower, isn't it, Alex? You knew that as soon as you walked away from that place, you were going to be cold and you were going to be lonely. In fact, you knew that your life was never going to be the same again."

# 34

As soon as he saw Rosie Maguire for the first time, Shahid Khan knew that she was going to change everything.

He had not taken any of the girls who had been offered to him in Syria. Women came to the Caliphate to serve as brides to the warriors fighting against the forces of Assad. Shahid had felt no desire for their company, for the arrangement of marriage, for the physical benefits of a shared bed. He had felt that a woman would distract him from his commitment to the cause. In this respect he was unlike many of the other soldiers who were fighting inside Iraq and Syria. He knew that Jalal had sensed this and recognized that there was something different about him, something special. Jalal had seen the discipline and the focus in Shahid's personality. This was one of the reasons why he had been chosen for the important operation in England.

Shahid had been working at the super-market for more than a month when he first noticed Rosie. He was shocked by the intensity of his attraction to her, and ashamed that he had no control over it. He walked past the deli counter where she worked two or three times in the space of a few minutes, each time looking at her, trying to catch her eye. On the last occasion she looked up and smiled. Just a tiny curl at the edge of her mouth, like she already knew what was going to happen between them. Then the smile was gone. But it was enough to convince Shahid that she liked him. It wasn't the kind of smile the other white girls gave him. It wasn't greedy or empty, a look of bored lust. There was meaning in it. It was as if Rosie were trying to say that she understood him.

The next day she wasn't there. Shahid was about to start working nights, so, the following afternoon, he came in early. He found her in the staff canteen. She was putting on a sweater at the end of her shift.

"I'm Shahid," he said. "I saw you."

"Oh, hi there."

That smile again. There was nobody else in the room.

"You finished? Going home?"

"Yeah. You?"

"Nah. Nights."

"What's that like?"

Before he had thought about his answer, Shahid said: "Lonely."

Rosie liked it that he had been honest enough to admit it. "I bet," she said. "Not many other people around, yeah? Nobody to chat to."

"I don't mind it that much," Shahid replied, not wanting her to think that he was complaining. "I put on headphones, get the place to myself."

"Your own playground."

She was not as striking as some of the other girls he had seen in Brighton, but she was more beautiful than all of them. The feeling Rosie gave Shahid when she looked at him was like a promise of all that was right and all that was wrong. He knew that it was not permitted for him to be with a woman if she was not Muslim, but Shahid had become lonely in Brighton. He had needs. He knew that it would be wrong to become involved with Rosie, that it was dangerous in the context of the operation, but an old part of him was suddenly awake again.

He began to think about her all the time. He wanted to see her. He found out when she would be working so that they would be in the supermarket at the same time. When Rosie was talking to him she made him feel calm. Shahid liked to make her laugh. He told her stories about the people who worked out at the gym and teased her about her taste in music. He was surprised that she found him funny. He did not know that he was capable of that with a woman. She brought new things out of him.

It was Rosie who had asked him out first. Shahid had not liked this and yet he had agreed straightaway. He felt that it should have been his place to make the invitation, but that his faith and his discipline had not allowed this. He had gone with her because he was compelled by his attraction to her. Just for a walk along the beach so that he could spend more time with her. A lot of white girls were racist and didn't want to be seen with a "Paki," but Rosie was different.

He had worn shorts and a T-shirt. She had worn a summer dress that had partly covered her shoulders. He tried to fight his feelings for her, but it was hopeless. He took photographs of her as they chatted in a café so that he could look at her face and the curves of her waist and her breasts when he was in his room later on. He had done similar things with Vicky, the girl who had betrayed him in Leeds. He had taken photographs of her to look at when he was alone. Vicky had sent him films of herself as well, disgusting films. Shahid had destroyed them. They were shameful. He did not want things to be the same with Rosie. He wanted what was between them to be pure. Vicky had turned out to be cruel and unkind. Rosie wasn't like that. There was something vulnerable about her, something that meant he would always be able to control her.

"So where did you say you were from?" she asked him. "What's your accent?"

They were in Starbucks on London Road. Rosie had ordered an iced coffee and a chocolate cookie. Shahid had paid for them.

"Leeds," he replied, without thinking. He should have said "Bradford."

"Yeah? So what you doing down here?"

"Trying to make a new start," he replied. "I like the seaside. Saving up enough money so I can go to college."

Shahid told Rosie things that he had told no one else. Truthful things. That his oldest brother, Imran, had been killed in a car accident when Shahid was seventeen. That his mother had died of liver cancer only a year before that. That he'd been into aikido as a teenager, used to fight with his brother and compete in competitions, but had given it all up after Imran died.

"What about your father?" Rosie asked. "Where's he?"

"Don't have any contact with him," Shahid replied. Two years earlier, Elyas Iqbal had been told by West Yorkshire Police that Shahid — or Azhar, as his father knew him — had been killed while fighting for ISIS in Mosul. "We don't get on," Shahid told her. "We fell out."

"Why's that?" Rosie had already told him that she had grown up in care in Nottingham. Her mother had been taken away from her by social services when she was ten because she had been addicted to heroin. Shahid felt bad telling her that he had no relationship with his surviving family. It felt like a waste of something Rosie would have given everything for.

"My dad's difficult," Shahid replied. "Conservative. Strict. Classic Pakistani immigrant, you know? Wouldn't let me breathe, man. Always judging me, telling me I wasn't doing stuff right."

"That must have been hard for you. I can imagine. And without your mum there, too."

Shahid felt the breath going out of him. The feeling of being listened to, of being understood, was almost overwhelming.

"Yeah, she was the one I got on with," he said, and felt the empty anger that was always there whenever he thought about his mother. "She encouraged me with stuff, you know? She was proud of my belts, the aikido and that. Sounds like it was bad for you, too. What happened to your mum? You ever see her?"

"Nah," Rosie replied, brushing the question away. "Don't know where she is or what she's doing. Never knew my dad, neither."

On their second date they went to the cinema. While watching the film, Shahid knew that Rosie wanted him to kiss her, yet he did not have the courage. He was constantly fighting against his faith and his discipline. It bewildered him that he could feel such a sense of longing for a woman who was infidel, at the same time as a determination not to betray himself. Other men wanted to be with her. Rosie had told him that. Shahid knew that she had already slept with other men. She was twenty and she was not a virgin. Shahid hated this about her and yet he wanted to be one of those men. He thought of her in the act of loving him. He thought of her tenderness and her soft skin and her caresses on his stomach and his back. It was torture. A woman had finally pushed Shahid Khan toward love, but she was not pure and she was not Muslim.

"I keep a diary," she said as they were waiting at the bus stop after the film.

"Yeah? What kind of things do you write about?"

"Stuff."

"Am I in it?"

"Maybe." She gave him one of her smiles, kind eyes promising limitless intimacy. "Maybe not."

Shahid had felt that people were watching them. Otherwise he would have kissed her. He didn't like the feeling of being judged, the Paki with the white girl.

"I write about feeling lonely," she said, looking back at the town. "About not knowing where I've come from, where I belong."

"That doesn't sound good."

"Sometimes it is. Sometimes it isn't. It's who I am."

Shahid was about to take Rosie's hand when he saw that his bus was coming.

"That's mine," he said, losing his courage. "I'd better go."

Rosie looked disappointed.

"Yeah?" she said. "You don't want to wait for the next one?"

"Nah. Gotta get back." Shahid knew that he had to find a way of getting this woman out of his system. "I'll see you at work," he said, stepping on board. He did not know how Rosie was planning to get home.

"Yeah, at work then," she replied, stepping aside to let other passengers on to the bus. "Thanks for the film, Shahid. I had a really nice time with you."

"Me too."

"Text me," she mouthed through the window, and waved as Shahid took a seat.

# 35

There was a gentle knock at the door. Kell wondered why Mowbray was interrupting them. He felt that he had Minasian where he wanted him and was frustrated by the disruption. Picking up the iPhone, he told Minasian to take a seat and walked into the next room.

Mowbray was hovering in the bedroom.

"What's going on?"

"It's the boss, guv. She keeps calling. Keeps threatening. Wants to know what's going on."

"Threatening? What do you mean?"

"She doesn't like it that we've got GA-GARIN here. Under our own steam. Off the books. It's making people nervous."

Kell felt a familiar burst of irritation with Amelia's tactics.

"Where's Simon?" he asked.

"Long gone. She ordered him home."

"What have you told her?"

"The truth."

The television in the bedroom was paused on Sky News. Kell handed over the iPhone and told Mowbray to encrypt the video, then to send it to Vauxhall Cross.

"That'll keep her quiet. Give her something to chew on." The image on the television was flickering. "I need more time with Minasian. I need to know what he's going to give us, how we're going to communicate, when we can next meet up."

"Sure," Mowbray replied, as though such concerns were far beyond his remit or understanding. Kell looked across his bedroom at the set of bookshelves. Mowbray had flattened down a framed photograph of Rachel.

"Did you . . . ?"

"Just in case Minasian came in here," Mowbray explained. "Didn't want him seeing . . ."

"It's all right," Kell replied, picking up the photograph. "Let him see her. Let him see what his people did."

There was a pile of papers on the floor, including a copy of the notes Kell had scribbled in Brussels after the first dinner with Riedle. He reached for them, a sudden spasm in the base of his spine as he turned around.

"Anything on the news about Sterndale Road?" he asked, nodding toward the television. "Twitter? Internet?"

"Bits and pieces."

Kell looked down at the notes. The pain was spreading across his lower back.

Power and control central to M's personality. Must retain a position of dominance.

"Sounds like the cops think it's a local issue," Mowbray was saying. "Riedle hasn't been formally identified."

Kell continued to read the notes.

Chameleon. Adapts himself to give people what they need for as long as he needs them.

He asked for Mowbray's phone so that he could continue to film the interview. He read the final note.

What does M <u>want</u>? What can we give him? Do we flatter, or squeeze?

Kell returned to the interrogation. Minasian was standing on the far side of the room. He had taken down two books. The first was a Penguin Classic of Isaac Babel's *Red Cavalry;* the second, which Minasian was reading, had a pale yellow cover. It occurred to Kell that he was looking remarkably relaxed for a man who had just been told that his father-in-law had arranged for his lover's murder.

"Larkin?" he asked.

"Yes," Minasian replied. *"Whitsun Weddings."*

"You know it?"

"Of course I know it." Minasian provided a brief glimpse of the intellectual hauteur that had so exasperated Riedle. "Why would I not?"

Kell shrugged. He could not think how to answer such a question. The Russian turned a page and ran a finger down several lines of verse.

"If you were to give this poem to a man from outer space, it would provide you with a perfect insight into the English character, English culture."

"I would agree with that."

Kell suspected that Minasian was repeating a clever remark that had been made by somebody else. He could hear a police siren outside and wondered how much time was left to them. The Russian continued to read the poem. He did not quote from it aloud or attempt to expand on his thesis. Indeed, Minasian seemed utterly satisfied by the act of reading, relaxed and self-possessed. He looked like a customer in a bookshop browsing the shelves on a lazy afternoon. Kell felt that he could understand why Riedle had become so covetous of Minasian's attention. There was a sealed-off aspect to his behavior; he could give the impression of being entirely comfortable in his own skin. For someone as needy and as romantic as Bernhard Riedle, such poise might at times have felt like a calculated insult.

"Shall we continue?" Kell asked, setting Mowbray's iPhone to record and placing it on the table.

"Of course." Minasian closed the Larkin, replaced both books, and sat down.

"I'd like to speak about the future."

Minasian picked up his empty cup of coffee and looked down at the dregs. He took a spoon from the tray and began tapping the side of the mug, like the prelude to an after-dinner speech.

"Of course," he said.

Kell tried to make himself comfortable, struck by the change in Minasian's mood. "It will be obvious to you why we were interested in your relationship with Bernhard Riedle. You will have worked out some time ago why I have brought you to my apartment."

"That is the only part I do not under-stand." Minasian produced a wolfish smile. "You have shown me so much of yourself, Thomas. Your taste. Your style. The things you possess and the things you lack. I now understand a great deal more about you. Why would you take such a risk?"

"I have nothing to hide," Kell replied, though he hated the idea of Minasian creep-ing around his personal effects. "I don't see it as a risk."

"I heard that there were difficulties be-tween you and MI6," Minasian continued. "I heard that after Istanbul you came into conflict with Amelia Levene. Perhaps you are now working for somebody else?"

"I'm flattered that you paid so much at-tention to me, Alexander." Kell wondered where the hell Minasian was getting his information. For an awful, debilitating mo-ment he wondered if Amelia had been right about Mowbray working for the SVR. "I can assure you that I'm still very close to Amelia."

"And will I be meeting her?"

It was a strange question. Would Minasian expect a powwow with "C" as a condition of his cooperation with the Service? Did his inflated sense of his own status and ability demand that? Or was he merely being mischievous?

"That's why I wanted to talk about the future," Kell told him.

"Ah, yes." Minasian produced a nod and a smirk. "The future."

A second spasm in Kell's lower back. He rubbed the base of his spine and sat straighter in the chair. Minasian seemed to log his discomfort. "I don't want you to work for us because you feel you have no choice," he said. "I don't want this to be personal. I don't want it to be about Istanbul or Odessa, about Kleckner or Rachel—"

"And yet you keep mentioning them."

Kell experienced Minasian's sarcasm as a taunt. He wondered what had happened in the few minutes he had been gone to transform his attitudes to such a remarkable extent. He continued:

"I want you to know that we understand your situation and that we would be sympathetic to any reservations you may have about the political and economic direction that your government has been taking in recent years."

Kell saw Minasian's contemptuous reaction and regretted that he had ever countenanced such a clumsy approach. It was foolish in the extreme. Officers were taught to give agents a secondary justification for betrayal and Kell had believed that it would be beneficial to do so in this instance. Minasian was a proud man, clever and self-assured; crudely to blackmail such a person, to force him into treason against his will, might have been counterproductive. Kell had wanted the Russian to feel that he was on the side of the angels, fighting the good fight for SIS; not because Kell had a video-taped confession of his affair with Riedle, but because he despised the corrupt pluto-crats and murderers in the Kremlin as much as he did. This had been naïve. He was not dealing with a rational actor.

"Is this the part where you tell me that my government is worse than your govern-ment?" Minasian was enjoying himself. "That the Kremlin steals from its own people, that my country has been robbed by its politicians?"

"The thought had occurred to me," Kell replied.

"You tell me that the greatness of Russia is being held back by the greed and cyni-cism, the violence of a cabal of men around the president, men like me and my father-in-law who keep him in power, just as he keeps them in positions of influence?"

Kell decided to run with the conceit.

"You don't need me, Alexander. You're doing my job for me."

Minasian smiled. "Do you really believe this about Russia?"

"I do," Kell replied. "And I fully expect you to respond by telling me that the West has caused all of Russia's problems."

"This is something I also happen to believe," Minasian replied. "It is something you choose not to think about. For obvious reasons."

"Obvious in the sense that the arguments made in support of that idea are morally and politically infantile?"

*"Infantile?"* Minasian appeared to enjoy Kell's choice of vocabulary. "Would you describe the sanctions against my country as 'infantile'? The deliberate strategic and economic isolation of Russia by the Western powers in the post–Cold War era. This is 'infantile'?"

"The sanctions are an expression of dismay."

"Dismay," Minasian repeated.

"Don't tell me you haven't had doubts in the past few years about the way Russia is heading."

"Thomas, I can tell you with one hundred percent certainty that I have never experienced any doubt about the direction in which my country is heading. I cannot say the same thing about the United Kingdom, or her allies."

"Then I guess we must agree to disagree," Kell conceded. "But it's interesting that you brought up Mr. Eremenko."

"Interesting why?"

"I wouldn't necessarily have described him as being 'helpful' to the future of Russia. All of the evidence we have assembled about his operations indicates that he has —"

Minasian tried to interrupt. "Please, I am not at all interested in what you may or may not mistakenly think about the activities of my father-in-law."

"He has shown himself to be violent, not least this afternoon, less than a mile away from where we are sitting."

"You have no proof of that."

Why was Minasian protecting Eremenko? Out of familial loyalty? Because he planned to work for him one day? Or because he knew of another reason why Riedle had been killed?

"This is a much larger problem than Andrei, isn't it?" Kell was now in a debate that he was determined to win. "This is a conversation about the future of Russia.

About building roads and schools and hospitals, instead of buying ski chalets and town houses in Notting Hill Gate. Whose side are you on, Alexander?"

"You do not need to educate me, or the Russian people, on building schools and hospitals." A little fleck of spittle landed on Kell as Minasian spoke. "We educate our children properly. We treat the sick in our hospitals without first checking that they have enough money to buy the doctor a new car."

"You're talking about America. You seem to think I work for the CIA."

Minasian reared back, as if Kell were operating at a level of intellectual discourse to which he had rarely sunk.

"Britain is finished," he said, waving his hand in front of him like a child sweeping toys from a table. "The United States certainly matters in international affairs. England is an irrelevance."

"That must be why so many of your countrymen are relocating here," Kell replied, and felt the tightening shame of his country's slow decline.

"You think I am so naïve? You think I am a victim of Kremlin propaganda, of brainwashing?"

"I never said that."

Minasian gestured outside. "You must know that there is no truth in this world, Thomas. Only versions of the truth. He who controls the past will control the future, no?" He produced a sinister grin. "And he who controls the present controls the past."

Kell seized on this. "Ah, yes," he said. "*Nineteen Eighty-Four.* Your favorite book."

The same look of irritation that had passed across Minasian's face earlier in their conversation was momentarily visible again. Kell felt that he could see, however briefly, the man within. Just as quickly it passed, like a single frame of film in the wrong reel. Minasian was restored to genial equanimity.

"How did you know this?" he asked.

"Bernie told me."

"Is that right?" There was an edge of wary suspicion in Minasian's reply. Kell knew that this was the moment to change the direction of the conversation. He had been foolish to think that he could persuade a pedigree SVR officer out of his beliefs. Such a man was not about to examine his prejudices for flaws, or to thank Kell for showing him the light on Kremlin malfeasance. After all, by bringing Kleckner to justice, Kell had dealt Minasian a near-fatal blow. The Russian would be as anxious to avenge Odessa as Kell himself burned to avenge Rachel's murder. By blackmailing him into working for the West, Kell was giving Minasian the best possible opportunity to do that. That was why Amelia had been so reluctant to touch him. He was a Trojan horse.

"I suggest we have another cup of coffee," he said. He was aware that they were running out of time. "Let's dump the politics. It was a mistake for me to engage you on issues that are extremely sensitive to both our countries."

Minasian picked up his empty coffee cup and handed it over.

"Look," he said, gesturing freely with both hands. "It is not necessary to avoid politics altogether." The Russian conveyed a sudden and unexpected sense that he could accommodate some of Kell's arguments. "I would like to cooperate. I was not completely truthful. I sometimes have profound doubts about the direction in which my country is heading. For this reason, I can see areas in which we can both usefully collaborate without a loss of dignity or common sense on my side."

"Go on," said Kell.

"On terrorism, for example."

"What about it?"

"Common ground."

"Common ground," Kell repeated.

Minasian sat down. "I don't want England to suffer," he said.

"What do you mean?" Kell could hear Mowbray talking on the telephone next door, his voice a low defensive rumble as he doubtless listened to Amelia's demands.

"What sort of things will you want from me?" Minasian asked. There was a note of surrender in the question.

"You know exactly what we will want," Kell replied. Though he was aware that Minasian was trying to manipulate him, he reeled off a shopping list of requirements. "Anything well informed on Ukraine, anything that will give us some idea of the Kremlin's long-term goals in the Middle East. The identities of SVR sources in the U.K. —"

"What about terrorism?"

"What about it? You keep mentioning that."

"I have information." Minasian looked down at the floor, apparently deep in thought. Then he met Kell's gaze. "An attack on U.K. soil is imminent."

Kell felt a chill sweep across his back.

"An SVR attack? The Kremlin is bringing the war to London?"

Minasian shook his head.

"Not us," he replied. "Something we know

about. Our sources. ISIS is bringing its war to London. On this issue, for example, I would be very happy to cooperate with the Secret Intelligence Service."

# 36

Less than a minute later, Mowbray walked into the sitting room. He did not knock. Kell turned to look at him, angered by the interruption.

"Need to speak to you, sir."

"What is it?" he said, walking into the bedroom and closing the door.

"Time's up," Mowbray told him. "Amelia's sending a car."

"When?" Kell asked.

He felt like a man who had woken up from a deep sleep. He was finding it difficult processing what Minasian had told him. He could not know if the terrorist attack was a diversionary tactic or a genuine threat.

Mowbray looked at his watch. "Fifteen minutes? Twenty? Depends on traffic, I guess."

Kell assumed the vehicle would be coming from Vauxhall Cross. It was still the rush hour, so there was the chance of a small delay.

"What about the film? Did you send it?"

Mowbray nodded.

"So where does she want to take him? Back to Claridge's?"

"Search me."

Kell reacted quickly. There was no time to guess at Amelia's strategy. He went back into the sitting room.

"Tell me more," he said.

Minasian frowned. "More?"

"About the attack. About ISIS. What have you heard?"

"It is just something I was told by a colleague in Kiev." Minasian was picking at the fabric of his trousers. "I do not know specific facts. The man is a British national from Leeds who has been given a clean-skin passport by elements in ISIS."

"That's it?" Kell had the strong impression that Minasian was plucking the story out of thin air.

"We call him by the cryptonym STRIPE," he added. "We believe that he traveled from Leeds to Syria in order to fight *jihad*."

"That's all you know?"

"It is all I can remember."

When Minasian saw that Kell was dissatisfied by this answer, he moved to reassure him.

"I will of course endeavor to discover more details so that the attack can be thwarted."

Though Minasian's motive to lie was obvious, Kell had to take what he was saying seriously. He had no choice. Besides, if the Russian was making it up in order to play for time, and the threat later proved to be false, Kell would turn him in. Minasian knew that.

"And how are you going to get that information to me?" he asked, trying to call Minasian's bluff.

The Russian reacted quickly.

"However you wish to proceed."

Kell felt like a tennis player being pulled around the court by a pro. He knew that he had no more than thirty minutes to arrange every element of his relationship with Minasian: channels of communication; language; crash meetings. Having run Kleckner for more than two years, Minasian would know all of the tricks, all of the pitfalls. In this sense, Kell was lucky to be working with a fellow professional, but it was still not enough time.

"How long are you staying in London?" he asked.

"We leave tomorrow."

Kell took out a packet of cigarettes. He looked around for Amelia's lighter and found it on the floor beside Minasian's chair.

"You're going back to Kiev together?"

Kell lit the cigarette and offered one to Minasian, who declined. He could sense that he was reluctant to answer the question. Secrecy and evasion were sown into his character. It was a few seconds before he replied.

"We are flying to Moscow together. I will be back in London in eight days."

"In exactly eight days?" Kell made the calculation. "Thursday next week?"

Minasian nodded.

"Why are you coming back?"

Kell suspected the reason, and was not surprised when Minasian confirmed it.

"We have a further appointment with the doctor," he said. "On Thursday morning. I have promised to accompany Svetlana. We arrive late on Wednesday evening, we will be staying at Claridge's, we leave whenever the doctor is satisfied. Possibly Saturday. Possibly Sunday."

"And your Service is happy for you to take this time off? You're not in London on any other business?"

Again Minasian hesitated. It was completely contrary to his nature to answer questions about his work, particularly from an enemy officer.

"I have one responsibility while I am here."

"Which is?"

"To make contact with an agent."

Kell wondered why Minasian was already cooperating so freely.

"Who?"

The Russian smiled. "Nobody on your side," he replied, sensing Kell's disquiet. "A Syrian official, not a British national."

Kell wanted to ask further questions about the source, but there was no time left in which to do so.

"Then I suggest that we meet on the Friday," he said.

Minasian looked at his watch, as though it contained an appointments calendar detailing his every move for the next three weeks.

"Of course," he said. "Friday morning or afternoon?"

"Afternoon," Kell replied.

"Where?"

"Do you know the Westfield shopping mall, here in White City?"

"I know of it," Minasian replied. "I have never been inside."

Westfield was within walking distance of Kell's flat. He knew the building well.

"There's a large branch of Marks and Spencer toward the back of the mall, in the northeast corner. Do you know that chain?"

"Of course."

"The men's section is on the first floor. It's a large area, a lot of room to move. Escalators, lifts, several exits. That's where we'll meet."

"I can check it out tomorrow. Walk the ground."

"Do that," Kell suggested, though he wondered when Minasian would have time before his flight out of the country. "I'll be there between two thirty and three. Do what you have to do to clean your tail. If you feel good about proceeding, find a white shirt in the men's department and pick it up. Carry it around with you. I will do the same. You see me with a white shirt, I'm happy. If you think we have a problem, wear a baseball cap or a hat of any kind and we'll abort. I will do the same. If you see me wearing a hat, no white shirt, go back to your hotel."

"I won't have any surveillance," Minasian replied firmly. It appeared to be a matter of personal and professional pride that Kell understood this. "We will not be disturbed."

"If you abort," Kell continued, ignoring

this, "go back to Claridge's. Somebody will make themselves known to you and we will make an alternative arrangement. It's imperative that we meet next week, even if you have to get out of bed at three o'clock in the morning and talk to me through a wall in your hotel."

There was a useful ambiguity built into this last statement. Minasian could interpret it in one of two ways: as a plea for more information about the imminent terrorist attack; and as a warning that Kell would not hesitate to turn him in to the SVR if he failed to make contact.

"I will be there," Minasian replied, meeting Kell's gaze.

"If anybody stops you or asks awkward questions, tell them you're buying classic British food to take back to Kiev. Marks and Spencer marmalade, branded chutney. Earl Grey tea. Tikka masala." Minasian nodded. "Once we've made eye contact, that's where you'll go. Downstairs to the food hall in the basement of Marks and Spencer. Put a stopwatch on it."

There was a momentary pause as Minasian committed the plan to memory. "A stopwatch?" he said. "I don't understand."

Kell took a long draw on the cigarette then stubbed it out.

"You can reach the basement car parks from the food hall," he said. "There are moving walkways in the wine section which will take you to different levels in the car parks. Go to the middle car park, level two. Exactly ten minutes after we have first made eye contact, walk to aisle forty-five. It's the one right in front of you. I'll go down to the car park by a separate route, drive past, and pick you up in a vehicle."

"Will you be alone?"

Kell could tell him nothing about Amelia's refusal to countenance the operation; he could not even be certain that he would be permitted to meet Minasian in nine days' time. After all, "C" was sending a car for his agent. If she intended to interview Minasian, however briefly, Kell's link with the Russian would be snapped. Amelia would want control of GAGARIN and saturation on the threat from STRIPE.

"I will be alone in the car," he replied. "But we will have people in other vehicles for backup. Making sure you're safe."

"As well as making sure *you* are safe," Minasian replied, with what Kell considered to be unnecessary emphasis. He greeted the remark with a patient smile, then outlined plans for a fallback if either man was unable to reach the first meeting.

"If one of us can't be in the men's section between half past two and three, we try again two hours later. Between half past four and five. Agreed?"

"Agreed." Minasian scratched the side of his neck. "What about making contact in the meantime?" he asked. "While I am away?"

Kell stood up, took a BlackBerry from a stash of three he kept in a nearby drawer and handed it to Minasian.

"This is PGP encrypted," he said. "If you learn anything about STRIPE that's time-sensitive — if you have a target, a date, in other words only if the attack is imminent — you can send that information to me in such a way that you will not be compromised. Otherwise I suggest we have no interaction and meet on Friday. I don't trust computers, I don't trust phones. Never have, never will." Right on cue, there was a prolonged buzz on the intercom. Kell ignored it. "Do everything you can in the next nine days to find out what's known to the SVR about this individual," he said. "His name. The number of the passport he was given, how it got to him, who he's working with. It's possible that my people already have him in their sights or know individuals associated with him. Anything that was gleaned by the SVR could be matched up with our intel. I need to know what he's planning to do, when he's planning to do it."

"Of course," Minasian replied.

Kell stood up and lifted the receiver just as the intercom began to buzz a second time.

"Hello?"

"Vehicle for Mr. Thomas?"

"We'll be down in five minutes."

Kell replaced the receiver and picked up Mowbray's iPhone. He stopped the second recording and put the phone in his back pocket.

"We've got a car for you," he said. Minasian looked up in surprise. "Time for you to be going."

Kell opened the connecting door and walked through to the bedroom. Mowbray was looking out of the window, curtains pulled to one side. Kell stood beside him and saw a bottle green SIS Vauxhall parked on a double yellow line outside his flat, hazard lights flashing.

"Got here quicker than I thought," he mumbled. "Cross kept saying time was a factor."

It didn't sound like one of Amelia's stock phrases; Kell wondered how many other officers were now involved in the effort to prevent him from forging a workable relationship with Minasian. It was a source of almost grotesque frustration to him that Amelia seemed so determined to keep the Russian at arm's length. Surely, once he had confronted her with the evidence about STRIPE, she would reconsider her position?

He walked back into the sitting room to find Minasian standing in front of the bookshelves. He was running his finger along the spines of some Dickens, almost on tiptoes as he peered up at the titles. Kell had an abrupt feeling that this might be their first and last encounter. Anything could happen in the next few days. Minasian's relationship with Riedle could be unraveled by the SVR and his career ended at a stroke. His marriage to Svetlana could collapse under the pressure of what had happened, placing Minasian at the mercy of Andrei Eremenko. And then there was the interference from Amelia. She could prevent Minasian and Svetlana reentering the U.K., citing sanctions against the Russian elite.

"When you come back next week, are you traveling under alias?"

Minasian shook his head. He appeared to have been wrong-footed by the timing of Kell's question.

"Better to do so," Kell told him. "I assume you have British documents, a British passport?"

With reluctance, but a faint trace of professional pride, Minasian conceded that this was the case.

"Use it," Kell told him. "Just to get through the border." He looked around for his house keys. "Time for us to go," he said.

Minasian looked at his watch. Kell walked past him and opened the curtains and the window. The air pouring into the room was cool and clean. The sound of children playing in a nearby garden was interrupted by a car alarm sounding on the opposite side of the building. Minasian rolled his neck and stretched his jaw, looking like a man who has emerged unscathed from a minor altercation on the street.

Mowbray came out of the kitchen and nodded at the Russian. Minasian did not appear to recognize him from the hotel in Egypt. Kell passed the second iPhone to Mowbray, indicating with a look that he should again encrypt the video and send it on to Amelia.

"We should go," he said, turning to Minasian, who was staring at the phone like a man in a trance. "Do you have everything?"

"I came only with my jacket. If you could

please now return my BlackBerry?"

"Of course."

Kell passed the battery, SIM card, and phone to Minasian, then led him toward the front door. They walked out of the building, leaving Mowbray inside the flat. When the driver saw Kell coming down the steps toward the street, he opened the door of the Vauxhall.

"Mr. Kell?"

He was a short, neatly turned-out man in his late fifties, tanned and silver-haired. Kell was surprised that he had used his surname in front of Minasian.

"That's right."

"I'm to take you to your meeting."

At first, Kell wondered if he had misunderstood. He looked across at Minasian, then back at the driver.

"To my meeting . . ."

The driver nodded toward the Russian.

"Your friend is to walk away."

Minasian could not hide his pleasure and pivoted around, grinning at the pavement. Kell felt a sense of impotent fury. He tried his best to conceal his annoyance and apologized to Minasian for what had transpired.

"My mistake," he said. "I thought they were sending a car for you."

"It is not a problem," Minasian replied. "I know London. I know where I am. I can walk from here." He looked up at the surrounding buildings, across the street at an unmarked Transit van. "No doubt your people will be following me all the way."

Kell did nothing to disabuse Minasian of the idea that he was under surveillance. They shook hands, Minasian's grip surprisingly soft.

"Look after yourself," he said.

"You too, Tom."

Without acknowledging the driver, Minasian walked north along Sinclair Road. He did not look back. Kell watched him. Just another Russian in London, just another pedestrian on the street. When he was about to vanish out of sight, Kell called out.

"Hey!"

He was not quite sure why he was doing what he was about to do. Minasian reacted to Kell's shout and turned around. Kell raised his hand, indicating that Minasian should stop. He began walking toward him.

"What is it?" Minasian asked as Kell caught up with him.

Kell knew that he had been overcome by a moment of sentimentality, but there was also good operational sense in what he was about to say. Agent care. Agent cultivation.

"What about Riedle?" he asked. "What about Bernie?"

Minasian stepped backward and frowned. He seemed to believe that Kell was taunting him.

"The funeral," Kell explained. "Would you like somebody to go? To represent you?"

Minasian reacted in a way that Kell could not have anticipated. With profound sadness, the Russian lowered his head, then reached out and placed a hand on Kell's shoulder. He looked at him with gratitude.

"You are kind," he said. "You do not need to do this. I will mourn him privately. All of my feelings for Bernhard were private. I am used to this."

Without another word, Minasian turned and walked away. There was a skip beside Kell, filled with bags of earth and smashed furniture. He leaned against it and watched Minasian until he was out of sight. He was heading in the direction of Westfield. Kell assumed that he would go directly to Marks and Spencer and walk the ground in readiness for their meeting. It was what he himself would have done.

In due course Kell turned and headed back toward the car. The driver was watching him as he approached the vehicle. There was a look on his face of small-minded bureaucratic distrust that irritated Kell intensely.

"Everything all right?" he said to him.

The driver did not reply.

"Where are we going?"

"I have a postcode, sir."

"What is it?"

The driver indicated with a tilt of the head that he was not prepared to divulge even this simple piece of information. "I have my orders," he explained.

Kell suppressed an urge to lean into the car and pick up the instruction sheet the driver had left out on the passenger seat. Instead he looked up at his flat and saw Mowbray's face in the bedroom window, half hidden behind twitching curtains. It was like catching a neighbor spying. He wondered how long Mowbray would remain loyal. Was it his fault that Amelia had sent the car? Had they cooked up the plan together?

"Do you need anything from your residence?" the driver asked. He had a pedantic, adenoidal voice. "I was told it would be a long night."

"Meaning?"

"Meaning that you should perhaps pack a bag."

Kell shook his head, no longer bothering

to disguise the fact that he had no idea what the hell was going on. He walked back to the front door and let himself into the flat. Mowbray was at the table in the sitting room, working on a laptop.

"You knew about this?" Kell asked.

"Knew about what?"

"The car. The driver."

Mowbray looked up, an expression of blank innocence on his face. "No, guv."

Kell trusted him as he would once have trusted Amelia or Rachel. That is to say, he did not trust Mowbray at all.

"What did she say to you on the phone? Did she threaten you?"

"Threaten me? What about?" Mowbray was not angry, but he seemed bewildered by Kell's questions. "She was just fucked off that you were doing stuff behind her back. Disobeying orders."

"Just me or you as well?"

"You and me both."

Kell took a moment. There was no point in making an enemy of Mowbray, in continuing to interrogate him.

"The second film," he said, trying to move on. "Did you encrypt it?"

"Just doing it now."

"Don't," Kell told him.

Mowbray again seemed puzzled.

"Something's going on." Kell was looking around for his lighter. "I don't want Amelia to see the second film until I know what's happening. Can you hold her off until morning?"

"I suppose."

Kell did not know what to make of Mowbray's reply. It was neither a guarantee that he would do what he had been asked, nor an indication that his loyalty to Kell had been bought out by SIS. Kell took his phone, went into the bedroom, and threw a change of clothes in an overnight bag. He grabbed some toiletries, picked up his jacket and wallet, and went back into the sitting room.

"Did you overhear any of the arrangements I made with GAGARIN? Lines of communication? Crash meetings?"

"No, guv."

Kell was pleased. "Good," he said. "So if Amelia asks you about any of that stuff, you won't have to lie to her."

Mowbray frowned. "No, I suppose not," he said. He closed the laptop. "What's going on, boss? How come they let GAGARIN walk? None of this feels right. Why is it you going in the car and not him?"

Kell persuaded himself to be reassured by Mowbray's questions. He found the lighter and slipped it into his jacket pocket.

"I have no idea," he replied. "No idea at all."

## 37

Kell was smoking as he opened the back door of the Vauxhall.

"Please extinguish your cigarette before entering the vehicle," said the driver with such banal, automated humorlessness that Kell was tempted to stub it out on the paintwork. Mowbray had gathered up his belongings and was already fifty meters away on Sinclair Road, heading south toward Kensington Olympia. Kell tossed the cigarette in the gutter, sat in the back seat, and closed the door.

"Where are we going?" he asked.

"I have my instructions, sir. I only have a postcode —"

"So you keep saying." Kell didn't bother buckling the seatbelt. "A postcode is all I'll need. What is it?"

"I'm afraid I'm not at liberty to divulge that, sir." Though Kell had spent more than two decades working alongside numberless job-for-life bureaucrats and middle managers, he was always astonished by the manner in which they spoke. "All I can tell you is that you should prepare for a journey of perhaps two or two and a half hours. Traffic dependent."

Kell was at the edge of his patience. He felt as he had on that wretched November day four years earlier when two SIS security gorillas had escorted him to the entrance of Vauxhall Cross, demanding — in tones of flat, emotionless condescension — that Kell surrender his pass at the gates "before leaving the premises." Kell had served too loyally, and achieved too much for Amelia Levene, to be treated with such disdain.

He sat back. Perhaps he was overreacting. He was tired and hungry and still angry with Amelia. Kell could not think why it was necessary to sit in a car for two hours in order to have a meeting with her. Who else would be there? In his state of bedraggled irritation, he would not have been surprised to find Amelia waiting for him in a coastal safe house alongside her opposite number in the SVR. Anything was possible. Why else had she been so reluctant to ensnare Minasian?

"Can we stop for something to eat?" he asked.

The driver had been listening to a debate about Greek debt on LBC radio. He said: "Sorry, what was that?" and turned down the volume.

"I said can we stop and get something to eat? Just a sandwich will do."

"Yes, sir. That should be possible. I'll stop at the next petrol station."

The next petrol station turned out to be Fleet Services on the M3, an hour outside London. Kell was followed around the rest area by the driver and watched at a discreet distance as he bought a Whopper at Burger King and a double espresso from Starbucks.

"Where did you think I was going to go?" he said, no longer bothering to disguise his contempt as they walked back toward the car. "Hide in the gents? Run out the back and hotwire a Ford Fiesta?"

Nothing more was said. Kell sat in the back, wolfing his burger, running through old e-mails on his iPhone, and suppressing a truculent desire to rub gherkins into the upholstery.

Fifteen minutes later, the driver took the exit for the A303. Kell now knew where he was being taken. Sure enough, just before half past nine, the Vauxhall entered the village of Chalke Bissett, where Amelia owned a small house. It was here, two years earlier, that Kell and Amelia had run the operation to flush out her kidnapped son. At the church in the center of the village the sat-nav became confused and began to send the Vauxhall back in the direction of Salisbury. Kell explained that he had been to the address many times before and directed the driver through the village and along the isolated lane that led to Amelia's property.

To his surprise, the driver did not insist on accompanying Kell to the front door. Instead, he turned the Vauxhall around and waited in the lane while Kell approached the house. It was almost dark, but he could make out a satellite dish and what looked to be a mobile phone mast on the roof. Tech-Ops at Vauxhall Cross had given "C" 's country retreat an upgrade.

Amelia took her time coming to the door. Kell had to knock twice before she appeared in the short corridor that led from the kitchen to the front of the house. She was wearing casual weekend clothes — there was a slight tear in the knee of her jeans — and looked as though she had been doing some gardening.

"You made it," she said. She was perspiring very slightly and carrying a half-finished glass of white wine. "Where's your driver?"

"Waiting for you to let him go," Kell replied.

Amelia peered out toward the lane and gestured at the Vauxhall. Kell saw the car move away.

"I made dinner," she said, leaving a faint mist of Hermès Calèche in the corridor as she turned toward the kitchen. Kell felt like a husband coming home late after a long day at work.

"I ate in the car," he replied.

He had not been back to the house since the Malot operation, but the place still looked and smelled the same. Fading wallpaper, worn rugs, furniture that had been in Amelia's family for generations. He saw two photographs of her son, François, who lived in Paris, and remembered Minasian's remark, earlier in the afternoon: *You have shown me so much of yourself. Your taste. Your style. The things you possess and the things you lack.* Amelia offered to take Kell's jacket, but he kept it on, immediately lighting a cigarette as a means of testing her mood.

"If you're going to do that, we'll have to go outside," she said. "Drink?"

Kell saw that there was a half-finished bottle of red wine in the kitchen and asked for a glass. Memories were coming back to him all the time. He recalled the elderly Barbara Knight masquerading as a cleaning lady, the team watching and listening to her every move on a bank of screens in the house next door. Kell wondered what had become of her, and of her feckless husband, whose name momentarily escaped him. In different circumstances, he would have enjoyed reminiscing about the operation with Amelia, but too much had changed between them. He opened the back door and took a seat at the head of a garden table. Amelia followed him, passing Kell his glass of wine.

"Thank you for coming all this way," she said.

"Don't mention it. Nothing I like more than surprises."

"Yes. I remember."

There was a smell of roast chicken coming from the kitchen. Kell was hungry.

"Why all the subterfuge?" he asked.

"No particular reason." Amelia sipped her drink. It would not have surprised Kell if she had added: "I just enjoy winding you up."

"The driver. A favorite of yours?"

"Increasingly, why?"

"Never mind." The easy rapport between them was bothering him. He had expected

Amelia to be in a less affable mood. "Bureaucrat. Company man. Looked like he hadn't told a joke since the mid-1980s. Not my cup of tea."

"Oh, poor Tom," Amelia replied, and Kell's patience snapped.

"What's that supposed to mean?"

Amelia leaned back in mock surprise. "Nothing!" she said, and Kell knew that he had overreacted. "I was just teasing you."

There was a prolonged silence. Kell continued to smoke the cigarette, but found the taste of it sour against the wine. She was behaving as if nothing she had done in the preceding twelve hours was of any consequence or concern. The order to release Minasian, her refusal to cooperate on surveillance, the reluctance to offer Kell a safe house. All of it appeared to have been forgotten.

"What's going on?" he asked.

"Isn't it obvious?"

"Not to me. I just spent the last few weeks reeling in an SVR officer for you. On my own time. Recruited him this afternoon. Only you don't seem all that enthusiastic about it."

"Can you blame me?"

Kell dropped the cigarette, putting it out under his shoe. Amelia looked down and appeared to suppress an urge to ask Kell to pick it up.

"What don't I know?" he said. "What are you keeping from me?"

He dreaded her reply. There had been so many secrets between them, so many lies. Amelia could finesse and conceal with greater skill than any person he had ever known.

"You know everything," she said. Her eyes contained an apology for earlier deceptions, as though she was keen to build a new and more trusting relationship between them. In feeling this, Kell knew that he was most probably deceiving himself.

"Then why are you acting this way?" he asked. "Why tell me to stand down? Why don't you want a piece of Minasian?"

"To protect you." Amelia stood up and walked back into the kitchen. Kell picked up his glass and followed her. She had opened the door of the oven and was pulling out the chicken.

"Protect me from what?"

She set the roasting tray to one side before answering.

"You don't see him straight. You're too close to him."

"You're not serious?" The question contained what Kell hoped was an appropriate level of contempt.

"Harold sent the tape," Amelia replied, finding a carving knife in a drawer beside the sink. "I watched it before you arrived. You're too easy on him. He tells you whatever he thinks you want to hear."

Kell took another sip of wine. It had been a long and difficult day. He did not want to give Amelia the pleasure of seeing him lose control.

"You think I don't understand him? You think I handled him wrong?"

"I didn't say that."

"Then what are you saying? That you don't believe we have a lone wolf? That he's lying about this kid from Leeds?"

Amelia secured the chicken with a fork and began to carve through a leg.

"What kid from Leeds? What are you talking about?"

Amelia had not yet seen that section of the recording. She knew nothing about the terrorist threat. Kell explained what little Minasian had told him and was stunned by her reaction.

"Sounds like he's just making it up."

Kell took a step toward her. "What?"

It amazed him that she was so certain in her conviction, so oblivious to any sense that she was being stubborn or obstructive, even though he himself had experienced identical misgivings about Minasian's revelation.

"Well, we certainly have no way of checking him out, do we?" Amelia was still carving, still not looking at him. "Unless Minasian gives you something actionable, a detail we could use to run this boy to ground, what he's told you is effectively worthless."

"Isn't that the point of having him as an agent?" Kell lit a second cigarette, blowing the smoke toward the food. Amelia cut him a look. "I see him again. I get more information. We try to stop the attack."

"Possibly," she conceded. "If the possibility of such an attack even exists."

"How can you afford to be so sanguine about this? He's a fucking clean skin."

At last, Amelia set down the knife and turned toward him.

"Tom, you know as well as I do that we get hundreds of threats like this every year. I grant you, this one may be genuine. It could be the case that Alexander Minasian is a noble humanitarian who wants to help prevent a terrorist attack on U.K. soil. It could be the case that the SVR just happen to have a line into the ISIS cell in Syria that obtained this false passport and funded a young *jihadi* back to Britain." She crossed to the stove and emptied a pan of gravy into a small porcelain jug. "It could also be the case that Minasian knew he had to give you something this afternoon in order to get out of your flat, so he made it up off the top of his head."

"Fine," Kell replied, holding up his hands in mock surrender. He was so exasperated by Amelia's attitude, so bewildered by her intransigence, that he did not feel it was worth continuing. She was not going to change her mind. She was only going to find more reasons to doubt GAGARIN. Added to this sense of frustration was his own nagging suspicion that she was right; Kell wondered why it had become so important to him to believe everything Minasian had told him.

"I'm sorry, Tom," she said, "but I just don't buy it. You think that you can get GAGARIN to cooperate on the basis that he's gay and working for a government that is aggressively homophobic. You think that you can offer him refuge from Andrei Eremenko, even though nobody has a clue who really carried out this afternoon's shooting."

"You don't think Eremenko had Riedle killed?"

"I have no idea!"

"Who else then? Who ordered it?"

Amelia was scalded by the handle of a pan

and dropped it into the sink with a clatter. Kell asked if she was all right but she brushed him off.

"Tom, we don't yet know who ordered it." He searched her face, looking for some tiny indication that she was concealing something, that SIS knew who was behind the assassination. "And we don't *have* to know. It's a police matter. The murder of Bernhard Riedle, tragic though it is, is not the responsibility of the Secret Intelligence Service." Kell tossed his cigarette through the back door. Amelia followed it with disapproving eyes, as if Kell's act of minor vandalism might start a fire in her garden. "Answer me this," she said. "When have you ever known a successful recruitment based on blackmail?"

Kell did not want to concede her point, but failed to provide an answer.

"When we work successfully," she continued, "what we do is based on trust, on empathy. It isn't ever about revenge or coercion. You know that."

"Of course I do," Kell replied.

"So when Minasian tells you how much he loved Bernhard Riedle, that he couldn't walk away from Sterndale Road because he felt like a child 'standing in the shower after a swim' — or whatever it was that he said

— all I see is a bullshit artist of the first order." Kell could picture Amelia studying the first video, looking for reasons to doubt Minasian, to push him away. "Here is a man whose career you undermined by exposing Ryan Kleckner," she said. "He has a personal animus against us — against *you*, in particular — that is every bit as toxic as yours against him. Alexander Minasian is the sort of person who will say and do *anything* in order to survive. He will never betray the SVR, and he will certainly never allow himself to be humiliated by you."

"So I'm the problem?" Kell felt another spasm in his lower back. Amelia saw him wince in pain but said nothing. "Because of Kleckner, because of Odessa, he won't deal with me? If somebody else runs Minasian, you think that he or she might produce something useful from him?"

Amelia was spooning slices of chicken and roast potatoes onto two warmed plates.

"You're not listening to me," she said. "Even in those circumstances, I doubt that GAGARIN would play ball. Nothing he tells us can be trusted. What's his motivation? He doesn't need money. He's married to the daughter of one of the richest men in Russia. A man like that probably already has several million dollars siphoned off in offshore accounts in readiness for his divorce and/or retirement. Minasian has no *ideological* motive for treachery. The only thing he really cares about is Alexander Minasian — his own survival, his own self-image, his own progress through life. He's not a Kleckner. He's not looking for kicks or to occupy center stage. He's a manipulator, a sadist. Coercion? Perhaps. But how does a man like that respond to being blackmailed by an enemy Service that has already got the better of him over Kleckner? By *thanking* us? No. He's going to want to *harm* us. So why bring the fox into the chicken coop, Tom? Why take that risk?"

"Because of the threat to hundreds, maybe thousands of lives."

"That's not why you're doing this. That's not why this is so important to you."

"Does it matter why it's important to me? I thought our job — I thought *your* job — was to save lives?"

Amelia stopped serving the food and turned to face him. There was suddenly great affection in her eyes, a look of respect and understanding borne of years of embattled friendship. He understood what she had meant by wanting to protect him, yet her protection was the last thing he needed.

"Of course I have a responsibility to keep

people safe," she replied. For a moment it looked as though she was going to come toward him, to try to take hold of his arms in a gesture of reassurance. "I just want to be sure that you understand what might be going on here."

"I understand, Amelia," Kell replied. He was beginning to feel patronized.

"Do you?" A wasp flew in front of her face and she flicked it away with her hand. "Minasian knows that it's only a matter of time before word leaks out about Riedle. Somebody is going to talk. So inevitably he'll be kicked out of the SVR." The wasp flew out into the garden. Amelia went back to serving the food. "In fact the only reason they might have for keeping him on would be his burgeoning relationship with SIS. Minasian confesses that he's been turned, Moscow sees that as an opportunity to use him as a double agent, he then sends us months and months of chicken feed."

"Aren't we getting a bit ahead of ourselves?"

"Perhaps," Amelia replied, though it was clear from her tone of voice that she considered the scenario to be completely plausible.

"What about the fertility clinic?" Kell asked. "What about Svetlana's baby?"

"What about it?"

To Kell's embarrassment, he found that he could not answer his own question. His desire to manipulate Minasian by controlling his wife's access to the baby they both craved felt sordid and reprehensible. "So we just give up?" he said, trying to salvage the argument. "We have a serving SVR officer by the balls who's just told me there is a home-grown, clean-skin *jihadi* planning a terrorist atrocity on British soil, but we let him go because we think he's a Trojan horse?"

Amelia did not answer immediately. She picked up two bottles of wine — one white, one red — walked past Kell, and carried them outside. She lit a candle at the table, then came back into the kitchen, took knives and forks from the cutlery drawer, tore off some strips of kitchen roll for napkins and invited Kell to pick up their plates. He did so. A loose roast potato rolled onto the floor. Amelia swore, picked it up, put it back on the plate without a word, then led him outside.

"Have a seat," she said.

Kell set down the plates and refilled their glasses of wine. Amelia thanked him. She looked up at the steep hill that bordered the northern side of the property, gathering her thoughts. A swarm of insects were buzzing around an outdoor light. Kell could hear a sheep moaning in the darkness.

"Look," she said, drawing what felt like a line under their earlier exchange. "I'm sorry. I owe you an apology."

"How so?"

"It was a mistake for me to tell you to pursue this. I wanted you to be working for us again. I wanted Minasian as badly as you did. You came to me with the revelation about his sexuality, it seemed too good an opportunity to resist. I should have known better. Minasian is a type. The high-functioning homosexual, forced to exist in secret, living a double life. We've seen it historically time and time again. That behavior breeds a love of intrigue and subterfuge, of acting and performance. Risk-taking. The guilty secret inside the gay man makes him feel ashamed and vulnerable, which leads to an absolute ruthlessness, not to mention a five-star talent for manipulation."

"That's all a bit old hat, isn't it?" Kell was surprised that Amelia was voicing such a reactionary theory. "Maybe fifty years ago you might have been able to make a case for that kind of behavior, but not today. What you're saying is basically homophobic."

"It *is* fifty years ago in Russia in terms of gay rights. It *is* fifty years ago in terms of what Alexander Minasian can do with his private life and — more importantly — can be *seen* to be doing with his private life in Moscow and Kiev. How is he any different from a Blunt or a Burgess, a J. Edgar Hoover or a Jeremy Thorpe? I'm not saying that *all* secretly gay men in the twenty-first century are sociopathic. Goodness me." With an exasperated intake of breath, Amelia looked out on her garden and took a moment to compose herself. "Look." She turned back to Kell, trying to lay the conversation to rest. "All I'm saying is that it's textbook. I should have avoided him at all costs. It was my fault. This was the wrong operation for you."

Kell felt that this answer was unequivocal and did not respond. Amelia interpreted Kell's silence as a demand for a more persuasive argument, and tried to provide it.

"There is also the added problem of the shooting this afternoon." She had picked up her knife and fork. "I must be frank. That's what's changed my mind definitively. I can't risk linking the Service to Riedle. I can't spare the resources. Furthermore, going after Andrei Eremenko is not an HMG

Requirement. Let him skirt around the sanctions. Let him sell forty percent of his petrochemical company to Svetlana. You may not have noticed, but we have other fish to fry these days."

Kell looked down at his food. "It's not about Eremenko," he said. "Since when is counterterrorism not a Requirement of Her Majesty's bloody government?"

Here Amelia was prepared to concede ground.

"Okay," she said. "If there's something on the clean skin that I can use, then sure. If Minasian gives you something credible, come back to me. But my advice to you would be to leave it. Your assessment of Minasian's character in the first instance was absolutely correct. He's a sociopath. Sadistic, manipulative, cruel. He has to win. He can't win by making you the hero."

Kell nodded, knowing that he would still get nothing in terms of cooperation from SIS. No surveillance, no technical support, no analysts. Once Amelia had made up her mind about something, there was no persuading her. Perhaps that explained why she had wanted him to come all the way down to Wiltshire; to give him the bad news in person, then perhaps to try to rebuild the broken pieces of their friendship.

"If that's your decision, then I guess that's the end of it," he said, and began to eat.

"You're sure?" she said.

"What choice do I have?"

For all his frustration, Kell recognized that he still had options. He had told Mowbray to delay sending the second film. Amelia knew nothing about Westfield, nothing about the arrangements he had made to meet Minasian. He could act alone in the next few weeks, running GAGARIN, gathering intelligence, only involving the Service at a later date if the product on STRIPE proved to be authentic. He had enough money to pay Harold, with Elsa Cassani in the wings should he need further backup. Better to function in this way, behind Amelia's back, than to risk being shut down altogether.

"What arrangements did you make for contacting one another?" she asked.

Kell was amazed by the timing of the question.

"I gave him a BlackBerry," he replied, saying nothing about the Westfield meeting. "PGP encrypted. All that clever stuff."

"What's the number?"

"I'll have to look it up." Kell could feel Amelia searching his face for the lie. She knew him too well. She did not trust him to

340

give up on GAGARIN altogether.

"That would be kind."

"Why?" he asked quickly. "You're going to give it to Cheltenham?"

"No harm, is there?"

"None," Kell replied. "Don't you trust me to tell you if GAGARIN gets in touch?"

"Of course I do," she said, caught out by Kell's question.

"Look," he said. "I'll leave it." He took a sip of wine, trying to give the impression that he was at peace with Amelia's decision. "I can see why it's dangerous to trust him. I can see that he could do the Service more harm than good. I left everything in Minasian's hands. He said he was flying back to Moscow tomorrow, that he'd be in touch on the number. If I hear from him, I'll tell you."

"Of course you will." Amelia dabbed her mouth with the kitchen roll, candlelit eyes studying Kell's face closely. He knew that she knew he was lying to her. Her next question proved it. "So you made no arrangement to meet again?"

"You didn't give us time!" He smiled as he laid out the lie. "I was about to talk about a second meeting when your driver showed up —"

She interrupted him. "What about the

filming? Had you continued to record the conversation?"

Kell remained poker-faced. He was not about to admit to Amelia that a video existed in which he and Minasian had arranged the Westfield meeting. He didn't want her watching the film or crawling all over his ideas. He wanted to be free to work without bureaucratic interference. Amelia had let him down so many times in the past that she was effectively forcing him to deceive her.

"Afraid not," he said, skewering a potato and cutting it in half. "I didn't think it was necessary, once he'd confessed."

Amelia nodded, seeming to accept this answer, but she was watching him with a forensic intensity. He wanted to change the subject — to talk about her garden, about François, about anything other than Minasian — but knew that to do so would be to reveal his guilt.

"Do you want me to walk you through what was said?"

She shook her head. "Not necessary. I assume you'll write it up?"

"If you like."

They ate in silence. The insects continued to buzz around the light, the sheep continued to moan in the distant field. Kell complimented Amelia on the food and told her that Minasian had been "considerably more talkative with the iPhone switched off," an observation to which she offered only a brief response.

"Yes. People are often more relaxed and candid if they feel they're not being recorded."

Kell poured more wine, his mouth as dry as Amelia's sun-baked lawn. He could lie to most people with ease, but lying to Amelia Levene felt like betraying a member of his own family.

"Tom?"

"Yes," he said.

Amelia put down her cutlery. "At one point this afternoon, Minasian seemed to suggest that he wasn't responsible for killing Rachel. I wondered how you were feeling about that?"

Kell experienced that old unsettling sense of Amelia peering into the hidden corners of his mind.

"I'll never know," he replied, hoping to make the subject go away. "Too late now, isn't it?"

"Did you believe him?"

"Not necessarily."

She moved a strand of hair out of her eyes, tucking it behind her ear.

"It occurred to me that this might be why you're so interested in him. Because he might lead you to the people who were responsible."

"So *you* believe him?"

Amelia indicated with a shrug that she was not at all sure. Wary of disappearing into speculations, Kell did his best to put an end to the conversation.

"I don't have any desire for vengeance," he said. "You think I do, but you're wrong." Even as he spoke the words, he knew that he was deceiving himself just as much as he was deceiving Amelia. "Rachel is gone. Minasian isn't going to bring her back, nor is he going to lead me to the men who ordered her murder. As far as I'm concerned he can go about his business. He can stay in the SVR, he can quit, he can work for Andrei Eremenko. He can try to get his wife pregnant at a fertility clinic, he can move to Barcelona and start a new life with a new man. None of it makes any difference to me. The only thing I care about is STRIPE. I want him investigated. Because if some brainwashed maniac comes back from Syria and kills two hundred people in the rush hour, I want to know that I'm not responsible. I want to know that I wasn't just sitting on the sidelines, waiting for it to happen."

# 38

Shahid walked Brighton Pier all the time. He knew where the crowds gathered, where the cameras were, where he would have the best chance of shooting the targets and then moving forward. He had a vivid fantasy of clearing the pier of structures and people, of all the shit that was contaminating Brighton, so that he could walk along it with Rosie at his side and breathe in the clean sea air, all alone. He liked to imagine that, after it was over, the police would comb through days of CCTV and spot him as he scouted the target environment, grainy footage of a holy warrior played time and again on the Net and the news, the great Shahid Khan preparing for his day of martyrdom, planting the seeds for England's future.

When Shahid had seen the pier for the first time, he knew that Jalal had made the wisest and most intelligent choice of target. It was a godless place, evidence of an entire society and culture on its knees. The enclosed areas were the worst. The noise and the smell and the greed of the arcades. Mothers with their stomachs displayed who likely did not know the fathers of their own children, frenziedly pumping coins into machines that lured and tricked them with promises of riches that never came. Men who were not at work during the day, day-trip tourists and teenagers hypnotized by fruit machines and arcade computers that made a game of war, a cartoon of despair and bombings, of the conflicts created by Western politicians. Infidel soldiers, Muslim victims — all inside a game designed to entertain children. It made Shahid toxic with violence. There were times, walking in that deafening place, when the screams of the customers and the stench of their food and the noise of their music became so much for him that he wanted to act in that very moment. Had he been armed, had Kris already supplied him with his weapons, Shahid would have taken them all in a moment of transcendental purity, cleansing the room, the pier, driving an entire way of life into the sea.

He had come here with Rosie. That was the only time that he had felt distracted in the target environment. At the southern end of the pier, near the rollercoaster, where he planned to finish after working his way south from the beach, they had kissed for the first time. He had no longer been able to stop himself. He had taken her around the waist so that she could feel his strength as he pulled her toward him. She had tasted of ice cream and perfume. She had opened her mouth and he had felt her lips and her tongue, lost in the sweetness of being able to tell her with his mouth and with his body how he felt about her, how attractive she was, how much she tormented him.

"God, I'm so glad," she said, breaking the kiss and looking into his eyes. "I've wanted you to do that for so long."

"Sorry," Shahid said, feeling embarrassed. He knew that he had been weak to wait and wondered if he had kissed her in the right way.

"Nothing to be sorry about," she said, and put her hand on the back of his neck. The touch of her fingers was gentle at first, then she pulled him toward her. It was a new side of her and it sent a pulse right through him. He knew that she wanted him as much as he wanted her. They were both losing their control.

As they walked back to the bus stop, holding hands, he became worried. He was more than ever convinced that Rosie had been sent by God to prove his commitment to Islam. He knew that God was making him choose between a life with a woman who was not Muslim and the afterlife of martyrdom, which was sublime. It was no choice at all. He liked Rosie, he would continue to see her, but it was pointless to get caught up in her. It was not the destiny of Shahid Khan, of Azhar Ahmed Iqbal, of Omar Assya, to be a husband or a man of the family. He was greater than that. He was a soldier in a war. A martyr. He had to fight his doubts and his lust. This was the will of God.

## 39

Amelia dropped Kell at Salisbury station the following morning and he took the train back to London. It felt like a farewell of sorts. Toward the end of dinner, the temperature had fallen in the garden. Amelia had gone inside to fetch a pashmina, leaving Kell alone at the table. He had immediately sent a WhatsApp message to Mowbray suggesting — in *en clair* language — that "the second movie" was a "mirage" that the "suits" didn't need to see. Mowbray had understood what was being asked of him, replying with the simple message: "I get it. Never saw the film." From that moment Kell had felt that his professional relationship with Amelia Levene had changed irrevocably. He had embarked on a deliberate strategy of deception. Whatever trust he had felt for her had vanished long ago. Should she discover that he was lying to her, Amelia's faith in Kell would be similarly degraded.

Eight days remained until the scheduled meeting with Minasian. Kell heard nothing from Amelia nor from Vauxhall Cross. He suspected that Amelia would put him under light surveillance — a quick look at his phones, a daily printout of his wi-fi activity — and therefore was conscious to go about his life as normally as possible. He made no attempt to contact Claridge's to confirm Minasian's reservation, nor did he check that Svetlana had made an appointment at the fertility clinic. He watched the cricket on Sky, read short stories by Isaac Babel, went to the movies, exercised at the gym. For the benefit of the snoops at GCHQ, Kell looked online at several articles about ISIS and ran Google searches on home-grown *jihadis;* it would have looked suspicious abruptly to abandon all interest in the potential threat from STRIPE. To test the intensity of any possible mobile surveillance, Kell took himself off to Paris for three nights, eating at his favorite restaurants — Brasserie Lipp and Chez Paul — and visiting the recently reopened Musée Picasso. At no point did he sense that he was being watched or followed. He dined with an old colleague from the Service whom he knew to be in regular contact with Amelia. Kell said nothing about Minasian or the threat from STRIPE, but hinted that there was a "small possibility" he would return to active duty in the near future, "depending on something in the pipeline which may or may not happen," an appropriately gnomic remark that he hoped would be conveyed back to "C." Kell checked the dedicated phone for a message from GAGARIN, but the Russian did not make contact. Kell was certain that he would appear at Westfield as promised, bringing with him detailed information about STRIPE that would allow SIS to make an arrest. He assumed that Svetlana Eremenko's passport would be flagged at Heathrow, but did not know if Amelia would bother to put eyes on Minasian at Claridge's. Assuming she did so, Kell had enough faith in the Russian's antisurveillance skills to shake off even the most sophisticated team that SIS could throw at him.

Friday dawned. Kell paid his habitual visit to the gym and swam forty lengths of the pool. A week earlier he had paid for a private locker in the changing room and deliberately left his watch inside it when he had finished dressing. He did not want to run even the small risk that Tech-Ops had

351

planted a tracking device in his personal effects. For the same reason, Kell put on a brand-new pair of shoes, purchased in High Street Kensington the day before. There were ways in which footwear could be "painted," making it possible for the Service to follow a subject over significant distances.

Outside the gym, Kell made a quick visual note of the five vehicles parked in the immediate area, then walked south toward Hammersmith Road to hail a cab. He had been certain that the surveillance threat against him was nonexistent, yet as he turned around in the back seat of the taxi, he saw one of the cars that had been parked outside the gym — a navy blue SEAT Altea — making a left turn onto Hammersmith Road. Kell had not committed any of the number plates to memory and could not be sure that it was the same vehicle. He was also aware that he was at the start of a long process of cleaning his tail and that it was not uncommon in such circumstances to imagine threats where none existed. Paranoia kept you sharp; suspicion was a useful accomplice. Kell continued to watch the car as the taxi headed southeast. It followed him to Cromwell Road, eventually disappearing at a set of lights close to the Natural History Museum. Kell did not get a look at the driver.

Kell had a simple objective: to throw off any surveillance, but not to be seen to be doing so. For that reason, he could not abandon his iPhone without good cause. To leave it at home — or to secure it in the locker at his gym — would look suspicious to Amelia. In Paris, Kell had dropped the phone on the street, causing a tiny hairline crack to appear in the lower part of the screen. This had given him an idea. He instructed the taxi driver to take him to a small shop on Gloucester Road, where he asked for the screen to be replaced. The owner of the shop told him that the job would take two hours. Kell promised to return before the end of the day. He had no intention of doing so — the meeting with Minasian would almost certainly run on too long — but planned instead to pick up the phone in the morning.

As soon as he had left the shop, Kell walked the short distance to Gloucester Road Underground station and waited for a District Line train traveling east. He made a cursory assessment of the passengers standing within a carriage distance of him on the platform, then boarded the train at the last moment. As far as he could tell, there was no suspicious activity in reaction to this. Standing close to the doors, Kell feinted to leave at Victoria station, watching the behavior of a young man who, moments earlier, had caught his eye while reading a copy of *The Guardian.* The man did not react. Kell had been suspicious of him not only because of the lightning-quick eye contact between them, but also because he assumed that someone of his appearance — hipster haircut, Converse trainers, turned-up skinny jeans — would more naturally read the digital edition of the *Guardian,* rather than a physical newspaper. The man eventually stepped off the train at Westminster.

Kell found a seat. He could see all the way to the rear of the carriage, but his view ahead was obscured by a large group of Spanish teenagers who had boarded the train at Victoria. On a straightforward clean, Kell would have stepped off the train at one of the stations, jumping back on at the last moment in order to expose or throw off a tail. He would have switched platforms and lines, allowing — for example — the first few trains at Gloucester Road to leave the station without him. But he could not afford to be seen to be acting abnormally. Instead, Kell got off at Embankment and walked through a narrow park running parallel to the river. A path connected the entrance at Embankment station to Waterloo Bridge. Kell walked underneath the bridge and found the rear entrance to Somerset House.

He had come to see an exhibition in the Eastern Gallery. This was how Kell had typically filled his days during his extended absence from the Service; should Amelia glance at his surveillance report, his behavior would not appear to be abnormal or out of character. He had walked the ground at Somerset House shortly before leaving for Paris and knew that the southern side of the complex was a warren of offices and corridors, splitting to all four points of the compass. In such an environment it was almost impossible to track a target without coming into contact with them. Kell stood in the lobby area for a count of sixty seconds and was followed inside by a woman of his own age wearing a gray business suit, carrying a cup of takeaway coffee. She was slim, wore black-rimmed glasses, and nodded politely at Kell as she passed him. Kell turned and went into the ground-floor bathroom, checked his clothing for any tags that may have been attached during his journey, then bought a ticket to the exhibition. He stayed there for the next twenty minutes.

As soon as he had left the Eastern Gallery, he took a lift to the first floor and emerged into the outdoor courtyard. Kell had not seen the woman in the business suit since she had walked past him in the lobby. He looked for her now, but did not spot her. There were members of the public seated at outdoor tables on two sides of the courtyard and Kell strolled past them, searching for repeating faces. If the young man on the train had been following him, it was likely that he had affected a change in his appearance. Kell could not see him. He bought himself a cup of coffee and a *pain au chocolat* in the café in the northeast corner of the courtyard, eating them at a secluded table indoors while pretending to read a book. Across the room, there was a bearded man wearing a dark suit who was not dissimilar in appearance to a businessman Kell had clocked at Embankment station. On closer inspection, however, Kell saw that he was a different person.

After finishing his coffee, Kell left Somerset House by the main entrance on the Strand. As he looked around for a cab, a young man wearing Converse trainers crossed the street ahead of him. He was of similar build and coloring to the *Guardian*-reading hipster on the Tube, but was wearing a black leather jacket and a blue baseball cap. Kell knew that experienced surveillance officers could change their outward appearance with relative ease, but that they were often obliged to continue wearing the same shoes. He waited until the young man had crossed the street, watched him walk in the direction of Covent Garden, then, when he turned to greet a friend outside the Lyceum Theatre, saw that he was an entirely different person to the one who had been sitting on the train. Kell smiled. He remembered the man in denim jeans and a brown tweed jacket who had spooked him at Bayswater station several weeks before and knew that he would always be plagued by such moments of paranoia. Still, on days such as these it was better to anticipate problems around every corner rather than to walk into a trap set for him by Amelia Levene.

He headed west in the direction of Trafalgar Square and walked north along St. Martin's Lane as far as Wyndham's Theatre. Kell was known within the Service as an avid reader and collector of rare books, so it made sense for him to browse in the windows of the secondhand bookstores in nearby Cecil Court; doing so afforded him the opportunity to glance up and down the pedestrianized colonnade every few moments, checking for foot surveillance. He saw nothing to raise his suspicions. Having bought a first edition of *The Whitsun Weddings,* he walked to Holborn station and boarded a Central Line train to Shepherd's Bush. By half past one, exactly an hour before his scheduled meeting with GAGARIN, Thomas Kell was walking into Westfield.

# 40

It was a soft target. That was the first thing Kell thought about whenever he found himself in Westfield. A handful of gunmen, armed with semi-automatic weapons, could stroll inside at any moment and murder two or three hundred people in less time than it took to make a skinny latte. The security guards were unarmed. Counterterrorism units in Paddington would take at least ten minutes to scramble. Members of the British public did not carry guns or knives. A reasonably well-organized terrorist cell — or lone wolf *jihadi* with combat experience in Syria — could wreak havoc in the heart of London before MI5 had got out of bed. That was the stark reality of Western capital cities in the early twenty-first century. That was the nature of the threat from men like STRIPE.

Kell walked around. Westfield was crowded with families of every race and creed, the new international London of Somalians, Bengalis, Saudis, Chinese. It was one of the emerging paradoxes of extreme Islam that the modern terrorist was blind to nationality and religion; every person in the mall — the Saudi doctor, the Iraqi exile, the Nigerian lawyer — was a legitimate target. Kell felt an exaggerated sense that he was one of the few white European faces in the building, and therefore easier to spot among the polyglot sea of shoppers and staff. Taking an escalator to the first floor, he felt a sense of kinship with Alexander Minasian, who was doubtless going through a near-identical antisurveillance routine somewhere else in London. It was even possible that Minasian was already inside Westfield and that the two men would pass one another in the mall. Kell imagined that the Russian had left Claridge's at dawn and taken an inexhaustibly complex sequence of trains and taxis and Tubes in an attempt to shake off the phantom agents of SIS and Andrei Eremenko. It was Minasian who had taught Kleckner about the joys of Harrods; he would almost certainly have spent an hour inside the store that morning, affecting changes in his appearance, doubling back along mirrored corridors, perhaps even lifting a security pass so that he could leave via the subterranean passage that led to the staff entrance on Hans Crescent.

Kell stopped at the top of the escalator. It occurred to him, not for the first time in his long career, that the business of agent-running was absurd. He knew that Amelia could not afford to put a team on him; he knew that the chances of Minasian being followed by the SVR were infinitesimally small. Kell could have met GAGARIN in broad daylight in the middle of Leicester Square and, chances are, nobody would have batted an eyelid. Yet he had spent nine days in a state of sustained paranoia, shuttling around London and Paris, renting out lockers at his local gym and handing in his iPhone for repair. As for Minasian, Kell could only imagine the obsessive lengths to which the Russian had gone in order to ensure his security. And yet it had to be done. If Minasian helped to stop an attack, if Kell's actions ensured the safety of the men and women obliviously going about their shopping in Westfield, then it would all have been worth it.

He was hungry. Kell made a clockwise circuit of the western section of the mall, purchased a small digital wristwatch in WHSmith, then ate a tagine at a branch of Comptoir Libanais, watching all the time for repeating faces or suspicious behavior. By the time he had finished eating, it was twenty past two. Kell sank a double espresso, picked up his bag, passed a group of schoolchildren being herded toward the cinema, and walked the short distance to the entrance of Marks and Spencer.

The women's section on the ground floor was empty. Nobody looking at dresses, nobody looking at skirts. Kell walked straight ahead toward the underwear department, passing a woman in full burka pushing a sleeping child in a buggy. To his left, there were rows and rows of pajamas and nightdresses; to his right, a huge poster of a model in pink lingerie. A bank of escalators led upstairs to the men's section and down to the food hall. Kell rode to the first level, using the height of the escalator to scan the open-plan floor for Minasian. The anxiety was in him now; the heart-quickening fear that his agent would fail to show. Kell wasn't worried about Amelia. He hardly even cared about surveillance. The only thing that mattered was GAGARIN's integrity. Had he gone back to Moscow to confess his sins? Had Eremenko confronted him and demanded that he divorce Svetlana? Or had Minasian kept his word, gathered the product on STRIPE, and brought it with him to Westfield? Kell could hear Amelia's voice in his head — *He has to win. He can't win by making you the hero* — and suddenly felt that he had been played. The Russian wasn't going to come. STRIPE was a fake and GAGARIN was a ghost.

Kell reached the top of the escalator. The men's section was straight ahead of him. Suits, jackets, trousers, shirts. He looked at his watch. It was exactly half past two. He had timed it perfectly. He turned to his left, made a complete anticlockwise circuit of the floor, found a Panama hat, and placed it in a handbasket that he carried back to the escalator. He had not yet seen Minasian. He walked toward the men's section and saw a row of white shirts stacked on a shelf close to the entrance. He turned and went back to the far end of the shop floor and placed two pairs of socks in the basket, trying to behave as naturally and as unobtrusively as possible.

Why wasn't Minasian there? Kell looked down at the basket and told himself to relax. Spying is waiting. He repeated the mantra, telling himself, over and over again, that agents always showed. In twenty years Kell had known a joe not to materialize only three times. They stuck to the rules. They did what they were told. After all, Minasian knew that SIS had enough compromising material on him to obliterate his career; there was no possibility that he would risk taking them on. He *had* to come. He *had* to show. GAGARIN had no choice.

Kell looked again at his watch. Already twenty to three. He turned around and looked back at the entrance. Thirty feet away he could see a husband and wife flicking through suits and an overweight man in his fifties holding up a mustard tweed jacket, checking his reflection in the mirror. Still no sign of Minasian. Kell picked up another pair of socks, dropped them in the basket.

Then there she was. Coming out of a changing room in the corner of the store. A slim woman in a gray business suit, wearing black-rimmed glasses. The woman who had passed him in the lobby at Somerset House. Kell immediately reached down into the basket and took hold of the rim of the Panama hat. If he put it on, it was a signal to Minasian. Get out. You are compromised. Abort.

He looked again. He could not see the woman's face. In breach of all sensible trade-craft, Kell walked directly toward her. He moved so quickly and with such purpose that the woman looked up, sensing him in her peripheral vision. Kell was walking toward her as though he was intending to introduce himself. And then he saw, to his intense relief, that he had made a mistake. It was not the same person. His eyes had played the old surveillance trick, turning her into someone else. She was much younger than the woman he had seen in Somerset House, but the gray suit was exactly the same. Doubtless it was a Marks and Spencer staple.

He turned and walked back toward the entrance. Time to pick up a white shirt and let Minasian know that the coast was clear.

Kell was passing the bank of escalators when he saw a man in his mid-thirties walking into the store ahead of him. Cheap denim jeans, a gray T-shirt, several days of stubble.

Minasian.

At first the Russian did not see Kell. He turned to his right, picked up a white shirt, then moved forward to look at a rack of suits. Kell passed within three meters of him and went to the stack of shirts. He picked up a white shirt of his own, tucked it under his arm, then walked directly toward him.

Minasian was barely recognizable, no trace of the slick metropolitan professional whom Kell had interviewed at Sinclair

Road. As he looked up and caught Kell's eye, there was an electrifying moment of understanding between them, invisible to any passerby, that confirmed that the meeting could safely go ahead. Then Minasian moved away. Kell put down the basket, placed the shirt back on the stack, and walked out of the store.

## 41

Mowbray had hired the Peugeot in his wife's name and left it overnight in Westfield. He had posted the keys and the parking ticket through Kell's front door just after nine o'clock the previous evening, with a note telling him where to find the vehicle. As soon as he had left Marks and Spencer, Kell took a lift to level 2 of the underground car park, paid for twenty-four hours of parking, and found the Peugeot. He sat behind the wheel and looked at his watch. Four and a half minutes had passed since he had seen Minasian. He knew that it would take less than thirty seconds to drive the short distance to aisle 45.

He could picture Minasian every step of the way. Down to the food hall, past the soups and the rows of checkout staff, the grandmothers buying chutneys, and the teenagers stacking shelves. The chill of the air-conditioning, the shrill robotic voice of

the automated warning on the walkways —
*Please hold the handrail while traveling . . .
Please hold the handrail while traveling* —
then the stale, uncirculated air of the subterranean car park. The lengths to which both
men had gone to protect themselves from
scrutiny, to seal off any possibility of suspicion or arrest, struck Kell with the full force
of their absurdity. Sitting in Mowbray's
rented car in the basement of that vast, soul-
less shopping mall, Kell wondered what had
gone so wrong between their two countries
that the SVR would not simply pass over, as
a matter of courtesy and respect, the file on
a brainwashed *jihadi* bent on causing mayhem in the United Kingdom. Why had it
required blackmail to obtain that information? Why had it required Kell to devise an
intricate system of signals and meetings
with a compromised Russian spy in order
to secure the safety of his fellow citizens?
Was the blood feud between their two
countries, the clash of systems and personalities, so toxic that it would allow for the
deaths of hundreds of innocent people? Kell
was under no illusions about the extent to
which people wanted — even *needed* — to
cause each other harm, but he felt cleaned
out by the political classes, exhausted by
the effort of trying to make a difference in a

world where no difference could be made.

He looked again at the watch. Eight minutes since he had left GAGARIN. He started the engine and pulled out. The wheels of the Peugeot squealed on the smooth concrete. Kell flicked on the headlights and looked for Minasian. He turned into aisle 45 and saw him immediately — the newly grown beard, the cheap denim jeans, the man on whom he had come to rely so heavily. Kell pulled up alongside him and Minasian opened the door. Within a minute they had left the car park, emerging into the clear, bright sunlight of a London afternoon.

# 42

The more time Shahid spent with Rosie, the more he opened up to her. He wanted somebody to know what he had been through in his life, the pain he had suffered, the sense of isolation he had known. It had taken sacrifices for Azhar Ahmed Iqbal to become Shahid Khan. It had been necessary for him to prove his worth on the battlefield and then to separate himself from his old life, even from his family. Shahid wanted Rosie to know at least some of this, so that when the time came she would look back and understand why he had been prepared to sacrifice his life for a cause much greater than himself.

There were obviously things that he could not tell her. It was too much of a risk. Though he knew that Rosie hated the police because of what they had done to her family, Shahid could not trust her with the full knowledge of what he had seen and done in the Caliphate. She would never understand, for example, why homosexuality was a sin in the eyes of God and therefore why it had been right for Shahid to take the life of the man in Raqqa. He and two other fighters had led the blindfolded man to the top of an apartment block, close to where Shahid had been living, and Shahid had pushed him to his death. Rosie could never be told this. If he began to explain his actions, to describe to her both the revulsion and the intoxicating sense of power that he had felt as he reacted to the baying crowd and pushed the man. If he told her that he had looked down at the dead body — the man's leg twisted and jackknifed at the knee, his smashed skull spilling blood onto the ground — and had felt liberated in that moment from all ordinary moral constraints; well, she would never be able to see sense and would inevitably betray him.

One night in July, Shahid had gone round to Rosie's flat and they had watched a DVD. When Rosie went out to buy pizzas, he had looked for her diary and read parts of it. He knew then how much she wanted him and felt confident when he undressed her later that night and took pleasure in her body. He knew that she had dreamed about him that way and so he let her touch him and suck him and give him the pleasure that he had wanted for so long. Afterward, though, Shahid had felt that they had gone too far and he left the flat. Rosie had been upset and had texted him. She asked if he was all right and if she had "done something wrong." Shahid had not responded.

Two days later, he invited her for a meal at an Italian restaurant in Brighton. He wanted her again. He wanted to be inside her this time. He used some of the money that Farouq had given him, because he thought he should take her somewhere nice, somewhere impressive.

It was over dinner that he started to tell Rosie more about his past. First, he told her about Vicky. He said that he had had a girlfriend in Leeds who had cheated on him. She had gone to live with another man in London. She had betrayed him and broken his heart. Then he told her that he had a secret, that if the police or anyone else knew about it, he would get into a lot of trouble. Rosie understood that he was telling her to keep her mouth shut. Shahid said that he was a good Muslim who had been horrified by what was happening in Syria and had gone there, secretly, to fight against Assad.

Far from being shocked, Rosie said that she admired his courage.

"I think that's amazing of you." She held his hand across the table. "Fuck, that's so brave."

"I believed in what I was fighting for," he told her. "I believed I made the right choice in going there. I never doubted myself. I never doubted my brothers and sisters who fought alongside me, against the regime."

"Brothers and sisters?"

"You know, fellow soldiers. The women out there living alongside them."

"Oh, yeah."

"Assad was killing innocent people, slaughtering them. Women and children. Women like yourself, Rosie, Muslim girls like Marwa and Hind at work. Butchered by Assad's cowards. I just felt like it had been going on too long. Their sisters in Pakistan, Afghanistan, murdered by Americans, killed by drone attacks. Women and children. Old men and babies. I felt like I had a responsibility as a Muslim to go out and fight for them. To protect them, avenge them."

"Of course you did."

In her diary Rosie had written that Shahid often seemed "unhappy about something, sad inside," so he knew that what he had told her might help her to piece him together. He knew her well enough to know that she would respect him for his honesty and admire him for what he had done.

He poured more water into her glass — he didn't like her to drink alcohol when they were together — and told her more about his reasons for going to Syria.

"Many times, back in Leeds, I'd be watching films, you know, on YouTube, wherever we could find it, wherever my friends could find the footage online, and I still remember the blood, the pregnant bodies carved open, the screaming on those films." He saw Rosie flinch. "I'm sorry to speak like this to you, but that's what drove me out there. It wasn't like I didn't feel anything. I cried again and again, you know? I wept for the fear those people lived under, of the attacks by Assad and the Americans. Their lives without hope, futures destroyed before they had started. Somebody had to do something to help them. It was the will of Allah, peace be upon him."

Rosie hesitated. It looked as though she was trying to work out how she felt about what Shahid had told her. Eventually she admitted that she did not understand the complexity of the politics in Syria and didn't feel that she knew enough about Muslims or what Shahid believed in.

"What about ISIS?" she said.

Shahid knew that he could tell her nothing about ISIS and the Caliphate. It was enough that she knew he had fought on behalf of oppressed Muslims. She would admire him if he told her this. Girls, Muslim or infidel, loved soldiers. They liked their men to be strong and brave.

"What about them?" he said.

"Did you come across them? They're fucking maniacs."

Shahid was silent. Rosie saw that he was annoyed.

"I don't mean to upset you," she said

"You're not upsetting me." He spoke quietly. "There's lots of lies and propaganda about ISIS put out by the West. They're not just about violence or whatever. Suicides. Bombings. That's all propaganda and lies."

"But it's on the news. Online."

"Yeah, but those guys, the guys that do that stuff, they're the radical ones. You always get men like that in war. They go too far. They're not thinking about the future and what's best for Islam. Some of them don't know their religion. They have no education."

Rosie was watching him very carefully.

"So you think what ISIS is doing might be right?" It looked as though she cared about his answer. "I'm not judging you,

Shahid. We're just chatting. You're my boyfriend, you can tell me anything. I trust you."

"And I trust you," he said, and stroked her wrist. It was the first time she had called him her "boyfriend" and he felt trapped by the word, even though he knew then that he could have all of her. "It's just that things were very complicated in my head for a long time. I was so angry, you know?"

"Sure."

"I just felt like I didn't belong, and my faith gave me that. I just felt like I wasn't worth anything. I'd grown up not feeling that I was like other lads, that I didn't have their opportunities on account of my skin, my background. You're a white girl. You don't know what that's like. I was brown. They called me 'nigger.' They called me 'Paki' and 'coon.' Me and my friends, we were third-class citizens. You grow up around that, you get stopped by the police because you're brown, because you're not wearing the right clothes, because your mum and dad are from a different country . . ."

"So you got confidence, you got strength from fighting?" she said, interrupting him. "I bet you did. I think it was brave of you to go out there. I wouldn't go out there! I wouldn't know what to do or where to start."

"It's not your fight," Shahid replied, and saw that he had confused her.

"I know it's not my fight."

"I didn't mean it like that. I meant that I wouldn't want you to see those things. To put yourself at risk. It's no place for a girl."

"Isn't that a bit sexist? You said there's lots of women out there."

Rosie started laughing. Shahid did not respond. He took a sip of the water and looked at the other couples in the restaurant.

"What was I going to do here in England?" he said. "Get a job in a corner shop? Drive a taxi? There were no opportunities for lads like me." Rosie nodded. Shahid often wondered what would happen to her, how she would remember him, after he was gone. "I'm glad I did it," he said. "I'm glad I did my duty as a Muslim."

"I'm glad, too."

They were silent for a while. The waitress came and spoke to Rosie. Did she want anything else? Dessert? Coffee? She didn't look at Shahid. When she had gone, he told Rosie that the waitress was racist, that she hadn't liked it that he was with a white girl.

"Don't be daft," Rosie said, laughing.

"That's silly. People aren't like that round here." Her eyes were soft in the candlelight. "Tell me more about Syria," she said. "Did you feel like you really changed things?"

"Changed things? Yeah. Definitely. But it will be slow. The fighting will go on for a long time."

"But how does fighting change anything? How does what ISIS or what these rebels are doing stop the bombings? I don't understand. Aren't they the ones *doing* the bombings?" Rosie forgot the name of the Syrian president and Shahid had to remind her. "That's right. Assad. If you want to stop his killings and his slaughter, then how does more fighting do that? An eye for an eye, yeah? If I attack you, you attack me."

"I would never hurt you," Shahid replied.

"I don't mean that. I mean the expression. The *idea*. They're starting to attack ISIS now, yeah? I've seen it on the news. British and American planes. Their bombers."

"Yeah, that's true. The Western governments fight them, but they can never win . . ."

"But that's what I'm saying to you! Nobody can win if you keep fighting. You get attacked in the street here in Brighton, you fight back, right, but you both end up in hospital."

"Not me," Shahid said proudly, and he could see the effect his words had on her. He remembered what she had written in her diary — *He makes me feel safe. I like the way he looks and smells. His arms turn me on. There's something a bit scary about him but I've always liked that, a bad temper. He's so gentle but he has these sudden outbursts and it's a bit frightening.* Shahid knew that he could say or do almost anything and this girl would go along with it.

"The attacks have been even worse under Obama than under Bush," he said. He liked teaching her. He liked the feeling of being able to educate those who were ignorant. "The Middle East — the whole region since the invasions, the illegal invasions and occupations of Muslim lands — has been unstable and corrupt. My Muslim brothers and sisters are at the mercy of politicians, Rosie. My government. *Your* government. The greed for oil and the slaughter of hundreds of thousands of innocent people was for the sake of what? For power and money? The only solution is to fight back. The only solution is to go back to a time when things were pure. When people like you and me lived side by side in harmony and the Americans, the West, had not reached this state of corruption. They are murderers, Rosie, much more than ISIS are murderers. Obama drones. He kills without looking. He sits in his White House armchair and presses a button and whole families die. They don't care about ordinary people. They never cared."

"Hey, let's change the subject," Rosie said. She forced a smile. "This is all getting a bit sad. We're meant to be having fun, no? I've had such a nice time. Food here's so good."

"Really good," said Shahid. He was worried that he had revealed too much, that she might become suspicious of him. "I'm sorry to be so political," he said. "It's just important to me. I don't like seeing ordinary people suffer."

"Me neither," Rosie replied quickly. "But I feel like you're so passionate about this stuff, that you believe in it so much, you should do politics or debates in public or something. That's the way to change things, isn't it? Not through wanting people to fight and get hurt. There are already so many wars, Shahid."

He allowed her to say that without contradicting her. Shahid wanted to explain to Rosie why it was necessary for people to die in order to create a better future, but he did not want to lose her. She would never understand.

They asked for the bill. Rosie went to the toilet while Shahid paid. When she came back, he saw that she had applied lip gloss. He could smell a fresh burst of perfume. She bent down and kissed him on the lips in front of everyone in the restaurant.

"I don't want to go home," she said. "I'm not tired. Let's go back to yours. Get a minicab."

# 43

"How are you, Alexander?"

"I am well. And how are you, Thomas?"

"Fine. Glad you could make it."

The smell of Minasian's cologne was one of the few consistent characteristics about him: his appearance had otherwise changed to such an extent that Kell felt as if he were sitting next to a new person.

"What is that?" Minasian asked, looking down into Kell's lap. Kell was holding the plastic bag from Goldsboro Books. He passed it across.

"I bought you something."

It was a blatant attempt to soften Minasian up, a gift that he hoped would help to establish a degree of rapport, even trust, between them. Kell knew that it was a risk, that Minasian would not necessarily respond to such a gesture; he might even think that Kell, by giving him a book of poetry, was playing on his sexuality.

"This is extraordinarily kind of you," he said, taking the book out of the bag, unwrapping it, and immediately turning to the copyright page. "A first edition."

"Bought it this afternoon." Kell had taken a slip road onto the A40, a triple-carriageway taking traffic west out of the city. "Have you seen the inscription?"

Minasian turned the page and erupted in laughter.

*"England is not an irrelevance,"* he said, quoting what Kell had written. "I like this very much. Very funny."

Kell glanced across and smiled. "We should talk about when we're next going to do this." He was following protocol. Always fix the next meeting with an agent as soon as you see them. You never know how long you'll have.

"Of course." Minasian knew the tradecraft. The Russian services applied exactly the same principles. "I will be free in Warsaw for two or three hours on the afternoon of July twenty-fourth. How easy will it be for you to travel?"

"I can be there," Kell replied.

Kell knew that Warsaw was dangerous. More SVR on the ground, more FSB. Minasian could be walking him into a trap. But he felt that he had no choice. If he was

going to run GAGARIN, this was the kind
of risk that he would have to take; he was
not always going to be able to call the shots.
They made an arrangement to meet at a
hotel in the center of the old city. Minasian
explained that Kell would be contacted in
his room by a third party who would give
him instructions on where and when they
should meet. Kell didn't like the sound of it
and said so.

"You seem to forget who's running who,
Alexander." He tried to keep an easy,
friendly tone in his voice. "That's not how
this works. You don't tell me where to meet.
I tell you."

He could feel Minasian bristling. The
fragile ego. The ceaseless will to power. His
mood could slip so quickly from affable
good cheer into hostile silence.

"Fine," he replied, staring out of the
window at the passing traffic. "You make
the arrangements."

Kell let him run out on the line and slip
the hook. It had been important to establish
authority over him, but he did not want Minasian to feel humiliated.

"Look," he said, maintaining an acquies-
cent tone. "It sounds fine. I know the Regina. Used to be the American embassy in
Warsaw, right?"

"That is correct."

"I'll get a room under the name Stephen Uniacke. But no third parties, okay? Nobody else comes between us."

"Agreed," Minasian replied.

"You have the BlackBerry I gave you?"

"Of course."

"So let's communicate on that. If you don't hear from me, we show ourselves in the lobby of the hotel between 2 P.M. and 3 P.M. local time. Same signal that we used today. If you're wearing a hat, I'm going home. We meet in my room ten minutes after eye contact."

A tiny nod of agreement. "Fine."

"Tell me about STRIPE," Kell said, trying to draw Minasian out of his sullen mood. "What have you found out?"

"First I wish to say something." Kell took an exit off the A40. He brought the Peugeot to a halt at a set of traffic lights. Minasian was rubbing his face as he said: "I want to establish some laws."

"Laws?"

"Rules."

The lights turned green. Kell moved forward. "I'm all ears," he said.

Minasian made a small adjustment to his hair.

"I have been doing a great deal of thinking." Another set of lights. Another column of traffic. "You were right about Andrei. He spoke to me. He told me that he knew about my relationship with Bernhard."

Kell was not at all surprised that Eremenko had taken his son-in-law to task, but was astonished that Minasian was telling him about it.

"He said to me in very straightforward words that I must give up that side of my life, my behavior with men, that I must concentrate on Svetlana. I must make the marriage work. I am determined to do this."

"Okay." Kell did not want to show his hand before he had heard everything that Minasian intended to say. He could not be sure if the Russian was being sincere or simply embarking on another elaborate manipulation.

"We have shaken hands on this and made a deal," he said. "We will have a child, if the IVF can work, and I continue to have my career with the SVR. In three years' time, Andrei has suggested that I leave the Service and take over the bulk of his business interests."

"And what does this have to do with you and me?"

"It is very simple." Minasian put the Larkin back inside the wrapping paper and placed the bag at his feet. "I will not survive if we continue in our relationship. I will be caught and I will be prosecuted. In all probability I will lose my life. I am asking you for clemency."

The traffic was moving steadily forward, the Peugeot boxed in. Kell was looking for a turning into a suburban cul-de-sac where he planned to park. What Minasian had said was exceptional, in his experience, and completely outrageous.

"Clemency! We're only just getting started."

"Not so."

Minasian had plainly run through every possible permutation of the conversation and now reached into the hip pocket of his jeans, pulling out what looked like a Duracell battery that he waved in Kell's eyeline. Kell made the turn into the quiet suburban street and pulled up in the shade of a chestnut tree. He switched off the engine.

"What's that?" he asked, though he knew the answer to his own question.

"A flash drive. Containing information. A lot of information." Minasian unscrewed the copper section of the battery and showed that it could be separated from the lower half, revealing a hidden USB connector. "The names of three inspectors on the

Iranian nuclear deal whose lives are in danger. Two of them resident in London, one in New York City. And detailed information on STRIPE."

Kell took the two sections of the flash drive and screwed them back together.

"And the identity of your Syrian agent in London?"

Minasian was aghast. "I cannot give you that, Thomas. I would sooner destroy my own career than reveal the identity of a source. I hope that you would feel the same way about me."

Kell had no choice but to say: "Of course, Alexander." He held up the battery. "Is he the guy telling you about STRIPE?"

Minasian looked away. "I cannot comment on that. It does not matter where the information came from. All I can tell you is that you must act on it quickly. Perhaps even in the next three days."

Kell felt a numb sense of dread.

"An attack is imminent? Where?"

"I do not know. *We* do not know. I am trying to discover this. I do not want to see innocent people die." Minasian turned away so that Kell could not see the look on his face. "I have taken a very great risk bringing it to you," he added despondently. "Only

388

a few people in my Service know about this threat."

"I see."

Minasian began to list the principal information contained on the flash drive as a series of verbal bullet points. "The name on the individual's passport. The number of this passport." With each detail, he struck the side of his right hand into the opposite palm. "The date of issue. The time and date of arrival of his flight from Cairo to Heathrow, eight weeks ago. It is all on there."

"I need more than that," Kell told him. "You said the threat could come at any moment. If we're too late —"

Minasian interrupted him.

"With this passport we believe he has opened a bank account at a branch of Santander in Brighton."

"Brighton?"

"Rented a one-bedroom apartment. Taken a job working as a night porter at a supermarket. With CCTV from the airport, and his place of work, you can surely make an arrest within twenty-four hours."

Kell experienced a countersurge of intense relief, like waking in the dead of night from a dream of sickness and death. He was going to stop a terrorist attack. He was going to be proved right. He tried not to give any indication of his gratitude, but clutched the flash drive tightly in his fingers as if it were a reward for every nerve and sinew he had strained in pursuit of his quarry.

"That sounds hopeful," he said.

It was oppressively hot. Kell turned the key in the ignition a single click and lowered all four of the electric windows. Minasian reacted to the cooling breeze that swept into the car, tilting back his head and stretching his neck.

"What I want in return," he said, "is to be left alone. I want our relationship to end."

"Then why did you agree to Warsaw?"

Minasian's reply was instant; he had anticipated the question before Kell had even framed it. "Because I knew that you would want to organize a second meeting. I knew that it would be the first order of business between us. I considered Warsaw suitable because I did not know if you would agree to my offer."

"I do not agree to your offer," Kell replied, adopting the same firm tone of voice with which he had rejected Minasian's idea of introducing a third party. "I will still want to meet you in Poland."

Minasian looked beaten. "Then it will be the last time," he said. He touched the stubble on his face and Kell saw that he was extraordinarily tired. "I will not be your agent. I will not be your creature. For my own peace of mind, for my own security and personal pride, I cannot work for the British government."

"And yet you've just given me a flash drive that you say —"

"Yes!" Minasian's face was a picture of frustration. "To save lives! To give you something that is of no cost to my country. You will stop this man. I have given you priceless information. If I were found to have done this, I would be charged with treason against the state. And what have you done for me in return? You have forced me into a position in which I am obliged to choose between my career and my marriage, my *survival.*"

It was a completely convincing display of emotional distress, so much so that Kell found himself sympathizing with Minasian's dilemma.

"You're being very melodramatic, Alexander," he said. "I haven't given you that choice at all. Things aren't nearly as bad as you're making out."

Minasian did not reply.

"Let me ask you something." Kell leaned an elbow out of the open window and turned in his seat. "Do you love Svetlana?"

"Excuse me?"

"Do you love your wife?"

"Of course."

"And did you love Bernhard?"

A lowering of the head, a melancholy glance out the window. "I thought that I did."

"Meaning?"

"Meaning that he provided me with things that my wife was not able to provide. I do not wish to discuss it with you. It is personal. This has nothing to do with our work."

"But what *does* she provide you with?" Kell needed to show Minasian why it would be impossible to continue in the life that he was choosing. "Money? Is that it? Is that why you married her? So you could afford to buy the right clothes, wear the right wristwatch, feel that you've climbed your way out of the gutter?"

The Russian flicked him a look of distilled anger. "I did not come from the gutter. How dare you say this. You know nothing about my childhood. You know nothing about my family."

"I know about your brother." Minasian's face was bloodless with surprise. "I know that he was killed in a war that was prosecuted by a man you keep defending, a government whose lies and greed are destroying your country."

Minasian shook his head. "So we are on this subject again. People are so keen to see duplicity in others, to see cruelty and violence in their supposed enemies. But they cannot see it in themselves."

Kell ignored this and pressed on. "Why don't you come and live here? Work for us for a while, start a new life? We'll keep you safe, the British government will protect you. SIS can give you a new identity. You can leave Svetlana, make a new start in London." Kell did not believe for one moment that Minasian would consider the offer, or even take it seriously, but he wanted him to hear it, because it threw his hypocrisy and self-interest into relief. "We don't make judgments about a person's sexuality. We don't condemn a man for working against a gangster regime. We think of men like you as heroes. You could be true to yourself. You could live an authentic life. You could help to destabilize the regime, to usher in a new era of openness and prosperity for Russia. Otherwise you're going to live out the rest of your days as — what word did you use? — a *creature* of the Kremlin, a creature of Andrei Eremenko."

Minasian was silent. He looked at the flash

drive in Kell's hand as though he regretted handing it over. Kell anticipated that he would try to turn the tables on him, and so it proved.

"You think that you have lived an authentic life, Thomas Kell?"

Kell responded quickly.

"I'm not lying to anybody," he said. "I'm not trapped in a sham marriage. I'm free to live the way I want to live, to say the things I want to say. I don't have a father-in-law with a briefcase of money in one hand and a gun in the other. I don't work for a Service that turns its back on its own people."

This last statement was false and Minasian knew it.

"Really?" he said, seizing his opportunity. "Your Service has always treated you with the respect and integrity that your work and your conduct deserved? That is not what I heard about you, Thomas. That is not what I heard about Witness X."

For the second time in their brief acquaintance, Kell wondered where the hell Minasian was getting his information. How did he know that he had been turfed out of SIS on false accusations of torture and given the code name Witness X? Had Kleckner told them?

"Whatever you think you know about Witness X, you know nothing," he said. "It was political pressure. I'm back in the fold."

"*Are* you?"

The question was laced with suspicion. Had Minasian intuited that Kell was running him behind Amelia's back?

"I don't understand," Kell replied, playing dumb.

"Never mind." Minasian allowed the moment to linger. "You know what I am talking about."

"Not sure I do," Kell replied, trying his best to look confused by what Minasian was saying. "My offer to you was a sincere one. If you want to start again, if you want to escape from the trap in which you have found yourself, we are here to help you."

"How *kind.*" Minasian summoned as much contempt as he could find and packed it into his voice. "You blackmail me, you set this trap and throw me into it, then you offer to get me out. How very noble. How very British."

"Just goes to show that England is not an irrelevance." Kell hoped that some bone-dry humor would rescue the conversation and he was pleased to see Minasian acknowledge it with a weary shake of the head.

"So you want me to give it all up and start again? That was your purpose all along?"

Minasian reached down to the bag at his feet. "Like Gordievsky, like so many others. Start a new life in quiet suburban England, the land of *The Whitsun Weddings*."

"I think it's your best bet." Kell was distracted by an elderly woman who had emerged from a house in the cul-de-sac. She was carrying a dead potted plant that she threw into a dustbin. "Nobody can go through their entire life living a lie," he said. "Deceit catches up with you. There is a reckoning."

"Do *you* find that?" Again Minasian tried to switch the direction of the conversation. "Do *you* find that lying is a sickness? Perhaps in a long career, a spy's constant exposure to deception leaves him feeling . . ." — Minasian searched for the correct term — "worn out."

"I don't think spying is a particularly healthy way of making a living, if that's what you're trying to say." Minasian seemed pleased by this response. The outlines of a vulpine smile cracked within his beard. Kell had not intended to make such a candid reply, but he enjoyed jousting with Minasian. "I don't think that I will do it forever," he said.

"Really?"

"Sure. But right now I'd rather be doing

this job than any other. And I'd rather be working for my Service than for yours."

Minasian looked disappointed. "We all feel that way about our own country, of course," he said. A car drove past them, leaving the cul-de-sac and heading out toward the main road. "I wonder if you have used spying as many people in our business tend to. As a replacement for the family. As a substitute structure for life."

"What are you talking about?"

"Your own marriage was unhappy. You had few friends from school or university. Your mother died when you were relatively young."

Kell again experienced the unsettling sense that Minasian knew far more about him than was normal. He said: "Not sure about your sources, Alexander. Some of Ryan Kleckner's information was faulty," but he was unsettled to see that the Russian did not react to the mention of Kleckner's name.

"Like me," Minasian continued, his knee knocking the gear stick, "you have not had any children. Like me, you suffered with an unsatisfactory marriage. You went to one of your English boarding schools, which are known to produce broken characters ideal for the life in MI6. A young man cannot grow up in an environment without girls, his parents and siblings far away, living for eight or nine months of the year in an institution that oppresses his spirit with rules and traditions . . ."

Kell knew what Minasian was trying to do and felt the discomfort of being picked apart.

"What is this?" he said. "Freud for beginners?"

"I do not mean to probe too deeply, Thomas. We all have our reasons for what we have done. I believe that you replaced one institution, one false and unhealthy structure, with another: the institution of secrecy and deception. I grew up in a country and a system that was hopeless and bankrupt, humiliated by the West, cornered and betrayed. So I joined the secret world for very different reasons to yours. I joined in order to make a difference."

"And you think I didn't?"

"I think you have no understanding of the Russian temperament. I think you imagine that we are all monsters, determined to taunt and punish the West, to make war, to make trouble, because we are suffering from a kind of collective psychosis."

"Can you blame us?" Kell replied.

"I *lived* through the humiliation." Minasian was as angry as Kell had ever seen him. "I lived through years of watching the West try to grind us into the dust. I joined the Service in order to improve the standing of my country. I wanted to help restore to Russia both a sense of national pride and a correct evaluation of my country's strength in international affairs."

"Well, good for you," Kell replied, amazed that Minasian expected him to swallow his self-delusion. "Most of your colleagues were just in it for the cash. Ex-KGB, in league with organized crime, laundering money offshore, money that belonged to the Russian people, then using it to buy up state assets. I'm sure you're aware of what happened. Just as I'm sure that you and your closest colleagues had nothing to do with it."

Minasian was so incensed by what Kell had said that, for a moment, it looked as if he were going to get out of the car. Kell tried to calm him down.

"Look, I'm only winding you up," he said. "A few bad apples in the FSB doesn't mean you're all contaminated." Kell was aware that they were wasting time. Minasian needed to get back to Claridge's. "All I was trying to say is that if you can imagine a life without five-star hotels, without designer clothes, without lunch at the Wolseley every time you come to London, we can make anything happen for you. We can set you free. It's probably too late to save Russia, but it's not too late to save yourself. Believe me, Alexander, a clear conscience and a restored sense of self-esteem is worth a great deal more than a life of lies lived in luxury. But if you want to stay in the Service, if you want to have a kid with Svetlana, if you want to work for your father-in-law in four or five years' time, get hold of his mining interests, have his ice hockey stadium in Helsinki transferred into your name, then I can't let you go. You're too valuable to us. Right now, I own you."

It was the wrong thing to say, the one lazy slip of Kell's tongue. He had spoken against his own best interests and provoked Minasian, feeding the rage inside him. Kell thought back to the notes he had scribbled in the wake of the dinner with Riedle, advice that he had now ignored. *Power and control central to M's personality. Must retain a position of dominance.* Yet he had not wanted to pander to Minasian's self-importance, to be distracted by his moods and volatility. He thought of him as a fraud and a bully; surely there was only one way to treat such people, and that was with a show of strength.

"You do not own me," Minasian replied, predictably enough.

"Of course not. But I demand results from you. If the product is good" — Kell took out the flash drive and waved it in the air — "and you help to save lives, we can talk about a deal further down the road."

"The product is good. The product *will* save lives. But it is the last thing I will give you. In Warsaw, we say good-bye."

What did Minasian have up his sleeve that he could afford to call Kell's bluff with such audacity? Kell took out a packet of Winston Lights and offered one to the Russian. Minasian shook his head, watching Kell carefully as he lit the cigarette.

"Let me ask you one thing," he said. "Have you ever recruited someone who can bring you information like this?"

"Frequently," Kell replied, blowing a column of smoke across the passenger seat.

"I don't believe you."

"Why is it so important for you to be the hero, Alexander?"

"Why is it so important for *you*?"

Kell smoked in silence, deciding on his reply. "To me belongeth vengeance," he said eventually. "And recompense."

Minasian looked baffled. "Excuse me?"

"You don't know your Bible?"

"I don't know *your* Bible."

"Vengeance is mine," Kell explained. "And payback."

Minasian frowned. "That is what this is for you? Revenge for the death of your girlfriend?" He leaned toward Kell, grabbing his arm at the upper part of the bicep. "I have told you that I had nothing to do with this. I have told you that I thought it was a terrible thing to do, beneath our Service."

"I want revenge," Kell repeated, and it was suddenly very clear to him how to proceed. He knew how to get what he wanted, how to set both of them free. "Let's make a deal," he said, removing Minasian's hand. "I want the names of the men who ordered Rachel's murder. I want to meet them in Warsaw. You bring them to me, you bring me their heads, you can go. Put me in a room with them and it will be the last thing I ask of you. After that, you can have your clemency, Alexander. After that, we say good-bye."

# 44

Rosie had been the first woman to provoke feelings in Shahid since his relationship with Vicky three years earlier. That part of himself — his ability to desire and to be desired — had been buried by Vicky's betrayal. It was as though Rosie had cleared away the earth from his heart and freed him to love again. Shahid had been unable to control his attraction toward her. He had felt both great shame and great happiness inside the mystery of this obsession.

After the restaurant they had gone back to his room in Rottingdean. Rosie had given herself to him. Shahid had been unable to resist. He had been inside her. He had drowned in her. Afterward, lying side by side in his narrow bed, she had told him that she loved him. Shahid had started to cry, his body shaking as Rosie held him in her arms.

"It's okay, it's okay," she whispered.

"What's the matter? Why are you crying?"

The moment was so overwhelming that it had made Shahid question everything. For the next few hours, with Rosie asleep beside him, and the morning sun slowly bringing light to his bedroom, he had sat with the shaming realization that he had allowed his love for Rosie to corrupt his faith. Satan had come into his heart in the form of lust and had polluted the purity of his mission. That lust was now sated, but he knew that it would return. God would continue to test him.

So Shahid prayed as the girl slept beside him. He asked God to show Rosie that she could accept Allah into her heart and become a Muslim. Only then could he marry her. Only then would he be able to lie with her again, without bringing shame and dishonor upon himself.

Yet a marriage between Shahid Khan and Rosie Maguire was surely not the will of Allah. God's will had already been made clear to Shahid by Jalal. It was the destiny of Shahid Khan to avenge the Prophet. A woman could not change that, especially a woman who was infidel. Shahid knew that his act of martyrdom would take him from Rosie, but that he would be rewarded in paradise with pleasures far greater than those he had known on this earth.

In that moment, pulling back the curtains so that the sunlight poured into the bedroom, Shahid realized what was obvious. His prayer had been answered. Rosie had been given to him by God to use for his pleasure. The love he felt for her was incomparable to the radiance of Islam that shone through him. She was simply a vessel through which God had shown him the strength of His love.

Understanding this, Shahid woke Rosie and told her that it was time for her to leave.

"What, now?" she said, still half asleep. The pillow had left a crease in her face and the makeup around her eyes was smudged.

"Now," he said.

"But you don't have work today."

"Going to the gym. You have to go."

He explained that she could get a bus back into Brighton from the stop at the end of the Close. Rosie sat up in bed, confused and tired. Shahid passed her the clothes that she had left on the floor. Then he went into the bathroom to wash himself.

# 45

Kell dropped Minasian outside Northolt underground station and watched him vanish into the late afternoon crowds. It was half past five. With decent traffic he would be home before six to run the contents of the flash drive through a laptop.

But he had made a simple, infuriating oversight. With his iPhone at the repair shop, Kell had no means of communicating with Amelia. He had made no record of her mobile or e-mail address, nor had he memorized the contact details of any mutual friends or colleagues who could put them in touch. It was an embarrassing mistake of the sort that would not have occurred had he been working in a larger team.

The shop was due to close at seven. Kell diverted south toward Earl's Court and was there in forty-five minutes. He collected the phone and drove back through rush-hour traffic to Sinclair Road, wondering if he should have taken the flash drive directly to Vauxhall Cross. But Kell could not be sure of its contents. He had to check the product for himself before exposing it to Amelia. If the SVR had implanted the flash drive with second-rate intelligence or — worse — some kind of malware or virus, he would look like a fool.

As soon as he was home, Kell unplugged the wi-fi in his flat and took out an old Vaio laptop that had been gathering dust in a cupboard. It started up first time. Kell disabled the laptop's Internet access, then unscrewed the flash drive and inserted the USB connector into the port. A flash drive icon immediately appeared on the desktop. He clicked on it and waited for the screen to populate.

Nothing happened.

Kell clicked on the icon a second time, with the same result. The flash drive failed to open. He wondered if it was a fault with the laptop and searched his desk for another device that he could use to test it. He picked up a portable hard drive containing backups of his photographs, as well as information relating to his finances and divorce. He inserted this into the Vaio. A new icon appeared on the screen. When Kell clicked on it, the contents of the hard drive opened up.

It was not a fault with his computer. There was a fault with Minasian's device.

Kell swore at the screen. He texted Mowbray to ask if he was free to come over. Perhaps he would know a technical trick, a way of opening it up and getting the information. But Harold did not respond. Kell tried phoning him, three times, but each time the call went to voice mail.

Kell hated this feeling. To be at the mercy of technology, of a piece of impregnable kit that refused to give up its secrets. In his long career he had known everything from the floppy disk to the fax machine, the short-burst radio to satellite phones the size of microwave ovens. In the presence of technology of any kind, Kell possessed what had once been described by a colleague as "suboptimal karma": photocopiers jammed if he went near them; computers crashed; phones dropped their signal. It was happening again.

He took out the BlackBerry. He was sure that there was a technical fault with the flash drive and that Minasian was not deliberately stalling. Finding his number, he tapped out a message for encryption and sent it.

The battery does not work. It needs to be replaced ASAP.

Kell did not know how long it would be before Minasian replied. He was certain that the Russian did not carry the BlackBerry around with him at all times; he could not even be sure that he had access to it at Claridge's. If Minasian was engaged on other SVR business, or having dinner with Svetlana in central London, it could be many hours before he replied — time in which STRIPE could be making the final preparations for an attack.

It was not yet eight o'clock. Kell decided that if Minasian had not responded by nine, he would breach all protocol and cold-call the Eremenko suite at Claridge's from a public telephone box. He had no other choice.

Ten minutes later he was preparing some food in the kitchen when the BlackBerry chimed.

Very embarrassed to hear this. I apologize. It was not my intention. I can replace it with a new one tomorrow.

Kell sent back a terse reply.

Tomorrow is too late. You know that. I need it now.

Minasian's response was immediate.

Not possible. I cannot get the battery from my office until the morning. Do not worry.

Kell could understand Minasian's position. The intelligence had most likely come from a file that was kept under lock and key by the SVR. Minasian could not risk a late-night visit to the embassy without raising suspicion. Nevertheless, he pushed for answers.

Anything is possible. Tomorrow could be too late. You know that. I need it now.

Still Minasian refused to act.

Tomorrow will not be too late. Trust me.

It was the last thing Kell was prepared to do. Yet he had no choice. He knew that Svetlana was scheduled to meet her doctor at the fertility clinic at nine o'clock the next day.

You have an appointment, yes?

There was a two-minute delay before Minasian replied.

Yes. At nine.

Kell was taking a risk, but he felt squeezed

by time. The plan was lazy and he was certain that Minasian would not go for it. It was bad tradecraft. The Russian would be passing sensitive information to a third party over which neither side had operational control. Nevertheless, he tapped out his reply.

Leave it for collection. Our friend who wrote the poem will pick it up.

Kell waited. Pasta was boiling on the stove. He put a metal spoon into the water and stirred it, freeing a clump of spaghetti that had stuck to the base. He opened a bottle of wine and poured himself a glass, staring at the BlackBerry, willing Minasian to understand what he was being asked to do.

The screen lit up.

The envelope will be there for collection from 9 A.M. Have a good evening.

## 46

Kell was awake at first light. To kill time, he went to the gym as it was opening and swam his habitual forty lengths of the pool. Mowbray had come round the night before in an attempt to open the flash drive, but after working on it from eleven until after midnight, had declared it "a cheap piece of shit which doesn't work" and driven the hire car home.

Kell took the Tube as far as Marble Arch, then walked the remaining mile to Upper Wimpole Street. He was close enough to the entrance of the clinic to see Minasian and Svetlana pull up in the Eremenko limousine at 8:55 A.M. The chauffeur stepped out and opened the back door on the street side. As Minasian walked beside his wife, Kell could see very clearly that he was carrying a brown manila envelope in his left hand. The chauffeur did not accompany the couple inside. Instead he returned to the limousine, pulled closer to the curb, then switched off the engine and put on the hazard lights.

Kell assumed that Svetlana would be the first appointment of the day and therefore that the doctor would see her almost immediately. He waited fifteen minutes before climbing the steps to the clinic and pressing the buzzer for the ground floor. Kell could see the Eremenko limousine reflected in a brass plaque on the side of the building.

He was buzzed inside. Kell pushed the door and found himself inside a residential lobby that had been converted for office use. There was a door to his right with a sign saying: RECEPTION, three others ahead of him stretching along a narrow corridor, each with the name of a doctor printed on a square plastic panel. Kell was clicked into the waiting room.

The smell hit him first. The disinfected potpourri of a dozen identical clinics visited with Claire in years gone by. The same stark, vacuumed chill in the waiting room, the same pale yellow paintwork. On the wall behind the reception desk, photographs of mothers and babies, of fathers cradling infants in their arms. Vases of fake fresh flowers, plastic cups beside a plastic water cooler, and always a lone woman in the corner of the room, distractedly flicking through the pages of a magazine. Kell avoided her nervous, shuffling eye contact and walked toward the receptionist. He could not stop thinking of Claire, of the agony and the frustration and the boundless expense of her infertility, and wanted more than anything to be out of the clinic as quickly as possible.

"Can I help you, sir?"

The receptionist had dyed blond hair and a forced, insincere smile inadequate to the emotional responsibilities of her job.

"My name is Mr. Larkin. I'm here to pick up a package."

Kell could see the manila envelope beside a black keyboard behind the counter.

"We were expecting you. Mr. Eremenko left it for you just a moment ago." She passed the envelope to Kell and gave an exhausted sigh. "He's still here. Would you like to wait for him?"

"No, thank you," Kell replied. He was already turning to leave. "Just tell him that I've picked it up."

# 47

Kell went out into the lobby, closed the door behind him, and walked up the staircase to a landing on the first floor of the building. He looked at the envelope. Minasian had written the name MR. P. LARKIN in block capitals on the front, with the words FOR PERSONAL COLLECTION ONLY in the top left-hand corner.

Kell opened the envelope. There was no flash drive inside, just a single piece of paper covered in neat, almost childish handwriting.

The man you are looking for is operating under the name Shahid Khan. He was born in Leeds in 1992 under a different identity — Azhar Ahmed Iqbal. He was presumed to have died in 2014 while fighting against the Assad regime in Syria. His parents moved to the United Kingdom in 1983. His mother died when he was sixteen years old. To the best knowledge that we have, his father continues to reside in Leeds.

Shahid Khan's passport was supplied to him due to a compromised official at the British Passport Office named James (Jim) Martinelli. The passport (number 653781818) was obtained by an associate of a former senior Iraqi intelligence officer, Jalal al-Hamd, now prominent within ISIL, via contacts with the Albanian mafia. Khan has been tasked by Jalal with carrying out a mass execution in the United Kingdom with the purpose of spreading fear and panic in the population and further escalating the confrontation between ISIS and the Western powers.

Khan returned to the United Kingdom on 16 May. He met with a Syrian associate of Jalal al-Hamd during this period who is the source of my information. We know that Khan took work as a night shelf-stacker at a twenty-four-hour Asda supermarket in Brighton Marina. He lodges in a room in the town of Rottingdean at 45 Meadow Close. The house is registered to a Mrs. Katherine Arden.

More information was obtainable in the flash drive. I do not know why it did not work. I did not intend to trick you or to make a mistake of this kind. We will meet again in thirteen days. As you know I am telling you this because there is strong indication that Khan will soon obtain a weapon and has closed his relationship with Jalal. In our own context, we would assume that this indicates his intention to act in the very near future. I wish you luck.

## 48

Kell dialed Amelia's private number.

"Tom. What is it?"

"Where are you?"

"Does it matter?"

If he had not been so determined that Vauxhall Cross should take immediate action on Khan, Kell might have paid closer attention to the curt, dismissive tone in Amelia's voice.

"I've heard back from our Russian friend."

There was a significant pause. "I see," she said.

"We have a serious problem."

"We do, do we?"

Kell felt a scratch of irritation, that old frustrated feeling of being held at arm's length.

"The boy from Leeds," he said, trusting that what he was telling Amelia would shake her out of her complacency. "I have a name. I have an address."

"I thought we agreed that you weren't going to continue with that relationship?"

"We never agreed that." Kell was amazed that he was being pulled into a conversation about trust when the threat from Khan was clear and present. He walked out of the clinic, passed the Eremenko Mercedes, and headed south along Upper Wimpole Street. "Anyway, does it matter?"

Amelia ignored the question.

"What do we know about this young man?" she asked.

Kell explained that Minasian's intelligence indicated an imminent attack, almost certainly in an area of high population density in or around Brighton.

*"Brighton?"*

"Brighton," he confirmed.

"Tom, come on. At no point have we ever had a significant threat directed at a small coastal town in England. Oxford Street, yes. Waterloo, yes. Manchester Piccadilly, perhaps. These people are about cities, they're about generating fear. Hitting at the heart of government. You know this. The greater the carnage, the greater the publicity. Brighton is simply not going to be on their radar."

"Are you prepared to take that risk?" Kell had come to a halt on the corner of Wigmore Street, lighting a cigarette as he spoke.

"You're prepared to have this on your record? A maniac starts shooting people in the Brighton Pavilion, takes out two or three hundred summer tourists on the pier, gets into the aquarium and kills scores of young children with their families, you'll live with that?"

There was a long silence. Kell could not make sense of Amelia's refusal even to countenance the possibility that Minasian was telling him the truth. Nor could he understand her lack of faith in his judgment. He had surely earned the right to be heard, to be treated with greater respect. It could only be the case that she knew something about GAGARIN, something about Khan or Brighton, that trumped his own intelligence, rendering it obsolete.

"All right," she said, as though she had been made aware of the foolishness of her position and had resolved to correct it. "I'll send someone to meet you. Where are you?"

Kell drew deeply on the cigarette.

"Amelia, I don't have time for a fucking meeting. I don't want some underling from the Office to finish his cup of tea, wander down to the Tube, get stuck in a tunnel, turn up to see me fifteen minutes late, listen to what I have to tell him, then wander back to work after stopping for lunch. He'll spend the afternoon filing a report that someone several rungs below you may, or may not, find time to read before the end of the summer. I am telling you that this intelligence is real. This threat is real. You need to act immediately."

It was always a mistake to try to pressure Amelia Levene, to adopt aggressive tactics or to lose control of one's equilibrium. Very slowly and very calmly she picked at the loosest thread of Kell's argument and began to pull.

"So you're telling me that anyone I send to listen to what you have to say would be so unmoved by the product that they would delay returning to the Office, stop for a sandwich, and write such a dreary CX on their return that it would never cross my desk?"

Kell flew at her. "For Christ's sake, I'm trying to impress upon you that time is a factor."

"And I understand that. And I can arrange for you to sit down with Jimmy Marquand within the hour. All it takes is a phone call."

"Jimmy?"

Marquand was an old colleague of Kell's, one of the high priests at SIS, a smooth career spook with fading hopes of replacing Amelia as "C." The last Kell had heard, he had been farmed out to Washington.

"Yes. Jimmy. Will he do?"

The question was deliberately snide, implying that Kell was demanding special treatment. Realizing that Marquand was his only hope of eliciting official help, Kell agreed.

"Fine," he said. "Tell him to meet me at Oxford Circus Tube. Ticket gates."

"Time?" Amelia asked.

Kell glanced at his watch. "As soon as he can get there."

"Eleven," she said.

# 49

Marquand was twenty minutes late.

Kell had been pacing up and down inside the station for almost half an hour. He eventually caught sight of Marquand at the top of the Victoria Line escalators. He was easily spotted. At fifty-two, Marquand boasted a lustrous blow-dried mop of hair that had earned him the nickname "Melvyn" from colleagues at SIS. He was looking tanned and fit and wearing a well-cut suit. The briefcase that usually accompanied him on official business was nowhere to be seen. Two dreadlocked, black-clad teenagers with piercings in most available orifices appeared to obscure Marquand's view of Kell until he had almost reached the ticket gates. When he looked up and spotted him, he nodded in a way that made Kell suspect that he had been briefed to be obstructive.

"Tom."

There was very little warmth in the greeting, only a sense of wariness, like meeting an old friend who has let you down too many times.

"How are you, Jimmy? Long time no see."

"Long time. Long time."

They shook hands and turned toward the exit, emerging into thick crowds on the corner of Regent Street. Kell remembered meeting Marquand in the spring of Amelia's disappearance and felt that something significant had changed in his manner in the intervening period. Three years earlier, Marquand had been nervous and agitated in Kell's presence, very much the junior man. He had all but begged Kell to come out of enforced retirement and to search for Amelia. On this occasion, however, he seemed altogether more poised and self-possessed, giving the impression that their meeting was an interruption in his day that he could have done without.

"I heard you were working in Washington."

Marquand pursed his mouth and said: "Yes, that's correct," as though Kell — a private citizen — had no right to be talking about SIS postings overseas.

"How did that work out for you?"

"Perfectly well, thank you. Came back in April."

In the space of a few minutes, Kell had

moved from a feeling of gentle optimism to one of intense irritation at Marquand's manner. Any respect or loyalty he might once have felt for Kell appeared to have leached out of him. His hauteur was all the more galling when Kell considered the sorry secret at the heart of Marquand's career — that in fifteen years he had failed to make a single truly significant recruitment. Why, then, was he the one acting like he was doing Kell a favor?

"Amelia said you had something you wanted to show us."

They were outside Hamleys, children loitering on the pavement, shoppers laden with heavy bags weaving through the crowds. Kell didn't need anybody to show an interest in his private life or to inquire after his state of mind, but he felt it was telling that Marquand had avoided the subject altogether. They had not seen one another in over two years. Marquand had been heavily involved in the operation to free Amelia's kidnapped son. For him to move straight to business indicated either that he was aware of the time pressure surrounding Khan or, more likely, regarded Kell as yesterday's man.

"I do," he said. Kell turned off Regent Street and led Marquand down a narrow pedestrianized passage. He took Minasian's letter from his jacket pocket, unfolded it, and passed it to him. "Take a look at this."

Marquand produced a pair of half-moon spectacles and put them on. "Now what do we have here?" he said. He began to read the letter, peering down at the contents like a man inspecting a bill for surcharges at the end of an expensive meal.

"It came from a Russian —"

"I heard." Marquand raised his hand to indicate that he did not wish to be interrupted. A man in torn jeans and a stained T-shirt walked past, offering Kell a copy of the *Big Issue.* Kell shook his head. Marquand appeared to be coming to the end of the letter. To his horror, Kell saw the ghost of a smile at the edge of his lips, as if Marquand was struggling to contain a fit of giggles.

*"Brighton?"* he said, with almost exactly the same measure of contempt as Amelia.

"That's what it says."

"Who's the source?"

"As I was saying, he's a Russian SVR —"

"Yes, yes, we know about him." Marquand's interruption was instant. "I mean, where is he getting his information?"

Kell understood immediately that Marquand was prepared to downgrade the intel-

426

ligence by doubting its veracity.

"I believe it's coming from a Syrian official in London, but I have no proof of that."

"So you don't know the chain of command?"

Marquand corrected his hair in a gust of wind.

"Chain of command?" Kell was bewildered that Marquand had used such a phrase.

"I mean the source, the transfer of information. How is a Russian SVR officer getting this kind of product? Is it coming out of a cell, is there somebody on the Syrian side who's reporting to Moscow?"

"Does it *matter*?" Kell replied.

"Of course it matters. We need to know that it's bona fide."

A young arm-in-arm couple walked past them, gazing into one another's eyes. Kell waited until they were out of earshot before responding.

"Jimmy, it's real. Now here's what I need you to do —"

Marquand shook his head and held the letter up in front of Kell, letting it flap in the wind.

"Come on now. You can't expect us to act on something like this without deeper investigation."

Kell took the letter, afraid that Marquand would allow it to blow away down the street. Then he looked at Minasian's neat, level handwriting, the careful spacings and schoolboy ink, and suddenly realized what Marquand had seen. A piece of adolescent fantasy, an SVR practical joke, hatched in Moscow and played on a man so desperate to prove his worth that he had fallen for it, hook, line, and sinker. In the same moment, Kell saw himself as others must have seen him: as a pedigree spy who had tripped on the career ladder and failed to stay the course. As an increasingly disheveled divorcé, drinking and smoking too much, worn out and frayed around the edges. Yesterday's man.

"I believe it's actionable," he said.

"Can you leave it with me?" The tone of Marquand's question betrayed his absolute commitment to do nothing of any consequence with the information that Kell had given him.

"You can take a copy," he replied.

"And how do you suggest I do that?" Marquand looked down the street, as if to indicate that photocopiers were not commonly found on pavements in that area of London.

"How about using your phone?" Kell suggested, his patience about to snap. He was tired of trying to persuade SIS that Minasian's product was valid, tired of trying to spur Amelia and her useful idiots into action. Dealing with them was like rattling the handle on a locked door and somehow expecting it to open. He was wasting his time.

"Tell you what," said Marquand, pinching the letter between his thumb and forefinger as Kell held it in his hand. "Why don't you make *us* a copy and file it through the usual channels?"

"The usual channels," Kell repeated.

"That is correct."

Marquand indicated that he was going to leave. There had been no trace of the years they had spent together as colleagues, no acknowledgment of the awkwardness of the situation, nor of Marquand's role in exacerbating it. Kell might just as well have been a stranger who had accosted him on the street.

"Always good to see you, Tom."

Marquand shook Kell's hand, smiled a patronizing smile, then turned and walked away. Doubtless he would return to Vauxhall Cross with reports of their erstwhile colleague's sorry and hilarious demise. Kell looked at Marquand's bouffant hair, at his neat tailored suit and polished City brogues, and could not prevent himself from a petty and yet liberating retort.

"Hey, Jimmy."

Marquand was halfway down the passage, about to join the flow of pedestrians heading north along Regent Street.

"Yes?" he said, turning around.

"Go fuck yourself."

# 50

Kell knew what he had to do. The plan came to him with absolute clarity.

He found a public phone box. He took out his phone, found the number for Falcon Security, and asked to be put through to Anthony White.

"May I ask who's calling, please?"

"Thomas Kell."

White was ex-SAS, the CEO of a private security firm that had made a fortune from more than a decade of conflict in Iraq, Syria, and Afghanistan. Amelia had employed him on the operation to rescue her kidnapped son in France. Kell had subsequently done a small amount of private-sector work for Falcon, after which White had offered him a permanent position. Kell had turned the job down.

The interior of the phone box was plastered with cards advertising the services of prostitutes. Kell looked down and waited for the receptionist to connect the call, the floor wet with water that had spilled from a crushed bottle of Evian. He heard the long, sustained sound of a phone ringing in an international location, then the crackle of White picking up.

"White."

"Anthony? It's Tom Kell."

"Tom! How are you? Good to hear your voice."

"I need a favor."

"Of course. What can I do for you?"

White was in his early forties, a six-foot Old Etonian whose charm, good looks, and faultless manners had proved as indispensable in the business world as his innate ruthlessness and capacity for violence. Kell had known him to kill a man at point-blank range. He was glad to count him as a friend.

"Where are you?" he asked.

"Dubai."

It wasn't the answer Kell had hoped for. Nevertheless, he pitched White on the open line, concealing his purpose as best he could.

"I'm going shooting at the weekend," he said. "Private party."

White immediately understood what was being asked of him. "I see," he said. There was an unmistakable note of pleasure in his voice, a love of adventure and mischief. White had the lowest boredom threshold of any man Kell had ever met and would plainly relish whatever scrape he was about to get into.

"I need some kit," Kell told him. "Wondered if I could pop into your London office and chat to someone? Sooner rather than later. I've got the Barbour. I've got the Wellington boots. It's the other stuff I need."

"Sure. What number are you calling from?"

Kell told him that he was speaking from a public phone box near Piccadilly Circus. White checked that he was still using the same mobile number and asked if Kell was on WhatsApp.

"Of course."

"And the kit is just for you?"

"Just for me."

It sounded as though White was in a moving vehicle. Kell pictured him in the back seat of an armored car, tanned and resplendent, pitching his services to a member of the Saudi royal family while running his hand up the thigh of a Russian ballerina.

"I can get this done for you, Tom," he said, the brisk, decisive confidence of the alpha male. "Can you give me an hour?"

"That would be ideal."

"And lunch when I get back to London. On me. I want to hear all about it."

Ninety minutes later, after a brief exchange of messages, Kell was in a branch of Caffè Nero at Victoria station, waiting for a man called "Jeff." White had said that he would be "easily recognizable as ex-Regiment," having evidently forgotten — in the relative confusion of making the arrangements so quickly — that Jeff had also been involved in the operation to release Amelia's son from captivity.

Kell saw that he had not changed. Jeffrey Quest was built like a prop forward but had the face of a saint. With his sandy-colored curly hair and ruddy-cheeked bonhomie, he might have passed for a farmer or the landlord of a much-loved rural pub. He was carrying a small red rucksack and a copy of the *Evening Standard* and nodded warmly at Kell as he caught his eye. He put the rucksack on the ground between them but did not shake Kell's hand.

"Nice to see you again, Mr. Kell. How have you been?"

"Well, thanks," Kell replied, sipping his coffee. "Want one?"

"Not for me, cheers. Bad for the ticker."

Jeff, who was in his early fifties, illustrated

his point by tapping his chest three times. Kell remembered the three bullets he had fired with a high-velocity rifle into the fleeing Luc Javeau, seconds before Kell himself would have been obliged to take the shot.

"Weapon's in the rucksack," he said. "Sig Sauer nine-millimeter with a spare magazine. Sixteen rounds. That be enough?"

"That's all I'll need."

"You know what you're doing? You've used one before?"

Kell was accustomed to the military's view of SIS officers as brain men and desk jockeys. He absorbed the inherent condescension and drained his coffee.

"I'm sure I can work it out," he replied. "Put a bullet in the chamber, point the barrel away from me, fire. That's how it works, right?"

Jeff smiled. "Something like that."

He explained that the gun was unregistered and untraceable and that "Mr. W" did not want it back. He was not going to ask why Kell needed it, nor did he want to know.

"I hope you won't find out," Kell replied, an ambiguous reply that Jeff struggled to understand. "Will you tell the boss I'm grateful to him?"

"Sure," he said. "Anything goes. He likes you."

Jeff stood up to leave. This time he shook Kell's hand.

"Thank you for this," Kell told him. "I appreciate it."

"No problem." Jeff nodded in a slow, reflective fashion, an affable man of apparent integrity who had lived alongside violence and conflict throughout his adult life. "Take care," he said, leaving the rucksack on the ground as he walked away. "Look after yourself, Mr. Kell."

## 51

The man Shahid knew as "Kris" had given him a strip of sleeping pills to use on the nights leading up to the operation. Shahid had taken only one, on the final evening, when prayer had failed him and he could not shake off the images of Rosie in his bed, her nakedness and her touch somehow more real to him, the memories richer and more shameful than anything he might do the following day.

He woke up later than he had expected, feeling no sense of nervousness or agitation, only the melancholy yearning for Rosie that had plagued him for the past several days. He felt a determination to carry out his duty with professionalism and courage so that he would be remembered for all time as a brave warrior of Islam who had chosen God over the woman he loved. Shahid ran a bath, then took the razor and carefully shaved his head, propping up the mirror behind the taps and repeatedly wiping it with a towel when the steam from the water fogged the glass.

He dressed in jeans, desert boots, a T-shirt, and denim jacket, sealed the poem he had written for Rosie in an envelope, and left it on the low stool beside the bookshelf. The police would find it and give it to her. He did not want to risk the poem getting lost in the post. It was important that Rosie read it so that she could finally understand why he had acted as he had acted, why he had not spoken to her since the night when she had stayed in his bed, why he was fixed on the path of martyrdom. He was sure that she would love him after this day because she would see that he was a great warrior. She would love him because he had realized that the cause, and the strength of his beliefs, were larger than the sanctity of his own life, larger than the lives of others. He was sure that she would respect him and come to see that there had been no choice for Shahid Khan other than to help to restore Europe to the age of the Prophet, to a time when life was pure, when the family was paramount, before the politics of greed, the wars prosecuted by the West, poisoned the earth. It was a beautiful idea. It was sublime. He had tried to express this idea in the poem. Rosie would read it and then she would understand.

Kris came in the van at two o'clock. Shahid was waiting for him outside the takeaway at the entrance to Meadow Close. He realized that it would be the last time he would ever see this place. Kris said that he had rented the van for two days after answering an advertisement in the paper, paid cash in hand so there was no trace back to him, no danger of numberplate recognition on a stolen vehicle. It was already a very hot day and he joked that this was good for Shahid.

"More people on the beach, more people on the pier. Sitting ducks, man."

Kris said that Jalal had been right to wait until the early evening. That was when the pier would be most crowded, when Shahid could do the most damage. That was how he could send out the loudest message to all corners of the earth. He would be a hero. Shahid told Kris that he did not think of the operation in terms of "damage." He thought of it in terms of "cleansing." Kris said that he understood this and slapped him on the back. Then they both climbed into the back of the van so that Shahid could take a look at the weapons.

There was a Glock 40 pistol with a spare

magazine. Kris demonstrated to Shahid what he already knew: that the Glock held eighteen rounds in each clip and that the empty clip could be dropped by pushing the release at the side of the grip. Shahid had fired an identical weapon in Syria.

Next Kris showed him the AK-47. It was fully automatic and there were four separate magazines, each with thirty rounds. Kris had brought a small backpack with him containing the spare magazines, as well as two hand grenades with a simple pin release.

"In case things go wrong," he said.

"They're not going to go wrong," Shahid told him.

## 52

There was a train leaving for Brighton at two thirty. Kell bought a ticket and jogged to the platform, boarding moments before the train pulled away from the station.

The train was not busy. He found a deserted section between two carriages and locked himself inside a toilet. He opened the rucksack and took out the Sig Sauer. Quest had provided two magazines, but no belt holster with which Kell could have concealed the weapon under his jacket. Kell was oddly grateful for the oversight. It was a hot day. He removed his jacket, wrapped it around the weapon and placed it back inside the rucksack.

There was unreliable wi-fi but a decent 3G signal on the train. Kell returned to the carriage, took a seat, and typed Khan's address into Google Earth. Rottingdean appeared to be a small village to the east of Brighton. A pin dropped on Meadow Close, a closed circle of suburban houses no more than a mile from the sea. The Close was surrounded on three sides by fields, to the north by more housing. There was a playground and two tennis courts to the south of the property.

Kell then typed "Asda" into the Search bar and was directed to the twenty-four-hour superstore at Brighton Marina. The store was located beside a complex of upmarket apartments backing onto a marina. There was a large car park to the west, a low white cliff to the north. A dual carriageway ran east to west along the top of the cliff, connecting Rottingdean to Brighton along a coastal road. It would have taken Khan less than half an hour to walk to work cross-country; only five or ten minutes by car or bus.

The train passed through Gatwick Airport. Hordes of pale-faced Brits with overweight suitcases were disembarking from a train on the opposite platform. Two young couples, tanned and chatting animatedly about a holiday in Ibiza, walked into Kell's carriage and slumped down at a vacant table. One of the girls had dreadlocks and a birthmark across her shoulder. She soon fell asleep against the window. Kell watched her face as it rocked against the glass, fields flashing by, the darkness of tunnels. He bought a cheese sandwich and a Coke from a passing catering trolley, then checked that he had enough cash to pay for the taxi in Brighton. He felt overwhelmingly underprepared for what he was about to face. Nothing had been planned in advance and he would have no support or backup. Kell could spend the next twenty-four hours in Brighton and find nothing. He could go to the house in Rottingdean and find Shahid Khan fast asleep in his bed.

The train pulled into Brighton station. Kell watched the girl being pushed awake by her friends, heard them joke with her about coming down from three successive nights of clubbing. He picked up the rucksack, waited until the other passengers had disembarked, then stepped off the train.

Bright sunlight streaming through the station. Families feeling the energy and pull of the seaside as they made their way along the platform. Kell took out his wallet and looked for his ticket. It was not there. He lifted out his credit cards and the money he had taken earlier in the day from an ATM, but there was no sign of it. He searched his trouser pockets but found nothing except a crushed box of matches and some loose change. He wondered if he had dropped the ticket on the platform or left it on the train. He could not even remember physically taking the ticket from the machine at Victoria station.

The jacket. Of course. Kell stepped to the side of the platform and reached into the rucksack. He pulled his jacket free of the pistol, rolling it out in his hands inside the bag until he felt the gun drop onto the magazines. The ticket was in the inside pocket. He put the jacket back in the rucksack, passed through the ticket barrier, and walked toward the taxi rank.

There was a long queue. Kell was obliged to wait for ten minutes, smoking as he listened to the squawk of seagulls and the perpetual automated drone of public announcements inside the station. Standing amid clumps of excited children, day-trippers from London shielded under hats and sun cream, Kell could not remember a feeling of such profound isolation. Even in the most solitary days of his career, in Kabul and Baghdad and Nairobi, he had always felt part of some larger structure. This day, though, had confirmed in Kell an almost infinite sense of separation from the everyday flow of life, beginning with his solitary laps of the pool, his visit to the clinic, and now concluding in the queue of a taxi rank in Brighton, surrounded by all the blameless excitement of an English summer crowd. He felt that he was heading toward some kind of personal reckoning: a confrontation not only with Shahid Khan, but with Minasian and Amelia and Marquand. With all of them. It was as though Kell wanted not only to prevent Khan from carrying out an attack, but also to prove something about his own courage and judgment. If he could stop Khan, he could silence them; even Claire. It was a case of rattling the handle on the locked door until somebody had the good sense to let him in.

"You're up, mate."

A shaven-headed man had tapped Kell on the shoulder, pointing out the next car on the rank. Kell thanked him and walked toward the taxi, holding the rucksack in his arms like a sleeping child.

"Can you take me to Rottingdean?" he said, climbing into the back seat.

"Rottingdean?" said the driver, immediately reaching for a sat-nav. "Sure. Got an address?"

## 53

Meadow Close was twenty minutes away. The driver took the same coastal road that Kell had looked at on Google Earth less than an hour earlier, pointing out the Asda Superstore at Brighton Marina as they passed along the top of the cliff. At the entrance to the Close, Kell instructed him to pull over and park on a quiet street beside a shuttered Chinese takeaway. There was a Renault Clio with a dent in the door parked outside the restaurant, a white van pulling away into traffic. Kell handed the driver a twenty-pound note and asked him to wait.

"I need to make several stops around Brighton this afternoon," he explained. "You free for the next couple of hours?"

"You got the money, I got the time," the driver replied.

"I'll be fifteen minutes."

Kell put on his jacket, shouldered the rucksack, and stepped out of the car.

There were no other pedestrians in the area. Traffic was passing along the main road, but the street leading into the Close was deserted. Kell walked downhill into a neat suburban estate of detached brick houses and bungalows with small, well-tended gardens. There were few cars on the street and no sign of any residents. Google Earth had put Khan's house on the far side of the Close. Kell walked anticlockwise around the loop, searching for number 45.

It was a small, two-story building with a strip of shattered tiles on the roof. Not as well maintained as the other properties in the area, not as neat and tidy. The grass at the front of the house had not been mowed for several weeks and the frames around the windows were warped and chipped. There was a large green Brighton & Hove City Council recycling bin to one side of a drive that was pockmarked with clumps of weeds. A narrow, gated passage ran from the drive alongside the house to the rear of the building.

Kell pressed the bell.

Movement inside. The panels of frosted glass on either side of the front door shimmered. Somebody was shuffling around in the hall. Kell heard the rattle of a chain being removed, then the voice of an elderly lady saying: "Just a minute, please."

She opened the door. A frail woman in her eighties with a lively and welcoming face. As she said: "Hello, yes, can I help you?" Kell caught the smell of stale smoke on her clothes.

"Hello. I'm here to see Shahid."

"Shahid?"

Did he even exist? Kell could not tell from the woman's reaction if she knew what he was talking about.

"That's right," he said.

"I'm afraid you've probably missed him."

"Probably?"

"Yes, love. I think he's just gone to work."

"Down at Asda?"

"Down at Asda, yes."

Kell feigned frustration, as if his day had been cursed with bad luck. "But he told me to meet him here."

"He did?" The elderly lady opened the door more fully. Kell assumed that she was the landlady, Katherine Arden. "He lives around the back." She nodded in the direction of the gated passage running alongside the house. "Did you telephone him, love?"

"That's the problem. He's left his mobile in his room."

"Oh, no."

It was a slick improvisation, the logic of

which remained unquestioned by the land-lady.

"He's teaching me Arabic," Kell continued. "We were supposed to have a lesson."

*"Arabic?"*

"Yes."

"I didn't know Shahid taught that."

"Part-time," Kell explained. "He's doing me a favor. He teaches me Arabic, I teach him the guitar."

"Oh! How nice." The elderly lady appeared to be distracted by a memory, then returned her gaze to Kell. "Guitar," she said. "He's either always at the gym or always at his work, far as I can tell. Either that or sleeping!"

"I'm Tom," said Kell, smiling warmly and offering the woman his hand.

"Kitty," she replied. "Would you like to come in?"

The hall smelled of food that had been deep fat fried, the living room of lily of the valley. There was a green sofa in one corner with a crisp white throw over the back. Kitty had been listening to Radio 2 when Kell had rung the bell. He could hear the low murmur of *Steve Wright in the Afternoon* on an old, pre-digital radio beside the window. There was a half-finished cup of tea on an upright piano beside the sofa, a folded copy of the *Daily Express* on a small circular dining table.

"Shahid's been here for the last couple of months, yes?" Kell asked. "Since he came to Brighton?"

"That's right. I don't mind having colored tenants, unlike some. My parents were in India."

"I see."

"All I want is clean and tidy. Reliable. Rent on time every month, no nonsense with girls or drugs."

"Shahid's your ideal man, then."

"Yes, he is, bless him. Nice strong lad. Good manners."

Kell was offered a cup of tea, but did not want to be delayed in kitchen chitchat when he could be searching Khan's room.

"Maybe it's best if I just drive down to the marina and see if he's there. If he doesn't have his phone, I can't reach him."

Kitty gave a resigned shrug. "I suppose."

"Maybe I could look for it? Take the phone down if I find it? He said it was charging in his room."

Kitty reacted to the suggestion not with suspicion, but with unbridled enthusiasm. It was as though Kell had offered to mow the grass and repaint the windows at the front of her house.

"That's very thoughtful of you," she said. "Yes, take it down to him. Let me find the key."

Two minutes later, Kell was following Kitty to the rear of the property. She walked in pale blue bedroom slippers. It was a point of stubborn principle to Kell that he had not taken the gun from the rucksack. He wanted to rely on his ability to outwit Khan, to foil his plan without recourse to violence.

They came to a separate entrance in the back garden, overlooking a field to the south. Kitty explained that her husband had converted the first floor into a bedsit "about a year before he died, poor thing."

She knocked on the door. She called out for Khan. When there was no reply, Kitty slipped a key into the lock and ushered Kell inside. There was a staircase immediately in front of them.

"You go up, love," she said. "I get too tired. I'll wait for you here."

It was a piece of luck. Kell climbed the stairs. The carpet was brown and worn through and there was a smell of Tiger Balm on the landing. Kitty switched on a light. Kell saw that there was a bathroom to his left, a bedroom on the right. He walked into the bathroom. Water was dripping from the shower and there were black hairs in the bath and around the plughole.

"That's the bathroom," Kitty called out, the first indication that she was apprehensive about Kell's behavior. Kell reappeared on the landing and smiled.

"So I see," he said, and went into the bedroom.

"Can you find it?" she said. "Can you see the phone?"

Kell knew that he would have less than a minute to look around before Kitty's suspicions deepened. There was a makeshift kitchen at the back of the room, an unmade bed in the far corner. The smell of Tiger Balm grew stronger the closer Kell came to the kitchen. The pictures on the walls were watercolors of seaside scenes, as well as posters of Mesut Ozil and Bruce Lee. No newspaper clippings on a corkboard, no *jihadi* literature on the bookshelves, no magazines with stories about Syria or ISIS. Kell could not even see a Koran. He went through the drawers in the kitchen and found only cutlery, a box of matches, and some cooking implements. No alcohol visible, no drugs or cigarettes. Just tins of food in the cupboards, packets of rice and pasta, a box of salt.

"Can't seem to find it," he shouted out,

opening the door of the fridge. It was empty save for two boxes of leftover Chinese takeaway, a carton of orange juice, and some kind of bodybuilding protein shake in a large plastic container.

Kell did not know what he was expecting to find. A gun? Some ammunition? Surely Khan would not risk keeping such things in the house. There was a laptop computer beside his bed. Without thinking through the legal consequences for any subsequent investigation, Kell scooped it up and put it in the rucksack, trusting that Kitty would not notice the shape change to the bag.

As Kell turned to leave he saw a low wooden stool near the door. There was an envelope on it. He shouted out: "Here it is, got it!" and picked up the envelope.

"Wonderful!" Kitty replied as Kell looked down at the address. Khan had written "Rosie" in neat black ink on the front. The envelope was sealed. Kell dropped it into the rucksack and took his iPhone out of his pocket.

"Found it," he declared to Kitty, trotting down the stairs and holding up the phone. "He left it charging under his bed."

# 54

The meter in the taxi was still running. Kell knocked on the window. The driver released the lock and Kell climbed into the back seat.

"Thanks for waiting," he said. "Can you take me to Asda at the Brighton Marina?"

They turned back into Rottingdean, heading downhill toward the coast road. The driver lowered his visor against the glare of the sun. Kell took the envelope out of the rucksack and opened it up.

It was a poem of war and love, written by Shahid in the self-aggrandizing style common to holy warriors of Islam. Kell understood immediately that Rosie was a non-Muslim girl with whom he had become romantically involved.

From the innocence and naïveté of my
   youth
I sprang into the path of God like a lion.
A lion of war and courage.

Willing to assist.
Willing to fight.
Willing to hate in order to love.

I will create a flow of blood
To stem a flow of blood.
All that is unclean will be cleaned by my
    faith.
All insults to the Prophet will be answered
    with death.
My insults will come in the form of
The blade, the bullet, the bomb.

You cannot know the courage inside me.
You will come to see it just as you saw the
    pure love inside me.
I will avenge all those who oppose me.
I will raise my voice as I raise my weapon
    for God.

Islam is my religion. God showers me with
    grace.
I live by the Koran. I will die for Allah.
I will fight the rulers, fight the traitors.
Those who await me are as beautiful as
    you.
They have not lost their virtue.
Only God can restore this purity to you.

The distant sea glittered in the afternoon

sunshine. Kell read the poem a second time and felt the burden of trying to locate Khan as a weight pressing down on him, a pressure that was close to intolerable. The poem. The soaked black hairs in the bath and around the plughole. Khan had shaved his body in preparation for an attack. He had deliberately left the poem in his bedroom for the police to discover in the aftermath of whatever atrocity had been planned by ISIS.

Kell's phone began to ring. A withheld number.

"Tom?"

It was Marquand. There was an unmistakable note of hesitancy in his voice.

"Speaking."

"The name you gave me," he said. The dismissive swagger that had characterized Marquand's mood at their earlier meeting had entirely vanished. He sounded rushed and contrite. "On the document. Can you confirm it?"

Kell knew, before he had even removed Minasian's note from his jacket, that Marquand had returned to Vauxhall Cross and run a search on STRIPE.

"Shahid Khan."

"Good God." In Marquand's quiet astonishment, Kell heard both a note of apology and the fear that SIS, through sheer bureau-cratic intransigence, had failed to prevent a massacre. "And the passport number?"

Kell read it out: "Six. Five. Three. Seven. Eight . . ."

It was enough. Marquand stopped him.

"Jesus," he said. "Where are you?"

Kell knew that he had won. He had finally persuaded them that Minasian had been telling the truth. But his moment of triumph had come too late, and there was no tri-umph to speak of.

"Brighton," he replied.

"You went there? You're already there?"

"Brighton," Kell said again.

"Can you get to a secure phone?"

Kell looked out of the window, shaking his head in disbelief. The taxi was pulling off the coast road onto a ramp leading down to the superstore.

"Who do you think is listening, Jimmy? Just say what it is that you want to say. The clock is ticking. I'm probably already too late. What have you found out?"

The taxi lurched to a halt behind an articulated lorry, like Marquand being bumped out of his complacency.

"Fine," he said, conceding immediately to Kell's request. "The passport official. Mar-tinelli. His name checks out. He's under investigation for passing fraudulently obtained documents to a loan shark in London. Kyle Chapman. One of the passports matches the information on your report. Same name. Same number. If Chapman sold it on to Jalal —"

Kell was ahead of him. He didn't need Marquand to join the dots.

"I get it," he said. "Well, it's nice to be believed. Hang on a minute."

Kell lowered the phone and told the driver to pull up and wait in the car park. He handed him another twenty-pound note and stepped out into blazing sunshine.

"I just need to go into Asda," he explained, speaking to the driver through the window. "I won't be more than five minutes."

*"Asda?"* said Marquand, overhearing what Kell had said. "You're in the marina?"

"I'm looking for Khan."

"You're going to confront him? Is that a good idea?"

"Got a better one?"

Kell waited for Marquand's reply, walking quickly through crowds of shoppers pushing trolleys back and forth in the car park. Two community buses had pulled up beside the entrance to the supermarket, dispensing slow-motion pensioners into the dizzying heat of the afternoon.

"Tell you what you could do," said Kell, spotting a young man with a shaved head stacking baskets near the automatic doors. It wasn't Khan. He was pale-skinned, undernourished. "Get me a copy of Khan's passport photo. I don't even know what he looks like."

"I'll try."

"And get a team to Brighton as soon as possible. I think he's active. I think he's going to do this thing within the next few hours. Get them to crowded public places. Plainclothes. The aquarium. The pier. The Pavilion. The beach. Whatever you do, don't call the Brighton police. Khan sees uniformed officers swarming all around him, he'll get spooked, live to fight another day. That's when we lose him. That's when he'll know he's been compromised by his own people and the link to GAGARIN will snap."

## 55

Asda was a vast prefabricated barn, as big
as an aircraft hangar, strip-lit and packed
with customers even in midafternoon on a
perfect summer day. Huge signs in fluorescent green offering discounted prices hung
from metal beams in the roof. Old ladies
with swollen ankles shuffled around the
flower stalls while children, high on sugar
and sunshine, screamed with boredom in
fruit and veg. Kell spotted a security guard
near the automatic doors and approached
him. He was checking the messages on his
phone.

"I'm looking for Shahid Khan," he said.

"Haven't seen him," the guard replied.

Kell walked deeper into the store. There
was an information desk ahead of him. A
poster bearing the slogan "Save Money. Live
Better" swayed overhead. He walked up to
the desk. A teenage girl with dyed blond

hair wearing a black waistcoat was stifling a sneeze.

"Bless you," Kell told her.

"Thank you. What can I do for you today?"

She had long-suffering eyes and an intelligent smile. There was a tattoo on her forearm, blue polish on her fingernails.

"I'm looking for Shahid Khan."

"Shahid?" The girl frowned, shook her head. "Not sure I've seen him today. Danny!"

She had called out to a passing member of staff, a man in his early twenties with a summer tan wearing outsized trousers and a high-vis jacket.

"Seen Shahid?"

"Nah," he said, hardly breaking stride. "Ask Rosie."

"Rosie," said Kell, his heart skipping a beat. "She's here?"

"Yeah. Think she's on the deli. Do you know where that is, sir?"

Kell said that he could find it and walked as quickly as possible across the store, past aisles of detergents and cereals, stalls with special offers on disposable barbeques. He reached the delicatessen and saw a young woman standing to one side of the serving counter arranging a display of cheeses on a disused wine barrel.

"Rosie?" he said, walking toward her.

She looked up. Kell saw that the object of Khan's affection, the focus of his poem of false courage and self-pitying love, was an attractive young woman — perhaps no older than twenty or twenty-one — with pale skin and eyes marked by tiredness and anxiety. Rosie had jeweled piercings in her ears and blond hair gathered up in a bun beneath a cheap white hat. She frowned when Kell reached out to shake her hand. Her grip was soft and lifeless.

"Hello."

She was on duty and too polite to say that she did not recognize this tall, well-dressed stranger, a man she had never seen before. Perhaps he was management.

"My name is Tom," he said. "Tom Kell. You're Rosie?"

"Yes," she said. There was a badge on her shirt with the name printed on it.

"I wanted to talk to you about Shahid."

In an instant there was a hardening in her gaze, a collapse in both spirit and civility.

"I don't want to talk about him."

"Why not?"

"I don't." She was moving to one side, bending to adjust the cheeses. "I just don't."

"Has he hurt you?"

462

She looked up, wounded. "Why would you say that?"

"Does he love you?"

Rosie reared back, as if the question was both an affront to her pride and an insight of astonishing power.

"Is he in trouble?" she said, afraid to look Kell in the eye. "Are you police?"

"I'm not the police," he replied. He was aware that their conversation could be overheard by a member of staff serving a customer at the nearby counter. He drew Rosie away from the area, trying to walk her toward a more private space. "Why would you think he's in trouble?" he asked, taking incrementally slow steps to one side of her so that she was obliged to move with him.

"He's troubled," she said. "He's confused. He's got all this stuff in his past."

Kell was touched by her desire to protect Khan, even as her expression betrayed that she feared both what he was capable of doing to her and what he might be capable of doing to others.

"Have you spoken to him today?"

There was a tell in her reaction. She shook her head and said, "No," but her hand covered her mouth as she said the word. She looked down at the polished floor of the supermarket.

"Not spoken verbally," Kell replied, trying to give her an outlet in which she could tell the truth. "Just by text. Snapchat? For example do you know where he is now?"

There was a long silence. A bald man in a pistachio green shirt and off-the-peg black suit walked past and said: "Good afternoon, Rosie!" with the insincere bustle of a middle manager on the make. Rosie said, "Yeah, hi, Mr. Samuels," and at last made eye contact with Kell.

"Who are you?" she said.

Kell lowered his voice.

"I work for the security services. I'm sorry to have to tell you this, but your friend is a concern to us. A very serious concern. Did he tell you about his time in Syria?"

Rosie's lips were bound together as she nodded slowly, like a child who has been caught in a lie. It was all the confirmation Kell needed.

"You won't be in any trouble, Rosie. I promise you," he said. "But you must help me find him. We can help him together. But we must do it now."

He had pushed too hard. He was the law, after all. He was the police and the enemy. He was the kind of man who had bullied her friends, the kind of man Khan had professed to hate. An instinctive clan loyalty flashed across Rosie's face. She would not be moved to help Kell. She did not trust him.

"I think you should go," she said.

"I'm afraid that's not going to be possible." Kell knew that this was just a moment of bravado. Push her and she would quickly snap. "This man is a threat to the public. If he does what I think he's going to do, and it's shown that you failed to help me, you could be in a lot of trouble."

"Are you threatening me?"

The question didn't suit her. The girl was too decent, too kind to fight. There was no real anger or violence inside her; only an awful melancholy, a frustration for what had been gained and what had been lost.

"I'm asking you to help me, Rosie. I'm asking you to help all these people." Kell swept an arm around the vast barn of the superstore, at all the shoppers and shelf-stackers and middle managers whom Khan would murder as nonchalantly as he would lift weights in a gym. "He's a sleeper agent for ISIS. He has been planning an attack in Brighton. I think you know that, or something like that. I can see it in your face. I can tell from the way that you've been talking to me. You know something, don't you?

You're scared and you don't know what to do."

She broke then. Quickly and straightforwardly. There was a slump in her posture. She reached into the back pocket of her jeans and began to mutter something that Kell could not hear. He asked her to repeat it.

"He called me at lunchtime," she said. "Asked me if I was on shift."

"And what did you say?"

Kell felt a tautness in his body, a quickening of the blood.

"I said I was off at five. I asked if he wanted to meet up."

"Yes . . . ?"

Rosie looked up. Kell saw that her lovely eyes were stained with tears.

"Then he sent this," she said. She passed Kell her phone. "He texted me this."

There was a message at the bottom of the screen.

Stay away from the pier tonight.

# 56

Kell took out his phone and rang Marquand. Rosie was standing in front of him, holding the top of her head with both hands as though trying to hold herself together. To Kell's frustration, the call went to voice mail. He left a message.

"Jimmy, it's happening this evening. In the next three or four hours. I've got a text here, sent to his girlfriend." Rosie was starting to shake, looking around the store as if searching for a route by which to escape. "Get a team to the pier in Brighton. All the way along. If he starts at the sea end, by the time anybody reaches him he could have killed fifty people."

Kell lowered the phone. Rosie was starting to cry. She said: "What's he doing? Oh, man, what's he doing?"

Kell reached out and took her hand. She was reluctant at first, flinching as he tried to touch her, but when he said, "We're leaving. You're coming with me," and put his hand on her back, the girl allowed him to steer her past the delicatessen counter, along an aisle stacked with bottles of cordial and mineral water, then behind the long line of tills at the checkout area. They moved quickly toward the exit. Rosie seemed grateful that she was at least with somebody who could take charge of her and tell her what to do. Kell passed the manager in the black suit and the girl with the tattoo who had helped him at the information desk. Neither of them appeared to notice that Rosie was leaving, nor that she was in tears.

"Did you text him back?" Kell asked, realizing that there had not been a reply to Khan's message on her phone.

"I tried calling him," she said. "He didn't answer."

"And did you tell anybody? A friend? Did you call the police?"

They walked outside into the blinding sunlight. Kell looked at Rosie for an answer. She indicated that she had told no one.

"I'm so sorry," she said. "I should have done something. I should have told someone. I don't like talking to the police."

"Show me a photograph of him," Kell said, looking around for his driver. "Have you got one?"

"Yeah," she said, quickly taking out her phone. She seemed to want to make up for not calling the police. "Got loads."

The driver was nowhere to be seen. Kell swore under his breath as he took Rosie's phone. There was a selfie of Khan on the screen, a clean-shaven, good-looking man in his mid-twenties wearing a crisp white shirt. He was smiling for the camera, for Rosie. There was a gold stud in his left earlobe, a medallion around his neck.

"Send this to me, send it to this number," he said, passing the phone back to Rosie.

In a trance of obedience, Rosie tapped Kell's number into her phone and sent the photograph to him via WhatsApp. Kell was still looking around for the taxi driver when he heard the photo ping into his iPhone.

"Send more," he said. "Three or four more, different angles, different perspectives. Whatever you've got. I need to send them out so that people have an idea what he looks like. And I need his contact details."

Rosie did as she was asked. They were now some distance away from the entrance to the superstore, wandering around the car park looking for Kell's taxi. There was still no sign of it. The driver had taken his money and run.

"I've sent two more," Rosie told him. Kell forwarded the photographs to Marquand, as well as the number of Khan's phone. There was a chance that he had left it switched on and that GCHQ could triangulate his position. No sooner had he done so than Marquand called him back.

"Tom?"

"Did you get the photographs?"

"Yes. Just now. And your message. SO15 is scrambling, I've given the number to Cheltenham. I'm very sorry, Tom. We should have listened to you."

"Forget about that." Kell looked up at the coast road and saw that a traffic jam had formed above the cliff. It would be quicker to walk to the pier. Ten minutes. Perhaps fifteen. "I'm going to go down there. I'm with the girlfriend." Rosie flinched. "She might be able to spot him."

"What else can you tell me about him?" Marquand asked.

Kell led Rosie toward the ramp that curved up to the coast road. His hand was on her shoulder as he steered her along the pavement.

"Tell me more about Shahid," he said to her, with Marquand on the line. "How tall is he?"

She looked up at Kell, squinting against

the sun. "What?"

"How tall is he? Shahid. Is he a big guy? Muscles?"

"Yeah. Goes to the gym. Does that stuff."

"Tall?" Kell asked.

"About your height."

"Did you get that?" Kell said to Marquand. "Six foot. Athletic build. Muscular. Shaved head."

Rosie reacted with disdain. "What? No he doesn't."

"Shaved head," Kell repeated. "Brown eyes. He's going to be solid. Military. Remember this is a guy who has seen action in Syria. He's trained, experienced. Tell '15 to be careful."

"They know what they're doing, Tom."

They were almost at the top of the ramp as Kell ended the conversation. He looked at his phone. He had only 13 percent power left, not enough for more than twenty or thirty minutes, much less if he kept talking to London.

"How much power in your phone?" he asked Rosie. His hand was still on her back and they were hurrying along the promenade like a couple running late for a wedding.

"How much what?"

Rosie looked at her phone and said that

she had more than 50 percent. As they walked, Kell typed her number into a message for Marquand and instructed him to call it if the battery on his own phone died. They were out in the summer crowds now, traffic backed up to the west all the way to the Grand Hotel, the shimmering beach packed as far as the eye could see. The pier was half a mile away, a pale charcoal blur in the intensity of sunlight and heat. Kell urged Rosie to walk more quickly, the rucksack starting to bite into his shoulder, the gun and the laptop knocking against his back. Skateboarders and cyclists were riding in single file along the promenade, dodging fallen ice-cream cones and dogs on leads. The clamor and energy of Brighton in that moment was so great that Kell felt the imminence of Khan's lethal plan as an inevitability: he would never be able to spot him among the crowds; he would never be able to give sufficient warning to the men and women and children who would stand in his way. The joy of an innocent summer day at the beach would be obliterated. Kell quickened his pace, urging Rosie to look for Khan, to search the crowds for his face.

"He could be in one of the cars," he said. "Keep looking at the cars and the vans. Motorbikes. Keep looking on the other side of the road."

A man carrying a poodle in a basket stepped across Kell and swore as Rosie blocked his path.

"Don't mind me," she said, releasing a burst of anger as she was forced to walk around him. The man ignored her and disappeared down a flight of steps toward the beach. Horns sounded in the queue of traffic behind them, drivers growing ever more frustrated in the stalled humidity of the late afternoon. As Kell broke into a jog, still several hundred meters from the pier, a moped passed within six inches of his right elbow, weaving in and out of the cars in a reckless slalom.

"We need to run," he told Rosie, but she was reluctant to do so, asking Kell to slow down because she had hurt her leg at work. Kell had no choice but to comply, checking his phone for an update from Marquand as he walked alongside her, moving as quickly as possible. There was nothing. Just a message from Claire and a message from Mowbray, both of which Kell ignored. The power on the phone was down to 10 percent. Two or three more calls from London and he would have nothing left.

He looked at the time. It was not yet six o'clock. Kell assumed that Khan intended to act at any point from six onward, if only because he had told Rosie to avoid the pier "tonight." Yet the early evening was the time when the greatest number of people would be coming back from the beach, when he could do the most damage. On this basis, there were ten minutes before an attack might begin. Kell did not know its nature, nor even if Khan would be acting alone. It was plausible that he was merely one piece in a nightmare jigsaw, and that several brainwashed ISIS thugs were currently descending on Brighton, looking to take control of the pier and to spread mayhem on the beach. It was then that Kell decided to take out the Sig Sauer, pulling the rucksack off his back and feeling for the butt of the gun beneath the laptop and his jacket. Waiting until a group of tourists had passed, so that he could act with relative discretion, he pulled the weapon out of the rucksack and slipped it into his hip pocket.

"What was that?" said Rosie. "Was that a fucking gun?"

"We won't need it," Kell replied. "I won't have to use it."

"Fucking hell," she said, "you've got a fucking gun. You're gonna kill Shahid." She slowed her pace and moved away from him, trying to release Kell's grip on her arm. It was like marching a prisoner to the gallows. Kell urged her to keep her voice down and held on to her with all of his strength, feeling the gun knock against his thigh as he put his arm around Rosie's stiffened back, squeezing her shoulder against him.

"It's going to be okay," he said. "Here's what we're going to do."

It helped to keep talking to her. Rosie calmed down as Kell explained his strategy. They would go to the entrance of the pier and he would leave her there. She had the chance to save hundreds of lives. All she had to do was stand, facing the road, and wait for Shahid to come. If she saw him, she must go up to him. She must do everything she could to stop him doing what he had come to do. Kell asked her if she believed that Shahid was capable of shooting her and she said "No" with absolute conviction. She began to cry then, but Kell squeezed her shoulder more tightly, holding her body against his own as they walked, explaining what he intended to do.

"He might start at the far side of the pier. Over there. At the French end." It was an odd description, but it made sense to Rosie. She looked south, in the direction of France, and followed Kell's hand as he illustrated the route he would take to meet up with her. "It means people can get away, but it means he has a chance of escape. I'll leave you at the entrance and I'll look for him on the pier. I'll run. It won't take me long. I'll be back with you in just a few minutes. Once I know the pier is clear, we can wait for him. We can wait for him together."

"Why don't we just call the police?" she said, and Kell explained that a counter-terrorism unit was already on its way to Brighton — might already *be* in Brighton — and that if Shahid got spooked by the police, or saw that the pier was being closed off to the public, he would walk away, only to try again when nobody knew where he was or what he intended to attack.

"That's fucking mad," Rosie told him. "We've just gotta stop him or all these people are gonna die."

"We will stop him," Kell told her. "We will stop him."

Moments later, his phone rang. It was Marquand, relaying the information that SO15 were airborne and twenty minutes out.

"Don't let them land on the beach," Kell said. "Don't let them show themselves on the pier. I don't want him spooked. I don't want him running away."

Marquand understood Kell's terrifying

gamble, the risk he was taking in not informing the police and clearing the pier. Kell
told him that he was armed and that he
intended to leave Rosie at the entrance to
the pier while he checked that Khan was
not active at the southern end.

"What if she walks?" Marquand asked.

"She's not going to walk," Kell replied,
making eye contact with Rosie so that she
knew that he was talking about her. "She's
a good person. She wants to stop this thing
as much as you and I do. She can get in the
way of this man and talk to him. I'm convinced of it." He was speaking for Rosie's
benefit, as much as for Marquand's. "If she
walks, she knows she's in a lot of trouble.
I've explained that. Rosie doesn't want that
on her conscience."

They passed a Ferris wheel and came to
the entrance to the pier. Kell told Marquand that he wanted to preserve the power
on his phone and he hung up. Rosie was
looking at the crowds mingling under the
clocktower with an expression of numb,
openmouthed dread.

"Just wait here," Kell said, aware of
cackling laughter at one of the food stalls,
of "Beat It" playing on a sound system. "Do
what I told you. If you see him, go up to
him. Don't be afraid. Give me your phone

in case mine dies. I won't be more than five minutes."

Kell passed underneath the clocktower and ran along the western deck, the beach beneath him still packed. He could picture Khan at the southern end of the pier, preparing to move with the fanatic's clinical and deadly efficiency from the fairground rides at the southern tip to the fish-and-chip stalls at the entrance. Kell could tell, simply by the weight of numbers around him, that the pier was packed along its entire length. The only limit to the devastation Khan might cause would be imposed by the amount of ammunition he was able to carry and by how quickly people were able to conceal themselves or run away. Kell was also aware that he had taken a grotesque risk with Rosie's life; he could not know how Khan would react if he saw her. Her presence might detain him momentarily; it might also catalyze him to an even greater rage.

He reached the first enclosed structure on the pier. He walked into a cave of arcade games and slot machines, a stink of vinegar and a frenzy of amateur gambling. He looked for Khan, but saw only kids and parents, eager young couples shoving coins into penny pushers. Ten seconds later Kell was back outside, a seagull passing within a few feet of his head, keeping pace with him as he ran south along the pier, gliding soundlessly on an updraft from the water below. Kell reached a restaurant, jogged around it on the western side, not so much looking out for Khan — there were simply too many faces to register and process — but trying to detect changes in the atmosphere of the pier: silence or screams, gunfire, the shock and panic of crowds. He heard a sunbathing pensioner on a white bench saying: "Slow down, love" as he ran past her. Kell then came to a second enclosed area, this one larger than the first: more penny pushers, more fruit machines, deafening pop music smothering the clicks and shouts of a game of air hockey played by young boys in shorts and T-shirts. Still no sign of Khan. Moments later Kell was outside again and moving toward the last section of the pier. He was in sight of a mini-rollercoaster, a packed bumper-car track to his right and, beyond it, farther west along the seafront, the rusted shell of the old, burned-out pier. He sprinted in the direction of the beach. Kell ran until he could feel himself at the point of exhaustion, his body and his face drenched with sweat. His lungs were stinging and he was gasping for air. If he had to use the gun, he doubted that he would be able to control his breathing sufficiently to be able to take an accurate shot. Kell had to stop the weapon from jumping out of his trouser pocket, holding it in his left hand as he ran, the rucksack repeatedly knocking against his back. Somebody else shouted: "Slow down, mate!" as Kell passed a stall selling fresh doughnuts and Brighton rock. He almost collided with a young child in a wheelchair.

At last Kell came to the first arcade and pushed his way through it, back through the noise and the stench of vinegar and the gambling crowds, until finally he could see the archway and the entrance to the pier. Rosie was standing to one side, waiting for Khan.

"You okay?" Kell asked her. He was starved of air, cursing the cigarettes he had smoked, the years he had lived, the distance he had run in fierce summer heat. He took off the rucksack and had to lean against the side of a fish-and-chip stall, trying to catch his breath. Rosie looked as if she had never seen a man in such a state of exhaustion.

"I'm all right," she replied. "How about you?"

There were still large numbers of people

milling around the entrance to the pier. Some had come up from the beach, others were holding buckets and windbreaks, heading down to the sea for an evening swim. Kell continued to search the crowds for Khan. The sound system was still playing Michael Jackson as seagulls squawked overhead. Drawing in a series of deep breaths, Kell looked at Rosie and handed back her phone.

"Didn't trust me not to call him, did you?"

"Never crossed my mind," Kell replied.

She was scanning the faces in front of her, eyes scrutinizing everything in her path.

"No sign of him," she said, but as Kell looked down at his watch, he heard a note change in Rosie's voice, as if all strength had suddenly left her.

"Oh, God," she said. "He's here. I can see him. He's coming from the road."

## 57

Kell looked up. At first, he saw nothing. Just sunburned faces and plastic buckets, pensioners in summer hats. England the way it used to be. Then, following Rosie's eyeline, he looked beyond the crowds toward the road, where a white van was pulling away from the curb. Directly in front of it, walking purposefully toward the entrance of the pier, came a young, dark-skinned man with a shaved head.

"That's him?" Kell asked, though he knew the answer to his own question. Khan was wearing black combat trousers and a dark waistcoat. There was a large red holdall slung across his back.

"Jesus," Rosie muttered. "Yeah, it's him."

Whatever relief Kell felt at having identified Khan evaporated as he came to terms with his appearance. He was decked out in the uniform of the mass killer: the holdall evidently contained weapons; the waistcoat was almost certainly packed with ammunition. Kell reached into the pocket of his trousers for the butt of the gun. The Sig Sauer felt tiny and inadequate in his hand. As he slipped the safety catch and took a step forward, he knew that he was going to have to shoot Khan. No plainclothes SO15 officer had intercepted him. Kell and Rosie were all that stood between Khan and a massacre on the pier.

"Shahid!"

Rosie had done something extraordinarily brave. Before Kell was aware of what was happening, she had passed him, walking directly toward Khan, waving her arms above her head. Kell saw the gunman register her voice, a look of horrified surprise on his face as he saw her coming toward him. In the same moment, Khan reached for the holdall, swinging it down in front of him so that he could unzip it and take out a weapon. Kell knew that he was so jacked up on hate and adrenaline that he intended to take Rosie as his first victim.

"Rosie, no!"

Kell could not let another young woman die. As he shouted, several people in the area seemed to sense for the first time that something was wrong. Kell took out the gun and felt the crowds around him come to a standstill. Instinctively, he shouted: "Everybody get back!" and waved his free arm left and right as Rosie continued to walk forward. Khan was still cradling the holdall in his arms, reaching inside it as he looked at Rosie with a mixture of rage and consternation.

"Shahid! Put the fucking bag down!"

Kell raised the Sig Sauer in the air, aiming high above the heads of the crowd. He did not have a clear shot to Khan and could not risk hitting a bystander. Rosie heard him and turned. She shouted: "No! Don't!" and Kell fired into the air in order to assert authority, to try to project control. The crowd around him scattered like birds disturbed from carrion, women screaming, men grabbing young children by the hand and pulling them away from the scene. In less than two or three seconds, there were fewer than six people left in the area. Kell shouted at them to move away, fearing that Khan's waistcoat was a suicide vest rigged to blow. Khan himself appeared to have been startled by Kell's gunshot and was struggling to pull the AK-47 from the holdall. Rosie, frightened by the sound of the gunshot, had ducked and was crouched down in the space between them, switching her frightened gaze between the two men.

All traffic in the area had come to a standstill. Even in this heightened atmosphere of anxiety and confrontation, Kell was aware of a Michael Jackson song blasting out from one of the stalls beside the pier.

"Drop the fucking bag!" he shouted at Khan, and heard a siren kicking up in the distance. Beads of sweat were streaming down Kell's face, but his breathing was steady and regular. To his intense relief, he saw the bag drop to the ground. Kell continued to move toward Khan, inching forward, but Rosie now stood up — counter to everything that Kell wanted or had expected of her in that moment — and came between the two men. Kell momentarily lost the line of sight to Khan.

In that instant, two things happened. Rosie began to speak, arms extended in front of her, palms together, as though in a gesture of prayer. She said: "Please don't do this, Shahid. It's not right. It's not you . . ." But as she spoke he took a grenade from the lower pocket of the waistcoat and held it up in the air, his face a rictus of defiance.

"Get back!" Kell shouted when he saw the grenade. There was screaming. Kell knew that any throw toward the pier or down toward the beach would create a bloodbath.

"Why did you come?" Shahid was shouting. "I told you to stay away!"

"I wanted to stop you," Rosie replied. Kell had drawn alongside her and was still pointing the gun at Khan's chest. He heard a man shout out: "Fucking shoot him!" but was so determined not to take a man's life that he waited, perhaps fatally, for Khan to make his move.

"Put the grenade down, Shahid," Kell told him. "This is not the way. God is showing you his purpose. God has sent us to stop you."

"What do you fucking know about my God, you fucking pig?" Khan shouted and held the grenade even higher. Behind him, a Union Jack cracked in the wind. Kell knew that he must fire, even as Rosie continued to implore Shahid to surrender.

"Look at these people," she screamed. "Look at them!" and pointed Khan to a group thirty or forty feet away on the road behind him. "Muslims!" she said. "Devout Muslims! A veiled woman! Children. With their father. A Muslim family! You want to kill them? Is that who you came to kill?"

Kell saw what Rosie had seen. A young family, exactly as she had described: the mother dressed in black purdah, two young children in each of her hands, their father beside them.

Khan turned and saw it, too. The area around him was now completely clear, people still moving backward along the coast road and toward the pier, those who had not run away watching the scene in fascinated disbelief.

Suddenly there was a violent noise from the pier, like the sound of a car backfiring. Kell thought that he heard a distant scream. Others reacted to the blast, faces turning to see what had set it off. For a sickening moment Kell believed that a second gunman was loose, that they had planned to herd the terrified public toward the center of the pier and to slaughter them. But there was no further noise, no more screaming. Kell assumed that somebody had set off a firecracker, perhaps on the beach, and turned back to Khan.

Rosie was still standing between them. Khan was facing her. Kell had a shot to Khan's head but saw him lower the grenade and bring it down toward his stomach, in what appeared to be a gesture of surrender. Khan seemed to have come to terms with the futility of his position. He spoke to Rosie, shaking his head, eyes glistening with rage.

"You ruined everything," he said. These

first words were barely audible but then, at last, the music from the pier was shut off and there was an absolute stillness. Kell saw that Khan was holding the grenade in his left hand, tight against his stomach, and that he was slowly raising his right hand as he addressed Rosie. Had Khan not taken a further step forward, toward the girl, Kell would not have looked as closely at his raised hand. But he saw the pin of the grenade clutched in Khan's fingers as he screamed out to his false God: *"Allahu Akbar!"*

Rosie was less than five feet away from the advancing Khan. Kell jumped forward, grabbed her around the waist, and pulled her back, the gun falling from his hand as he ran with her as far as they could manage before her weight threw him off balance and they toppled to the ground. Kell was on his side. He rolled over and smothered Rosie's body with his own so that she was entirely protected as Khan was obliterated by the grenade, a noise of such force and power that Kell was momentarily numbed by a ringing silence in his ears. As Rosie struggled and writhed beneath him, Kell heard only the sound of sirens and of screaming.

He prayed that Shahid Khan had died alone.

## 58

Brighton Pier reopened forty-eight hours later.

Only one person in the crowd had taken a video of what had happened, capturing Kell's face and recording the confrontation with Khan, right up to the moment of his suicide. When the woman attempted to sell the film to a national newspaper, the D-Notice Committee acted swiftly over the forty-five-second footage, persuading the editor to pixelate Kell's face in order to protect his identity. Seven photographs, taken on smartphones by members of the public who had been standing behind Kell at the northern end of the pier, showed Khan's face in full and Rosie's in profile. Kell could not be identified from any of the pictures, all of which had appeared online within an hour of Khan's suicide.

SIS, Special Branch, and the Security Service could neither confirm nor deny that the middle-aged man who had saved the life of Rosie Maguire was an undercover intelligence officer tasked with stopping Shahid Khan. The Watson Report would later commend both Rosie and "Officer B" for their bravery in "extraordinarily testing circumstances," noting that "Officer B" "undoubtedly saved countless lives by his quick-thinking and courage." Both Jim Martinelli and Kyle Chapman faced lengthy prison sentences for facilitating the creation and distribution of several falsely obtained passports.

Only one person in the crowd suffered minor injuries as a result of Khan's suicide, a fragment of the grenade piercing her forearm as she instinctively raised her hand to protect her face. Rosie was taken to hospital and later obliged to sign the Official Secrets Act, forbidding her from discussing, either in public or in private, any element of her interaction with Thomas Kell. In lengthy conversations with MI5 and SIS, Rosie made it clear that she had no intention of trying to sell her story to the press or to appear on television. She was ashamed of her relationship with Khan and wanted to hide from the glare of publicity, not least because she had faced the inevitable backlash from online trolls who had attacked her for "sleeping with a terrorist." Rosie nevertheless became the public face of the incident, her bravery lauded by the press next to photographs of the "Heroine of the Pier" that had been culled all too easily from Facebook and Instagram.

Kell, by contrast, vanished into anonymity, his identity protected by law, his actions adjudged by one broadsheet commentator to be typical of the "brave men and women who work in the shadows of our intelligence community, tracking our enemies, securing our safety, tackling the threat from Islamist terror head-on, all too often without commensurate reward or recognition." The intelligence that had led "Officer B" to the pier was widely, and erroneously, credited to a "long-running MI5 surveillance operation against Shahid Khan." Amelia Levene basked in the glory of a successful SIS counterterrorism coup and was personally congratulated by the prime minister at 10 Downing Street. Kell and Rosie were both invited to attend the same event. Rosie declined on the grounds that she "wanted to forget all about it"; Kell knew that his presence would oblige Amelia to lie to the prime minister about his suspension from the Service, his recruitment of Minasian, and the assassination of Bernhard Riedle.

Consequently he sent his regrets.

Inside Vauxhall Cross, however, Kell was the man of the hour. SIS laid on a four-course lunch, opened up the cellar, slapped him on the back, and told him that "things just hadn't been the same" since his inauspicious departure from the Service some four years earlier. Wags made jokes about the "miraculous transformation" of "Witness X" into "Officer B." Jimmy Marquand apologized for the "hesitancy" he had shown toward Kell in Oxford Circus and made it clear that he was pushing for "the highest civilian honor possible, a George Cross if HMG can be persuaded." In a meeting in her office attended by Marquand and two senior members of the Service whom Kell had never seen before, Amelia thanked him for his contribution to "the fight against terror" and expressed her admiration for the "tenacity" he had shown in pursuing Minasian, "often against my express wishes." Kell knew that this was Amelia's way of admitting that she had been wrong, without going to the trouble of making an outright apology.

Privately, Amelia was more effusive, inviting Kell for a drink at her flat in London at which she explained that a stream of intelligence coming out of Moscow from a senior source in the FSB had made her "blasé" about the need to recruit Minasian. Furthermore, she had been convinced that Kell's attitude toward the Russian had been skewed by his feelings for Rachel, and concerned that any deeper investigation into Riedle's murder would embroil the Service in a scandal that it could ill afford. Kell accepted her apology and did not add his own theory that the pressure of the top job — the plate-spinning chaos of SIS global "Requirements" — had affected Amelia's judgment. She had found it easier to say no to a friend than to go to the trouble of backing Kell's hunch that GAGARIN was telling the truth. It was no more or less complicated than that.

"What do you want to do about Minasian?" she asked as she poured him a second Talisker in the living room. Kell had come from the pool at his gym and was aware that his skin was giving off a vague odor of chlorine.

"I want to see him," he replied. "We agreed to meet."

"Why?" she asked.

"To thank him. And to see if he'll keep working for us. That is, if you *want* him. Perhaps your source in Moscow is so compelling that you feel you have no need for another one."

Amelia slid him a look. "Tom, don't," she said with a soft smile. She took a sip of her wine. "Of course we would love to continue to run him. I think that Minasian is very unlikely to agree to that, not least because he knows that after Brighton you won't shop him to Moscow."

"Won't I?" Kell asked.

Amelia knew him too well. "You're not that cruel."

There was a moment of silence. A couple was walking past the house, turning the corner into Markham Street.

"We have unfinished business," he said.

"What sort of unfinished business? You mean the mole you were worried about?" Amelia searched Kell's face for a reaction. "Minasian knew about Witness X because Kleckner told him. It was all over Moscow at the time."

Kell shook his head. He had meant Rachel. He wanted the names of the men who had killed her. That was the deal he had struck with Minasian. *Tell me who ordered her murder. The truth will set you free.* But he could not say this to Amelia.

"Just agent stuff," he told her. "Friendship. Loyalty. Trust. Mistrust."

"Why do I feel that you're hiding something?" she asked.

"Because *you're* always hiding something. You apply the same characteristics to other people."

"Ouch."

Amelia allowed Kell's criticism to pass. He wanted to tell her the truth. Kell needed Amelia to know that he was not yet clear of his grief, that he had not absolved her of responsibility in Rachel's death, that the desire for vengeance ran through his blood like an infection. Instead he told her that he had promised to let Minasian go in return for the information about Shahid Khan. That was his intention in going to Warsaw. To set him free.

"You want to go as a private citizen, or as part of a team?"

In all of the commotion that had followed Brighton, Amelia had never raised the subject of Kell's future status as an employee of SIS. This was the closest she had come to acknowledging the elephant in the room. Perhaps it was a case of personal pride: she did not want to give Kell the opportunity to turn her down. For his part, Kell was still not yet sure that he wanted to come back. He needed to see Minasian and to get the names. Then he would have a clearer idea in his mind of what he wanted to do.

"I don't feel strongly either way," he said.

Amelia placed her wineglass on a table beside her and stood up.

"Go and see him," she said. "I'll protect you."

## 59

Amelia's words were in Kell's mind as he landed in Warsaw four days later. It was late on a Thursday evening. Minasian had confirmed the meeting for the next afternoon. In the only exchange between the two men since Brighton, Kell had texted the encrypted phrase: "White shirt OK for tomorrow?" to which Minasian had replied: "See you there." It was enough to demonstrate that the Russian considered himself clear of surveillance and would keep to the arrangement they had made to meet in the lobby of the Regina hotel between two and three o'clock. It was a sketchy plan, not least because there was a danger that Minasian might try to double-cross Kell and put third parties into the hotel, perhaps even with the intention either of trying to eliminate him in his room or on the streets of Warsaw. Aware of the threat, Amelia had arranged for the local SIS station to watch Kell at all times. They had booked a suite at the Regina under the name "Stephen Uniacke," but Kell was to stay at a different hotel some distance away. A first-posting SIS officer took over the Uniacke alias and spent a fitful night in the room, a gun under his pillow as he waited for phantom Russians to strike.

Kell's driver was a Pole on the SIS payroll who carried a firearm and was old enough to remember the heat of the Cold War. He took Kell to a nondescript hotel a mile from the Regina, where he held a brief meeting with Max Stenbeck, the formidable — and formidably young — Head of Station in Warsaw. Stenbeck, who had fought with the Royal Marines in Afghanistan before transferring to SIS in 2007, congratulated Kell on Brighton and assured him that he would be safe "at all times." To Kell's frustration, Stenbeck also guaranteed that "every word" of his conversation with Minasian in the Uniacke suite would be picked up and recorded by a Tech-Ops team in the next room.

"We will have eyes on you," he said. Kell knew that he would have to obtain the names of the men who had killed Rachel in such a way as to avoid Stenbeck's microphones. Amelia would want to know every move that he made in the room with Minasian and would likely do everything in her power to prevent Kell from pursuing Rachel's killers.

"The risk from Minasian is very low," Kell assured him. He hoped that his newly minted reputation for courage and perspicacity would persuade Stenbeck to accept this analysis without demur. "If Minasian wanted me dead, he'd have done it in London. He wants to be reassured that we won't shop him to Moscow. He wants me to let him go."

"And do you intend to do that?"

Kell shrugged. "I haven't decided yet."

Later Kell went for dinner alone, sipping a beer at one of the tourist restaurants in the old town, thinking of Brussels and the dead Riedle, of the long days and nights he had spent luring him in. Could it be said that Riedle had died so that dozens of people in Brighton might survive? Kell could not make the link in his mind; Riedle was dead because Eremenko had willed it. He had not been a necessary sacrifice. Riedle had been murdered because of his sexuality and because Minasian had lied to him. Kell could absolve himself of personal responsibility, but felt no sense of justice, just as he had felt little euphoria in the hours and days that followed Brighton. He had acted bravely — yes — but it was the girl who had stopped Khan. Without Rosie's love, and the effect of that love on a brainwashed young man, dozens of people would have died. Kell had simply been cynical enough to recognize that he could use her; just as he had been cynical enough to use Bernhard Riedle. This was the grammar of his trade and the structure of his personality: a facility for deceit and manipulation was as much a part of Kell's character as his decency and capacity for love.

He was sitting at a table toward the center of a cobbled square in the medieval center of Warsaw. A few meters away, a man dressed as a druid, his clothes and face entirely covered in silver paint, was sitting as still as a waxwork, hovering in midair as if held up only by a wooden staff. Children stared at him, straining on their parents' hands. Close by, men were selling the summer's fad gadget, a luminous rocket that fired high into the night sky before returning to earth with the accuracy of a boomerang. At the next table, four young people of varying nationalities were struggling to find anything to say to one another, sitting through long pauses and communicating in fractured English. Kell had been watching them for almost an hour. One of them, a Frenchwoman in her late twenties, kept looking at Kell, as though imploring him to join them and to inject some life into their conversation. A part of him wanted to accept the tacit invitation. He could have smiled and pulled up a chair, found out the group's stories, and made them laugh. But he knew that he could have no part in it. This was more than a sense of being restricted by his responsibilities toward Minasian; Kell felt completely separated from the everyday to-and-fro of life, to the extent that he could not even imagine communicating with strangers.

He realized, finishing his beer and asking for the bill, that he had felt like this for too long. It was time to change things. He needed to organize his life so that he was no longer so isolated, so compromised. He was tired of being alone.

## 60

When Kell walked into the Regina hotel the following afternoon, he found the small lobby deserted. It was just before two o'clock. As he took a seat on a sofa in the center of the room, he caught a movement in his peripheral vision and turned to see two guests checking in at a reception desk tucked away in the southeast corner of the lobby. Almost a dozen bags were strewn on the ground behind them. The guests sounded tired and agitated. Classical music was playing. Kell could hear a fountain in the courtyard behind him. He was wearing a white shirt and carrying a baseball cap that he placed on a plumped cushion beside him. A waiter appeared, crossed the lobby, and asked Kell if he wanted a drink. He ordered an espresso. Then he took out his BlackBerry and iPhone and checked for messages. There was a text from Stenbeck, who was in a room directly underneath the

Uniacke suite, informing him that an MI6 security detail was waiting outside the hotel. There was no word on the BlackBerry from Minasian.

At ten minutes past two, Kell looked up to see Minasian coming through the revolving door at the entrance to the hotel. He was carrying a plastic bag and wearing a white polo shirt. He was clean-shaven and appeared to have lost weight. He made momentary eye contact before turning toward the reception desk. Kell finished his espresso, left a fifty-zloty note under the cup and saucer, and walked toward the bank of lifts on the far side of the lobby. He could hear Minasian talking to the receptionist in English. He stepped into a lift and rode up to the top floor. Kell knew that it would not be necessary to text the Uniacke room number to Minasian. A man of his resourcefulness and experience would be able to discover such information as easily as he could order a cup of coffee.

And so it proved. Exactly ten minutes after Minasian had walked into the hotel, there was a soft tap on the door of the suite. Kell had closed the curtains and conducted a sound check with Tech-Ops in the room below. He took a moment to compose himself, then opened the door.

"The hero of Brighton."

Minasian had prepared a wolfish smile. He stepped into the room and set the plastic bag on the ground. Kell closed the door behind him. To his astonishment, the Russian immediately grabbed him in a bear hug and slapped his hands against Kell's back, muttering: "Congratulations, Tom, congratulations," as he squeezed ever tighter. Kell did not know if Minasian was frisking him for a microphone or weapon, planting some kind of tracking device on his sweater, or behaving in an authentic way. He had come to trust Minasian and to doubt him in equal measure. There were days when he thought that Riedle had misread his character to a disastrous extent; and days when he believed that Riedle had seen through to the cold center of his pitiless and corrupted personality.

"It's good to see you, Alexander. I'm glad you could make it."

Minasian shrugged, suggesting that he had experienced no difficulty in keeping to their scheduled meeting. He crossed to the far side of the suite and briefly popped open a curtain, as though expecting to see a surveillance officer crouched on the window ledge with a boom microphone.

"You did it," he said.

"Did what?"

"Brighton." Minasian turned and beamed another telegenic smile. "You stopped Shahid Khan. You stopped this monster. You saved the lives of hundreds of people."

Kell knew what Minasian wanted him to say.

"I didn't do anything," he replied. "You made it all possible. You were the hero, Alexander. The British government — the British people — owe you a debt of thanks that we can never repay."

Minasian was silent as he absorbed the compliment, trying to appear modest. It was cold in the room, the air-conditioning working hard against the fierce Warsaw summer.

"Hot outside," Minasian said. "Cold in here."

"So it's not just the British who like to talk about the weather."

Minasian did not appear to understand the joke and gave no reaction. He walked back to the door, picked up the plastic bag, reached inside it, and pulled out a gift-wrapped present.

"I bought you something," he said.

He passed the present to Kell.

"That was very kind of you." Kell knew from the shape and weight of the package that it was almost certainly a book. As he

505

unwrapped it, he laid a private bet with himself that Minasian had bought him some Isaac Babel. He was mistaken.

"A first edition of Graham Greene's *Brighton Rock*," Minasian exclaimed with evident satisfaction. "It is the American edition, not the British. I hope this is satisfactory."

"More than satisfactory," Kell replied. He was genuinely pleased with the gift. "Did you inscribe it?"

"Please?"

For once, Minasian's faultless English had failed him.

"Did you write in it?" Kell explained, answering his own question by opening the book to the title page. In Minasian's neat, schoolboy handwriting he had written:

"He who thirsts for an answer must stock up with patience." Isaac Babel

Kell felt a chill run through him. "It's a great quote," he said.

Such was the ambiguity of Minasian's dedication that he could not know if it referred to the Khan operation, to Rachel, or to something else altogether.

"You know it?"

"I didn't," Kell replied.

Minasian was watching him intently. He

sat down on a corner of the large double bed and bounced briefly, like a customer in a shop testing the springs. Kell offered him a drink from the minibar. Minasian asked for sparkling water.

"I imagine that everything we say is being listened to," he said as he unscrewed the cap. "Recorded by your people. That we are not alone."

Kell smiled at him. "What would you do in my place?" he replied.

"I would do what you have done."

The two men were silent for a moment. Kell no longer felt the desire to spar with Minasian, to wrestle with his moods or to fight against his charm. He wanted only two things: to resolve the nature of his relationship with MI6 and to know the truth about Rachel's death. Everything else was of no consequence.

"First things first," he said. "Thank you for the book." He tapped the cover twice and placed it on a side table beside a flatscreen television. "I want to repeat what I said. The information you gave us . . . in my twenty-year career, few agents have ever provided me with intelligence of that value. I know that you obtained it at great personal risk and under circumstances of severe duress. I doubted that you were telling me the truth — we all did, in fact — but you proved us wrong."

Minasian lowered his gaze. It struck Kell that something had altered in his demeanor. He was more relaxed, but somehow more resigned in spirit than at their previous meetings.

"How is everything with Svetlana?" Kell asked. "With your father-in-law?"

Minasian looked up. His expression said: "What do you know that I do not know?"

"Everything okay?" Kell asked.

Minasian's voice dropped to a conspiratorial whisper. "I am doing some business with him later this evening," he said. "Here in Warsaw. At six o'clock."

"With Andrei?"

Minasian nodded. "We are meeting at Most Gdanski. The Gdansk Bridge," he said. "Then afterward to dinner. The father-in-law and his — I have always liked this expression in English — errant son."

"Most Gdanski?"

Kell wondered why Minasian was telling him this. Why disclose that there would be a meeting on Polish soil between an SVR officer and a Russian oligarch? Was he giving Kell a warning, or trying to lure MI6 to the meeting? There had been a strange tone of fatality in Minasian's voice ever since he had walked into the room. Kell had to remind himself that he was in the company of a supreme manipulator; that Minasian possessed a matchless ability to switch his moods to suit the requirements of any given conversation. He repeated lines to himself from the notes he had taken after meeting Riedle: "Adapts himself to give people what they need for as long as he needs them." Kell did not want to be dragged into another conversational tug-of-war.

"Why are you telling me this?" he asked, deciding that it was best to be unequivocal in his approach.

"Am I not supposed to tell you things like that?" Minasian had a smirk on his face. "I thought I belonged to you? I thought I was your creature?"

"Alexander . . ."

Minasian raised his hand, acknowledging that he had gone too far. He apologized for making a "bad joke" and took a long swig from the bottle of water.

"You don't belong to me any more," Kell said, seizing the opportunity formally to break their relationship. "You never did. You were never anybody's creature. Last time we met, you asked for clemency. You asked me to set you free. I will keep my word. If you give me what I asked for, when you walk out of here, MI6 will have no further hold on you. Our offer of asylum still stands, of course. You can continue working for the SVR and provide us with intelligence should you wish. But those are your decisions. You can do what you want. You are a free man."

Minasian took a long time to respond. He stared ahead at the black television screen, scanned the pictures in the room, each as bland as the last. There was the noise of a child running in the corridor outside and a parent scolding it in a language Kell did not recognize. Minasian coughed to clear his throat.

"It's funny," he said, returning to his mournful tone. "I thought about your offer a great deal. Could I change things? Could I change Russia? I thought about Ryan Kleckner, about his reasons for what he did, but I am a different sort of man. I believe Ryan acted as he did because he needed the excitement. He wanted to feel special in some way. Validated, better than the rest. In this sense, he was not unlike Shahid Khan, no? Young men seeking approval and power, and finding it in chaos. Seeking to exert control over themselves by exerting it over other people."

"That's an interesting way of thinking

about it," Kell replied.

"I worked for you because I had no choice. And I was glad in the end to do it because it provided me with an opportunity to save lives. I liked the power that this gave me. I cannot deny it. For once, Alexander Minasian, the man who had recruited agents and run them with comparative success, was now on the other side of the fence. *I* was the agent. I was the man at risk. But as soon as I saw the news from Brighton, I knew that I did not want to continue. I knew that I wanted to see you here today so that I could explain myself."

"Explain yourself?" Kell had a grim feeling that the Russian was going to produce a new piece of information, a revelation that would throw everything that he had come to understand about Minasian into chaos.

"I have come to feel that lying is a kind of sickness. That prolonged exposure to deceit leaves a person feeling worn out. Either as an agent, or as the controller of that agent, the constant process of lying, of subterfuge, of concealment and second-guess, is exhausting. It is bad for the soul. Would you agree, Tom?"

The observation chimed with Kell so deeply that he could only mutter a cracked "Yes" before lapsing into silence.

Minasian continued.

"What I mean to say is that I have lived so much of my life in a secret way. In a false way. I have not been true to myself. I have not been true to my wife. I have not been true to my Service. I have not been true to you."

"What do you mean, to *me*?" Kell asked, and felt a further tremor of discomfort.

"I could work for you," he continued. "You could work for me. We could work together. But would we *change* anything?"

"Doesn't Brighton prove that we could?"

Minasian waved a dismissive hand. "I don't mean at the level of counterterrorism. There will always be effective policing. I mean at the level of policy. The projection of power. Let's be honest. What can a spy do that a drone cannot? Are we more useful than a software virus, a piece of malware, a security camera, a satellite, a mobile telephone?"

Kell realized what was happening. Minasian was talking himself out of the SVR and into a permanent job with Andrei Eremenko. That was why the two men were meeting in Warsaw. Minasian needed to rationalize his decision to end his career as an intelligence officer by claiming that the business of human intelligence — of recruitment, of agent-running, the entire trade that both of them had known all their adult lives — was obsolete. And he needed Kell to validate that choice. There had to be a fault in the system rather than a fault with Alexander Minasian. It was a symptom of his narcissism.

"I believe that we are better," Kell replied. "I believe that deeply. I believe in human beings. I believe in relationships."

"Then you are more romantic than me," Minasian replied. "More optimistic. I believe that so much of what we do in our business is pointless."

"Well, I think if we go into life expecting it to deliver results for us all the time, we're going to be disappointed," Kell told him.

Minasian smiled appreciatively. "Yes," he said. "He who thirsts for an answer must first stock up with patience."

"Exactly."

Minasian chose this moment to take out the encrypted BlackBerry and to return it to Kell.

"I believe this is yours."

"Keep it," Kell told him.

"I would rather not." Minasian looked at the phone as if it were something he wanted to throw into a bin. "I do not trust them."

"Me neither."

Kell removed the battery from the Black-Berry and placed it in a drawer beside the bed. It seemed a good opportunity to move the conversation into more fruitful territory. He longed for a cigarette and had no compunction about pulling back the curtains and sliding open the door onto the balcony. Let Stenbeck's headphoned wonks live with the street noise and the birdsong. He needed nicotine and fresh air. Besides, what Kell now wanted to discuss with Minasian was his own private business. It had nothing to do with Stenbeck or Amelia.

"You will smoke?" Minasian asked.

"Yeah. Want one?"

Minasian shook his head. He took another long swig of water. Kell watched his Adam's apple moving up and down, a barometer of his concealed anxiety. The Russian stood up and settled in a chair closer to the open door. Kell stood outside in the shade provided by a high wall. It was still fiercely hot. He lit a cigarette and took the smoke deep into his lungs.

"So about that," he said.

"About what, please?" Minasian asked.

"Patience. Answers. Rachel. You were going to tell me."

"Yes." Minasian appeared to be overcome by regret. He shook his head slowly and

514

looked at the ground. "I was going to tell you about that."

## 61

The personal and business affairs of Andrei Eremenko had been under investigation by Carnelian Solutions for nineteen months. Carnelian styled itself as a "global consultancy" offering "political and business risk assessments," "investigative due diligence," "on-the-ground client security and protection," as well as "in-depth analysis of trends in global finance and economics." More than half of its 125-strong workforce had backgrounds with national intelligence services. One such employee was a former MI6 officer named Jane Shilling who had retired from the Service nine years earlier to join the board at Carnelian on a salary three times greater than that which she had enjoyed at Vauxhall Cross. A friend of Amelia Levene, and a former girlfriend of Jimmy Marquand, Shilling had run the clandestine investigation into Eremenko's operations on behalf of a wealthy Russian client with a grudge as limitless as his bank balance.

In the aftermath of the Riedle shooting, Amelia had instructed Marquand to make "delicate inquiries" into the relationship between Eremenko and his son-in-law. Carnelian had provided SIS with information about Eremenko in the wake of Rachel's assassination, so Amelia told Marquand to make Shilling his first port of call. Marquand's former lover was now married and wary that "Melvyn" was trying to reignite a romantic fire that, for her, had been extinguished more than a decade earlier. But she agreed to meet Marquand for lunch at Sheekey on condition that he treated whatever she might tell him in the strictest confidence and "pass no judgment on our methods."

"What methods are those?" Marquand had asked, trying to separate a razor clam from its shell.

It transpired that, with the help of a former officer in the Shin Bet, Carnelian now had control of three of Eremenko's five mobile phones and had successfully planted listening devices in his homes in London, Verbier, and New York.

"We couldn't manage Moscow," she confessed. "Tried. Too risky."

Shilling had handed Marquand a file that demonstrated Eremenko's culpability in the Riedle shooting to a 90 percent degree of proof. Carnelian had hacked text messages and voice mail recordings in which Eremenko expressed his anger with Minasian for his relationship with Riedle, as well as his concern that the affair, if discovered, would end his son-in-law's career with the SVR. Carnelian had also traced two payments of fifty thousand pounds to the bank account of a known associate of the Turkish hit man suspected of carrying out the Riedle assassination. Shilling had believed that this would mark the end of her interaction with MI6, but a subsequent conversation, picked up by microphones placed in Eremenko's London office, caused her to summon Marquand to a second meeting three weeks later.

They met in a branch of Itsu on Notting Hill Gate.

"What's up?" Marquand asked as he sat down. Plates of sushi and edamame beans passed their table on a help-yourself conveyor belt. "You sounded worried on the phone."

"It's Minasian," she replied. "Eremenko has given the order. Warsaw. Tonight. They're going to kill him."

## 62

Kell rolled up the sleeves of his white shirt and took another drag on the cigarette. Minasian was sitting in the hardbacked chair on the other side of the sliding doors, propped forward like a man in a hospital expecting to hear bad news. His elbows were on his knees and he was staring at the ground. Kell felt that Minasian was too ashamed to look at him.

"I did not tell you the truth about Istanbul," he said.

"Go on." Kell knew, in the way that a person can sense themselves becoming sick, that nothing good was going to come of what Minasian was about to tell him.

"The person who killed Rachel Wallinger was French. His name was Sebastien Gachon. He had many personalities, many pseudonyms. He operated on that occasion using the name Eric Cauques. Gachon was also responsible for the murder of our agent,

Cecilia Sandor, and her boyfriend, Luka Zigic. The orders to remove all of them came from Moscow."

Kell choked on the word "remove" but said nothing. Sandor had been Paul Wallinger's lover, an SVR honeytrap orchestrated by Minasian. Kell could see a sheen of sweat on Minasian's forehead and on the back of his neck. He had not yet looked up.

"Where is Gachon now?" Kell asked.

At last Minasian made eye contact.

"Dead," he said.

"How?" To Kell's surprise he felt relief rather than anger that he would not have a chance to confront Gachon face-to-face. He was a hired killer; it was enough that he was dead. The person that mattered was in Moscow. That was the name he wanted.

"Car crash," Minasian replied. "Outside Lyons."

"When?"

"Six months ago."

"Moscow arranged it?"

"It was an accident."

Kell walked past Minasian, picked up a notepad and pen from the suite, and returned to the balcony. He stubbed out his cigarette.

"How are you spelling the surnames?"

Minasian recited the letters — G A C H

O N — and did the same for Cauques. Kell wrote them down and put the notepad in his back pocket. He would have Elsa run the names and produce a file. He wanted to see the face of the man who had shot Rachel. He wanted to know with absolute certainty that he was dead.

"Anybody killed with him?" he asked. "Anybody else in the car?"

Minasian shook his head. Kell took out a second cigarette and lit it.

"Who gave the order in Moscow?"

Minasian walked out onto the balcony.

"May I have one?" he asked, indicating the packet of Winston Lights in Kell's hand. Kell closed the door, shutting out the last of the microphones. The suite was the only room on the top floor in this section of the hotel and their conversation could not be overheard.

"Sure."

Kell passed Minasian a cigarette and lit it for him with Amelia's gold lighter. There were two iron chairs on the balcony. Minasian sat in the closest of them, putting on a pair of sunglasses.

"The order was given by my immediate superior. He has since been replaced. He took the blame for the failure of the Kleckner operation."

521

"He took the blame rather than you?"

Minasian nodded. "It was thought that he had acted rashly. That he was too concerned to keep the Kleckner product flowing, at any cost. He became paranoid. His methods became unnecessarily violent."

"That's how you would describe the death of this young woman?" Kell was appalled that Minasian would so casually refer to Rachel's murder. " 'Unnecessary violence'?"

Minasian held up his hands. "Forgive me, Tom. My use of English was incorrect."

"Take off your sunglasses."

"Excuse me?"

"I don't like talking to people when I can't see their eyes. Especially yours. I find it difficult to know whether they're telling me the truth."

Reluctantly, and with a look of offended pride, Minasian removed the glasses and hooked them onto his shirt.

"I am trying to tell you the truth," he said.

"Trying." Kell turned the word over, exhaling a funnel of smoke as he studied Minasian.

"What was the name of your superior?"

There was a fractional hesitation before the Russian said: "It does not matter."

"It matters to me."

"He is still with the Service. It will be difficult to find him."

"Why? Because you're leaving the SVR?"

Minasian's composure cracked. "How did you know this?"

"Isn't it obvious?" Kell ground out the cigarette. "You've lost faith in what we do. You're meeting your father-in-law on neutral ground this evening. He's made you an offer, hasn't he?"

Minasian did not bother concealing this. "You see a lot, Tom," he replied. "Yes. I have decided to move on. A new career."

"So what did you mean when you said that you hadn't told me the truth about Istanbul? Was there somebody else involved? Why aren't you giving me more details? What is it that I still don't know?"

Minasian took his time. He looked like a man carrying a terrible secret. Kell did not believe that he was speaking to someone who had undergone a profound change in temperament; he still knew that the Russian was capable of layered subterfuge and chameleonic shifts in personality. Nevertheless, in these moments Minasian's discomfort seemed precise and authentic. He did not want to have to tell Kell what he was about to tell him.

"I lied to you at your apartment in London," he said. "I was shocked by what had happened to Bernhard. I was angry with you and I was grieving. I did love him, whatever you may think or whatever Bernhard may have told you. I did not always treat him well, but I did not set out to destroy him."

"What you felt for each other is private. It's none of my business," Kell replied.

"But you loved Rachel?"

"Yes, I did." Kell wondered at the good sense of revealing what he was about to say, but something in him wanted Minasian to know how he felt. "I got over it. I hardly had a chance to know her. It was the sense of what had been wasted — the potential in her. That was what was taken away. Not just from me, but from her family, her friends."

"I could have stopped it."

Kell took a sharp breath.

"There was a communication with Moscow. My superior gave the order. He instructed me to engage Gachon. I did this. I am very sorry, Tom. I was angry with you because of the humiliation in Odessa. Your people had injured me and you had taken Kleckner. I wanted to strike back at you. I could have stopped him, I could have made out that I never received the communication. I could have told Moscow what others said later, after it was too late. That the murder of this woman — of Rachel Wallinger — was senseless and wrong. But I did not do that. There is blood on my hands. I lied to you."

A plane was flying high overhead, east to west in the cloudless sky. Kell looked up and understood why Minasian had confessed. It was an act of vengeance, a means of regaining control over him after a long period of humiliation. He could walk out of the room knowing that Kell was powerless against him. Minasian's suffering, his apparent mood of anxiety, of mournful resignation, was a façade. He was drawing sadistic satisfaction from the impact of his words, even as he feigned remorse.

Kell opened the sliding door and pulled back the curtain. He turned to face Minasian.

"Go," he said, indicating the door of the suite.

"Tom, please."

Kell had known for a long time that Minasian had been responsible for Rachel's death. He had needed to think otherwise in order to recruit him, to run him, but his instincts had been right all along.

"Our business is concluded," he said.

Minasian stood up. He walked toward Kell, seizing him by the arms.

"I need to know that you forgive me."

"No, you don't."

"What do you mean by that?"

Kell removed his hands, feeling the strength in Minasian's arms. "You know what you're doing, Alexander. You know what you've done. We both understand that."

Minasian took a step back.

"I can see that it is pointless trying to persuade you," he said, going into the suite. Kell followed him, saying nothing. He felt an impotent rage at his failure to protect Rachel, at the futility of his lust for vengeance, even at his failure physically to attack Minasian, to fight him. In this last moment between them, all of it felt meaningless. Kell's humiliation, his anger at Gachon, at Amelia, at Moscow — none of it was of any importance when set against the fact that Rachel was lost.

"We have said all that we will ever say to one another."

Kell reached for the door. Bowing his head, the Russian walked out into the corridor.

"I am truly sorry," he said, turning back to face him. "Whatever you may think, whatever you may believe. What I did was wrong and I regret it deeply."

"Good-bye, Alexander," Kell said, and closed the door.

## 63

Kell went back onto the balcony and sat in the hot sun. In a moment of extraordinary clarity, he knew that his career as a spy had come to an end. He wanted nothing more to do with it. Far from a desire to go after Minasian, Kell felt a profound empathy with the words he had spoken to him just a few minutes earlier. The Russian had articulated the doubt with which Kell had wrestled for too long. Spying was a sickness that had hollowed him out. It had cost Kell his marriage; it had cost Rachel her life. How had Minasian put it? "The constant process of lying, of subterfuge, of concealment and second-guess, is exhausting. It is bad for the soul." Whether or not he had been speaking from the heart was immaterial. It no longer mattered to Kell whether Minasian had been telling the truth. What he had said was indisputable. The profession they had chosen had left both of them broken and

528

compromised and alone.

There was a loud knock on the door. Kell walked back into the suite. Max Stenbeck was standing in the corridor. He was a rotund man, bespectacled and prematurely bald. Kell did not know him well enough to determine if the weary look on his face indicated confusion or annoyance.

"What the hell happened?" he said.

"Minasian left."

"So I see."

Kell ushered him inside. "You didn't hear our conversation?"

"None of it." Stenbeck pulled the sliding door on the balcony until it clicked shut. "None of the mikes worked. Heard him come in. Heard you tell him that the British government couldn't thank him enough for Brighton, blah blah blah — then nothing. Fucking kit."

Kell was not surprised; he had known technical failures of this kind several times before in his career. He took out his iPhone and saw that Stenbeck had sent him three text messages during the meeting with Minasian, each of them warning him that their conversation was not being picked up.

"Sorry," he said, indicating the phone. "Only just saw these."

Stenbeck perched on the same corner of

the bed that Minasian had briefly made his own. He did not test the springs.

"I was sitting with Tomasz thinking I've got another Philby–Elliott on my hands." Stenbeck was referring to the notorious SIS recording of Kim Philby's confession to his MI6 counterpart, Nicholas Elliott, which was drowned out by the sound of Beirut traffic. "We literally had no idea what was going on in here."

"Don't worry about it," Kell told him. "He didn't say anything incendiary."

"How long ago did he leave?"

"About ten minutes. I thought you had a car outside?"

"They didn't see him go," Stenbeck confessed. "Minasian must have used a side entrance."

"Must have."

Kell was hungry and took a packet of peanuts from a tray above the minibar. He offered Stenbeck a drink.

"No, thanks," he said. "So what happened?"

Kell knew that he could carry off an attitude of gnomic indifference and that Stenbeck wouldn't confront him about it. He was Amelia's newly anointed saint: the hero of Brighton, the man who had brought down Ryan Kleckner. He was untouchable.

"We talked," he said, opening the peanuts. "We decided to end our relationship. I thanked him for Brighton. He thanked me for letting him go."

"That was it?"

"That was it."

Kell found that he could hardly summon the energy to lie.

"What about when you went onto the balcony?"

"How do you know we went out there if the microphones weren't working?"

It was a first indication that Stenbeck was suspicious of him. Kell assumed that Amelia had planted the seed of doubt. *Keep an eye on Tom. He has issues with Minasian. Personal issues.* Stenbeck looked over his glasses at the sliding door and gave a cool reply.

"Because that was open when I came in. Because you like to smoke. And because I gave up on the tech, opened the window to get some air, heard you talking outside your room, but couldn't make out what you were saying."

Kell smiled. He liked Stenbeck. He was a fellow traveler, not a company man like Marquand. He had the look of someone who loved the game, who had entered it for the right reasons. Kell wondered if he

531

should just tell him everything — about Gachon, about Minasian's decision to greenlight the hit on Rachel — but he couldn't be bothered to deal with the blowback. It was over. The past was a foreign country.

"He gave me a present," he said, picking up the copy of *Brighton Rock.* "American. First edition."

"In return for *The Whitsun Weddings*?"

Kell was swallowing a mouthful of peanuts and felt his throat go dry. After Brighton, Amelia had asked for a detailed account of his relationship with Minasian. Kell had obliged her. He had not anticipated that she would circulate the report to the Head of Station in Warsaw.

"Not bad," he said.

Stenbeck frowned, as if Kell were trying to draw him into a confrontation he had no interest in joining.

"I'm just intrigued," he said.

"Sure."

There was an awkward silence. Kell filled it by walking outside. Clouds had gathered over the old town. It was threatening rain.

"So where did he go?" Stenbeck asked, joining Kell on the balcony.

"I have no idea."

Kell felt the lie as no more than a necessary protection against Amelia's snooping.

"None? You don't know where he went? Nothing about meeting his father-in-law? Nothing about seeing Andrei Eremenko?"

It had been a long time since Kell had been outmaneuvered in a conversation. What did Stenbeck know? Had he heard the exchanges with Minasian and lied about the microphones?

"Why do you ask?" he asked.

"Because we've had some information."

"What kind of information?" Kell inhaled on the cigarette and looked up at the darkening sky.

"Minasian thinks he's meeting his father-in-law tonight. Here in Warsaw. Did he mention that?"

Kell found himself saying: "No. All he told me is that Eremenko has offered him a job."

"I'm afraid that's not true."

"In what way is it not true?"

"Eremenko is in London. We had a confirmed sighting at Claridge's within the last forty-five minutes. The man he has sent to meet Minasian in Warsaw intends to kill him."

## 64

Kell knew that he was holding a man's life in his hands. If he revealed that Minasian was going to the bridge to meet Eremenko, MI6 could save him. If he did not, Minasian would be killed.

"Why does Eremenko want to get rid of him?"

Stenbeck shrugged. "More boyfriends. More fucking around. He was being watched twenty-four seven; they realized he was still cheating on Svetlana. Alex can't keep it in his trousers. The father-in-law has had enough."

"And he was happy to leave the Service."

It was a piece of information Kell had not yet divulged. Stenbeck reacted with surprise. "He told you that?"

Kell nodded.

"So Minasian is no more use to him." Stenbeck understood how Russian elites functioned. "Eremenko's power base is undermined. He wants Minasian out of the picture before he gets a chance to embarrass him in the private sector. Easier to screw around when you're not answerable to the SVR."

"Exactly." Kell dropped the cigarette and kicked the butt toward the edge of the balcony. He was asking himself the same question, again and again. Do I protect the man who took Rachel from me? Or do I lie and let him meet his fate?

"Where did this intel come from?"

Stenbeck explained that Carnelian had been listening to Eremenko's conversations on behalf of a Russian client. Jimmy Marquand had been digging around, looking to tie Eremenko to the Riedle shooting. Carnelian had handed him what they knew.

"So what are you planning to do?" Kell asked.

"Me?"

"Yes, you. The Service. Amelia. What does she want to do about Minasian?"

"She thinks that you should decide," Stenbeck replied.

"She said that?"

Stenbeck nodded. Kell picked up the first edition of *Brighton Rock* and opened it to the first page:

Hale knew, before he had been in Brighton three hours, that they meant to murder him.

"She doesn't care, one way or the other?"

"I didn't say that," Stenbeck replied.

Kell felt that he was being tested; that Amelia had eyes and ears in the hotel suite and was somehow watching his every move.

"I have no way of contacting Minasian," he said. "And we can't exactly ring up Svetlana."

"No."

In that moment, he made the decision to save Minasian's life. Amelia believed that Kell was a decent man. He did not want to let her down.

"All I know is that he's meeting Eremenko on a bridge somewhere this evening."

In some ways it felt like an act of surrender. Kell wished that he possessed the ruthlessness to abandon Minasian to his fate. An eye for an eye. But he knew that he would not be able to live with such an act on his conscience.

"He told you that?" Stenbeck was suddenly jolted out of his mood of indifference. "A bridge? Where?"

"The Gdansk Bridge," Kell replied.

Stenbeck appeared to know the location.

"Why didn't you say so before?"

"You didn't ask."

"What time?"

"Six o'clock."

Stenbeck shook his head. "He told you that as well?"

He returned to the corner of the bed and sat down, deep in thought.

"There is, of course, another theory," he said after a long period of contemplation.

"And what's that?" Kell asked.

"That's it's a trap. That they have no intention of killing Alexander Minasian. The real target of the operation is *you.*"

## 65

"You'd better explain that one to me." Kell felt a sense of frustration that was all too familiar. "Perhaps there are things you know that I don't."

Stenbeck began to work from memory. Kell was impressed by how much of the detail of his written report he had absorbed.

"When you met Minasian in London, the second time. After Westfield. You drove north, along the A40. Correct?"

"Correct."

"But it was Minasian who suggested Warsaw? He was the one who sowed that idea in your mind, not the other way around?"

"Also correct."

"He said that he was going to be here this afternoon. July twenty-fourth. He was very precise about this. A window of opportunity, away from prying eyes, for only two or three hours."

"Nothing unusual about that," Kell replied. "Minasian knows his own schedule, he knew when he would and wouldn't have the opportunity to see me."

Stenbeck nodded. "Of course. And as an intelligence officer himself, he knew that your first order of business would be setting the next meet."

"What's your point?" Kell asked.

"I'm saying that he came prepared. He wanted to meet you here. He wanted to see you, to act like you were the hero, to be told that he was free of his obligation to the Service. But he had another agenda. He wants to walk you into the arms of the men he and Eremenko have hired to kill you."

Kell sat in an armchair positioned between the bed and the window. He was not at all convinced by what Stenbeck was telling him.

"You're saying that Minasian and Eremenko are working in tandem? That both of them — for different reasons — want me out of the picture?"

"I'm saying that it's a possibility. Why else did he tell you about the Gdansk Bridge? Why be so specific? If information is power, why is he handing that power to somebody who has no need for it? Why did he feel it was necessary to tell you what he was doing and where he was going this evening? Unless he *wanted* you to be there?"

Kell tried to interrupt, but Stenbeck wasn't done.

"What happened with the BlackBerry?" he said. "You gave Minasian a phone at the first meeting, right? Used it only once, to confirm today's meeting?"

Kell nodded. He knew the tail that Stenbeck was chasing.

"Did he give it back to you or did you ask for it?"

"I didn't ask for it." Kell reached into the drawer and removed the BlackBerry. It was the first time that he had begun to doubt his own mind. "He gave it back to me. He wanted to give it back."

Stenbeck leaned backward with a look of quiet triumph on his face, as though his theory could now brook no argument. Kell worked through the logic. Eremenko knew that he was under surveillance by Carnelian. He had sworn revenge against his son-in-law in order to mislead MI6. What had been heard on the tapes had been misinterpreted by Marquand. A man had been sent to Warsaw not to kill Minasian, but to kill Kell.

"But why?" Kell asked. "Minasian knows where I live. Eremenko could have had me taken out at any moment in the last six weeks. I'm not exactly difficult to find."

"Not on British soil," Stenbeck replied instantly. "That way he starts a war. They do it here, it's an accident. Plausible deniability. Minasian is playing on your decency. He knows that you won't be cruel enough to let him die. You'll have to be the hero. You'll have to come and save him." Kell was astonished by Stenbeck's frankness. "Why else did he give you back the phone? He knows that you have no way of contacting him now. You'll have to go to the bridge to warn him in person. That's when you get killed."

"Not if you come with me," Kell replied. "Not if we take a team down there, get in ahead of him, find out who we're dealing with."

Stenbeck reacted with astonishment.

"Are you serious? You think London would sign that off? I'm not putting my people in the line of fire to protect an SVR officer who may or may not be trying to assassinate one of my colleagues. Alexander Minasian is not your responsibility."

"He saved lives, Max. Hundreds of lives. Eremenko is trying to kill him because he's ashamed of his son-in-law's sexuality. It's that simple. Power and homophobia, with a dash of the psychopath for good measure.

Believe me. This is not a secret plot. I am not the target. This is Eremenko taking Minasian out of the equation because it's his *will*."

"I'm afraid I profoundly disagree."

Kell stood up. "Then I guess I'm on my own."

# 66

They came to an arrangement.

Stenbeck knew that it was pointless trying to prevent Kell from contacting Minasian. Warsaw Station would have to help him, with or without clearance from London.

"Minasian doesn't want to kill me," Kell insisted.

They were still in the suite, Kell finishing off the last of the peanuts.

"That may well be the case," Stenbeck told him. "But it's my responsibility to think otherwise. I don't want to be the man who lost Thomas Kell to an SVR trap."

He took out a map of Warsaw and showed Kell the location of the Gdansk Bridge. It was no more than a ten-minute walk from the Regina, north along the river. There were tram stops on the bridge at both ends and a walkway for pedestrians and cyclists running along the southern face, overlooking old Warsaw and the Vistula River. Stenbeck explained that there was a ramp at the far end of the bridge, leading down toward the Warsaw Zoo.

Both men anticipated that Minasian would most likely be waiting at one of the two tram stops or at a point somewhere on the walkway overlooking the river. If Eremenko planned to have him killed, the attack could occur in several different ways: a gunman could emerge from a passing tram; conceal himself among the waiting passengers; or approach Minasian on the walkway and shoot him in plain sight. If, on the other hand, the meeting was a trap, Minasian might try to lure Kell off the bridge, to get him into a vehicle or to take him into the more secluded, forested areas on the eastern side of the river. A gunman could be waiting at a prearranged location. Kell's murder would be made to look like an act of petty crime, rather than a professional hit. Kell continued to insist that he was in no danger, but Stenbeck refused to believe him. To avoid giving any further fuel to his theory, Kell did not tell him that Minasian had confessed to culpability in Rachel's death.

It was almost half past five. There were only thirty minutes until the Russian was due on the bridge. Stenbeck left the suite for a moment. He returned carrying a small canvas bag. He closed the door behind him and walked up to Kell. He reached into the bag and pulled out a gun.

"Take this," he said. "Just in case."

"Thank you."

"I believe you're familiar with the brand."

The gun was identical to the one Kell had used in Brighton.

"All too familiar," Kell replied, forcing a smile.

There was a belt holster for the weapon that Kell hooked onto his trousers. Stenbeck had arranged to put a driver on the road outside the zoo. Stenbeck himself would follow Kell at a discreet distance, watching for threats and variables as he approached the first tram stop on the western side of the river. With the gun concealed by his jacket, Kell walked out of the Regina ahead of Stenbeck at exactly 5:40 P.M., moving east toward the river. His only goal was to prevent the attack on Minasian. After that, he was done.

The streets were crowded with pedestrians walking around the restored medieval city. Watching them, Kell had no idea if he was alone or operating under a blanket of SVR surveillance. There was no way of knowing and no time to check. He passed a bronze sculpture of Marie Curie and lit a cigarette.

Dogs were barking on leads and couples holding hands in the evening sunlight. There was a small park set back from the highway that ran along the shore of the Vistula River. Adults and children were cooling their bare feet in the waters of a small lake, columns of water shooting up in jets from a fountain. Kell thought of Brighton and the innocent summer day smashed by the hate of Shahid Khan. He could see the Gdansk Bridge in the distance, now just a few hundred meters away. He thought of Rosie and wondered what had become of her.

His phone rang. It was Stenbeck.

"How are you doing?"

"Fine," Kell told him. "Anyone on me?"

"Hard to tell."

For the first time, Kell felt a sense of trepidation. He wondered if he was being wilfully naïve; if his desire to save Minasian was an act of sentimental weakness that the Russian had played upon as easily as he had manipulated the hapless Bernhard Riedle. Taking out a cigarette, Kell began to smoke, looking out across the river to the eastern side, at the undeveloped banks of forest and makeshift urban beaches, the sand dotted with sunbathers. Was this where Minasian planned to take him? What was waiting for him on the other side of the bridge?

"Fucking hot," said Stenbeck.

"I noticed. Any sign of our man?"

"None."

Kell hung up and continued toward the bridge. He entered the station at five minutes to six. Cars were passing on the carriageway overhead. Beneath the bridge, traffic was moving in both directions along the highway that skirted the river. There were only half a dozen passengers waiting for trams on either side of the platform. The tramlines disappeared to the east beneath a canopy of green steel girders that formed a tunnel across the Vistula. At the far end of the tracks, in a vanishing point of gleaming steel, Kell could see a cone of bright yellow sunlight.

He called Stenbeck.

"No sign of Minasian," he said. "I'm going to the other side."

"You'll be alone as you cross," Stenbeck told him.

Kell passed a corkscrew concrete staircase and joined the walkway running along the southern side of the bridge. He was aware of two women following him and a cyclist coming fast in the opposite direction. The walkway was separated from the tramlines by a screen of girders, the green steel plates marked with graffiti, the spaces between them grown thick with weeds and cobwebs. There was no way of leaving the walkway without climbing through onto the tracks or jumping into the river on the other side. Kell was caged in. He reached for the butt of the gun.

The cyclist passed him, a flash of helmet and Lycra. Kell turned to see that the two women had stopped a third of the way across the bridge, seemingly to look at the river. The only other person he could see was Stenbeck, a few meters behind them. Kell was now halfway across the bridge. He tossed the cigarette down into the water and quickened his pace. A bell in the old city chimed six o'clock.

He reached the tram stop on the eastern side. It was deserted save for a man standing on the far side of the platform. He was wearing a white polo shirt and leaning against a concrete pillar. Minasian.

"Alexander."

Minasian looked up. Kell knew straightaway, from the look on his face, that Stenbeck had been wrong. Minasian was not expecting to see him.

"Tom? What are you doing here?" He was shouting across the tramlines. "Andrei will see you. He will see us."

Kell had not yet released the gun. Minasian glanced down and saw that Kell was armed.

"Andrei isn't coming," Kell called back. They were no more than twenty feet away from each other, their voices almost drowned out by the noise of the traffic passing overhead.

"What do you mean he's not coming? Why did you follow me here? You said it was over. Why did you come?"

To Kell's astonishment, he saw that Minasian looked frightened.

"Andrei wants you dead," he said, walking across the tramlines so that he came within a few feet of the Russian. "He's not even in Warsaw. He was seen two hours ago in the lobby of Claridge's."

Minasian shook his head. "That is not true," he said, trying to force a smile that would disguise his disbelief. "I had a message from Andrei twenty minutes ago. He is coming here at any moment. He is on the next tram."

Kell was close enough now to reach out and to touch Minasian's arm. "Our Station has intelligence that this meeting was set up in order to kill you. You need to come with me. You are not safe."

"This is a trap," Minasian replied, stepping back to break Kell's hold on him. "A clumsy trap. You blame me for Rachel, you are reacting impulsively."

"This is not about Rachel. I promise. Whoever gets off that tram is most likely the same person who murdered Bernhard. But this time he will have come for you."

"You are insane to say this!" Minasian glanced to his left. As if sent to confirm a prophecy, a tram was gliding in from the east. Minasian looked utterly alone.

"Alexander," he said. "It's over. If you want to be safe, you must come with me. Your life is in danger."

Minasian looked past him. He saw Stenbeck standing on the opposite side of the tramlines.

"Who is that?"

"A friend," Kell replied. "He can take you to our embassy. He can make you safe. He will get you back to London and protect you."

The tram was less than a hundred meters away, slowing as it approached the station. Kell was certain that the gunman was on board. He walked back across the tracks, hoping that the Russian would follow him. He felt that he had only seconds before the doors of the tram opened and Minasian was shot.

"Tell me," he shouted. "After London. In

the last two weeks. Have there been other men? Have you been tempted?"

The question unlocked the last of Minasian's reluctance to act. Kell saw a secret pass across his face, the memory of a man, of a body, of a night without Svetlana. It was this that Eremenko had known about, the catalyst for his decision finally to be rid of the son-in-law who had betrayed him.

"Andrei knows," Kell said. "He has you followed. Everywhere. You swore to remain faithful to his daughter and you broke your word. He wants you dead." He held out his hand, imploring Minasian to cooperate. "Come with us," he said. "You wait here, on this platform, in this place, you will not survive."

The bell rang out on the tram. Kell heard the hiss and crackle of electricity in the cables overhead. At the last instant, Minasian made up his mind and stepped in front of the tram. He was across the tracks just as the front carriage passed him, sending a breeze sweeping upward into Kell's face. Kell grabbed him, pulled him toward Stenbeck, and felt a wave of nausea that he had saved the life of a man who had killed the woman he loved.

"This cannot be correct," Minasian told them. Stenbeck was studying him, still trying to work out if Kell was being sucked into a trap.

"The car is down below," he said, nodding in the direction of the zoo. "Let's go. Let's go quickly."

Passengers were leaving the tram. Kell looked back at them as he pushed Minasian toward the top of the path. He was sure that he saw a man looking in their direction from the platform, eyes concealed by sunglasses, relaying a message into a mobile phone.

"What is going to happen to me?" Minasian asked. "I do not understand."

A mother and her young child were walking up the path from the road. Kell stepped to one side to allow the child to pass.

"Don't worry about that now," he said. "Let's just get to the car."

Stenbeck was on the phone to the driver, telling him to start the engine. They were halfway along the path. Kell looked back up and saw the man in sunglasses looking over the rim of the bridge. He was still talking into the phone. It was one of the hottest days of the summer and he was wearing a black leather jacket.

"We need to move," he said.

He held Minasian tighter by the arm. Stenbeck was ahead of them, trying to locate the car.

"Where the fuck is Krzysztof?" he said, looking east toward the zoo, panning his eyes along the forested banks of the river.

Kell looked back up toward the bridge. The man in the sunglasses was following them. Kell remembered Simon's description of Riedle's killer: squat, dark hair, balding at the back. Early thirties. Greek or Turkish. He was certain it was the same man.

"You recognize that guy?"

Minasian turned, looking toward him. "No," he said.

Stenbeck had located the car. He was sweating profusely, pale English skin flushed by the evening sun.

"Coming any second," he said as Kell saw the man place a hand inside his leather jacket.

"Gun," he said.

Simultaneously, Minasian and Stenbeck said: "Where?" and followed Kell's eyes up the ramp toward the bridge. The man did not withdraw his hand from the jacket. Instead he reacted to the sudden squawk of a siren nearby. Kell turned in the direction of the zoo. A handcuffed prisoner was being bundled into the back of a police vehicle. A man in plainclothes standing beside the vehicle was holding a scoped rifle. At the last moment, as he was forced down into the back seat, the prisoner glanced up at the ramp and appeared to signal to his accomplice. Seeing this, the man in the leather jacket immediately turned and walked back up the path toward the bridge.

"Jesus," said Stenbeck. "They got him."

"What's happening?" Minasian asked.

Kell realized that Stenbeck had tipped off the ABW. They had conducted a search of the area beneath the bridge and found an armed man. Kell looked at Stenbeck, who confirmed his suspicion with a brisk nod. Krzysztof pulled up beside them in a Lexus. Stenbeck opened the back door and pushed Minasian inside.

"Get in," he said.

Kell was watching the man in the leather jacket. Eremenko's housetrained assassin.

"You see that man?" he said, climbing into the back seat and pointing up toward the bridge. "The one in the leather jacket? Short. Dark hair."

The Russian looked out of the window.

"Yes?" he said.

"That's the man who shot Bernhard."

Minasian looked appalled.

"What did you say?" He pressed his face closer to the window. His forehead bumped against the glass as Krzysztof pulled away from the curb.

"Your father-in-law sent him. The SVR had Gachon. Eremenko has that guy."

"And that was his buddy," Stenbeck added, indicating the plainclothes ABW team behind them. "You were being walked into a trap. Your friend Tom just saved your life."

"I don't believe you." Minasian was craning in the back seat, trying to see what was behind him. "None of this is true. You are setting me up. Put me out of the car. I want to confront this man."

Kell held Minasian by the arm. "Not today," he said. "We're going home."

"He killed Bernhard."

Against all expectations, Kell found that he was touched by Minasian's expression of despair.

"Another time," he said, sinking back in his seat as the car moved south toward central Warsaw. "We lose the things we love."

## 67

They drove to an SIS safe house on the western side of the city. Minasian was taken inside by Krzysztof, leaving Stenbeck and Kell on the street.

"What happens now?" Stenbeck asked. "He's your source, Tom."

Kell shook his head and looked down at the cobbled road.

"Minasian is nothing to do with me," he said. "Amelia will want to get him back to London. They'll do a trade. In return for telling her everything he knows, she'll set him up for a new life in the U.K. Quid pro quo."

"Don't you want a piece of that?" Stenbeck was astonished at Kell's nonchalance.

"I'm done," Kell told him. "Getting out."

*"What?"*

Kell did not have the patience to explain himself. He had reached the point of no return. He was grateful that nobody had been harmed on the bridge, but sick of vengeance and sick of death. He thanked Stenbeck and wished him well. He assured him that he would write up a report of the incident and tell Amelia that Stenbeck had acted at all times with professionalism and integrity.

"I appreciate that. Thank you."

Stenbeck ordered a car to take Kell back to his hotel. He packed his bags, checked out, and hailed a taxi that took him to the railway station. There was an overnight train leaving for Berlin at half past eleven. Germany seemed a good place to aim for. He could disappear for a while.

Kell bought a ticket and ate a kebab at a counter inside the station. He had switched his phone to mute, but when he saw Amelia's name light up on the screen he decided to answer.

"Max says you've left. What's going on?"

"It's simple," Kell replied. "My dealings with Minasian are finished. I've brought him to you. Call it a parting gift."

"What do you mean 'a parting gift'? I don't understand."

He wondered where she was calling from. The grace-and-favor flat? The fringes of an official meeting?

"I've decided to stop," he said.

"Stop?"

"Move on."

There was a pause as Amelia absorbed what he had said.

"But I want you to come back. I *need* you to come back."

"It's no good, Amelia. I'm done."

Kell felt no pleasure in telling her this. He did not enjoy the feeling of walking away from a challenge, nor did he like letting Amelia down.

"Too much has happened," he said. "I don't enjoy the work any more. I think of it as unhealthy."

"Unhealthy? But you just had the greatest triumphs of your career!"

Kell could hear the consternation in her voice. He knew that he would never effectively be able to explain to her why his life was more important to him than his career. For Amelia, the two things were inextricable.

"Those weren't my triumphs," Kell replied. He was being disingenuous because he wanted the conversation to end. "Carnelian saved Minasian. Minasian stopped Brighton. If it weren't for Rachel, I would never have gone after him. And what was the end result? Riedle dead, Minasian's marriage and career finished —"

"Tom, for goodness' sake. You must be tired."

"Very," Kell replied. They were showing the platform number for the Berlin train. "It's simple," he said. "I don't want this life any more, this divided life. I can't remember a time when what I did for a living made me happy. Fulfilled. I don't feel as though I was making a difference to anyone or anything. It was all just moves on a board."

"Tom, please. Just come home. Come back to London. We'll talk. You've been through hell in the last few years. I owe you. The Service owes you. Let's find a way."

"No," he said. "I am deeply grateful to you, Amelia. I thank you for everything you have done for me. Even for what you have *not* done, because I learned from that. It has been an honor to know you and to serve alongside you. I think you are a remarkable woman. I think you are devious and cunning, too. You are *complicated*. We are all complicated. But I want no further part in your secret life."

"This is senseless. You're tired. Come back."

"I won't be coming back for a long time." Kell put a handful of coins on the counter and picked up his bags. "I just want to live, Amelia. I want to start again."

# ACKNOWLEDGMENTS

My thanks to:

Sally Richardson, Charles Spicer, April Osborn, Dori Weintraub, Paul Hochman, and the team at St. Martin's Press.

Julia Wisdom, Kate Stephenson, Lucy Dauman, Jaime Frost, Kate Elton, Roger Cazalet, Oliver Malcolm, Liz Dawson, Claire Ward, Richard Augustus, and everyone at HarperCollins.

Will Francis, Kirsty Gordon, Jessie Botterill, and Rebecca Folland at Janklow & Nesbit in London. To Luke Janklow, Claire Dippel, Stefanie Lieberman, and Dmitri Chitov at the New York office.

To Jeff Silver at Grandview, Jay Baker, Jon Cassir, and Matt Martin at CAA, and Ged, Colin, Claudia, and Oliver at Raindog.

I am also indebted to: Sarah Gabriel (www .sarahgabriel.eu), Elizabeth Best, Caroline Pilkington, Ian Cumming, Salomé Baudino, Paolo Risser, Laila Danesh, Helena Tedal,

Nick Lockley, Melissa Hanbury, Stanley and Iris Cumming, Barney Bristow, Damian Lewis, Rory Carleton Paget, Ludmilla Linkevich, Masha Hayward, Vera Obolonkina, Leyla Sabauri, Peter Frankopan, Ben Higgins, Mark Pilkington, Rowland White, Amos Courage, Bard Wilkinson, Boris Starling, Peter Caddick-Adams, James Maby, Kam Heskin, Alice Kahrmann, Dr. Charlotte Cassis, Ron Amram, Eliza Apperly, Fatema Jan, Elij Kutsal, Chris Morgan-Jones, Marta Januszewska, Aurore de Broqueville, Nick Green, Raymond Lief, and Natasha Fairweather.

Thank you to Roddy Campbell, Constance Watson, Ian Johnson, Chelsea Carter, and everyone at www.vrumi.com for the office. I discovered the Montaigne epigraph in John Yorke's book, *Into the Woods*. Deeyah Khan's extraordinary film *Jihad: A Story of the Others* helped me better to understand the choices made by Azhar Ahmed Iqbal. Mark Lilla's essay "Slouching Toward Mecca" (*The New York Review of Books*), Ben Taub's "Journey to Jihad" (*The New Yorker*), and " 'We' and 'You,' " by Owen Bennett-Jones (*London Review of Books*), were all extremely useful.

# ABOUT THE AUTHOR

**Charles Cumming** is the author of the first Thomas Kell book, *A Foreign Country,* as well the *New York Times* bestselling thriller *The Trinity Six*, and others including *A Spy by Nature* and *Typhoon.* He lives with his family in London.